JOHN VARLEY

Demon

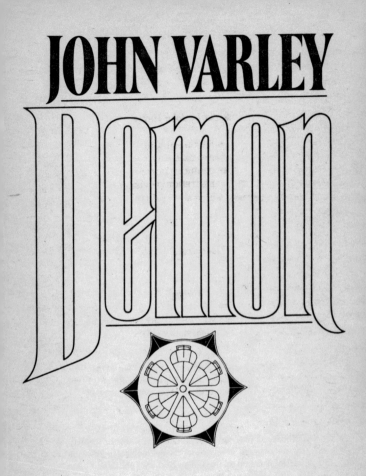

ACE BOOKS, NEW YORK

DEMON

An Ace Book / published by arrangement with
the author

PRINTING HISTORY
Berkley trade paperback edition / June 1984
Berkley edition / November 1985
Ace edition / May 1987

ISBN: 0-441-14267-2

Ace Books are published by The Berkley Publishing Group,
200 Madison Avenue, New York, New York 10016.
The name "Ace" and the "A" logo
are trademarks belonging to Charter Communications, Inc.
PRINTED IN THE UNITED STATES OF AMERICA

10   9   8   7   6   5   4   3

This book is dedicated to:

Irving Thalberg,
for the conceit;

Vlad the Impaler,
for the concept;
and

Edward Teller,
for the context.

PROPHECY

In the year 2024 the most important single thing which the cinema will have helped to accomplish will be that of eliminating from the face of the civilized world all armed conflict. With the use of the universal language of motion pictures the true meaning of the brotherhood of man will have been established throughout the Earth. . . . All men are created equal.
> —*D. W. Griffith*, 1924
> (Director of "The Birth of a Nation,"
> adapted from the novel *The Klansmen*)

Music will always be the voice of the silent drama. There will never be speaking pictures.
> —*D. W. Griffith*, 1924

All right, D. W., take three. . . .

DEMON

Being the Third Book in
The Gaean Trilogy
In which certain events described
in TITAN and WIZARD
come to their conclusions,
And containing an account of
The End of the World.

SHORT SUBJECTS

Stupidity got us into this
mess—why can't it get us out?

—Will Rogers

COMING ATTRACTIONS

The location scout was the first into the valley.

Like most of Gaea's genetically tailored beings, the scout did not have a sex. It had no mouth and no organs of digestion. What it did have was a pair of cinemascope eyes and a magnificent spatial sense.

The scout clattered over the valley on spindly rotors, hovered, and turned slowly. It saw a rushing river beneath twenty-meter cliffs. Above the cliffs was a plateau of sufficient size, and ringing the plateau were trees more than sufficient for the needs of the approaching Crew. It felt warm contentment, like a kitten who has found a bowl of milk. This was the place.

It flew over the trees, spraying them with an attractant pheromone. That done, it made several passes over the plateau, dropping spores. It settled at the edge of the plateau, already beginning to feel tired. Its rotor withered and fell away. Walking on long, feathery legs, it circled the location, stopping every hundred paces to poke a seed into the ground with a long sharp organ growing from its belly.

With the last of its strength it made its way into the woods and died.

In twenty revs the plateau was covered with bushes a meter high. Spaced around the location were klieg trees, already twenty meters high and getting bigger at the rate of two meters per rev.

Forty-five revs after the death of the scout the advance party of carpenters, teamsters, and vintners arrived. Carpenters were hairless animals the size of grizzly bears, all alike except for their teeth, which were wildly specialized. Some had beaver incisors, capable of gnawing down a tree with a few dozen bites. Others had a single projecting tooth two meters long, notched on one edge, which could saw beams and planks from raw timber. There were carpenters with trapezoidal teeth. These could bite the end of a plank in tenons,

2

ready for dovetailing. Others had drill-bit teeth. Twisting their heads vigorously, they could ream out a mortise.

In Gaea, a team of forty carpenters was called a union.

All the carpenters had quite human hands, except that each finger ended in a nail shaped for a different utility. The palms of the hands were as different as human fingerprints. Some were hard and horny, some were deeply grooved or pebbled, while others were smooth as a jeweler's rubbing cloth. With these hands the carpenters could plane and sand wood to a wondrous luster. The distance from the end of the thumb to the end of the little finger of each carpenter was exactly the same: fifty centimeters.

In a few revs, the platforms, soundstages, archives building, and scores of chapels had begun to take shape.

The vintners were one-purpose creatures. All they did was move onto the location and devour clusters of small white grapes. The plants that bore the fruit were not grapevines, but the fruit were, for all practical purposes, grapes. The vintners ate them all, then fell into a torpor from which they would never emerge. But in thirty revs they could be tapped for an excellent white chablis.

The teamsters were something else again. In a place where a union of carpenters was well within the norm, the teamsters stood out as weird.

Teamsters looked something like hippos, but were five times the size of elephants. They were land whales mincing along on six legs just thick enough to support them in Gaea's low gravity. Three of them arrived at the valley and started eating the plants that had grown from the scout's spores.

There were many kinds of plants. Each variety went to a different stomach. The teamsters had eleven separate sets of digestive organs.

When the field was cleared, the teamsters moved to the side and fell over, somnolent as the vintners. Their legs withered until the animals were little more than bulging bladders lined with row upon row of nipples in a bewildering variety of shapes and colors. But the teamsters retained their mouths for a little longer. They would eat the union of carpenters when construction was done.

Gaea's operations were always tidy.

* * *

Things started to really pop when the production crew began trickling in.

There were hordes of skittering little bolexes, brainlessly pointing themselves in all directions and whirring fruitlessly, too stupid to know they needed re-loading. They spotted the teamsters and began fighting for a teat like piglets after a weary sow. Their excited cries sounded like *meet! meet! meet!*

Close behind them were the arriflexes, accompanied by producers, and behind them were the lordly panaflexes, each with its attendant executiveproducer. The production species hung back with nothing to do while their photofaunal symbiotes gorged on silver nitrate, pyroxylin, and other chemicals, each going to its proper holding bladder. All the producers looked much the same, except for their size. The execs were the largest and the only ones with a voice. From time to time, for reasons having nothing to do with communication, one of them would grunt *unch, unch*.

As the bolies, arries, and panas chowed down, others of the Crew filtered into the site, dodging carpenters, who were putting the finishing touches on their work with Swiss Army fingernails. There was a gaggle of twenty-meter booms, stalking through the chaos like solemn storks. Groups of grips and bestboys quickly broke up, guiding others to their work sites. Painters sucked stains and dyes from the teamsters, then spread them over the bare wood with their long perforated tails. Elephants arrived, pulling rumbling carts full of costumes, props, carpets, make-up, and portable dressing rooms. These were real Earth elephants, bred from imported stock. In Gaea's gravity, elephants did not lumber; they pranced, supple and frisky as cats.

Pandemonium was taking shape.

Humanoids, androids, homunculi, and a few genuine human beings made their penultimate entrances, signaling it would not be long before the appearance of the Director Herself.

Some of these human-based and human-derived hybrids were workers, others mere extras. Some were the shambling undead, from which even the brainless constructs seemed to recoil. A very few were stars. Luther swept in with fire in his demented eyes and took his apostles straight to their spare chapel. Brigham and his boys rode in on horses to find the Temple not yet ready for them. There were recriminations, and conniption fits. Marybaker was there, and so was Elron. It was rumored that Billy Sunday was in the neighborhood, and perhaps even Kali. It was going to be quite a festival.

As each bolex, arriflex, and panaflex finished eating, the appropriate producer attached itself and the two moved off as one. Like the producers, the photofauns were enough alike that one could serve as model for all, except in size. The most important thing about a panaflex was the size of its single, glassy eye, and the width of its horizontal anus, which was precisely seventy millimeters.

A panaflex had only one urge: getting the shot. It would do anything to get the shot—take a ride on a copter, dangle from a boom, go over a waterfall in a barrel. Its unblinking eye ogled everything, and when it was ready, it shot film. Somewhere in its innards guncotton and camphor and other unlikely substances came together under considerable pressure to form a continuous strip of celluloid. That strip was coated with photoreactive chemicals to produce a full-color negative. The strip moved behind the panaflex's eye and was exposed in discrete frames by a muscle-and-bone pulldown and shutter mechanism Edison would have recognized.

The producer rode on the back of the panaflex, facing the rear, ready for the emerging film, which it ate. Naturally, this required a close contact to prevent fogging by ambient light. It didn't faze the producer, who was always hungry for film. By eating it, the producer also developed and fixed it.

When they in turn defecated, the product was projector-ready footage, which was why Gaea called them producers.

It was sixty revs after the preliminary scout first discovered the site and found it good. The flacks and hypes were returning from their forays into the woods, laden with game. These were ape-like creatures: two of the few predatory species Gaea had ever produced. Gaea was not good at predators. A hype would have fared poorly in an African jungle. But in Gaea, most of the fauna were not good at flight, either, simply because they had no predators. The principal source of meat, the smilers, did not have to be stalked—they didn't run—or even killed. Meat could be harvested from them in long strips, doing no harm to the smiler. Many a smiler steak was sizzling in the commissary building as the first great feast was prepared and laid out on long trestle tables with immaculate white cloths and big crystal jugs of chablis. A breathless quiet fell over the site as all awaited the arrival of Gaea. It was broken only by the excited *meet, meet, meeeet* of the bolexes as they jostled each other for position.

The ground began to tremble. She came through the woods. There was a reverent gasp from the assembled Priests as her head came into view over the treetops.

Gaea was fifteen meters tall. Or, as she preferred to have it, "fifty foot two, eyes of blue."

They were blue, too, though they couldn't be seen behind the largest pair of sunglasses ever constructed. Her hair was platinum blonde. She wore enough heavy canvas, dyed light blue, to rig a Spanish galleon. The cloth was cut and sewn by tentmakers into a knee-length dress. She wore moccasins the size of broad-beamed canoes. In face and figure, she bore an uncanny resemblance to Marilyn Monroe.

She paused when she reached the clearing and looked over all her subjects and all their works. At last she nodded: it was good. The lights on the klieg trees turned to face her and the massive lips parted in a smile, revealing even white teeth big as bathroom tiles. All around her, bolexes and arriflexes whirred admiration.

A chair had been built for her. It groaned as she settled into it. All her movements seemed slow. A blink took almost a second. The panaflexes had learned the trick of undercranking so that she seemed to move at normal speed while her minions scampered like mice.

Dressers scrambled up ladders behind her, armed with rakes for her hair, buckets of nail polish, cans of mascara. She ignored them; it was their job to anticipate her movements—something they were not always able to do. She looked at the big screen that had been erected facing her chair.

The Pandemonium Traveling Film Festival was about to begin. The klieg trees dimmed, turned off; the valley darkened. Gaea cleared her throat—a sound like a diesel engine—but when she spoke, it was pitched in the feminine range. Very loud, but feminine.

"Roll it," she said.

NEWSREEL

It was common knowledge that World War V started in a defective twenty-cent Molecular Circuit Matrix in a newly-installed firecontrol computer four miles below Cheyenne Mountain, Wyoming.

An investigation eventually led to the apartment of Jacob Smith, thirty-eight, of 3400 Temple, Salt Lake City. Smith had tested the MCM and allowed it to be installed in Western Bioelectric's Mark XX "Archangel" Brain Array. The Archangel had then replaced the aging Mark Nineteen in defense of the New Reformed Latter-Day Saints Territories, commonly known as the "Norman Lands."

The story was as apocryphal as that of Mrs. O'Leary's cow. But it was leaked to an eager young reporter for one of the global newsnets, where it eventually became the lead item in the nightly special: "World War V: Day Three." On Day Five Jake Smith was again in the news as a lynch mob dragged him from police headquarters and hung him from a lamp post in Temple Square, not thirty yards from the statue of another famous Smith, no relation.

By Day Sixteen the news anchors were trotting out historians who spent their time debating whether the current unpleasantness should be called World War III, IV, V, the Fourth Nuclear War, or the First Interplanetary War.

There were reasons to support the interplanetary designation, since in the early days some Lunar and Martian settlements had sided with one or another of the Terran factions, and even a few La Grange colonies began tiptoeing toward a foreign policy. But by the time Jake Smith was hung all the Outlanders had declared neutrality.

In the end, the decision was made in an office on Sixth Avenue, New York City, Eastern Capitalist Confederation, by a network logo design analyst. The overnight Arbitrons on the numeral V were strongly positive. The V looked sexy and might stand for Victory, so World War V it was.

The next day, Sixth Avenue was vaporized.

* * *

The global networks recovered. By Day Twenty-nine all were embroiled in the question: *Is This IT?* By "it," they meant the Holocaust, the Four Horsemen, the Final War, the Extinction of Mankind. It was a tough question. Nobody wanted to commit too strongly either way, remembering the egg on the faces of so many who cried doom at the outbreak of the Fizzle War. But all the nets promised to be the first with the news.

That it had resulted from a malfunction surprised no one. The strike by the Norman Territories against the Burmese Empire was obviously an error. Neither combatant had any grievances against the other. But shortly after the failure of the MCM in Wyoming, the Burmese had plenty of reason for anger.

The Moroni VI satellite, in near-Earth orbit, made its move somewhere over Tibet, mirved fifty miles above Singapore, and began evasive action. All six warheads strewed decoys in their wakes, and were preceded by twenty similar but harmless mirvs intended to soak up the ABM's and lasers. The Burmese computer barely got a glimpse of the onrushing horde. It decided the Moroni VI was going for ground-bursts at a minimum of twelve targets. About the time it reached that decision, the ten-megaton warheads exploded thirty miles over the province of New South Wales. The resulting burst of gamma radiation produced an electromagnetic pulse, or EMP, that blew out every telephone, vidscreen, transformer, and electric sheep-shearer from Woomera to Sydney, and caused the sewage system in Melbourne to run backward.

The Burmese Potentate was a headstrong man. His advisors pointed out that the EMP tactic should have been followed by invasion if Salt Lake City really intended to go to war. But he had been in Melbourne at the time of the attack. He was not amused.

In two hours, Provo, Utah was radioactive rubble, and the Bonneville Fun-city vanished.

It was not enough. The Potentate had never been able to distinguish one Occidental religion from another, so he fired a missile at Milano, The Vatican States, for good measure.

The Council of Popes convened in St. Peter's. Not the old one, which had been torn down to make way for an apartment block, but the new one, in Sicily, which was glass and plastic. For five days they conferred until the Spokespope emerged to announce the Papal Bull as a Gabriel warhead fell toward Bangkok.

What Pope Elaine did not announce was another sense-of-the-meeting resolution that had been summed up by vice-Pope Watanabe.

"If we're going to hit the B.E.," Watanabe had said, "why not 'accidentally' send one to those fuckers in the B.C.R.?"

So shortly after Bangkok was flattened by a one-megaton airburst, a second Gabriel fell on the outskirts of Potchefstroom, Boer Communist Republic. That it had been targetted for Johannesburg hardly seemed to matter.

So WWV, as it soon came to be abbreviated, lurched along in a back-and-forth exchange with everyone waiting for one nation or another to launch that all-out strike which, at county fairs, carnivals, and fireworks displays, is known as the blow-off. It would come as a solid wave of missiles aimed at hardened military sites, population centers, and natural resources, and would be accompanied by plagues and deadly chemicals. At the time the war started, there were fifty-eight nations, religions, political parties, or other affinity groups capable of unleashing such an attack.

Instead, the bombs kept dropping at the rate of about one every week. At first it looked like a free-for-all. But in three months alliances stabilized along surprisingly classical lines. The newsnets began calling one side the Capitalist Pigs and the other the Commie Rats. The Normans and the Burmese, oddly enough, ended up on the same side, while the Vatican was on the other. There were more vermin—the newscasters had names for them all—who would occasionally step up and kick a giant in the shin. But by and large the war soon came to resemble one of those contests Russians used to be so fond of during the First Atomic War. Aslosh with vodka, they would take turns slapping each other's face until one of them fell down.

The record for such a contest was established in 1931 and never beaten, when two comrades went at each other for thirty hours.

At the rate of one five-megaton bomb per week—just about one kiloton per minute—the Earth's nuclear stockpiles were estimated to be good for eight hundred years.

Conal "The Sting" Ray was a Capitalist Pig. Like his mates, he spent little time thinking about it, but when he did, he thought of himself as Canadian Bacon.

As a citizen of the Dominion of Canada, the oldest nation on Earth, Conal was in no danger of being drafted, and in less danger than most of being vaporized. For one thing, no nation was seriously engaged in raising armies. War was no longer labor-intensive. And only one bomb had been dropped on the Dominion. It had hit Edmonton, and the main reason Conal noticed it was because the Oilers no longer showed up for their Canadian Hockey League dates.

That Canada had once been a much larger nation was a fact no one had ever imparted to Conal—or if someone had, he had not been interested enough to remember it. Canada had survived by surrendering. Quebec had been the first to go, followed by British Columbia. B.C. was part of the Norman Lands, Ontario was an independent nation, the Maritimes had been swallowed up by the E.C.C. to the south, and most of southern Manitoba and Saskatchewan were owned by General Protein, the Corporation/State. Canada huddled between the western shores of Hudson Bay and the foothills of the Rockies. Yellowknife was its capital city. Conal lived in a suburb of Fort Reliance, a town called Artillery Lake. Fort Reliance had a population of five million.

Conal had grown up with two passions: hockey, and listening to comic books. He was terrible at hockey, being simply too fat and too slow. He was usually the last to be chosen in pick-up games. When he played, he was always installed at the goal, on the theory that though he wasn't quick, it would be hard to shoot around him.

On his fourteenth birthday a bully kicked snow in his face and Conal found a new passion: bodybuilding. To his surprise and everyone else's, he was damn good at it. By the time he was sixteen he could have been Mr. Canada. In true Charles Atlas fashion, he sought out the bully and forced him through a hole in the ice covering Artillery Lake, after which the bully was never seen again.

The name Conal meant "high and mighty" in Celtic. Conal began to feel his mother had named him well, though he was only five foot eight. And there was something in Mrs. Ray's heritage that, when he learned of it, provided Conal with his fourth great passion in life.

So it was that on his eighteenth birthday, Day 294 of the War, Conal took the morning sleigh to the spaceport at Cape Churchill, where he boarded a ship bound for Gaea.

* * *

Aside from a trip to Winnipeg, Conal had never in his life been outside Canada. This trip was considerably longer: Gaea was almost a billion miles from Artillery Lake. The fare was expensive, but George Ray, Conal's father, no longer dared thwart his son's desires. The boy had done nothing but eat, play hockey, and lift weights for three years; it would be nice to have him out from underfoot. A billion miles sounded about right.

Saturn impressed the hell out of Conal. The rings looked solid enough to skate on. He watched the ship dock with the huge black mass of Gaea, then dug out his oldest comic book, "The Golden Blades." It was the story of a young boy who received a pair of magic skates from an evil sorcerer and how he learned to use them. In the end the boy—who was also named Conal—mastered the skates and cleaved the wizard's head with a mighty kick. Conal fingered the soundlines bordering the final panel, heard the familiar meaty *thunk* as the skate opened the wizard's skull, watched the blood gush and the foul brains glisten on the page.

Conal doubted he could kill the Wizard with his skates, though he had brought them. In his mind, he saw himself wringing the life from her with his bare hands. In a more practical vein, he had also brought a pistol.

His quarry was Cirocco Jones, formerly Captain of the Deep Space Vessel *Ringmaster,* erstwhile Wing Commander of the Angels, *sub rosa* Hindmother of the Titanides, the one-time Great and Powerful but long-deposed Wizard of Gaea, now called Demon. He planned to stuff her through a hole in the ice.

It took Conal a month to find Cirocco Jones. In part it was because the Demon was not eager to be found, though she was not running from anything in particular at the moment. The other reason it took so long was that Conal, like so many before him, had under-estimated Gaea. He had known the World/God was large, but he had not translated the numbers into a picture of just how much territory he had to deal with.

He knew that Jones was usually found in the company of Titanides, and that Titanides usually stayed in the region known as Hyperion, so he concentrated his search there. His month of searching gave him time to become accustomed to the one-quarter gravity inside Gaea, and the dizzying vistas Gaea's mammoth interior presented. He learned that no Titanide would tell a human anything about the "Captain," as they now called Jones.

Titanides were a lot bigger than he had expected. The centaur-like creatures had played prominent roles in many of his comics, but the artists had used considerable license in portraying them. He had expected to see eye to eye with them, whereas the truth was they averaged three meters. In comics, Titanides were male and female, though one never saw any sexual organs. In reality, Titanides all looked female and their sexuality was impossible to comprehend. They had either male or female organs—completely human in appearance—between their front legs, and male *and* female organs behind. The anterior male organ was usually sheathed; the first time Conal saw one he had a feeling of inadequacy he had not experienced since his first week with the barbells.

He found her in a place called *La Gata Encantada*. It was a Titanide pub near the trunk of the largest tree Conal had ever seen. The tree was, in fact, the largest in the solar system, and beneath it and in its branches was the largest Titanide city in Gaea, called Titantown.

She was sitting at a table in a corner, her back to the wall. There were five Titanides seated with her. They were playing an elaborate game with dice and wondrously carved chessmen. Each player had a gallon-sized mug of dark beer. The one beside Cirocco Jones was untouched.

She looked small, slouched in her chair among the Titanides, but she was actually just over six feet. Her clothing was black, including a hat that resembled the one Zorro wore in one of Conal's favorite comics. It left most of her face in shadow, but the nose was too grand to hide. There was a thin cigar clenched in her teeth and a blue-steel .38 tucked into the waistband of her pants. Her skin was light brown, and her hair long and streaked with silver.

He stepped up to the table and faced her. He was unafraid; he had been looking forward to this.

"You're not a wizard, Jones," he said. "You're a witch."

For a moment he thought he had not been heard over the clatter and roar in the pub. Jones did not move. Yet somehow the tension of his blazing aura moved out and electrified the air. The noise gradually died away. All the Titanides turned to look at him.

Cirocco Jones slowly lifted her head. Conal realized she had been looking at him for some time—in fact, since before he approached the table. She had the hardest eyes he had ever seen, and the saddest. They were deep-set, clear, and dark as coal. She looked at him, unblinking, from his face to his bare arms to the long-barreled Colt in the holster on his hip, his hand opening and closing a few inches from it.

She took the cigar from her mouth and showed him her teeth in a carnivorous grin.

"And who the hell are you?" she asked.

"I'm the Sting," Conal said. "And I've come to kill you."

"Do you want us to take him, Captain?" one of the Titanides at the table asked. Cirocco waved her hand at him.

"No, no. This appears to be an affair of honor," she said.

"That's exactly right," Conal said. He knew his voice tended to get high and squeaky when he raised it, so he paused a moment to slow his breathing. She wasn't going to let these animals do her dirty work for her. It seemed she might make a worthy opponent after all.

"When you came here, hundreds of years ago, you—"

"Eighty-eight," she said.

"What?"

"I came here eighty-eight years ago. Not hundreds."

Conal refused to be distracted.

"You remember someone who came here with you? A man called Eugene Springfield?"

"I remember him very well."

"Did you know he was married? Did you know he left a wife and two children back on Earth?"

"Yes. I knew that."

Conal took a deep breath, and stood straight.

"Well, he was my great-great grandfather."

"Bullshit."

"It is not bullshit. I'm his grandson, and I've come here to avenge his murder."

"Mister . . . I don't doubt you've done a lot of crazy things in your life, but if you did that, it would be the craziest thing you *ever* did."

"I came billions of miles to find you, and now it's just between you and me."

He reached for his belt buckle. Cirocco jerked almost imperceptibly. Conal never saw it; he was too busy unbuckling his belt and throwing it and his gun to the floor. He had liked wearing that gun. He had worn it since his arrival, as soon as he saw how many other humans went armed; he thought it a pleasant change from the Dominion's stuffy firearms laws.

"There," he said. "I know you're hundreds of years old and I know you can fight dirty. Well, I'm ready to take you. Let's step outside and settle this honorably. A fight to the death."

Cirocco shook her head slowly.

"Son, you don't get to be a hundred and twenty-three years old by doing everything honorably." She looked over his shoulder and nodded.

The Titanide behind him brought the empty beer mug down on the top of his head. The thick glass shattered, and Conal slumped to the floor into a pile of orange Titanide droppings.

Cirocco got up, tucking her second gun back into the top of her boot.

"Let's see just what sort of dirty trick he really is."

There was a Titanide healer present; she examined the bloody scalp wound and announced the man would probably live. Another Titanide pulled the pack from Conal's back and started going through it. Cirocco stood over him, smoking.

"What's in it?" she asked.

"Let's see . . . beef jerky, a box of shells for that cannon, a pair of skates . . . and about thirty comic books."

Cirocco's laugh was music to the Titanides because they heard it so seldom. They all laughed with her as she passed the comics around. Soon the place was buzzing with tinny balloonchip voices and sound effects.

"Deal me out, folks," she told the people at her table.

Conal woke with the worst headache he had ever imagined. He was being bounced around, so he opened his eyes to see what was causing it.

He found himself suspended head down over a two-mile drop.

Screaming hurt his head badly, but he was unable to stop. It was a high-pitched, child's scream, almost inaudible. Then he was vomiting, and nearly choked on it.

He was bound in so much rope he might have been wrapped by a spider. The only part of his body with any freedom was his neck, and it hurt to move that, but he did, looking wildly around.

He was strapped to the back of a Titanide with his head on the monster's huge hindquarters. The Titanide was somehow climbing a vertical rock face. When he leaned his head all the way back he could see the thing's rear hooves scrabbling on ledges two inches wide. He watched in horrified fascination as one ledge broke away and a shower of stones fell up and up and up until he lost sight of them.

"The bastard threw up on my tail," the Titanide said.

"Yeah?" came another voice, which he recognized as Cirocco Jones's.

So the Demon was somewhere near his feet.

He thought he would go mad. He screamed, he pleaded with them, but they said nothing. It was impossible that the thing could climb such a slope by itself, and yet it was doing it with both Conal and Cirocco on its back, and doing it about as fast as Conal could have walked on level ground.

Just what sort of animal *was* this Titanide?

They brought him to a cavern midway up the cliff. It was just a hole in the rock, ten feet high and about as wide, forty feet deep. There was no path of any kind leading to it.

He was dumped, still in his cocoon of rope. Cirocco wrestled him into a sitting position.

"In a little while, you're going to answer some questions," she said.

"I'll tell you anything."

"You're damn right you will." She grinned at him again, then hit him across the face with the barrel of his own gun. He was about to protest when she hit him again.

Cirocco had to hit him four times before she was sure he was out. She would have hit him with the gun butt, except that would have pointed the barrel at her, and she hadn't lived to be one hundred and twenty-three by doing stupid things like that.

"He shouldn't have called me a witch," she said.

"Don't look at me," Hornpipe said. "I would have killed him back at *La Gata*."

"Yeah." She sat back on her heels and let her shoulders sag. "You know, sometimes I wonder what's so great about reaching one hundred twenty-four."

The Titanide said nothing. He was loosening Conal's bonds and stripping him. He had been with the Wizard for many years, and knew her moods.

The back of the cavern was ice. On a hot day like this one, a trickle of water flowed over the rock floor. Cirocco knelt beside a pool. She splashed water on her face, then took a drink. It was icy cold.

Cirocco had spent many nights here when things got uncomfortable down at the rim. There was a stack of blankets as well as several bales of straw. There were two wooden pails: one for use as a latrine, and the other to catch drinking water. A hammock was suspended between two pitons driven into the rock. An old tin washboard provided the only other amenity. When she had to stay for a long time, Cirocco would string a clothesline across the mouth of the cavern to catch the dry updrafts.

"Hey, we missed one," Hornpipe said.

"One what?"

The Titanide tossed her a comic book which had been stuffed into Conal's back pocket. She caught it, and watched the Titanide work for a moment.

There was a heavy stake embedded in the floor of the cave. The naked bodybuilder had been tied to it, sitting down, and his ankles fastened to stakes about three feet apart. It was a totally defenseless posture. Hornpipe was tying Conal's head to the post by wrapping a wide leather strap around his forehead.

The man's face was a wreck. It was crusted with dried blood. His nose was broken, and his cheekbones, but Cirocco thought his jaw was okay. His mouth was swollen and his eyes were tiny slits.

She sighed, and looked at the crumpled comic book. The cover said "The Wizard of Gaea," and showed her old ship, the *Ringmaster*, in its death throes. Even after this long she hated to look at it.

It was a dedicated book, in that all the characters were named and could not be changed by the purchaser. Most of Conal's books had provision to punch in one's own name for the hero.

The characters were familiar. There were Cirocco Jones, and Gene, and Bill, and Calvin, and the Polo Sisters, and Hornpipe the Younger, and Meistersinger.

And, of course, someone else.

Cirocco closed the book and swallowed to get rid of the heat at the back of her throat. Then she sprawled in the hammock and started to go through it.

"Are you really going to read that thing?" Hornpipe asked.

"You can't read it. There are no words." Cirocco had never actually seen a book like "The Wizard of Gaea," but she understood the principle. The colors glowed, or strobed, or glistened and felt wet to the touch. Buried in the ink were microscopic balloonchips. When you touched a panel the characters in it delivered their lines. Sound effects had replaced the old printed tzings, ker-pows, braka-braka's and screeches.

The dialogue was even worse than Conal's in *La Gata,* so she simply looked at the pictures. The story was easy enough to follow.

It was even accurate, in its broad outlines.

She saw her ship approaching Saturn. There was the discovery of Gaea, a thirteen-hundred-kilometer black wheel in orbit. Her ship was destroyed, and all the crew emerged inside after a period of weird dreams. They took a ride on a blimp, built a boat and sailed down the river Ophion, met the Titanides. Cirocco was mysteriously able to sing the Titanide language. The group got embroiled in the war with the Angels.

The characters screwed a lot more than she remembered. There were very steamy scenes between Cirocco and Gaby Plauget, and more between Cirocco and Gene Springfield. The last was an utter fabrication, and the first was out of sequence.

Everyone was armed to the teeth. They carried more weapons than a battalion of mercenaries. All the men bulged with muscles, worse than Conal Ray, and all the women had tits the size of watermelons that kept bursting free of the skimpy leather hammocks supporting them. They encountered monsters Cirocco had never heard of, and left behind nothing but bloody gobbets of flesh.

Then it got interesting.

She saw Gaby, Gene, and herself climbing one of the huge cables that led to the hub of Gaea, six hundred kilometers above. The three of them made camp, and the shenanigans started. It appeared to be a love triangle, with Cirocco involved with both her companions. She and Gaby plotted by the campfire, exchanging words of undying love, things like "Oh, God, Gaby, I love your hands on my hot, wet pussy."

The next morning—though Cirocco remembered the trip as having taken a lot longer than that—at their audience with the great Goddess Gaea, Gene was offered the position of Wizard. He lowered his head humbly to accept, and Cirocco grabbed him by the hair, pulled his head back, and slit his throat from ear to ear. Blood spilled down the page, and she kicked his head contemptuously out of the way. Gaea—who was a lot more chickenshit than Cirocco remembered her—made Cirocco Wizard, with Gaby as her wicked assistant.

There was a lot more. Cirocco sighed and closed the book.

"You know what?" she said. "He may be telling the truth."

"I thought so."

"He could be just a fool."

"Well, you know the penalty for foolishness."

"Yeah." She tossed the comic away, picked up one of the wooden pails, and threw two gallons of ice water into Conal's face.

He awoke gradually. He was being pushed and pinched, but it all seemed far away. He didn't even know who he was.

Finally he knew he was naked, bound beyond any hope of escape. His legs were spread wide and he couldn't move them. He couldn't see anything until Jones pried one of his blood-crusted eyes open. That hurt. There was a strap immobilizing his head, and that hurt, too. In fact, everything hurt.

Jones was in front of him, sitting on an overturned pail. Her eyes were as deep and black as ever as she studied him dispassionately. Finally he could stand it no longer.

"Are you going to torture me?" The words came out slurred.

"Yep."

"When?"

"When you tell me a lie."

His thoughts were moving around like glue, but something in the way she looked at him inspired him to work it out.

"How will you know if I'm lying?" he said.

"That's the tough part," she admitted.

She held up a knife, turned it in front of his face. She put the edge lightly along the top of his foot and drew it slowly toward her. There was no pain, but a line of blood appeared. She held it up again, and waited.

"Sharp," he ventured. "Very sharp."

She nodded, and put the knife down.

She took the cigar from her mouth, knocked off some ash, and blew on the tip until it glowed fiercely. She put the glowing tip about a quarter inch away from his foot.

The skin began to blister, and he felt it this time; it wasn't like the knife at all.

"Yes," he said, "yes, yes, I understand."

"Not yet, you don't." She held it right there.

He tried to move his foot within the bindings, but the Titanide's hand appeared from behind him and held it rock steady. He bit his lip, he looked away; his eyes were dragged back. He started to scream. He screamed for a long time, and the pain never got any better.

Even when she took it away—in five minutes? ten?—the pain remained. He sobbed helplessly for a long time.

At last he could look at it again. The skin was burned black in a circle about an inch around. He looked at her, and she was watching him again, as emotional as a stone. He hated her. He had never hated anyone or anything as he hated her then.

"That was twenty seconds," she said.

He wept when he realized she was telling the truth. He tried to nod, tried to tell her he understood what it meant, that twenty seconds was not a very long time, but he could not control his voice. She waited.

"There's one more thing you should understand," she said. "The foot is fairly sensitive, but it's a long way from being the most sensitive part of your body." He held his breath as she quickly flashed the tip near his nose, just long enough for him to feel the heat. Then she drew a fingernail slowly from his chin to his crotch. He felt faint heat all the way down, and when her hand stopped, he heard and smelled hair being singed.

When she took her hand away without burning him down there, an astonishing thing happened to Conal. He stopped hating her. He was sorry to see the hate go. It had been all he had left. He was naked and he hurt everywhere and she was going to hurt him some more. Hatred would have been a nice thing to hang onto.

She put the cigar back in her mouth and clenched it in her teeth.

"Now," she said. "Just what sort of deal did you make with Gaea?"

And he began to cry again.

It went on forever. The sad thing was that the truth was not going to save him. She thought he was one thing, when he really was something else.

She burned him twice more. She didn't put the cigar to the black spot, where the nerves were dead, but to the raw, swelling edges where the nerves were screaming. After the second time he concentrated his entire being on telling her whatever she wanted to hear.

"If you didn't see Gaea," Jones said, "who *did* you see? Was it Luther?"

"Yes. Yes, it was Luther."

"No it wasn't. It wasn't Luther. Who was it? Who sent you to kill me?"

"It was Luther. I swear, it was Luther."

"Is Luther a Priest?"

"...yes?"

"Describe him. What does he look like?"

He hadn't the faintest idea, but he had learned a lot about her eyes. They were far from expressionless. There were a million things to be read in them and he was the world's best student of Cirocco's eyes. He saw the changes in them that meant agony and the smell of burning flesh, and he started to talk. Halfway through his description he realized he was delineating the evil sorcerer from "The Golden Blades," but he kept talking until she slapped him.

"You've never met Luther," Jones said. "Who was it, then? Was it Kali? Blessed Foster? Billy Sunday? Saint Torquemada?"

"Yes!" he shouted. "All of them," he added, lamely.

Jones shook her head, and Conal heard, as though from afar, the sound of whimpering. She was going to do it, he saw it in her eyes.

"Son," she said, and sounded sorrowful, "you've been lying to me, and I told you not to lie." She took the cigar from her mouth, blew on it again, and moved it toward his crotch.

His eyes bulged as he tried to see it. When the pain came, it was exactly as bad as he had imagined it would be.

It was hard for them to bring him back to life, because he would have preferred to remain dead. There was no pain in death, no pain. . . .

But he did wake up, to all the familiar pain. He was surprised to find it didn't hurt . . . down there. He could not bring himself to even think the word for the place she had burned him.

She was looking at him again.

"Conal," she said. "I'm going to ask you one more time. Who are you, what have you done, and why did you try to kill me?"

So he told her, having come full circle back to the truth. He hurt badly, and he knew she was going to torture him. But he no longer wanted to live. There was more pain ahead, but there was peace at the end.

Jones picked up the knife. He whimpered when he saw it, and tried to make himself small, but it didn't work any better than it had before.

She cut the rope binding his left foot to the stake. At the same time, the Titanide loosened the knots binding his head to the post. His head fell forward, his chin hit his chest, and he kept his eyes firmly closed. But he eventually had to look.

What he saw was a miracle. Some of his pubic hair had been singed, but his penis, shriveled in fear, was unmarked. Beside it was a small piece of ice slowly turning into a puddle on the rock floor.

"You didn't hurt me," he said.

Jones looked surprised. "What do you mean? I burned you three times."

"No, I mean you didn't *hurt* me." He gestured with his chin.

"Oh. Right." Oddly, she looked embarrassed. Conal began to

taste the thought that he might live. To his surprise, it tasted good.

"I don't have the stomach for this," Jones admitted. Conal thought that, if she didn't, she put on a damn good act. "I can kill cleanly," she went on. "But I hate inflicting pain. I knew, in the state you were in, that you couldn't tell heat from cold."

It was the first time she had done anything like explain her actions. He was afraid to question her, but he had to do something.

"Then why did you torture me?" he asked, and immediately saw it was the wrong question. Anger showed in her eyes for the first time and Conal almost died of fright, because of all the things he had seen in those eyes nothing was so terrifying as her anger.

"Because you're a fool." She stopped, and it was as if twin doors had been closed over a roaring furnace; her eyes were cool and black again, but red heat glowed just beneath.

"You walked into a hornet's nest and you're surprised you got stung. You walked up to the oldest, meanest, and most paranoid human being in the solar system and told her you were going to kill her, and then you expected her to play by your comic book rules. The only reason you didn't die is my standing orders that if it looks like a human, let it live until I can question it."

"You didn't think I was human?"

"I had no reason to assume it. You might have been some new kind of Priest, or maybe some completely different practical joke. Sonny, in here we don't take *anything* at face value, we..."

She stopped, stood up, and turned away from him. When she turned back, she seemed almost apologetic.

"Well," she said. "There's no point in lectures. It's none of my business how you've lived your life; it's just that when I see stupidity I always want to correct it. Can you handle him, Hornpipe?"

"No problem," said the voice from behind him. He felt the ropes loosen; everywhere they came away caused pain, but it was wonderful. Jones squatted in front of him again, and looked at the ground.

"You've got a few choices," she said. "We've got some poison that's fairly painless and works quick. I could put a bullet through your head. Or you could jump, if you'd rather meet it that way." She spoke as though she were asking if he preferred cherry pie, cake, or ice cream.

"Meet what?" he said. Her eyes came up again, and he saw mild disappointment; he was being stupid again.

"Death."

"But . . . I don't want to die."

"Most people don't."

"We're out of poison, Captain," the Titanide said. He lifted Conal as though he were a rag doll, and started toward the mouth of the cave. Conal was not at his best. He felt far from the strength he normally possessed. He fought, and the nearer he came to the edge the stronger he grew, yet it meant nothing. The Titanide handled him easily.

"Wait!" he shouted. *"Wait!* You don't have to kill me!"

The Titanide set him on his feet at the edge of the drop, and held him as Jones put the muzzle of his gun to his temple and pulled back the hammer.

"Do you want the bullet or not?"

"Just let me go!" he screamed. "I'll never bother you again."

The Titanide did let him go, and it surprised him so badly he did a wild dance on the edge, almost fell over, went to his knees and then his belly and hugged the cool stone with his feet hanging over the edge.

They were standing ten feet from him. He got to his knees slowly and carefully, then sat back on his heels.

"Please don't kill me."

"I'm going to, Conal," she said. "I suggest you stand up and go out on your feet. If you want to pray or something, I'll give you time for that."

"No," he said. "I don't want to pray. And I don't want to get up. It doesn't really matter, does it?"

"That's always the way I figured it." She raised the gun.

"Wait! Wait, please, just tell me why."

"Is that a last request?"

"I guess so. I . . . I'm stupid. You're so much smarter than I am, you can squash me like a . . . but why do you have to kill me? I swear, you'll never see me again."

Jones lowered the pistol.

"There's a couple of reasons," she said. "As long as I've got a gun on you you're a harmless fool. But you might get lucky, and there's nothing I fear so much as a lucky fool. And if you'd done to me what I've just done to you, I'd come and I'd find you, no matter how long it took."

"I won't," he said. "I swear it. I swear it."

"Conal, there are maybe five humans whose word I trust. Why should you be number six?"

"Because I know I deserved what I got, and I'm eighteen years old and made a dumb mistake and I don't ever, *ever* want you angry with me again. I'll do anything. *Anything.* I'll be your slave for the rest of my life. I'll do anything you want me to do." He stopped, and knew to the depths of his soul that what he had just said was the truth. He remembered how little good the truth had done him a few hours ago. There had to be some way of proving to her that he spoke the truth. At last, he had it. A solemn oath.

"Cross my heart and hope to die," he said, and waited.

The bullet didn't come. He opened his eyes, and saw Jones and the Titanide looking at each other. At last the Titanide shrugged, and nodded.

MUSICAL INTERLUDE

Not long after Conal's arrival at Gaea, a ship named *Xenophobe* broke out of its circum-Saturn orbit and headed for Earth at maximum acceleration.

The *Xenophobe*'s departure had nothing to do with Conal. The ship and others like it had maintained orbit around Saturn for almost a century. The first one had been owned and operated by the United Nations. When that body died, ownership had passed to the Council of Europe, and later to other peace-keeping organizations.

None of the ships had ever been mentioned in any of the treaties and protocols signed between Gaea and various Earth nations and corporations. When Gaea had entered the U.N. as a full voting member, she had thought it the diplomatic thing to ignore their existence. The ships' purpose was an open secret. Each had carried enough nuclear weapons to vaporize Gaea. Treaty or no treaty, Gaea—

a single sentient being—massed more than all terrestrial life forms put together; it seemed wise to successive generations to have the capability of destroying her should she exhibit unforeseen powers.

"The truth is," Gaea had once said to Cirocoo, "I can't do shit, but why tell them that?"

"And who would believe you?" Cirocco had responded. Cirocco thought Gaea was secretly pleased to rate so much attention, such an unprecedented show of unanimity from the historically fractious peoples of Planet Earth.

But with the war about to enter its second year, *Xenophobe*'s cargo could be put to better use at home instead of being squandered in space.

Gaea noted its departure.

A being in the shape of a 1,300-kilometer wagon wheel cannot be said to smile, in any human sense of the word. But somewhere in the pulsing scarlet line of light that served Gaea as a center of consciousness, she was smiling.

Half a dekarev later, the Pandemonium Traveling Film Festival began showing a double feature to packed houses: *The Triumph of the Will*, by Leni Riefenstahl, and *Dr. Strangelove, or How I Learned to Stop Worrying and Love the Bomb*, by Stanley Kubrick.

In Gaea, time was doled out by the rev.

One rev was the time it took Gaea to rotate once on her axis: sixty-one minutes, three and a fraction seconds. The rev was often called the "Gaean hour." Metric prefixes were then used to describe any other length of time. The kilorev, called the Gaean Month, was forty-two days long.

Two kilorevs after *Xenophobe* left Saturn (to be shot down near the Moon's orbit by the Commie Rats), the mercy flights began. It was the first time Gaea had revealed any unforeseen powers.

It had been known that Gaea was an individual, aged specimen of a genetically engineered species called *Titan*. She had five younger sisters in orbit around Uranus, and an immature daughter waiting to be born from the surface of Iapetus, a moon of Saturn. Rare interviews granted by Gaea's Uranian sisters had established the Titan method of reproduction, the nature of Titan eggs, their method of promulgation and distribution.

It was also understood that Gaea, the senile Titan, had been known to employ manufactured beings that were not individuals with anything like free will, but rather extensions of herself in the same way that a finger or hand was an extension of a human's existence. These were called "tools of Gaea." For many years one of these tools had been presented to visitors as being Gaea herself. When Cirocco killed that particular tool, Gaea promptly manufactured another.

That tools and seeds could be combined came as no surprise to Cirocco. After ninety years of living with the insane God, little could surprise Cirocco.

The resulting organism was very much like a spaceship. Gaea released these sentient, steerable, immensely powerful seeds by the score as soon as she knew the *Xenophobe* was destroyed and nothing was likely to replace it. All of them shaped orbit for Earth. Of the first waves, ninety-five percent were destroyed before reaching the atmosphere. Year Two of the War was a nervous time; everyone was shooting first and not bothering to ask questions later.

But gradually the nature of the seeds was established. Each headed for a site of nuclear carnage, landed, and began shouting that salvation was at hand. The seeds spoke, played music calculated to lift the spirits of the broken creatures fleeing the holocaust, and promised medical care, fresh air, food, water, and unlimited vistas in the welcoming arms of Gaea.

The global nets picked up the story, dubbed the seeds "mercy flights." At first, it was hazardous to board one, as many were shot down attempting to leave Earth. But few hesitated. These were people who had seen horrors that would make hell itself seem like a summer resort. Before long, the combatants ignored the flights of Gaea's seeds. They had more important matters to consider, such as which million people to murder this week.

Each seed could carry about one hundred people. Frightful riots developed when the seeds landed. Children were often left behind as adults pushed beyond all civilized limits threw their children from them for the chance to board the seed.

No newsnet reported it, but the trip back to Saturn was miraculous. No injury was too severe to heal. The horrors of biological warfare were all cured. Everyone had plenty to eat and drink. Hope was reborn during the mercy flights.

* * *

Gaea's interior was divided into twelve regions. Six were in permanent daylight, six in endless night. Between these regions were narrow bands of failing or rising light—depending on one's direction of travel or state of mind—known as twilight zones.

The zone between Iapetus and Dione contained a large, irregular lake, surrounded by mountains, known as Moros. Moros means Doom or Destiny.

The coastline of Moros was irregular and precipitous. The southern part of it included scores of peninsulas, each defining a narrow, deep bay. The peninsulas were for the most part anonymous, but each bay had a name. There was the Bay of Fraud, the Bay of Incontinence, the Bay of Sorrow, the Bay of Equivocations, and Bays of Forgetfulness, Hunger, Disease, Combat, and Injustice. The list was long and depressing. The nomenclature, however, was logical, provided by early cartographers armed with lists from Greek mythology. All the bays were named after children of Nox (night), the mother of Moros. Moros was the eldest; Fraud, Incontinence, Sorrow, *et al.,* the benighted younger sibs.

The easternmost of the line was known as Peppermint Bay. The reason for the name was simple: nobody wanted to live in a place called the Bay of Murder, so the Wizard changed it.

There was one settlement on the Bay: Bellinzona. It was a sprawling, noisy, dirty place. Half of it clung to the almost vertical stone of the eastern peninsula, and the rest extended onto the water on pontoon piers. The islands of Bellinzona were artificial, standing on piles, or harsh knuckles or rock standing straight out of the black waters.

The city Bellinzona most resembled was Hong Kong. It was a polyglot city of boats. The boats were tied to piers or other boats, sometimes twenty or thirty deep. The boats were made of wood and came in every style humans had ever imagined: gondolas and junks, barges and dhows, smacks, wherries, and sampans.

Bellinzona was three years old when Rocky came to it, and already ancient with sin and decay, a giant felonious assault on the face of Peppermint Bay.

It was a human city, and the humans were as various as their boats, from every race and nation. There were no police, no fire department, no schools, courts, or taxes. There were plenty of guns, but there was no ammunition. Even so, the murder rate was astronomical.

Few of Gaea's native races frequented the city. It was too wet for the sand wraiths and too smoky for the blimps. The Iron Masters of Phoebe maintained an enclave on one of the islands from which they bought human children to be used as incubators and first meals for their hatchling stages. From time to time a Submarine would come to feed on the city, biting off large chunks and swallowing them whole, but for the most part the Bellinzona sewage disposal system kept the sentient leviathans distant. Titanides came to trade but found the city depressing.

Most Bellinzonans agreed with the Titanides. There were those who found romance in the place—raw, husky, and vital, "Fierce as a dog with tongue lapping for action, cunning as a savage. . . ." But unlike old Chicago Bellinzona was not hog butcher, tool maker, stacker of wheat. Food came from the lake, from manna, or from deep wells tapping Gaea's milk. The main things the city produced were dark brown stains in the water and plumes of smoke in the air; some part of Bellinzona was always burning. In its damp byways one could buy stranglers' nooses, poisons, and slaves. Human meat was sold openly in butchers' stalls.

It was as if all the misery of the tortured Earth had been brought to this one place, distilled, concentrated, and left to rot.

Which is exactly as Gaea had planned it.

On the 97,761,615th rev of the twenty-seventh gigarev, Phase-Shifter (Double-Sharped Lydian Trio) Rock'n'Roll stepped from his longboat and onto the end of Pier Seventeen on the outskirts of Bellinzona.

Cirocco Jones had once said of the Titanide that "It just shows you how a system designed to simplify things can get out of hand." What she meant was that any Titanide's *real* name was a song that told a great deal about the Titanide but could not be transliterated into any human tongue. Since no human had ever learned to sing Titanide without Gaea's help, it made sense for them to adopt names in English—the preferred human language in Gaea.

The system was useful—to a Titanide. The last name was that of his or her chord. Chords were like human clans, or associations, or extended families, or races. Few humans understood what the chords meant, though many could recognize the distinctive pelt each possessed, like Scottish tartans or school ties. The second, parenthetical name indicated which of twenty-nine ways had been employed to give birth to the Titanide, who could have from one to four parents. The first name celebrated the third important factor in any Titanide's heritage: music. They all chose musical instruments as first names.

But the system had broken down with Phase-Shifter. The Wizard had decided his name was just too outrageous to use. She dubbed him Rocky, and the name had stuck. It was a triumphant ploy for Cirocco, who had been plagued by the nickname for over a century. Now, having given the name to the Titanide, she found no one ever called her Rocky, if only to avoid confusion.

Rocky the Titanide moored his boat to a piling, looked around him, then up at the sky. It might have been late evening. It had been like that in Moros for three million Earth years, and Rocky had not expected it to change. There were clouds falling from the Dione spoke, three hundred kilometers overhead, while to the west sunlight yellow as butter streamed through the arched roof over Hyperion.

He sniffed the air and immediately regretted it, but sniffed again, cautiously, searching for the spoiled-meat scent of a Priest or the worse odor of Zombie.

The city seemed somnolent. Existing in perpetual fading twilight, Bellinzona had no rush hours or dead times. People did things when the spirit moved them, or when they could no longer put them off. And yet there was a pulse to the activity. There were times when violence hovered in the air, ready to be born, and times when the lazy beast, sated, coiled itself and nestled into a nervous sleep.

He approached an old buck human roasting fish heads over a fire in a rusty bucket.

"Old man," he said, in English. He tossed a small packet of cocaine, which the human snatched from the air, sniffed, and pocketed.

"Guard my boat until I return," Rocky said, "and I will give you another like that one."

Rocky turned and clattered down the dock on four adamantine hooves.

* * *

The Titanide was cautious, but not too worried. Humans had needed a long time to learn their lesson, but they had by now learned it well. When the ammunition ran out, Titanides had stopped being gentle.

They never had been, really, but they were realistic. There is no sense arguing with an armed human. For the better part of a century, most humans in Gaea had been armed. Now the bullets were gone and Rocky could walk the docks of Bellinzona with little fear.

He outweighed any five humans taken together, and was stronger than any ten. He was also at least twice as fast. If attacked by humans he was capable of kicking heads from bodies and pulling off limbs with his bare hands, and he would not hesitate to do so. If fifty of them ganged up on him, he could outrun them. And if nothing else worked, he had a loaded .38 revolver, more precious than gold, tucked into his belly pouch. But he intended to return the weapon, unused, to Captain Jones.

He was a formidable sight, trotting through the twilight city. He stood three meters high and seemed almost a meter wide. Centauroid in shape, he was an altogether smoother construction than the classical Greek model, and the details were all wrong. There was no join line between the human and equine parts of him. His whole body was smooth and hairless but for thick black cascades growing from his head and tail, and pubic hair between his front legs. His skin was pale lime green. He wore no clothing, but was festooned with jewelry and splashed with paint. Most startling of all to a human who had never seen a Titanide, he appeared to be female. It was an illusion: all Titanides had big, conical breasts, long eyelashes and wide, sensual mouths, and none grew beards. The top meter-and-a-half of him would instantly be identified as a woman in any culture on Earth. But sex in a Titanide was determined by the organs between the front legs. Rocky was a male who could bear children.

He moved down the narrow finger piers between the endless rows of boats, passing small groups of humans who gave him plenty of room. His wide nostrils flared. He smelled many things—roasting meat, human excrement, a distant Iron Master, fresh fish, human sweat—but never a Priest. Gradually he came to more traveled lanes, to the broad floating thoroughfares of Bellinzona. He clattered over bridges arched so high as to be nearly semi-circles. They were easy to negotiate in Gaea's one-quarter gravity.

He stopped at an intersection just short of the Free Female Quarter. He looked around, aware of the squad of seven human Free Females stationed at the interdiction line and as unconcerned about them as they were about him. He could enter the Quarter if he wished; it was human males the guards were watching for.

There were few other humans about. The only one he noticed was a female Rocky judged to be about nineteen or twenty years old, though it was hard to tell the age of a human between puberty and menopause. She sat on a piling with her chin in her hands, wearing low-cut black slippers with blunt toes. They had ribbons that laced around her calves.

She looked up at him, and instantly he knew other humans would judge her insane. He also knew she was not violent. The madness did not bother him; it was, after all, only a human word. In fact, the combination of insanity and non-violence produced the humans Rocky most admired. Cirocco Jones, now *there* was a madwoman. . . .

He smiled at her, and she cocked her head to one side.

She rose up on her toes. As her arms came up and out she was transformed. She began to dance.

Rocky knew her story. There were thousands like her: trash people, without a home, without friends, without anything. Even the beggars of Calcutta had owned pieces of sidewalk to sleep on, or so Rocky had heard. Calcutta was only a memory. Bellinzonans frequently had even less than that. Many no longer slept at all.

How old could she have been when the war came? Fifteen? Sixteen? She had survived it, had been picked up by Gaea's scavengers, and had come here, stripped not only of her physical possessions and her culture and everyone who had ever mattered to her, but of her mind as well.

Still, she was wealthy. Someone, certainly long ago on the Earth, had taught her to dance. She still had the dance, and the ballet slippers. And she had her madness. It was worth something in Gaea. It was protection; bad things often happened to those who tormented the insane.

Rocky knew humans could not see the music of the world.

The few humans around to witness, had they even noticed her dance, would not be hearing the sounds she created for him. To Rocky, the Titantown Philharmonic might be playing just behind her as she leaped and whirled. Gaea was wonderful for ballet. She hung in the air forever, and made walking on the tips of one's toes seem the natural gait for humans—insofar as they could be said to *have* a natural gait. Human dancing was a source of giddy excitement to Rocky. That they could *walk* was a miracle, but to *dance*....

In complete silence she created *La Sylphide* there on that filthy pier, on the edge of humanity's garbage bin.

She finished with a curtsy, then smiled at him. Rocky reached into his pouch and found another packet of cocaine, thinking it little enough payment for the smile alone. She took it and curtsied again. On impulse, he reached into his hair and pulled out a single white flower, one of many braided there. He held it out to her. This time the smile was sweeter than ever, and it made her cry.

"*Grazie, padrone, mille grazie,*" she said, and hurried away.

"You got a flower for me, too, dogfood?"

Rocky turned and saw a short, powerfully built human buck, or "buck canuck" as he liked to style himself. The Titanide had known Conal for three years, and thought him beautifully insane.

"I didn't think you went in for human—"

"Don't say 'tail,' Conal, or I'll remove some teeth."

"What'd I say? What's the big deal?"

"You couldn't possibly understand, being tone-deaf to beauty. Suffice it to say that your arrival was like a turd falling into a Ming vase."

"Well, I try." He shrugged his fleece-lined coat up around his shoulders, looked around, and took a final puff on the stub of his cigar, then tossed it into the murky water. Conal always wore the coat. Rocky thought it made him smell interesting.

"You seen anything?" Conal finally asked. He was looking at the seven sisters guarding the Quarter. They were looking right back at him, weapons held loose but ready.

"No. I don't know the town, but it seems quiet to me."

"Me, too. I was hoping your nose'd smell somthing I ain't been able to see. But I don't think anybody's been here for quite a while."

"If they had, I'd know it," Rocky confirmed.

"Then I guess they can go ahead." He scowled, then looked up at Rocky. "Unless you want to talk her out of it."

"I couldn't, and I wouldn't," Rocky said. "There is something badly wrong. Something has to be done."

"Yeah, but—"

"It's not that dangerous, Conal. I won't hurt her."

"You sure as hell better not."

They had bargained for a while, Cirocco and Conal, on that first day. It had been years ago, but Conal remembered it well. Conal had held out for lifetime servitude. Cirocco said that was too long: cruel and unusual punishment. She offered two myriarevs. Conal gradually came down to twenty. The Wizard offered three.

They settled on five. What Cirocco didn't know was that Conal intended then, and intended now, to fulfill his original promise. He would serve her until he died.

He loved her with his entire soul.

Which is not to say there had never been wavering, never a bad moment. It was possible to sit alone in the dark, unguarded, and begin to feel some resentment, to taste the idea that she had treated him badly, that she had done things to him that he didn't deserve. He had sweated many a "night" away, unsleeping in the eternal Gaean afternoon, feeling rebellion growing inside and knowing absolute terror. Because sometimes he thought that, far down in a place he could never see, he hated her, and that would be an awful thing, because she was the most wonderful person he had ever seen. She had given him life itself. He knew now, as he had not known then, that it was not something he would have done. He would have shot the stupid meddling fool, the idiot with his comic books. He'd shoot him today, if he ever encountered such a fool. One round, right through the head, *wham!* as was only right and proper.

The first few kilorevs had been tough. He was still amazed he had survived them. Mostly, Cirocco did not have time to worry about him, so he had been left behind in the escape-proof cave. He had a lot of time to think. As he healed, he took a look at himself for the first time in his life. Not in a mirror; there were no mirrors in the cave, and that drove him crazy for a while because he was so used to admiring the flow of muscles in his mirror, and because he wanted to see how disfigured he was. Eventually, he began looking in different directions. He started to use the mirror of past experience, and he was not pleased at what he saw.

What did he have? Adding it up, he came up with a strong body (now broken), and . . . his word. That was it.

Brains? Forget it. Charm? Sorry, Conal. Eloquence, virtue, integrity, restraint, honesty, gratitude, sympathy? Well. . . .

"You're strong," he told himself, "but not now, and, let's face it, she can beat you any time she needs to. You had a certain beauty, or so the girls said, but can you take credit for that? No, you were born that way. You had health, but not right now; you can hardly stand up."

What was left? It came down to honor.

He had to laugh. "An affair of honor," Cirocco had said, just before the Titanide clobbered him from behind. So what the hell was honor, anyway?

Conal had never heard of the Marquis of Queensbury, but he had picked up the rules of gentlemanly behavior. You don't shoot a man in the back. Torture is contrary to the Geneva Conventions. Always fire a warning shot in the air. Tell your opponent what you're going to do. Give the other fellow a fighting chance.

That was all very well, for games. Games were played by rules.

"Sometimes you have to pick your own rules," Cirocco told him, much later. But by then he had already figured that out.

Did that mean there were no rules at all? No. It just meant you had to decide which ones you could live with, which ones you could *survive* with, because Cirocco was talking about survival and she was better at it than anyone in the history of humanity.

"First you decide how important survival is," she said. "Then you know what you'll do to survive."

With enemies, there were no rules. Honor didn't enter into it. The best way to kill an enemy was from a great distance, without warning, in the back. If the need arose to torture your enemy, you ripped his guts out. If you had to lie, you lied. It didn't matter. This is the *enemy*.

Honor only arose among friends.

It was a hard concept for Conal. He had never had a friend. Cirocco seemed an unlikely place to start—seemed, in fact, a damn good candidate for the worst enemy he ever had. No one had ever hurt him a thousandth as much as she had.

But he kept coming back to his list. His word. He had given his word. Naked, defenseless, seconds from death, it had been all he had left to give, but he had given it honestly. Or so he thought. The trouble was, he kept thinking about killing her.

For a while he didn't think survival was worth it. He stood for long hours on the edge of the precipice, ready to jump, cursing himself for the groveling he had done.

The first time she came back, after an absence of over a hectorev, he told her what he had been thinking. She didn't laugh.

"I agree that one's word is worth something," she said. "Mine is worth something to me, so I don't give it lightly."

"But you'd lie to an enemy, wouldn't you?"

"Just as much as I had to."

He thought that over.

"I've already mentioned this," she said, "but it bears repeating. An oath made under duress is not binding. I wouldn't consider it so. An oath I haven't given freely is no oath at all."

"Then you don't expect me to live up to mine, do you?"

"Frankly, no. *I* see no reason why you should."

"Then why did you accept it?"

"Two reasons. I believe I can anticipate your move, if it comes, and kill you. And Hornpipe believes you'll keep your word."

"He will," Hornpipe said.

Conal didn't know why the Titanide was so confident. They left him again, quite soon, and he had more time to think, but he found himself going back over the same old paths. An oath given under duress . . . and yet, his Word.

In the end, there was nothing else. He had to jump, or he had to keep his word. Starting with that scrap dignity, perhaps he could build a man the Wizard might honor.

Conal and Rocky entered the Free Female quarter.

Each of the seven guards had to scrutinize Conal's pass, and even then there was an obvious reluctance to let him through. Since the establishment of the quarter two years earlier, not one human male had gone more than fifty meters beyond the gate and lived to tell about it. But the Free Females, by their very nature, were the one human group that acknowledged the Wizard's authority. Cirocco Jones was a goddess to them, a supernatural being, a figure of legend come alive. Her effect on the Free Females was much the same as a certifiable, living, breathing Holmes would have had on a group of fanatic Sherlockians: whatever she asked for, she got. If she wanted this man to pass into the zone, so be it.

Beyond the guard post was a hundred-meter walkway known as the Zone of Death. There were drawbridges, metal-clad bunkers with arrow slits, and cauldrons of flammable oils, all designed to slow an assault long enough for a force of amazons to be assembled.

A woman was waiting for them. She carried her forty-five years with a serenity many hope for but few achieve. Her hair was long and white. In the manner of Free Females at home, she wore nothing above the waist. Where her right breast had been there was now a smooth, blue scar that curved from her sternum to her seventh rib.

"Was there any trouble?" the woman asked.

"Hello, Trini," said Conal.

"No trouble," the Titanide assured her. "Where is she?"

"This way." Trini stepped off the dock onto the deck of a barge. They followed her to another boat, not quite as imposing. A rickety plank bridge took them to yet a third boat.

It was a fascinating journey for Rocky, who had always wondered what human nests looked like. Dirty, for the most part, he decided. Very little privacy, either. Some of the boats were quite small. There were tiny cockles with canvas awnings, and others open to the elements. All were stuffed with human females of all ages. He saw women asleep in bunks placed as far from the makeshift highway as space would allow. More women tended cooking fires, and babies.

At last they came to a larger boat with a solid deck. It was near the outside of the quarter, quite close to the open waters of Peppermint Bay. There was a big tent on the deck. Trini held a flap open and Conal and Rocky entered.

There were six Titanides in a space that might have held five comfortably. Rocky's arrival made it seven. Besides Conal, the only other human was Cirocco Jones, who was at the far end of the tent, wrapped in blankets, reclining in something that might have been a very low barber's chair. It put her head no more than a foot off the deck, where it was cradled between the yellow folded forelegs of Valiha (Aeolian Solo) Madrigal. The Titanide was drawing a straight razor slowly across Cirocco's scalp, putting the finishing touches on a shave that left the Wizard's head bare from the crown forward.

She raised her head, causing Valiha to coo a warning. Rocky noted that her head wobbled, that her eyes were not focusing well, and that, when she spoke, her speech was slurred, but that was to be expected.

"Well," Cirocco said. "Now we can begin. Cut when ready, doc."

Conal knew all but two of the Titanides. There was Rocky and Valiha, and of course Hornpipe, and Valiha's son Serpent. Valiha and Serpent looked like identical twins except for their frontal sex organs, even though Valiha was twenty and Serpent only fifteen. For a long time Conal had been unable to tell them apart. He nodded to Viola (Hypolydian Duet) Toccata, whom he knew only slightly, and was introduced to Celesta and Clarino, both of the Psalm chord, who nodded gravely to him.

He watched Rocky move in and kneel at the Captain's side. Serpent handed him a black bag, which he opened, producing a stethoscope. As he was fitting it to his ears, Cirocco grabbed the other end and put it to her bare head. She tapped her head with her fist.

"Dong...dong...dong..." Cirocco intoned, hollowly, then started laughing.

"Very funny, Captain," Rocky said. He was handing gleaming steel scalpels and drills to Serpent, who was in charge of sterilization. Conal moved closer and sat beside Rocky. Cirocco reached out and took his hand, grasped it strongly.

"So glad you could come, Conal," she said, and seemed to find it funny, because she started laughing again. Conal realized she was drugged. One of the Psalm sisters had pulled the blankets away from Cirocco's feet and was sticking pins in them, twirling them between thumb and forefinger.

"Ouch," Cirocco said, with no real feeling. "Ouch. Ow."

"Does that hurt?"

"Nope. Can't feel a thing." And she started to giggle.

Conal was sweating. He watched Rocky bend over, pull the blanket from Cirocco's chest, and put his ear to her heart. He listened in various places, then listened to her head. He repeated the process with the stethoscope, not seeming to have much faith in the device.

"Isn't it awfully hot in here?" Conal asked.

"Take off your coat," Rocky said, without looking at him.

Conal did, and realized that, if anything, it was cold in the tent. At least the sweat on his body felt clammy.

"Tell me, doc," Cirocco said. "When you get through, will I be able to play the piano?"

"Of course," Rocky said.

"That's *great*, 'cause I—"

"—never could play it before," Rocky finished. "That one's terribly old, Captain."

Conal couldn't help it; *he* had never heard that one. He laughed.

"What the hell are you doing?" Cirocco roared, trying to rise. "Here I am about to die, and you think it's funny, do you? I'll—" Conal never heard what she'd do, as Rocky was calming her. The rage was gone as quickly as it appeared and Cirocco laughed again. "Hey, doc, will I be able to play the piano?"

Rocky was smearing a purple solution over Cirocco's forehead. Three of the Titanides began to sing quietly. Conal knew it was a song of calming, but it didn't do anything for him. Cirocco, on the other hand, relaxed considerably. It probably helped if you understood the words.

"You can wait outside, Conal," Rocky said, without looking up.

"What are you talking about? I'm staying right here. Somebody's got to be sure you do it right."

"I really think you ought to leave," Rocky said, looking at him.

"Nuts. I can take it."

"Very well."

Rocky took a scalpel, and quickly, neatly, cut a large backward "C" from the crown of Cirocco's head to just over her eyebrows. With his purple-tinted fingers, he drew the flap of skin to the right, exposing the bloody skull below.

* * *

"Take him outside," Rocky said. "He'll be all right in a few minutes."

He heard Celesta trotting outside with Conal's limp body, just as he had earlier heard Conal hitting the floor, but Rocky never took his eyes from his work. He had known Conal would faint. The man had been practically screaming the fact for ten minutes. Any Titanide healer would have heard the symptoms, though they were inaudible to the human ear.

If there was one area of unqualified Titanide superiority, it was the ear.

It had been a Titanide ear that had first heard the odd sounds coming from Cirocco's head. They were not sounds that would register on a tape recorder—may not have been sounds at all, in the human sense of the word. But successive Titanide healers had heard it: a whisper of evil, the muttering of betrayal. Something was in there that shouldn't be. No one had any idea what it was.

Rocky had studied human anatomy. There had been talk of finding a human doctor to do the operation, but in the end Cirocco had rejected it, preferring to be in the hands of a friend.

So now here he was, preparing to open the skull of the being who stood in his world much as Jesus Christ stood to the human sect known as Christians.

He hoped no one realized how terrified he was.

"How's it look so far?" Cirocco asked. She sounded better to Rocky: much more relaxed. He took it as a good sign.

"I can't figure it out. There's this big black numeral eight in a white circle . . ."

Cirocco chuckled. "I thought it'd be inscribed 'Abandon hope, all ye who enter here.'" She closed her eyes for a moment, breathed deeply. "I thought I could feel that for a minute," she said, her voice shaking.

"Impossible," Rocky said.

"If you say so. Can I have a drink?"

Valiha held a straw to her lips, and she took a swallow of water.

"It's as I thought," Rocky said, after listening carefully. "The trouble lies deeper."

"Not much deeper, I hope."

Rocky shrugged as he reached for the drill. "If it is, it is beyond my powers." He connected the drill to a batteryplant, tested it, hearing the high-pitched whine. Cirocco grimaced.

"Tell me about rock and roll," she said.

Rocky put the point of the drill to Cirocco's skull and turned it on.

"Rock and roll was the fusion of several musical elements present in human culture in the early 1950s," Rocky began. "Rhythm and blues, jazz, gospel music, some country influence . . . it all began to come together under various names and in various styles around 1954. Most of our chord agree it achieved its first synthesis in Chuck Berry, with a song called 'Maybellene.'"

"'Why cancha be true?'" Cirocco sang.

Rocky moved the drill point to a new site, and looked at Cirocco suspiciously.

"You've been doing some research," he accused.

"I was just curious about your chord name."

"It was a grace note in musical history," Rocky admitted. "For a while it possessed an attractive energy, but its potential was soon mined out. This was not rare in those days, of course; a new musical form seldom lasted two years, much less a decade."

"Rock and roll lasted five decades, didn't it?"

"Depends on who you talk to." He finished the second hole and began on the third. "A species of music known as 'rock' persisted for a long time, but it had abandoned the zeitgeist."

"Don't use them big words on me. I'm just a dumb human."

"Sorry. The creative energy was expended in increasingly byzantine production, overwhelmed by technological possibilities it did not have the balls to exploit or the wit to understand. It became a hollow thing with a glitter exterior, more concerned with process than thesis. Craftsmanship was never its strong point, and soon was forgotten entirely. An artist's worth came to be measured in decibels and megabucks. For lack of a replacement it stumbled along, dead but not buried, until somewhere in the mid-90s, then was ignored as serious music."

"Harsh words from a guy whose last name is Rock'n'Roll."

Rocky had finished the fifth hole now. He started another.

"Not at all. I merely do not wish to deify a corpse, as some scholars do. Baroque music is still alive so long as there are those who play and enjoy it. In that sense, rock and roll lives, too. But the possibilities of baroque were depleted hundreds of years ago. The same with rock."

"When did it die?"

"There's some debate. Many say 1970, when McCartney sued the Beatles. Others put it as late as 1976. Some prefer 1964, for various reasons."

"What do you prefer?"

"Between '64 and '70. Closer to '64."

He now had a series of eight holes drilled. He began using a saw to cut between them. He worked in silence, and for a while Cirocco had nothing to say. There was just the sound of the bone saw and, outside, the quiet lapping of the water against the side of the boat.

"I've read critics who speak highly of Elton John," Cirocco said.

Rocky just snorted.

"What about a rock revival in the 80s?"

"Rubbish. Are you going to mention disco next?"

"No, I won't mention it."

"Good. You wouldn't want my fingers to slip."

Cirocco screamed.

Rocky's hand almost slipped on the rotary saw. He had never heard such agony in a human voice. The scream was still rising in pitch and volume, and Rocky wanted to die. What had he done? How could he be causing so much pain to his Captain?

She would have ripped the skin from her face but for Valiha's strong arms. As it was, every muscle in Cirocco's body stood out like cables. She fought, the scream dying for lack of air. Its very silence was more painful to Rocky's ears. She began to bite her tongue; Serpent moved in and jammed a piece of wood between her teeth, but it was only in one side. The tension was uneven. Rocky heard her jawbone crack.

Then it was over. Cirocco's eyes opened, and moved cautiously back and forth, as if looking for something about to spring on her. The stick of wood was bitten nearly in two.

"What was that?" she said, slurring the words. Rocky gently

felt her jaw, found the fracture, and decided to fix it later.

"I was hoping you'd tell me." He leaned over to let Serpent mop the sweat from his face.

"It was...like all the headaches in the world, all at once." She looked puzzled. "But I can hardly remember it. Like it's not there, or never was there."

"I guess you can be thankful for that. Do you want me to go on?"

"What do you mean? We can't stop now."

Rocky looked down at his hand, which had stopped shaking. He wondered why he'd ever studied human anatomy. If he hadn't been so damn curious someone else could have been handling this.

"It just seemed like a warning," was all he would say. Though he had told no one, he actually had a pretty good idea what he would find under Cirocco's skull.

"Open it up," Cirocco said, and let her eyes close again.

Rocky did as he was told. He finished his last cut, and lifted the section of bone away. Beneath was the dura mater, just as Gray's had said it would be. He could see the outlines of the cerebrum beneath the membrane. In the middle, in the great longitudinal fissure between the two frontal lobes, there was a swelling that should not have been there. Cruciform, inverted, like some unholy devil's mark...

The mark of the Demon, Rocky thought.

As he watched, the swelling moved.

He cut around it, lifted the membranes from the gray matter beneath, and looked down at a nightmare. The nightmare looked back, blinking.

It was pale white, translucent, except for its head. It looked like a tiny snake but it had two arms which ended in miniscule clawed hands. Its body nestled into the longitudinal fissure, and it had a tail that descended between the hemispheres.

Rocky saw all that in the first few seconds; what he kept coming back to was the thing's face. It had outsize, mobile, troglodyte eyes set in the face of a lizard. But the mouth moved; it had lips, and Rocky could see a tongue.

"Put that *back!*" the thing shrieked. It started to burrow between the lobes of Cirocco's brain.

"Tweezers," Rocky said, and they were slapped into his palm. He grabbed the demon by the neck and pulled it out. But its tail was longer than he had thought, and still was lodged firmly in the fissure.

"The light! *The light!*" the creature was piping; Rocky had it by the neck, so he squeezed harder and the thing began to gurgle.

"You're choking me!" it squealed.

Nothing would have pleased Rocky more than to twist its vile head off, but he was afraid what that might do to Cirocco. He called for another tool, and used it to gingerly separate the halves of the brain. He could see, down deep, that the monster's tail was embedded in the *corpus callosum*.

"Mother," Cirocco said, in an odd voice. She began to cry.

What to do, what to do? Rocky didn't know, but he did know one thing: he could not close her head until the creature was removed.

"Scissors," he said. When he had them, he inserted them between the halves of the brain, down as far as he could go, until he had the tip of the demon's tail between the blades. He hesitated.

"No, no, no—" the thing screamed when it saw what he was doing.

Rocky cut.

The thing screamed bloody hell, but Cirocco did not move. Rocky held his breath for a long time, let it out, then looked again. He could see the severed end of the tail down there. It writhed, then came free from its mooring, the nature of which Rocky did not know. But it was loose, anyway, and Rocky almost reached for it with the tweezers, then remembered his prisoner—who had turned quite blue. He handed it to Serpent, who popped the squalling obscenity into a jar and sealed the lid. Rocky removed the severed bit of tail.

"Captain, can you hear me?" he said.

"Gaby," Cirocco murmured. Then she opened her eyes. "Yes. I can hear you. I saw you get it."

"You did?"

"I did. I'm not sure how. And it's gone. It's all gone. I know."

"Gaea will not be happy this day," Valiha sang. "We have her spy." She held up the jar. Inside it, the creature writhed, sucking on the end of its amputated tail.

"Sorry about that," Conal said, as he sat beside Rocky. He looked at Cirocco a bit queasily, but he was in control. "That looks normal, doesn't it, Rocky? Didn't you find anything?"

Valiha held up the jar. Conal looked.

"Somebody help him," Rocky said. "It's time to close up."

* * *

Eleven revs after Rocky had sewn Cirocco's head back together, the Pandemonium Theater began another double feature: *Rock Around the Clock*, with Bill Haley and the Comets, and *Donovan's Brain*.

As usual, no one knew why Gaea had selected these particular movies from her vast library, but many people attending noticed she did not seem happy. She hardly watched the screen. She fidgeted and brooded. She got so agitated that at one point she accidentally stepped on two panaflexes and a human, killing all three.

The corpses were quickly eaten by Priests.

EPISODE TEN

No one dreamed the war could last for seven years, but it did.

Like any war, it had its ups and downs. There was one five-month period when no bombs fell and some dared hope it was over. Then Dallas was hit, and the exchanges were renewed. Four times huge flights of missiles arced from one area of the globe to another— massive "Sunday Punches" designed to end the conflict once and for all. None of them did so. Combatants fell by the wayside when they reached the point where no one survived capable of directing the attack. But a hard core of about two dozen nations were dug in so securely they could well be fighting for two centuries.

Fully seventy percent of the weapons malfunctioned in one way or another. "Dud" bombs fell in hundreds of cities, spewing plutonium, notifying the residents that another bomb would soon follow. Editorials were written deploring the greed of munitions makers who had cut corners on government contracts, thinking no one would ever know the bombs were defective. Company presidents were lynched; lynching became a world-wide mania, something to take one's mind off the war. Generals were skinned alive, diplomats drawn and quartered, premiers boiled in oil, but nothing seemed to help. The ones who mattered were in bunkers five miles deep.

There were peace efforts. The usual ending to a conference

was the vaporization of the host city. Geneva took a beating, and so did Helsinki, and Djakarta, and Sapporo, and Juneau. Eventually, negotiators were shot on sight if they tried to enter a city.

After seven years the war no longer appeared on the evening news. All public news-gathering operations had been destroyed. All satellite time was used for encoded military messages, and no one had a television to receive a broadcast, anyway. About a hundredth of the Earth's nuclear arsenal had been expended, and another twentieth destroyed before it could be used. There was still a lot left.

There were not many people, though.

It had been three years since a crop of any consequence had been brought in. Those few who survived on the surface scrounged for canned food, hunted, and ate each other. But there was little game left, animal or human.

Since the beginning of the war messiahs had been proclaimed at the rate of three or four per hour. Most of them claimed to know how to stop the war, but none of them did. Most of them were dead, now, and soon the Earth would be, too.

For seven years the Outlanders had been walking on eggs. Quick to declare neutrality at the outset of the war, the Lunar and Martian cities and the orbital colonies hoped only to stay out of the way while civilization collapsed down on Earth. Opinion varied as to whether the three Lunar nations could survive without support from Earth. There were almost a million people living on the moon at the outbreak of the war. The Martians figured to hold out twenty years, but no more than that.

Outnumbering these planet-bound settlements were the O'Neil colonies. There were hundreds of them, with populations ranging from five to a hundred thousand. Most were located at L4 and L5, points of gravitational stability sixty degrees in front of and behind Luna. There were also sizable clusters at L1 and L2, despite the perturbations that tended to make the structures drift out of the libration points; with a small thruster, even the largest colony could remain stable with minimum energy expenditure.

Those thrusters came in handy for something else as the war dragged on. Quietly, not making a big fuss about it, some of the O'Neils began converting into space vehicles. The newer ones had drives that were more than adequate already. Others needed some time, and took the slowest of orbits, but a migration began of all those who felt they could survive without the Earth.

There were a lot of places to go, none of them very good. One tried to make it in orbit around Mercury, where the free energy was intense. It proved to be *too* intense. A few took up orbit around Venus, and in Trojan orbit with Venus. Many more went out to the neighborhood of Mars, or to the Earth's Trojan points. The problem was to get far enough away from the Earth to seem not worth shooting at and unlikely to hit, while staying close enough to the sun to survive.

A very few decided to take the big leap. They converted their homes into starships and headed out.

Conal heard about these events from refugees arriving during the seventh year of the war. An inescapable image came to mind: he saw the Earth as a blackened globe, cracking apart, girdled in flame. Tiny mites were scurrying away in droves.

"Rats leaving a sinking ship," he told Cirocco.

"And what would you expect rats to do?" she countered. "Go down bravely? The rat's about the smartest animal there is, and the toughest. The rats don't owe the ship a damn thing, and neither do those ellfivers."

"No need to bite my head off."

"I'll keep doing it as long as you think it's a good idea to trust psychopaths. Anybody who *can* get away from the Earth right now and *doesn't* is saying she believes it's okay to lie down with a mad dog. Those ellfivers are the sane escaping the asylum. And maybe the grave."

When he had the time, Conal liked to hang around the Portal just outside Bellinzona, improving the breed.

The Portal was just what the name implied: the port of entry for all the wretched refuse who flocked to Gaea's shores. On Gaea's outer surface was the catcher that retrieved Gaea's returning eggs or the now-infrequent human ships seeking refuge. From there the people were taken to Gaea's equivalent of Ellis Island, far down in her bowels, where they were processed. The immigration procedure had once been complex and time-consuming. Now it was simplicity itself: holy people to the left, mortals to the right. Messiahs, priests, preachers, pastors, shamen, gurus, juju men, dervishes, monks, rabbis, mullahs, ayatullahs, vicars, necromancers, prelates, and popes all were taken directly to an audience with Gaea. The rest were loaded into capsules with what they could carry on their backs. There was a short ride through Gaea's circulatory system to a sphincter valve that squeezed them out, twenty at a time, into a small cave that Cirocco called "the asshole of the world."

Since all the refugees came out at the same place, the Portal attracted a certain element that hoped to prey on weakness or ignorance. Like pimps standing sentry in a big-city bus station, these people were on the lookout for immigrants who had something that could be sold at a profit. Sometimes it was their meager material goods. Sometimes it was a lot worse than that.

It was a strange game Conal played. He had played it many times, though Cirocco said he was a fool to do so. He would have kept doing it even if he thought she really meant that, but he knew she didn't, and Hornpipe had confirmed it.

"It is a worthwhile foolishness," the Titanide had said. "It is a Titanide thing to do." Titanides didn't care if a cause was lost, and it didn't worry them that they could not stamp out all the evil in the world. If they saw a chance to do some good without getting themselves killed, they did it, and so did Conal.

Which was not to say he went about it rashly. Some of the Portal layabouts ran in gangs, and took a dim view of anyone interfering in their activities. Conal would hang back, out of their way, and look for the chance to stalk the hunter as he led his prey to a dark, private place. When that chance came, when he had come in behind a Portal Rat and taken him by surprise, Conal killed him. Murderer, thief, slaver, or babylegger—it was all the same to Conal. There were no jails in Bellinzona, no middle ground between the quick and the dead.

More often he would have to watch as people got the living shit beat out of them and were stripped naked and left bleeding. Then he would take the victim to one of the jack-leg medicine men who served the function of hospitals in Bellinzona.

Today seemed like a good day. Looking around, he spotted a group of four Vigilantes wielding clubs that bristled with rusty nails. There were also three Free Female archers standing well away on high ground. With any luck at all, he would not have to do anything. The mere presence of these protective societies had driven many of the vermin away.

Increasingly, the pickings had been small at the Portal. More and more people arrived without so much as a stitch of clothing, wearing a vacant look: the walking corpses of Graveyard Earth. Most had been at the edge of death when rescued, some after suffering horribly for years. Gaea healed their bodies, but either could not or would not do anything about their minds.

Today's group was different. Fully half of them were not only clothed, but carried packs and suitcases brimming with booty. Conal could hear the jackals start to murmur. A Free Female bow twanged and an arrow shaft appeared in a man's throat; it qualified as a gentle warning in Bellinzona. The Vigilantes began laying about them with their clubs, but soon were forced onto the defensive. Conal began to edge back. He didn't plan to die in a riot.

He saw a particularly interesting duo just as he was about to leave. A short, thirtyish woman with some kind of painting on her face carried a small bundle in her arms, walking beside a stunningly beautiful young woman who must have been six feet tall. Both women wore brilliant, padded synsilks: spacer's clothes. The tall one carried most of the baggage, but the short one had a large synsilk pack.

Conal groaned. It was like watching a treasure-laden Spanish galleon sail into a nest of pirates. They had no idea what was about to happen.

It came quickly. A small figure darted from the crowd, punched the small one in the face, and grabbed the bundle. Conal realized it was an infant. The mother started to chase the man, but was suddenly hemmed in by the rest of the gang, who would strip the two women clean while the point man made off with the real prize.

There was nothing he could do to help the women. There were at least six men attacking them. So he would follow the man with the baby, because of all the things that could happen in Gaea he felt being sold to the Iron Masters was the worst. He was already after the man when the screaming began. Against his will, he looked back.

It was like a tornado. The women had knives in each hand, and knives in their boots, and they were whirling madly, shrieking at the top of their lungs, slashing and stabbing. One man took seven wounds before he had time to fall down and start to die. Another tried to hold his throat together as a second blade entered his bowels. Four were down, then five, as others moved in with knives drawn.

It was too bad, really. It was the most amazing display of sheer, furious will to fight he had ever seen, but he didn't see how the two could hold off an army. They were going to take a fine honor guard to hell with them, but they were going to die. The least he could do was save the child of the older warrior.

He had almost waited too long, mesmerized by the carnage. The fleeing kidnapper was approaching the main bridge to Bellinzona when Conal finally got through the crowd and into the open.

He was a hundred meters behind the man when he left the bridge. The fleeing man was small and quick. He darted in and out of the crowd, and then he outsmarted himself. Knowing a running man is conspicuous, he slowed down, glancing over his shoulder to see if anyone was back there. If he had kept running for another minute, Conal might well have lost him, and if Conal had kept running one second longer, he would have been spotted. But this was Conal's game, and when the man looked back, he saw no sign of pursuit.

The man saw nothing the second time he looked back, nor the third. There was nothing to be seen the fourth time, either, and for a very good reason. Conal was in front of him by then.

It wasn't too hard to figure out where the man was going; the location of the Iron Masters' trading post was well-known. There was no sense in keeping a kidnapped human baby any longer than you had to; most humans took a dim view of babylegging. So Conal positioned himself on a narrow pier and waited.

The man came hurrying along, still intent on pursuit from behind. Conal had the feeling the man had heard those screams and they had rattled him. He did what Conal had expected, which was hold the baby up in front of him while he went for Conal with a knife in his right hand. Conal grabbed his wrist and broke it; the man cried out and the knife fell. With his other hand, Conal reached around and stabbed the man in the back. He dropped the baby and Conal caught it, then pulled his knife out and eased the man down onto the wooden dock.

He made sure the baby was all right, then knelt beside the kidnapper.

Man. Okay, in Bellinzona, thirteen or fourteen years was enough to make you a man. It still didn't feel right to Conal. He still looked like a boy. He was Japanese, Conal thought. That wasn't rare, either. The human population of Gaea was roughly proportional to the population of Earth, which meant there were a lot more brown and black and yellow skins than white.

The boy was in a lot of pain, babbling something in his native tongue, and it looked like it was going to take him a while to die. Conal held up the knife and raised his eyebrows in what he hoped was a universal questioning gesture. The boy nodded excitedly. Conal slipped the blade between the ribs and into the heart, and the boy was dead in a moment.

He wiped the blade and put it away.

"The big hero," he muttered. It was a shitty world when you couldn't kill a baby-murdering human carcinoma and feel good about it. As usual, Cirocco had the last word. There were just not a hell of a lot of things you could do in this life that didn't taste bad in one way or another.

There was the problem of what to do with the baby.

He could think of several things. There were religious orders and some other organizations that took in orphans. Of these, the strongest was the Free Females—also, in his opinion, the likeliest to provide proper care for an infant.

The baby was bundled in some sort of spacer's carrying pack; it was not immediately obvious how to unfasten it. But he finally managed. He looked in the pertinent place, and shook his head. Okay, so the Free Females wouldn't want the little guy. Who was the next best?

He had a funny thought. It was impossible, of course, but what if . . . ?

So he headed back toward the Portal.

They were still there, still alive. Unless something happened soon, though, they would not be alive much longer.

There was a crowd of about a hundred of the toughest, meanest types Bellinzona had to offer, standing in a semi-circle fifty meters away from the rock wall where the two women were cornered. The area in between was littered with bodies. Conal stopped counting after two dozen. There were many more than that. He stood at the back of the crowd, trying to figure out what had happened.

The clue was in the bodies. Most of the ones close to the two women had died of knife wounds. The more distant ones had wounds seldom seen anymore in Gaea: round wounds about the size of a dime. His guess was confirmed when one of the people in the crowd threw a spear, and one of the women shot him in the stomach. Conal ducked. The crowd moved back, but inexorably began to close in again. The temptation was just too great.

It was a stand-off. No one in the crowd knew how much ammunition the two had left. Had they charged as a group the mob could have overwhelmed them, but there was no organization among these jackals.

He thought about it, and saw the irony. Obviously, the two had a limited number of bullets, or they would simply have shot everyone within range. Nobody in the crowd wanted to soak up a bullet just to enable someone else to grab the treasure. So the outcome, in minutes or hours, would be for the women to run out of bullets, in which case they could be attacked again—but then it wouldn't be worth it.

Conal took another look at the tall one. Seventeen, he thought. Maybe eighteen. Long blonde hair, fierce blue eyes. She was beautiful, as he had already observed. But there was something else about her, something she shared with the older woman—her mother? It was a look that said she would die on her feet, fighting, that she would never be taken alive. He respected that. He had learned what it meant to be taken alive, and it was never going to happen to him again, either.

Another spear was thrown, and the tall one snapped off another shot. This one went through the spear-thrower and into the heart of a man standing behind him. Nice gun, Conal thought.

Where were the Free Females? he wondered, then saw them. They were also backed to the wall, but one was dead, another badly wounded. The third crouched by her sisters, an arrow ready, looking very frightened. The two groups were twenty meters apart, and the newcomers showed no signs of wishing to join up with the archer. Who the hell *were* these people, anyhow? Apparently they didn't trust anyone. He hadn't seen anybody so suspicious since ... well since Cirocco Jones. It wasn't going to be easy to rescue the

Until that moment, he hadn't realized he *was* going to rescue them. He wasted a few minutes trying to talk himself out of it. Looked at reasonably, it seemed the most foolhardy thing he had tried since the day he swaggered into a bar and told the most dangerous woman alive he planned to kill her.

He looked down at the face of the baby boy.

"What the hell do you have to smile about, mister?" Conal asked him. Then he turned and hurried back over the bridge.

"A hundred, did you say?" the Titanide named Serpent raised a dubious brow.

"Hell, Serpent, you know I can't count to twenty-one without opening my fly. There's *about* a hundred, maybe a hundred twenty."

"Describe the smaller one to me again?"

"Drawings on her face. A real fright mask. The other one—"

"They are tattoos," Serpent said.

"You mean they don't come off? How do you know?"

"She has a third eye drawn on her forehead, doesn't she."

"Yeah . . . yeah, I think so. Her hair was bouncing around a lot. They were pretty busy trying to look six ways at once. . . . How did you know?"

"I know her."

"Then you'll come?"

"Yes, I think I will." He looked around the big warehouse that served the Titanides as a trading post, picked up two other Titanides with his eyes. "In fact, I think we'll make it a troika."

They sounded like the Apocalypse minus one as they thundered over the wooden bridge. Conal, clinging to Serpent's back, wished he had a bugle. It was the friggin' cavalry to the rescue, by God. The people in the back of the mob spent only a moment gaping at the sight, then scurried like hyenas from a carcass. They ran anywhere they could go. Many of them jumped into the putrid waters of the lake.

But a lot didn't have time to flee. The Titanides waded in, weaponless, and began breaking necks.

Conal had worried the women might fire at these apparitions, ntly their suspicious natures didn't extend to Titanides. lert for an opportunity to break through and get away from the wall. Then Serpent lifted Conal and tossed him over the heads of the circle of people.

He landed on his feet and just managed to stay on them, stumbling forward, holding the baby out in front so they wouldn't be tempted to shoot him. He had been gone for almost a rev, and during that time the women had been stoned by the crowd. He tripped over a large, loose rock, fell, and crawled around the makeshift barricade of luggage they had been crouching behind.

He looked up into the face of the blonde amazon. Nineteen, he decided. There was a line of drying blood down the left side of her face. He felt a surge of anger; he wanted to kill the bastard who did that. There was more pressing business, however, such as the gun she held to his temple. He held out the baby and put on his most winning smile.

"Hi. I'm Conal, and I think this belongs to you."

Another of Cirocco's favorite aphorisms: Never Expect Gratitude. Her upper lip curled contemptuously, and she jerked her head toward the older woman.

"Not me. It's *hers*."

TRAVELOGUE

At about the same time Conal was charging to the rescue in Bellinzona, an angel came to Cirocco Jones in Phoebe.

She stood at the edge of the three-kilometer cliff that marked the northern highlands and watched the angel approach from the south. Beyond the angel was a dark mountain. It had four distinct peaks, each a different height. To Cirocco, it resembled a broken bottle planted butt-first in the ground, with dirt heaped up around it. Others had seen a ruined belfry. Cirocco admitted the aptness of that analogy: there were even bats circling it. Or at least they looked like bats. The peak was twenty kilometers away. To be seen at that distance, the bats had to be the size of jetliners.

Cirocco knew the place well. She had spent some time there many years ago. It was not something she liked to remember.

The angel swept above her, circled to lose altitude, then hovered by beating his brilliant wings. He was unwilling to set foot on Phoebe. Cirocco knew that hovering was taxing for an angel, so she did not waste words.

"Kong?" she shouted.

"Dead. Two, three hundred revs."

"Gaea?"

"Gone."

She thought it over for a second, then waved her thanks.

Cirocco watched him into the distance, then sat down on the edge of the cliff. She removed her boots—lovely brown knee-length things of Titanide manufacture, supple and waterproof—folded them into a small, flat bundle, and stowed them in her pack. Then she shouldered the pack, checking its straps and the few items attached to her belt, turned around, and began climbing down the cliff.

An Acapulco cliff-diver would have beaten her down the side of that cliff, but nothing else human could have. With bare feet and hands, ignoring the rope coiled in her pack, she moved down the difficult, near-vertical slope faster than most people could have gone down a ladder. She did it without giving it much thought. Her hands and feet knew what to do.

She had thought about this from time to time, when other people reminded her that something she was doing was remarkable. She knew she was no longer quite human. She also knew she was a long way from being super-human. It was all a matter of perspective. Some of it was a matter of learning from every event in one's life, and Cirocco did that well. Most of her mistakes were decades behind her. Some of it was knowing one's limits, high as they might be. An observer watching her progress down the cliff would have thought she was in an awful hurry, taking insane chances. Actually, she could have done it a lot faster.

Cirocco looked to be between thirty-five and forty years old, but it depended on where you looked. The skin on her hands and neck and face looked more like thirty; the wiry arms and marathon legs seemed older, while the eyes were older still. A hard woman to judge, was Cirocco Jones. She looked very strong, but appearances are deceiving. She was *much* stronger than she looked.

When she reached the gentle hills at the bottom of the highland cliffs she put on her boots and began to run, not because she was in a big hurry but because there was nothing else to do and it was her natural gait.

She covered the twenty kilometers in a little over a rev. She would have done it faster, but there had been three rivers to swim. It didn't take long to scale Kong Mountain. It was just a steady upward slope until the jagged multiple peaks were reached, and she had no need to climb them. There was a broad highway leading into Kong's den.

She took the last part slowly. It wasn't that she didn't trust the angel. If he said Kong was dead, then he was dead. But the smell of the place brought back unpleasant memories.

The rock arched over her and soon she was walking in gloom. Twice she had to detour around twenty-meter lozenges sitting in the middle of the path. These were the "bats" she had seen from a distance. They were actually more of a cross between a reptile and a garden slug, massing ten or twelve tonnes. With their pterodactyl wings folded against their bodies, they might have been mistaken for collapsed circus tents. They certainly did not seem to be alive, but they were. They would sometimes hibernate for as long as a myriarev. They flew by crawling on their slug-foot to the top of one of Kong's spires, detaching themselves, and gliding for days at a time. As far as Cirocco knew, they were harmless. She never had figured out what they ate, or why they flew. She suspected they had been made merely to give the place the proper atmosphere. In Gaea, that was not an unreasonable assumption to make.

She reached the end of the passage and cautiously looked over the edge.

The floor of the cavern was a hundred meters below her. It was a passable copy of the chamber through which a foot-high rubber model of a gorilla had stalked in a movie from the 1930s. There was a shallow lake and many rock formations resembling stalactites and stalagmites—all of them much bigger than could have been formed through geological processes in Gaea's three million years. Like many places in Gaea, it was a carefully constructed setting.

But it was a ruined setting. Many of the rock formations had been snapped off. The lake was churned to sludge, the muddy shoreline pocked with footprints three meters deep. The water had a pink tinge. And centered in the weak, slanting rays of light that found their way through the vaulted ceiling was the star of the show; the mighty Kong, eighth wonder of the world.

Cirocco remembered when he'd looked better.

He was on his back, surrounded by Lilliputian swarms of Iron Masters who were busy dismantling him.

They went about it with their customary thoroughness, speed, and efficiency. A rail line had been run in through the southern entrance of the mountain. Cirocco knew it would connect with a funicular down the slope, probably joining a new spur from their Black Forest roadbed, in turn joining the main Phoebe-Arges line. A train idled at the railhead, a 2-10-4 chromium-plated steam engine presiding over twenty hopper cars normally used for iron ore from the Black Forest, now full of bits of Kong. The Iron Masters were good at railroads.

They were good at a lot of things. They had Kong down to a head, a torso, and part of an arm. There were massive bones being sliced up by noisy steam-powered saws.

It was gruesome, but fascinating. Cirocco had expected Kong would stink to high heaven after three hundred revs—almost two weeks. Not that the place didn't stink—it had in the best of times, she recalled, because it had never occurred to Kong to shovel out the tonnes of manure he generated every kilorev or even to step outside to relieve himself. But he did not appear to be rotting.

This annoyed Cirocco. Okay, so there was no law saying he had to rot, but the bastard *ought* to rot.

Still, there he was, hacked away up to his surprisingly complex ribcage, looking as fresh as the day he was slaughtered. Iron Master crews were cutting at his body with big flensing knives on long sticks, detaching hunks of pink meat, lifting them with hooks powered by a donkey engine and a tall mast like the ones loggers erect deep in the forest.

Another hectorev and he'd be gone.

It was no loss to Cirocco. She doubted anything could ever make her feel sorry for the great, idiotic beast. If anybody wept for him, she would invite the bleeding heart to spend a year in Kong's dungeons, watching him bite the heads off live Titanides. His huge head was turned toward Cirocco. Funny about Kong: he didn't look like a gorilla. His was a chimp's head, complete with silly-putty lips and flapping ears. His pelt was orangutan-brown and matted with filth.

There were only two things about the scene that really interested her, aside from the good news of his demise. Who had killed him? And why did the Iron Masters have his one remaining arm strapped down with heavy cables?

Meet, meet, meet, meeeeeet!

Cirocco turned slowly at the sound, spotted the little bolex perched ten meters above her in a rocky niche. It goggled down at her, quiet now.

Ah *ha!* she thought.

"C'mere critter," she crooned, climbing up after it. "Here boy, c'mon, I won't hurt you." She made all the whistling and tongue-clicking sounds appropriate to summoning a puppy, but the bolex squealed and backed into its niche, which was deeper than Cirocco had supposed. She tried reaching in for it, but it just retreated farther. She pulled back, stymied for a moment.

She considered asking the Iron Masters for help. They'd quickly blow the little bugger out. Then she had a better idea. She went back down to her ledge and began to dance and sing.

Cirocco was an excellent singer but Isadora Duncan would have had nothing to fear from her. Nevertheless, she worked at it, making enough noise so some of the Iron Masters looked up from their work for a moment—only to look back, doubtless filing away one more example of indecipherable human behavior in their cool, tin-foil brains.

Soon the bolex peered out. Cirocco danced faster. Its glassy eye glistened. She saw it stick out for a zoom shot, and soon it was scampering down, its eye held rock-steady. No bolex had ever been able to resist action.

When it got close enough she grabbed it. The bolex squealed, but it was defenseless. It kept shooting. Cirocco knew it must have run out of film long ago if it had come here with the Pandemonium Festival. And sure enough, the associateproducer attached to its back was dead. She peeled it off—they held on like leeches, long after they had become nothing but film canisters—and let the bolex go. It continued to shoot as it backed away, backed away, obviously ecstatic at the shots it was getting until it fell off the ledge and crashed on the rocks below.

Cirocco got out a knife and slit the assosh up the middle. Inside it was quite dry, and sixteen hundred feet of super-eight film was coiled on a reel delicate as a seashell.

She pulled out several feet of the film, held it up to the light, and squinted at it. Not much detail could be seen, of course, but it was quite clear there were two figures wrestling. One was brown and one was white. The white one was naked, and female. There could be little doubt who it was.

It must have been spectacular, but that was no suprise. Gaea had few budget restrictions. Cirocco could imagine the scene: Kong, master of all he surveyed, standing in dumb puzzlement as the obscene circus encamped, perhaps giving the fifteen-meter woman a wary eye. Kong was programmed to kill Titanides and human males, and to imprison human females. But Gaea would not have smelled right. None of the other mad creatures associated with Pandemonium would have looked like food or likely captives, either. And without that, Kong was essentially a pussycat. He was lazy, and he was stupid. Gaea's big problem had most likely been getting him to put up a fight.

Cirocco *almost* felt sorry for Kong.

"Gaea deeded the corpse to us."

She turned to face the Iron Master who had joined her on the ledge.

"Fine," she said. "You can have him."

"She said you were welcome to a percentage, should you happen by."

She studied the Master. From the amount of gleaming brightwork on his body she knew him to be a Tycoon, high in the hive hierarchy. She could see herself reflected in his carapace. It was chrome plating. Chromium was rare in Gaea. The Iron Masters worked hard to scrape what they could find from deep shafts in the Black Forest of Phoebe. For a while there had been a thriving trade in antique automobile bumpers, but the war had interrupted that.

Cirocco was deeply ambivalent about the Masters. It was impossible to like creatures who incubated their young in human infants. On the other hand, she did not hate them as so many humans did. Perhaps they were "monsters," but only if you concede that eating veal or baby lamb chops made humans into monsters. They were not nearly the threat to human children that the children's own parents

and neighbors were. Baby stealing was a cottage industry in Bellinzona. The Iron Masters never stole anything; they paid for what they
got, and they paid top dollar, and they bought only a few. Compared
to any general, from Caesar to the ones currently rearranging the
Earth, the Iron Masters were saints.

Still, they were creepy, the most alien of Gaea's sentient races.
The best thing about them was their utter reliability.

"Why should I be entitled to a percentage?" Cirocco asked the
Tycoon.

"One never asks Gaea why."

"You ought to try it sometime." But that was no use; Cirocco
was never going to get a rebellion going among the Masters. This
one still regarded her impassively—if something with no obvious
eyes can be said to regard. It reminded her of a picture in an old
book, something from her childhood. Owl, from *Winnie-the-Pooh*.
It was tall and tubular, with little peaks on top that might be ears.
Its metal body flared into a skirt near the ground, its odd feet barely
visible behind it. The creature had a great many arms—Cirocco never
knew just how many—that all fit into recesses as neatly as a blade
into a jackknife.

"For my percentage, I'll take a ride back to Ophion."

"Done." The thing turned and started to waddle off, penguin-
like.

"What will you do with him?"

The Iron Master stopped, and turned again.

"We will find uses." Which was the creature's way of saying
"none of your business," Cirocco realized. In a century of dealing
with the engineering, trading Masters, she had learned very little
about them. She didn't even know if there really *was* something like
living matter anywhere inside their metal bodies. For a while she
had entertained the notion that the ones she saw were all robots, that
the real masters never left their carefully guarded island in the Phoebe
Sea. She did know that when an Iron Master lost an arm, it did not
grow it back; it built a new one, and bolted it on.

"Why do you have him tied down?"

There was a pause. The Tycoon turned slowly to look at Kong,
then back to Cirocco. Was it amused? She didn't see how, but that
was what she felt.

"He is still lively."

Cirocco looked, and felt hair prickle all up and down her neck. Kong's eyes had opened. He was looking at her, his great brow furrowed. His only remaining arm, which ended at the elbow, had lifted and drawn the cables taut. His eyes rolled and he seemed to be trying to turn his head, but he was too weak. He returned his gaze to her again, forgetting about the problem of the pinned arm.

His lip curled in a tentative, chimp smile that seemed almost wistful.

Later, sitting on the back of the train and watching Kong Mountain dwindle in the distance, Cirocco wondered about it.

When would he die? She had watched them take out what must have been his heart, and it was not beating. Reflexes? Like twitching, severed frog's legs? She doubted it. There had been awareness in those eyes.

Gaea built to last. She had not designed him to get old, to reproduce . . . or to die. So maybe when the gangs finally chopped his brain up, he could rest.

And maybe not.

She found that she *did* feel sorry for him.

Cirocco reached the main east-west line just north of the Phoebe Sea. She hopped an eastbound freight, thinking it would take her as far as the Arges River, but found the industrious Iron Masters had extended it over fifty kilometers since her last visit to Phoebe, no more than six kilorevs ago. And they were at work at the railhead. They'd be in Tethys soon, she realized. She wondered how they would cope with the sand.

Of course, the sand would be a problem for her, too, but she knew how she would deal with it.

She left the Masters and all their works behind, began running toward the northeast corner of Phoebe. Ahead, Tethys loomed up the curve of Gaea, yellow, desolate, and unforgiving.

She ran all the time except when the forage was very good. Cirocco knew ten thousand edible plants in Gaea, over a thousand animals, and even some places where the soil itself could be eaten. There were an equal number of poisonous plants, some of them very similar to the safe ones.

Phoebe was not friendly territory—if such a thing existed any longer. As she began to tire she gave some thought to resting before crossing Tethys. She had been awake for about ninety revs, and running a good part of that time.

She found a deep pool in the Phoebe-Tethys twilight zone. The land there was mountainous and rocky, full of springs and blue lakes. The water in them was not cold. Casting about, she found a deposit of blue clay.

She sat down and removed her boots, then her shirt, which she stuffed into one boot, and her pants, which she put in the other. She removed a slender coil of rope from her pack, then put her boots in the pack and sealed it, along with ten kilos of rocks. She knelt in the clay and began twisting and crushing some broad leaves. When the leaves bled a sticky sap, she worked it into the clay.

Soon the clay was pliable. She rolled in it, rubbed it over every inch of her body and into her hair. When she got up, she was a blue demon with white eyes. The layer of mud was an eighth of an inch thick, but did not crack or flake as she moved.

She dipped the rope in the pool. It began to swell. She fastened one end to a bush at the edge of the water. Then she stepped into the water and submerged, paying the rope out behind her—the rope which had now become a strong breathing tube.

At two fathoms the weak light of the twilight zone was gone. She groped her way onto a silted ledge and settled onto her back with the weighted pack on her stomach. She put the other end of the tube in her mouth and slowed her breathing.

After one minute of self-hypnosis she was deeply asleep.

Three hours was as long as she could sleep anymore. She opened her eyes in the cool darkness.

Something slithered by her; she grabbed it and twisted, then pushed off for the surface. Just short of it, she paused and looked for danger above the water, then cautiously put her face into the air. Nothing. Satisfied, she climbed out and looked at her catch. A highlands rock eel, far south of its normal range. She thought about a fire, rejected it, and tossed the creature back into the pool. Highland eels cooked up fine, but were stringy and bitter raw.

The blue mud peeled off like rubber. It was a wonderful insulator.

She had learned many things in her long life. One was to be as comfortable as you can be all the time. And that meant dry boots, even if one had to sleep underwater. With satisfaction, she opened her pack and retrieved them. It was a wonderful pack, and they were wonderful boots. In her ranking of important things, dry boots came far ahead of food, and slightly before water.

She dressed, pulled on the boots, and started to run again.

Whenever possible, Cirocco avoided Tethys altogether. This time she would have to cross it. She holed up in the last patch of scrub brush, took out her tiny spyglass, and scanned the landscape ahead for sign of sand wraiths. She didn't expect to see them this far north; the condensation from the north wall, though hard to find, was beneath the surface, and deadly to the silicon-based wraiths. Still, she hadn't come this far by relying on her expectations.

The habit of traveling light had been ingrained for twenty years. Camouflage was an art she had studied at least that long. When God really *is* looking down from the sky—looking for *you,* and ready to kill—it pays to be both quick on your feet and hard to see. Her pack held ten kilos of the barest essentials. With the things in it, and the knowledge in her head, she could blend in anywhere.

Cirocco estimated it would be thirty-nine degrees on the sands.

No matter; she knew what to do.

She stripped once more, stuffed her clothing in her pack, and began digging at the base of one of the bushes that seemed dead. But the parched branches were only the top of the plant, and the least interesting part. They radiated away waste moisture.

When she reached the swollen roots a spurt of water washed over her bare feet. She knelt, cupped her hands, and drank. It was alkaline, but bracing.

With her knife she severed a nodule on one of the roots, then cut it open. A slippery yellow sap oozed out, which she squeezed into her hands and began rubbing over her body. Her skin was the color travel brochures referred to as "bronzed." It was a nice color, but several shades too dark for the sands of Tethys. She kept rubbing until she was the proper yellow-brown. The sap smelled like juniper. It was also a cure for acne, a property wasted on Cirocco.

There were a dozen scarves in her pack. She selected two of the proper hue, closed up the pack, then wrapped one scarf around her dark hair and the other around the pack itself. When she was done she was almost invisible.

Barefoot, she scrambled down the last rocky outcrop of Phoebe and down to the rolling dunes. She began to run.

Two hundred kilometers later, more than halfway across Tethys, she saw someone.

She did what seemed prudent: dived into the sand, wriggled until she was almost totally covered, like a stingray on the ocean floor, and waited.

She was pretty sure who it must be. She felt goosebumps, as she always did, then the feeling faded. It was possible she was going insane. Gaby had died here, a hundred kilometers to the south, twenty years before.

Cirocco didn't care. She stood up. She was coated in sand. The sweat which had been cooling her so efficiently as she ran now drenched her, began running down her body, leaving clean streaks as it went.

Gaby shimmered in the merciless heat haze, coming down the near side of a dune four hundred meters away. She was nude, as she always was when she came to Cirocco. And why not? Why should a ghost take clothing to the spirit world? She was milk-pale. At first that had made Cirocco uneasy, as if Gaby had been drained of blood. Then she remembered that Gaby had always been pale, before Gaea. She and Cirocco had been the only tanned people in a world of weak sunshine. And then Gaby had been dead. In death, she must have been quite black, though Cirocco had not seen it and never asked those who had.

"You're safe!" Gaby shouted, still coming toward her.

"Thank you! For how long?"

"All through Tethys."

Cirocco waited while Gaby vanished behind the last dune, then marched up the far side. Gaby paused for a moment at the top, then started down. Her feet left deep prints in the sand. She was terribly beautiful. Cirocco heard herself sob. She went to her knees, then sat back on her ankles. Her shoulders slumped wearily.

Gaby stopped fifty meters away. Cirocco could not speak; her throat was too thick, and she could not draw a proper breath.

"Are they all right?" she finally managed to say.

"Yes," Gaby said. "Conal found them. Saved their lives."

"I knew that boy would turn out useful. Where is he taking them?"

"Where you're going. You'll get there ahead of them."

"Good." She ransacked her brain. There were forbidden topics. "Uh . . . is it . . . are they . . ."

"Yes, they're still part of the key. Not all of it."

"The key to what?"

"I can't tell you that now. Do you still trust me?"

"Yes." Unhesitatingly. There had been bad moments, but . .

"Yes. I trust you."

"Good. I wanted to—"

"I love you, Gaby."

The image started to waver. Cirocco cried out, then jammed the heel of her hand into her mouth. She could see the dune through Gaby's body.

"I love you, too, Rocky. Or is it Captain, now?"

"It's whatever you want."

"I can't stay. Gaea's in Hyperion. She's moving west."

"But she won't go into Oceanus."

"No."

Gaby was the little woman who wasn't there. Just an outline, a wish, an hallucination . . . and she was gone.

Cirocco sat there for almost a rev, pulling herself together, staring at the footprints on the dune where Gaby had been. In the end, as before, she did not go over to touch them. She was terrified to discover they really weren't there at all.

The northern Thea ice-shield began in twilight and curved south and east. Cirocco ran along its edge, in blessed coolness.

There was no question of crossing Thea to the north. The mountains were not impassable—nothing really was, in Cirocco's experience; she had crossed them once in two kilorevs—but she did not have time for it. The fast way through Thea was over the frozen Ophion, which flowed right down the middle of the region of eternal night.

When she stopped, she was knee-deep in snow, and still naked. It was the work of a few moments to open her pack, reverse her clothes and boots so the white side was visible, and camouflage her pack and hair with white scarves.

She ran, but eventually got tired again. To be sleepy so soon was a sign she was overtaxing herself. She noted it, and looked for a safe haven.

Her requirements were spartan. She dug a hole in a snowbank, crawled in, and packed snow in behind her. As she fell asleep, she remembered that no more than fifty kilometers ahead was the spot where a certain Robin of the Coven had buried herself in snow—tired, frightened, and ignorant of the danger—to wake up with a case of pneumonia. Robin had almost died in Thea.

Cirocco simply slept. Three hours later she woke up, brushed off the snow, and started to run again.

It was six hundred kilometers and most of the way across Metis before she again felt the need to sleep.

There were those in Gaea who would not have believed it, but Cirocco Jones—rumored to be capable of regenerating a severed leg, of shape-changing into a serpent, a vulture, a cheetah, and a shark, of wrestling a dozen Titanides and of being able to pass unnoticed through a brightly lighted room—this same Jones had her limitations. The stories were exaggerations. It was true, she *did* have a hex power, and she could charm people into believing she was not there, and when she had lost her left foot seventy years ago she *had* grown it back, but she doubted she could manage a leg. And she could not remain awake forever, like a Titanide.

It was an appalling need, when one thought about it. To become defenseless, to simply lie there while something crept up bent on murder. . . .

She was in the south of Metis, in the region below the great Poseidon sea, beyond the swamp named Steropes that was Metis' most prominent feature. Here the land was savannah: level, grassy, dotted with windswept trees. In Africa, big cats would be sitting in the trees—or at least Cirocco had always envisioned it that way, though she knew little about Africa. But in Gaea the trees were bright red and leafless. They looked like diagrams of the circulatory system, with the big trunk branching to finer and finer capillaries.

Cirocco planned to sleep like a cat in one of those trees.

She stripped again, wrapped her pack in a red scarf. With her knife, she made deep gouges in the tree trunk. Red sap began to flow. She rubbed it over her skin, gradually becoming a scarlet woman. When she was completely painted she climbed the tree and made her way out on a horizontal branch thirty meters above the ground. She hooked her feet over the branch, letting her knees fall on either side, made a pillow out of her folded hands, and put her head down. In a moment, she was asleep.

In Dione, she finally slowed down.

Dione was safety—from Gaea, if not from humans.

She passed to the south of the long lake known as Iris, through mountainous countryside and into the forest surrounding Eris lake, until she reached the river Briareus, one of the longest rivers in Gaea.

At a bend in the river, over a hundred kilometers south of Moros, Peppermint Bay, and Bellinzona, she came upon a treehouse that would have made the Swiss Family Robinson envious.

It was built in a tree of the same species as the one that sheltered Titantown in Hyperion. Though only one hundredth the size, the tree dominated that part of the forest like a cathedral dominates a small European town. The main structure of the house was three stories high. Parts of it were built of red brick, or faced with stone. The windows had sliding glass panes and multi-colored curtains. Other structures were scattered at different levels in the branches, all of different design. There were straw beehives roofed with pitch, an ornate gazebo, something that looked like part of the onion-domed Kremlin. All of this was connected by broad, railed paths that rested on branches, or by rope suspension bridges. The tree grew from bare rock surrounded on three sides by rushing water and on the fourth by a deep pool. Fifty meters upstream was a ten-meter waterfall.

Cirocco walked over the main bridge. It swayed only a little under her weight. She had seen it bobbing crazily with a dozen Titanides on it.

On a wide, covered porch with a view of the pool, she paused to remove her boots and stand them outside the front door, as was her custom. The door was not locked. She entered, already sure—though she could not have told how—that no one was home.

It was cool and dim in the parlor. The sound of falling water came through the windows. It was soothing. Cirocco relaxed. She pulled off her shirt, having to peel it away from her skin in some places. When she removed her pants and set them on the floor they looked as if she were still in them. She couldn't smell herself anymore but thought her odor must be frightful if her pants were so stiff.

Ought to take a bath, she thought. Thinking that, she plopped on a low couch and was instantly asleep.

She sat up and knuckled her eyes. She yawned till her jaw cracked, then sniffed the air. She smelled bacon.

At her feet were her clothes, washed and folded neatly. Beside them was a steaming cup of black coffee and a monstrous yellow orchid. The orchid was sniffing the coffee. It looked up. . . .

The creature was a hermit squirrel, a two-legged mammalian with a long thick tail that borrowed the empty shells of Gaean snails and made them into mobile homes. The orchid was part of the shell.

It zipped back inside and slammed the door as Cirocco reached for the coffee.

She got up and went through the music room, where a hundred instruments hung on the walls or sat on special stands, through the vox-breeding room, lined with cages, sipping her coffee as she went. The next room was the kitchen. Standing in front of the stove poking at the sizzling bacon was a man well over two meters tall. He wore no clothes, but he was perhaps the one human in Gaea who truly did not need them. He could never seem naked.

Cirocco put her empty cup on the table and embraced him from behind. She could no longer reach his neck, so she kissed his broad back instead.

"Hello, Chris," she said.

"Morning, Captain. Breakfast'll be ready in a minute. You awake yet?"

"Jus' about."

"You wanna shower first, or eat?"

"Eat, then shower."

He nodded, then walked to the window.

"Come here. I want to show you something."

She went to him, trying to feel alert. She leaned out the window.

"What is it? All I see is water."

"Right." He picked her up and tossed her out the window. She squalled all the way down, and hit with a huge splash. He watched for her head. When she came up, sputtering, he called out, "See you in five minutes."

He went back to the stove, still chuckling, and broke ten greenish eggs into the bacon grease.

FIRST FEATURE

What we want is a story that
starts with an earthquake and
works its way up to a climax.

—Sam Goldwyn

ONE

Soon after Cirocco's arrival at the treehouse, a party of seven—
three Titanides and four humans—crested the last hill to look down
at the bend of the river Briareus. They saw the great rock, the great
tree, and Chris's treehouse sprawled in it.

In the time it had taken the party to travel the two hundred
kilometers from Bellinzona to Briareus, Cirocco had run almost
halfway around Gaea's rim.

They could have moved faster. One of their number refused
to ride a Titanide, so the whole group had slowed rather than leave
her behind. Several of the other six had noted how little the seventh
seemed to appreciate this fact.

After a short pause during which the Titanides sang praises of
the magnificent view and composed a few songs of arrival, the group
moved down the faint trail to the river.

Conal was in love again.

Not that he was unfaithful to Cirocco. He still loved her, and
always would. But this was a different kind of love.

And not that this one was going to be his lover, since she hated
him totally. Still, love was love, and it didn't cost anything to hope.
And she hated everybody. He couldn't believe anyone could hate
everybody forever. Maybe when she got over it she'd notice what
a fine fellow Conal Ray was.

Conal was not exactly thinking these things as they began the
final leg of their journey to Briareus, though they were going through
his mind. He was in a pleasant state between sleep and waking,
stretched out on the broad back of Rocky the Titanide. He had spent
most of the trip asleep. Working for the Captain, who might go a
full hectorev without sleep and who never seemed to tire, he had
learned the value of getting all the sleep he could get. His was an
infantryman's philosophy: pleanty of sacktime in a dry bed, a full
belly, and he was content with life.

He only woke up when the women had one of their high-voltage, shrieking arguments. At first he had feared they would come to blows, in which case one of them would surely die. But they always stopped short. He finally decided they always would, and was able to enjoy the shouting matches for the great theater they were. The *curses* those women knew! It broadened his vocabulary, and deepened his love.

Conal turned on his side and went deeper into sleep. Though the path was steep and rocky, the ride was smooth as a gurney rolling on linoleum. It had been said that Titanides were the most comfortable mode of travel ever discovered.

Titanides did not exactly appreciate being considered a mode of travel, but neither did they resent it. They carried only those they wished to carry. Very few humans had taken a ride on a Titanide.

Phase-Shifter (Double-Sharped Lydian Trio) Rock'n'Roll didn't mind carrying Conal. Since the day of his operation on Cirocco Jones, almost five myriarevs ago, he and Conal had been the closest of friends. Sometimes that happened between a Titanide and a human. Rocky knew of Chris and Valiha, who had loved each other for twenty years, and of Cirocco Jones and Hornpipe, who were sometime lovers and also grandmother and grandson—though it was not that simple a relationship, as no Titanide family tree is ever simple. He had heard of the great love Gaby Plauget had had for Psaltery (Sharped Lydian Trio) Fanfare.

Rocky had never made physical love to Conal, did not expect to, knew Conal would be shocked to know Rocky would like to. And it was not quite what humans think of as love. Chris Major had learned that about Valiha and it had hurt him. Nor was it the love one Titanide could feel for another. It was something else. It was something any Titanide could see. All at once, and with no good excuse, everyone knew this or that human was so-and-so's human, though they had the taste not to put it in those words. Rocky knew Conal was his human, for better or worse.

He wondered if Conal thought of him as "his" Titanide.

Behind Conal and Rocky rode Robin and Valiha.

Robin was emotionally exhausted. She was not looking forward to meeting Chris again after all these years.

He had stayed in Gaea, she had returned . . . but not gone home.

She no longer had a home. She had risen as high as one could go in the Coven, had been for a time the Black Madonna, head of the Council. She had won every honor her society could bestow, at an age younger than any before her.

She had been, and still was, miserably unhappy. It had been a tough twenty years. She wondered what it had been like for Chris.

"Valiha, do you know if . . ."

The Titanide turned her head around. Robin wished she wouldn't do that. Titanides were frighteningly supple.

"Yes? What is it?"

Robin had forgotten what she wanted to ask. She shook her head, and Valiha returned her attention to the path. She looked exactly as Robin remembered her. What had she been? Five? That would make her twenty-five now. Titanides didn't change much from their third year, when they were mature, to somewhere around their fiftieth, when they began showing signs of age.

She had forgotten so many things. The timelessness of Gaea, for instance. They had been traveling a long time but she had no idea how long. They had camped twice and she had been so tired that she had slept better than she had in years. It had been long enough for her nose to heal, and for the wound in her shoulder to improve.

A long time, as only Gaean time could be.

How had it been for Chris?

Valiha (Aeolian Solo) Madrigal was worried about Robin.

It seemed such a very short time since the young witch had boarded the ship for her return to the Coven. Valiha, Robin, Chris, and Serpent had gone for a picnic. The Wizard was not there, but her presence was felt, just like the other unseen presences: Psaltery, Hautbois, and Gaby.

Then Robin had left them.

Now she was thirty-nine Earth years old, and looked forty-nine. She had this insufferably marvelous mad child who burned all the time. The child was more Robinish than Robin was. And there was this . . . embryo.

Valiha knew about human infants, had seen thousands of them. But she never lost her sense that something was wrong.

She peeled back the blanket and looked at it. So small it hardly seemed to fill her palm, the infant looked back with pale blue eyes and grinned. It only had a couple of teeth. It waved a tiny hand at her.

"Mama!" it said, then gurgled happily.

That was about the limits of its powers of speech. It was learning to walk and talk. Within a few years it would master other skills. This was a stage Titanides did not go through. Titanides skipped infancy and the biggest part of what humans would think of as childhood. They walked a few hours after birth, talked shortly after that.

There was something else humans had to learn which this infant had not even started on yet. Titanides never learned it; on the other hand, Titanides never had to be carried around, so it wasn't a problem. Valiha twisted and handed the child back to its mother.

"Its diaper is full again."

"*He,* Valiha. Please. *His* diaper is full." Robin took him.

"I'm sorry. His sex just seems so irrelevant at this point."

Robin laughed bitterly.

"I wish you were right. But it's practically all that's important about him in this lousy world."

Valiha didn't want to get into that. She turned and thought of Chris again. It would be nice to see him. It had been almost a myriarev.

Serpent (Double-Flatted Mixolydian Trio) Madrigal had seen Chris many times over the last myriarev. He spent a lot of his time with Chris.

He viewed himself as uniquely lucky. Though Chris had not participated in the trio that gave birth to Serpent, he had acted like a father to the child for his first four years. Serpent had a Titanide father—forefather and hindfather in the same individual—and two mothers: Valiha, his hindmother, and a foremother who was now dead. But none of his parents had been quite like Chris. He knew parenting was different for humans. He had only to look at the cheerful idiot in Robin's arms to understand why that must be so. But though Titanide childhood was short, it was there, and quite different from adulthood. As Titanides grew they tended to get serious—*solemn,* in Serpent's view. *Too* solemn. They lost much of their sense of play.

Humans did that, too, but they didn't go overboard about it. No Titanide father would have taught him to play baseball. Titanides liked to race, but beyond that sports were foreign to them. It hadn't been easy to organize the leagues Chris and Serpent had set up in sports ranging from baseball and football (Chris had called it Polo at first, then threw away the mallets and just let the kids kick the ball) to tennis, hockey, and cricket, but they had done it. They had found that a Titanide raised with team sports will continue playing well into adulthood. Serpent was the best bowler in the Key of E Thunderers, the champion cricketeers of the Hyperion League.

There were a lot of reasons Serpent wanted to talk to Chris. One was his recent realization regarding the World Cup. It had been held on Earth four years earlier, in spite of the war. The matches had been spread around the globe to avoid making a tempting target. Even so, three games had ended early when stadium, players, and spectators were incinerated. Eastern Siberia had eventually claimed the Cup.

But there was simply no possibility of any games this year, a World Cup year. There were no arenas left. By default, the World Cup should be decided in Gaea. Serpent planned to organize it.

The thought so excited him that he increased his pace, only to remember for the hundredth time the tail-end charlie. He slowed, and looked over his shoulder at her, trudging along when she could just as well be riding.

He had *offered* her a ride, hadn't he?

He snorted. It was her own fault if her feet were sore.

Nova had more than sore feet. Like her mother, she had never been known for having a long fuse. By now she was ready to explode.

Only a year ago she had known the shape of life, all the turnings of the world. The Coven floated at LaGrange Two, solid and steady and real. Then the Council had decided to move it. Too many O'Neils had been blown up. No one could tell what the maniacs on Earth would do next. So preparations had been made and the mighty engines started. The witches of the Coven proposed to fly to Alpha Centauri.

At the start of the year, Robin had been Black Madonna. Now, Robin was nothing. She had narrowly avoided execution. Her manner of leaving allowed no possibility of return. It was a staggering fall, and it had brought Nova down, too. She was a stateless person. Her entire culture was on its way to the stars.

And, of course, there was *him*.

What a way to sum it up, she thought. A being so terrible that a whole new set of pronouns were needed. *He. Him. His.* The words hurt her ears like grotesque laughter.

All that wasn't enough. Now there was this awful place.

Upon entering it she and Robin had fought for their lives. They had killed almost a hundred people. The magnitude of the carnage had overwhelmed her. She had never killed anyone before. She knew *how*, but found theory and practice were completely different things. She had been sick for days. Not an hour passed that she didn't see the heaped bodies leaking blood, or the wolf packs of children tearing the clothes off the corpses.

Robin expected Nova to treat these monstrous animals as if they were people. To be *friends* with them, Great Mother save us.

They all expected her to talk with this Conal abomination, this twisted, reeking, hairy, graceless, pinheaded lump of muscle whose finest hour would have been an early abortion. They were on their way to see yet *another* male. Apparently there hadn't been enough of them in Bellinzona; her mother felt they had to tramp through the jungle to find this one.

Everything about Gaea was awful. The temperature was wrong. She sweated buckets every day. Climbing was all wrong. She was always too light, and kept stumbling as learned reflexes played her false.

It was too damn dark.

The air smelled of decay, and smoke, and wild things.

It was *too big*. The Coven, on the rim of Gaea, would have rolled around like a BB in a truck tire.

And it *never changed*. Nobody ever closed the windows and let night come, or opened them for a decent day. The concept of time was not the same in here. She missed the nice little half-hours and the comfortable cycles of days and weeks. Without them, she was adrift.

She wanted to go to sleep and wake up to find it had all been a dream. She would go to the Council and she and Robin would have a good laugh over it. Remember that place you went when you were a kid, mother? Well, I dreamed we went there, and you had a baby. A *boy*, would you believe it?

It wasn't going to happen.

She sat down on the trail. The yellow Titanide named Serpent, which looked exactly like its mother but which she was supposed to believe was a male, stopped and called something to her. She ignored it. It waited for a moment, then went on. That was fine with Nova. She could see the treehouse now. She would go to it when she felt ready. Or maybe she'd just sit here and die.

The last member of the party was the happiest of the lot.

He had been near death three times in his short life, but he did not know that. His mother had been his first potential murderer. Robin had thought long and hard on it, when she saw what she had miraculously brought forth from her troubled womb into a troubled world.

Most recently he had almost been killed by a babylegger. His memories of that were vague. It had all been over so quickly. He remembered the man who had smiled down at him. He liked the man.

There were a lot of new people. He liked that. He liked the new place, too. It was easier to walk here. He didn't fall down so much. Some of the new people were very big, and they had a lot of legs. They were many exciting colors, so bright and vivid that he laughed in delight every time he saw them. He had learned a new word: Tye-Nye.

A bright yellow Tye-Nye was carrying him now. He was satisfied with the ride. Only two things marred an other wise perfect afternoon. His ass felt wet, and he was wondering if it was about time for dinner

He was just about to mention these points when the Tye-Nye handed him to mother. Mother put him on the Tye-Nye's back, and he watched the Tye-Nye's long, fluffy pink hair bouncing above him him as his mother changed his diaper. The Tye-Nye turned her head around, and he found that hilarious. And mother was laughing! She hadn't been doing that much lately. Adam was ecstatic.

Robin opened her shirt, lifted him, and he found the nipple. And now the world was perfect.

* * *

The group reached the far end of the suspension bridge and began to file across. Adam was asleep now. Robin was ready to sleep. Nova was more than ready, but still lagged far behind the rest.

They passed under an arched gateway with the name of Chris's treehouse painted on it: Tuxedo Junction. Robin wondered what it meant.

Pandemonium was on the move again.

Gaea, as she moved through the forest of northern Hyperion, pondered recent events. She was not happy, and when Gaea was unhappy those around her always knew it. One elephant failed to get out of her way in time. She kicked it without breaking stride. The elephant flew into the air and landed a hundred meters away, torn in half.

She was deciding on the program for the next encampment. After much thought she decided on Kurosawa's *Seven Samurai*. Then she remembered the other two, waiting at Tuxedo Junction. Chris and Cirocco. Well there was that film from 1994, it had nine in the title, didn't it? Surely her librarian could ferret it out.

Then she had it, and laughed aloud. The second feature would be Fellini's *8½*.

TWO

Chris deftly flipped fried eggs out of the copper pan and onto an earthenware plate. The pan was almost a meter across. All his cookware was outsized. Most of his guests were Titanides, who loved to eat as much as they loved to cook.

He was only a mediocre chef, but Cirocco didn't seem to mind. She used her fork to make a gesture of thanks as he removed the first plate and set the second batch of eggs before her. She sat at the high table on a high stool, her feet hooked around the crossbraces, her elbows set wide and her head held low as she shoveled it in. Her wet hair was tied back out of harm's way.

Chris pulled a stool over to the table across from her and hitched himself up onto it. As Cirocco tore into her fourteenth egg, Chris began eating the two he had fixed for himself, and watched her over the table.

She seemed pale. She was thin. He could count her ribs; her breasts were hardly there.

"How was the trip?" he asked.

She nodded, then reached for her coffee cup to wash down the last mouthful of eggs. The job required two hands. It was a Titanide cup.

"No problems," she said, and wiped her mouth on the back of her arm. Then she looked surprised, gave him a guilty glance, and picked up her napkin. She wiped her arm first, then her mouth.

"Sorry," she said, with a nervous giggle.

"Your table manners don't concern me," he said. "This is your house, too."

"Yeah, but that's no reason to be a pig. It just tastes so good. Real food, I mean."

He knew what she meant. She had been foraging for a long time. But he smiled at the description of the food. The "bacon" was meat from a smiler with swine genes in its ancestry, in the baffling Gaean system of crossbreeding that would have driven Luther Burbank to the madhouse. The "eggs" came from a shrub common in Dione. Left unharvested, they would eventually hatch a many-legged reptile that scattered the plant's seeds in its excrement. But the fruit tasted very much like real eggs.

The coffee, oddly enough, was real coffee, a hybrid adapted to the low light of Gaea. With the collapse of the Earth-Gaea trade it had become as profitable to grow coffee in the highlands as cocaine, the traditional Gaean export. Coke glutted the market, but coffee was hard to get.

"Kong's dead," she said, around another mouthful.

"Really? Who did the job?"

"Do you need to ask?"

Chris thought it over, and could come up with only one likely candidate.

"You going to tell me about it?"

"If you'll slap some more bacon in that pan." She grinned at him. He sighed, and got up.

As the bacon began to sizzle, she told him what she had seen in Phoebe. While she talked, she finished her second helping. She got up and rinsed her plate, then stood beside him and sliced hunks off a huge loaf of bread and arranged them on a tray for toasting.

"I figure he's *got* to die when they cut his brain up. Doesn't he?" She squatted and slid the tray into the bottom drawer of the stove, beneath the firebox where the radiant heat would warm it slowly.

"I guess so." Chris made a face.

She stood and unbound her hair, shook it out, and ran her fingers through it. Chris watched, noted that it was almost entirely white now. It reached far down her back. He wondered if she would ever cut it again. Before her brain surgery, five years earlier, she had seldom let it get below her shoulders. Then her head was shaved, and she seemed to have found a new affection for long hair.

"Anything else I should know?" he asked.

"I talked with Gaby again."

Chris said nothing, but continued to turn the bacon strips. Cirocco started rummaging through a cabinet.

"What did she say?"

Cirocco came up with a Titanide curry-comb and began running it through her hair. She said nothing for a time, then sighed.

"I saw her twice. Once about three hectorevs before I went to Kong's mountain. Again in Tethys, not long afterward. The first time she told me Robin was returning to Gaea. She didn't say why. She has children with her."

Chris said nothing. Not long ago, he would have, but he had begun to wonder about a few things since then. Things like the definitions of "rational," the meaning of magic, the line between the quick and the dead. He had always thought himself a rational man. He was civilized. He didn't believe in sorcery. Though he had lived twenty years in a place with a "God" he had talked to, had loved a "Demon" who had once been a "Wizard," he took none of these words with their literal definitions. Gaea was a bush-league God. Cirocco was remarkable, but she had no magical powers, for good or evil.

In the face of the things he had witnessed or heard about, why should he worry about one measly resurrection?

But it had given him a lot of trouble. Gaby had died in his arms. He would never forget her horrible burns. The first time Cirocco told him she had seen Gaby, he had exploded. Later, he had been gentle, fearing his old friend was getting senile. But senility was too easy an explanation. Even if rationality was down the drain, pragmatism was still valuable, and Chris thought of himself as a pragmatist. If it works, it's there. And Cirocco's conversations with Gaby had been very good at predicting the future.

"When will she get here?" he asked.

"Here in Gaea? She's here already. In fact, she should be getting near the Junction by now."

"She's coming here?"

"Conal's bringing them. There'll be some Titanides with them, too. What's the matter? Don't you want them here?"

"It's not that. It'll be great to see her again. I never thought I would." He looked around the kitchen. "I was just wondering if I have enough on hand for guests. Maybe I should run over to the Hua's and see if they have—"

Ciroco laughed, and put her arms around him. He looked down at her face, and recognized the glint of mischief there.

"Don't be such a housewife, Chris," she said, and kissed him. "The Titanides are better at that, and they like it, too."

"Okay. What do you want to do?" He embraced her, let his hands slide down her back to her buttocks, and lifted her easily.

"First, let's get that bacon and toast off the stove before they burn. I've decided I'm not as hungry as I thought."

"No?"

"Well, not *that* way. I've been running all over this stinkin' wheel with nothing to look at but Iron Masters." She slipped a hand between them, down his belly, and squeezed. "Suddenly your homely face seems oddly attractive."

"That's not my face, old woman."

"It'll do," she said, and squeezed again.

At the completion of her thirteenth decade, boredom was one of Cirocco's chief fears. She had been spared the depredations of aging, the dulling of the senses and mental powers. It was conceivable that someday bedding down with a lover and performing the ancient rituals of coitus would pall. That was the day she would be ready to die.

But so far, so good.

They were in the crow's nest, a garret rising over the main house at Tuxedo Junction. There were windows in each of the six walls. One ladder went down to the third floor, and another up to a belfrey that housed Chris's carillon. Two dozen ropes ran along one wall, through holes in the floor and ceiling.

"Yowee!" Cirocco cried, and stretched an arm toward the ropes. She selected one and gave it a yank. The largest brass bell above them gave a joyous peal.

"That good, huh?" Chris said, and collapsed on top of her.

"I tell thee thrice," she said, and rang the bell two more times. Then she wrapped her arms and legs around him and hugged as hard as she could.

There were good and bad things about living in Gaea. Some things, such as the unchanging light, Cirocco hardly noticed anymore. The passing of day into night was just a vague memory. One of the good things she usually didn't notice was the low gravity. The one time she did notice it was during the act of love. Even a man as large as Chris did not weigh much. Instead of becoming an oppressive burden, his body was a warm and comforting presence. They could lie this way for hours if they wanted to, he utterly relaxed, she in no danger of being squeezed. And she loved that. Once a man was inside her, she always hated to give him up.

Chris raised himself slightly and looked down at her. He glistened with sweat, and she liked that, too.

"Did she say anything about . . ." He didn't know how to finish the sentence, but it didn't matter. Cirocco knew what he meant.

"Nothing. Not a word. But I know it's coming, and soon."

"How do you know?"

She shrugged. "I don't. Call it sexagenarian intuition."

"It's been a long time since you were a sexagenarian."

"What are you talking about? I've made it there twice. I'm a double sexagenarian, plus ten."

"I guess that makes you twice as sexy as anyone, plus ten."

"Damn right. I—"

They both heard it at the same time. Not far away, Titanide

voices were raised in song. Chris kissed her and went to stand in the window looking down toward the bridge. Cirocco rolled on her side and looked at him. She was pleased at what she saw, but wondered what Robin would think.

From the waist down, Chris was the hairiest human she had ever seen. He might have been wearing trousers made from bearskin. It was light brown, like the hair on his head, and nowhere less than ten inches long. It was soft and fine, the nicest possible pelt to wrap one's legs around.

Chris was turning into a Titanide. He'd been doing it for five myriarevs now. There was no hair at all on his chest or arms. His beard had stopped growing long ago and now his chin was smooth as a boy's. In the right light, his face could pass for that of a twelve-year-old. There were other things here and there that would surely startle Robin . . . such as his tail. The fleshy part of it was only about six inches long, but he could twitch it and make the long hair fly like a frisky horse. He was smugly proud of that tail, and no more in control of it than a dog. It twitched back and forth in excitement as he looked down at the party crossing his bridge. He turned, smiling.

"It's them," he said, and his long ears stood up straight, higher than the crown of his head. Cirocco's mind flew backward a century and a quarter, to a movie which had been old even then: cartoon boys shooting pool and turning into donkeys. A little wooden boy, and her mother holding her hand there in the darkness . . . but she could not remember the title.

"I'm going to meet them," he said, starting down the ladder. He paused. "You coming?"

"In a minute." She watched him go, then sat up in the huge straw-filled bag they had been using for a bed. She pushed the thick mass of white hair away from her face, stretched, and looked out the window opposite the one where Chris had stood.

Gaby was out there. She was sitting on a tree limb level with the belfry, not more than fifty feet away.

"Was it good?" Gaby asked.

"Yes." Cirocco felt no embarrassment or resentment when she realized Gaby might have been out there for a long time.

"You'll have to be careful with him. He's in great danger."

"What can I do?"

"There are some things I don't know." She looked sad, then shook it off. "Two things," she said. "One, he's the father of both of them. He might as well know it, because Robin is pretty sure of it already."

"Chris?"

"Yes. You'll see it. With Nova, anyway. The boy, too."

"Boy? What boy?"

"Two," Gaby went on. She grinned. "Don't strangle the girlchild. She'll drive you crazy, but put up with it. She's worth the effort."

"Gaby, I—" Then Cirocco gasped, as Gaby rolled off the limb and dived toward the pool below. She had one glimpse of her, arms pointed down, toes straight behind her, then the apparition was swallowed up in the greenery.

She listened a long time, but there was no splash.

THREE

The Titanides prepared a feast. From their happy singing, Robin assumed they were oblivious to the human tensions around them. She was wrong. The Titanides knew more about what was going on than Robin did, but they also knew they were powerless to affect any of it. So they employed a tactic that had worked reasonably well for almost a century. They left human affairs to the humans.

Robin had forgotten how good Titanide food could be. Shortly after her return to the Coven, just before the birth of Nova, she had ballooned to twenty kilos over her fighting weight. Ruthless dieting had taken it off, and kept it off for twelve years.

At some point she had lost interest in eating. Keeping slim had not been a problem for five years. During that time she had to remind herself to eat at all. Nothing tasted good. Now, digging into the heaping plates of food the Titanides offered, she wondered if she was going to have to be careful again.

It was a curiously joyless, brittle occasion. Chris, Cirocco, and Conal smiled a lot but spoke little. Nova, of course, had taken her plate to the most distant corner of the room. She ate furtively as an animal, always watching Cirocco.

"Nova," Robin called to her. "Come join us at the table."

"I prefer it over here, Mother."

"Nova."

The girl dragged her feet and scowled, but she came. Robin wondered how much longer she would do that. The virtue of obedience was strong in a Coven child, where families were quite different from the traditional human model. Nova owed Robin total allegiance until her twentieth birthday, and a great deal of respect after that. But she was eighteen now. A year or two years... it had little meaning in Gaea.

There were small blessings, though. The two of them had not fought since arriving at Tuxedo Junction. Robin was grateful for that. The fights tore at her heart. When fighting, it helps to know without doubt that one is right, and Robin hardly ever knew that anymore.

In fact, Nova hadn't said a dozen words since they got here. She had sat silently, either looking at her hands or at Cirocco. Robin followed her daughter's gaze to the Wizard—sorry, she corrected herself, to the *Captain*—who was singing some incomprehensible bit of Titanide to Serpent, then looked back at Nova.

Great Mother save us.

"Have you had enough, Robin?"

Flustered, Robin shook off her surprise and tried to smile at Cirocco. She dipped a spoon in the bowl of baby food the Titanides had prepared, and put the spoon in Adam's mouth.

"Me? Yeah, I'm doing great. It takes him longer, though."

"Could I talk to you? In private?"

There was nothing Robin wanted to do more, but suddenly she was frightened. She scraped food from Adam's mouth and gestured vaguely.

"Sure, as soon as—"

But Cirocco had already come around the table and lifted the baby. She handed him to Chris, who seemed pleased.

"Come on. Chris will take good care of him, won't you, old man?"

"Sure thing, Captain."

Cirocco was pulling Robin's elbow, gently but insistently. The little witch gave in. She followed Cirocco through the kitchen, out onto one of the railed walkways lying atop a horizontal branch, and up a gentle rise to a separate building half-hidden in the branches. It was five-sided, made of wood. The door was so low Cirocco had to bend over to enter. Robin was able to walk through with an inch to spare.

"This is a weird place."

"Chris is a weird fellow." Cirocco lit an oil lamp and set it on the table at the center of the room.

"Tell me about it. Valiha warned me he'd changed, but I never..." Robin trailed off, having finally looked at the interior of the pavillion.

All the walls were copper. Hammered into the metal were a hundred designs, some of them quite familiar to Robin, others foreign. Still more seemed to remind her of things deeply buried.

"What is this?" she whispered.

Cirocco gestured to the largest of the artworks. Robin moved closer and saw a stylized woman, angular and primitive as a hieroglyph. She was nude, pregnant, and had three eyes. A serpent coiled around her from one ankle to the opposite shoulder, where it reared its head and stared into her face. The figure gazed back at the snake, unblinking.

"Is this... supposed to be me?" Her hand went involuntarily to her forehead. It was the location of her tattooed third Eye. She had earned it over twenty years before, and without it, would have been unable to return to Gaea.

She also bore the tattoo of a serpent that wound around her leg, across her body, and up to her breast.

"What *is* this?"

There were two straight-backed wooden chairs in the room. Cirocco pulled one toward the center and sat in it.

"You probably should ask Chris about that. I think of it as a memorial. He liked you. He didn't expect he'd ever see you again. He built this."

"But it... it's *weird.*"

"As I said, so is Chris."

"What's happening to him?" Robin said.

"You mean physically? He's getting what Gaea promised him so long ago."

"It's disgusting."

Cirocco laughed. Robin flushed again, then knew Cirocco was not laughing at her, but at some private thought.

"No, it's not," she said. "It's only startling. You're seeing it all at once. I saw it day by day, and it looked entirely natural and right. And as for startling . . . you shocked him more than he shocked you."

Robin had to turn away. She knew what she looked like.

"It's called age," she said, bitterly. The terrible fact was that she looked a lot older than Cirocco.

"No. You've aged, but that's not the shocking part. In your own way you've changed as radically as Chris has. Some terrible fear has marked your soul."

"I don't believe that. Failure and disgrace, yes. Not fear."

"Fear," Cirocco went on, inexorably. "The Great Mother has deserted you. Your center is gone. You no longer burn; you float, your feet unable to reach the womb of the earth. You have no place to stand, no Umbilicus."

"How do you know these things?" Robin screamed.

"I know what I see."

"Yes, but the words, the . . . the secret words . . ." Some of them were from Coven ritual, from ceremonies and exorcisms Robin knew she had never mentioned to the Wizard. Others were from the darkest corners of her own soul.

"I've had some guidance. Right now, I want to know your purpose here. Why did you come? What do you hope to do?"

Robin wiped away tears and pulled a chair closer to Cirocco. She sat down, and eventually was able to look at the older woman.

She told her story.

Robin had come to Gaea, like so many others, to be cured.

Gaea was a god who never gave anything away. Robin had been told she must prove herself, do something heroic, before a cure was possible. She had not been inclined to do so. Her condition had not been impossible to live with. She had dealt with it before: when her hand began to tremble with the onset of a seizure, she had simply amputated her little finger.

But through the persuasion of Gaby Plauget, Robin had embarked on a trip around the interior of the wheel, accompanied by Gaby, Cirocco, the Titanides Psaltery, Hautbois, Hornpipe, and Valiha, and Chris Major, who was also seeking a cure.

Gaby and Cirocco had an ulterior motive. They were seeking an ally among the eleven regional brains of Gaea. Gaby was seeking a lot harder than Cirocco was; the Wizard had been a hopeless alcoholic who had to be dragged into the enterprise. Some of those regional brains were allies of Gaea. Some were enemies. The lines had been drawn during the Oceanic Rebellion while humans were still living in caves.

Gaby's plan had been nothing less than the overthrow and replacement of Gaea herself. She had been out to recruit a new God. The mission had cost her life, and possibly much more. It had cost Cirocco her status as Wizard. It remained to be seen whether it had cost the Titanides their survival as a race.

The only ones who seemed to have benefitted from the abortive quest were Robin, Chris, and the Iron Masters. Robin and Chris had been cured. The Iron Masters had, for reasons unknown, been allowed to expand from their tiny island in Phoebe until they now challenged the Titanides for dominance of the great wheel.

And at the end, Robin had headed for home, intending to live happily ever after.

"It was great for a while," she said, and smiled at the memory. "Chris was right. There *was* a great deal of *labra* in growing back a finger. I recommend it as a way to amaze your friends."

She knew Gaby and Cirocco had dismissed labra as the female version of macho. They had been wrong, but it didn't really matter. The fact that it was Gaea who had replaced Robin's severed pinky had continued to gnaw at her, and in the end hollowed out both Robin and her victory.

It was as meaningless as the third Eye, which was supposed to confer infallibility. In practice, the wearers of the Eye were bullies who could do no wrong, sanctimonious as any Pope.

"I left the Coven already at semi-mythical figure," Robin went on. "I came back . . . I don't know a word for it. The Coven had never seen anything like me."

"Superstar," Cirocco supplied.

"What's that?"

"Archaic word. It's somebody whose reputation exceeds all reasonable bounds. Pretty soon, they start to believe the reputation."

Robin considered it.

"There was some of that. Yes. I moved up as quickly as I wanted to. I could have gone faster, but ... I wasn't sure I should."

"You heard a voice," Cirocco suggested.

"Yes. It was my own voice. I think I could have been proclaimed the Great Mother herself. But I knew I wasn't. I knew I wasn't even very good."

"Don't be too hard on yourself. You were damn good, as I recall."

"Damn fast. Damn strong. Damn mean and a cast-iron bitch. But where it counted, to *me*" — and she thumped her chest — "right in here, I knew what I was. I decided to get out of public life. There are places we can retreat ... something like nuns. Isn't that what nuns do?"

"So I've heard."

"I was going to meditate for about a year. Then I was going to have a child and devote myself to raising her. But I didn't have time. The next thing I knew, I was pregnant."

She was silent for a moment, looking back on it. She chewed her lower lip, and at last looked back at Cirocco.

"This was a year — more than a year — after I got back from Gaea, you see. On Earth it could have just slid by. But in the Coven, we have to artifically—"

"I remember. I know what you're talking about."

"Yeah, but see, the women at the birth centers *know* who came in to have it done. When I started to swell up ..." She sighed, and shook her head. "The awful thing is, if it had happened to someone else, she might have been burned. We haven't burned anyone for Christianity for ... oh, fifty years. But it looked like there were just two possibilities. Either I'd had carnal relations with a Christian demon, or ... it was the Gynorum Sanctum, the union of a mortal woman with the Holy Mother, perfect and blameless."

Cirocco studied her as she lowered her head into her hands.

"Did they really buy that?" she asked.

"Oh, they did and they didn't. There's a conservative faction that holds all the teachings to be literally true. Anyway, it sealed my fate. I'm not saying I didn't help it along. For a while there I think I *did* believe the Great Mother had come to me. But every time I looked at Nova's face, something told me it was someone else."

Cirocco shook her head wearily. So much could have been avoided if she had not been busy while Robin was getting ready to leave.

Stop it, she told herself. You were busy for a while, sure, but then you were drunk for almost a kilorev.

"Did you ever suspect where the baby came from?"

"Not for a long time. Like I said, it was a lot easier to take it as it came. It wasn't till later I consciously questioned it."

"I could have told you Gaea would leave you with a parting practical joke. She did the same thing to me, and Gaby and August, right after we first got here. We were all pregnant. We had abortions." She paused, and looked at Robin again. "Do you . . . did you have any feeling about . . . who the child's father might be?"

Robin laughed.

"Go look at her. Isn't it obvious?"

"Nova's got your mouth."

"Right. And she's got Chris's eyes."

Chris was in the basement, looking for a film projector.

It was perhaps a semantic fallacy to have a "basement" in a treehouse, where all levels were above the ground, but Chris had managed it. A trapdoor in the floor of the main building led to a hollowed-out area in the trunk of the great tree. This room eventually received everything Chris had never managed to find a use for. There was a lot of it.

Conal, standing on the ladder and holding the lamp high as Chris threw objects from one pile to another, surveyed the miscellany with dismay.

"Aside from being a compulsive architect," he observed, "you've also got a bad case of pack-rat-itis."

"I think it's terminal," Chris agreed. "Still, you could say the same thing about the Smithsonian."

"What's that?"

"It's nothing, now that you mention it. Blown up many years ago. But it was a museum. And there aren't any museums in Gaea." He straightened, wiped a mixture of dust and sweat from his face. "It's a dirty job, but somebody ought to do it."

"The Titanides have a museum."

"Point taken. But the oldest thing in it is not much older than Cirocco. They haven't been around that long. We don't have any *human* museums in Gaea. If there are any left on Earth, they won't be around much longer. So why not start here?"

Conal took another dubious look at the piles of junk.

"Confess, Chris. You just can't throw anything away."

"Guilty." He reached deep into a stack of oddments, and came up with an ancient Kodak Brownie. "But you never know when you'll need something."

"Yeah, but where do you *get* it all?"

Chris shooed Conal up the ladder, followed him out, and shut the trapdoor behind him. Conal followed him through the maze of doors and rooms until they reached the space Chris had set aside as his workshop. It was actually several rooms, and in them Chris was able to do everything from glassblowing to repairing computers.

He set the projector on a workbench and began taking it apart.

"I just pick things up here and there," he said. "That's how it started. Nowadays, all the Titanides who come calling bring a gift. They do a lot of trading. No telling what they'll pick up. Not much stuff gets here from Earth anymore, but in the old days just about anything might come in. Settlers brought most of their possessions. This was back before the War."

He got the side panel off and peered in, blowing away clumps of dust. He poked a finger into the mechanism, made a wheel turn. He pulled a long glass bulb out of the projector and flipped it toward Conal, who snagged it. "Test that out, would you? I doubt it's any good. I'll probably have to blow another one."

Conal turned toward the electrical bench. He clamped the bulb and took two insulated wires with bare ends, touched one to the brass casing and the other to the dull metal tip. He flipped a switch, and the filament glowed brightly.

Chris brought the projector over and set it near the bulb.

"So it *does* work, huh? That'll save some time." He took it and screwed it back in place, then connected several devices together on the workbench and finally touched two wires to contacts on the projector's motor. It hummed and there was the faint smell of ozone, but nothing else happened. Chris muttered and tried a new arrangement of transformers. Still nothing. He looked up, to see Cirocco and Robin enter the room. Trailing a little behind them was Nova.

"Cirocco," Chris said, "I can go find a new motor for this thing and rig up a way to make it run the film drive. Or..." He gestured to her, then to the projector. "Do you think you can heal it?"

She gave him an odd look, then shrugged and walked to the workbench. She looked at the projector, put her hands on it, and frowned. Sparks crackled; Robin gasped, but Cirocco merely blinked. Something clattered briefly and then stopped. Cirocco leaned closer, oblivious to the blue Jacob's ladders that arced in the gaps between her fingers. Just for a second Conal saw a dreamy blurring of her eyes, then she straightened and put the tip of her thumb in her mouth.

"Bastard burned me," she muttered, sucking on it.

Chris raised an eyebrow, then punched the projector's power button. It stuttered, then ran as smoothly as such an old machine ever would.

No one said anything. Conal fetched chairs as Chris threaded Cirocco's film through the projector. He had no take-up reel, but it hardly mattered, as he assumed no one would want to see this more than once.

Cirocco and Robin tacked a sheet over the far wall.

"Shouldn't we invite the Titanides?" Robin asked.

"Motion pictures upset them," Cirocco said.

"We're not sure what it is," Chris added, answering the question in Robin's eyes. "Their brains don't seem equipped to handle it. They get nauseous, like they were seasick."

He started the projector.

In a moment there was a retching sound from the doorway. Conal turned and saw Nova fleeing the images on the screen. He thought about going after her, but knew it was a silly notion. He turned back to the film.

Gaea bit the head off a second man. This one was dressed in an orange robe. The first had been in a traditional priest's collar and black vestments.

It was a warm-up for the match with Kong. The giant ape could be seen hovering in the background of some of the shots. The bolex who shot them had been more concerned with the eating of the holy men. Each shot was rock-steady and carefully framed.

The fight began. Gaea and Kong grappled. Kong went sailing

over Gaea's head to land on his back. He seemed stunned as Gaea lumbered over and pinned him. Gaea was thrown off the great beast. He came after her. There was a gap, and Kong was down again. Gaea hovered over him, then pounced.

She seemed to be doing more than just pinning him this time. Conal couldn't figure it out. He stared at the screen, his mouth dry, fascinated and ashamed of it. Finally he had to look away. He studied Chris, Cirocco, Robin . . . anything but the screen.

"I would have sworn he was asexual," Cirocco said at one point.

"It was well-hidden," Chris said. "She had to drag it out of him."

"Great Mother preserve us," Robin whispered.

Conal looked back. He hadn't thought it was possible for a female to force sex on a male. Perhaps it wouldn't have been, but Kong was badly injured. Blood gushed from a hole in his chest as Gaea straddled him. She washed herself in it.

"Turn it off," Conal pleaded. Cirocco glanced at him, her face stony, and shook her head. He could leave, or he could watch. He dragged his eyes back.

Gaea staggered, seeming drunk. She ran into the stone wall of the cave, and fell onto her side. The screen went black for an instant, then lit again. Gaea was on her side, still nude. The blood was drying on her face and hands. She rolled onto her back. She moaned. Her stomach was heaving up and down.

"She's giving birth," Chris said.

"Yeah," Cirocco growled. "But giving birth to what?"

The end of the film ran through the shutter mechanism and trailed down to the floor. The white screen flickered and lit three pale faces until Chris mercifully shut it off.

It was a camel, and it was dead.

The camel had been born alive and Gaea had caused it to be included in the entourage from Kong mountain to the current site of Pandemonium, trying to think of a use for it.

She had not planned on a camel. She didn't plan much of anything these days. She was enjoying chaos. It was a hell of a lot more fun than running the friggin' world.

Gaea gave birth to things simply because it seemed the proper function for a god. She was as surprised as anyone else at what came out. Her mind had fragmented into many parts, each independent, some crazier than the others, but all quite mad.

Mental note: Show *The Three Faces of Eve* one day soon.

The part of her that supervised her equivalent of a uterus didn't tell the rest of her what it was up to. She was satisfied with the arrangement. After three million years a surprise was worth something. Once a kilorev her body presented her with something new. In the past year she had borne a litter of dragons, a four-meter tiger, and a creature that was half Model-T and half octopus. Most of them did not live long, lacking such items as hearts or noses. The rest were mules. Her subconscious couldn't be bothered with the fine details.

But the camel was pretty good. It was a full-grown dromedary, mean as the welfare department, and now it was dead because she had decided what to do with it. She was going to put it through the eye of a needle.

It was a large needle, granted. There was a big funnel, and machinery to grind the camel fine.

With a hundred cameras rolling, Gaea mounted the scaffolding above the funnel and poured the first barrel of camel puree into it.

Three revs later, tired and peckish, she called a halt. About half the camel was through and the rest would just be a matter of tedious work. Besides, the footage she had could be edited with shots she'd have taken of the funnel after it was cleaned out.

She settled in her chair to watch the day's double feature, which was *Lawrence of Arabia* and . . . she couldn't remember. She twisted and squirmed in her seat, impatient.

When was Cirocco going to get started?

Gaea was waiting for the Main Event.

FOUR

Robin, wake up."

Robin was instantly alert. She saw Cirocco looming over her. "Nothing's wrong. Don't be afraid."

"I'm not." She rubbed her eyes. "What time . . ."

Cirocco smiled as she saw Robin remember where she was.

"You've been asleep for about seven hours. Is that enough?"

"Sure." Cirocco was still whispering, so Robin did, too. "But . . . enough for what?"

"I want you to come with me," Cirocco said.

Nova kept her eyes closed and didn't move while her mother dressed. After Robin had left the room, shutting the door behind her, Nova sat up and crept to the door. She opened it a fraction of an inch, saw Cirocco and Robin talking quietly in the hallway. They moved out of her sight. She heard them going down the stairs to the first floor.

From the second-floor bannister she could see them in the main room, then heard the front door open and shut. She hurried back into the room she shared with her mother and Adam. She glanced to his crib, and was surprised to see he was gone. She knew Robin hadn't taken the little monster, so she assumed Cirocco had.

By leaning out the window she could see the far end of the suspension bridge. She leaned—then darted back in quickly. The two women were crossing it. Cirocco had the baby.

She was dressed, down the stairs, and had her hand on the doorknob before she stopped to think.

It wouldn't work.

Nova had a fair idea of her own capacities. On her home ground it was just possible she might tail Cirocco without being discovered. But Cirocco was too good. She seemed to feel eyetracks on her skin, to sense a passing thought. That Nova could follow such a woman through a jungle she didn't know was beyond the realm of reason.

But Great Mother, she ached to be with her.

At first Robin had not realized they were following a path. It was not well-defined, but it was there. They had to duck some low branches and climb over fallen trees. Still, the trail was there. Robin searched her meager knowledge of the ways of wild animals, wondering if this was a game trail, then realized what little she knew applied to Earth, not Gaea. Who could tell why a Gaean animal behaved as it did?

"Do you trust me, Robin?"

"Trust you? Sure, I guess so. Why?"

"Guessing isn't enough. Think it over."

Robin did, following along behind the woman she still thought of as the Wizard. She felt clumsy, weak, and very old. Ahead, Cirocco was lean, lithe, and seemed to grow from the ground under her feet.

Trust her? Robin could think of a lot of pro's and con's. The Wizard had been an alcoholic when Robin had known her. Did they ever get cured, *really* cured? Wasn't it possible that, when things got bad, she would dive back into the bottle?

Robin took another look. No, she wouldn't. She didn't know how she could be so sure, but she was. There had been a fundamental change in the woman.

"I trust you to keep your word. I believe that if you say you'll do something, I can count on it being done."

"It will, if I'm alive."

"I trust you to do what you think is right."

"Right for who? You, me, or everyone? It's not always the same."

Robin knew it wasn't, and gave it some more thought.

"For everyone. I think you'd tell me if you had to do something that you thought best, but was going to hurt me."

"I would."

They walked on in silence for a time, then Cirocco half-turned and gestured for Robin to walk beside her. The path was wide enough for two at that point. She took Robin's hand and they walked together.

"Do you trust me to keep a secret?"

"Sure."

"I didn't phrase that right. There are some things I have to keep secret from *you*. I can't tell you why. Part of it is the old golden rule of the so-called 'intelligence community.' What you don't know, you can't tell."

"You're serious, aren't you?"

"I ain't playing games, kid. There's war here just as sure as there's war on Earth. In some ways, this one is just as ugly."

"Yeah, I trust you to do that. At least, until I know more."

"That's good enough." She stopped, and turned Robin to face her. "Just relax and look into my eyes, Robin. I want you to relax completely. Every muscle is loose, and you're starting to get sleepy."

Robin had been hypnotized before, but never so easily. Cirocco didn't talk a lot, didn't use any tools. She simply looked into Robin's eyes and her pupils grew big as the Phoebe Sea. She murmured quietly and touched her palms to Robin's cheeks, and Robin relaxed.

"Let your eyes close," Cirocco said, and Robin did. "You will sleep, but you don't need to go deep. You can feel things, smell things, and hear perfectly well, but you'll see nothing. Do you understand?"

"Yes."

Robin felt herself being lifted. It was nice. She heard a wind rustling through trees. There was a smell like over-ripe strawberries. She felt herself bounce as Cirocco jogged along the path. Then she was turning around. This went on for an unmeasurable time, until all sense of direction was destroyed.

She didn't care. Mostly she felt Cirocco's strong arms beneath her back and under her legs, felt her hard stomach muscles against her hip, smelled the distinctive, slightly sweet odor she associated with the Wizard. Her mind built pleasant fantasies. It had been a long time without a lover.

She felt good. Better than she had since . . . since those long-ago days sailing down the Ophion with seven companions toward an unknown destiny. There was something to be said for being swept off one's feet by forces—or Wizards—beyond one's control.

"Nova wasn't asleep when I came in to get you," Cirocco said.

"She wasn't?"

"No. She followed us down the stairs. Then she watched us

out the window. I thought she was going to tail us, but she didn't."

"She's not a fool."

"I can see that. She's...difficult."

Robin laughed. "If you'd been demoted from the Virgin Daughter to an outcast and a refugee, you might be difficult, too."

"Why did she come? She seems to hate you."

"Part of her does, I think. I failed so hugely, my fall was so great...it was like I did it to her, too." Robin stopped, wondering why she was saying these things with no pain, then remembered she was hypnotized. That was fine with her. They needed to be said.

"She came out of obedience? It doesn't sound like her style."

"You don't know the Coven. It was obligation...and fear. I don't think my beloved sisters will make it. I think they're going to freeze out there. But by the time the question was put, I didn't have a vote. Nova didn't think they'd make it either.

"And...she didn't feel like she had a lot of choice. It was tough for us. For ninety days, after Adam was discovered, we didn't exist. My third Eye saved my life, but only just."

"Why did she have to go? You were the one with the child."

"Ah, it didn't matter. She was a freak, you see. She found out about Adam when he was six months old. She tried to kill him. I stopped her. Then both of us concealed him, but we knew it couldn't last. And it all came out in the end. It took every ounce of my former prestige to swear that he was a girl. No one looked, but they all knew."

"What do you mean, Nova was a freak?"

"The only child in the Coven with a brother. Guilt by association with me, the great sinner." She sighed. "Aren't people wonderful?"

"They're about the same everywhere."

Cirocco said nothing for a while. Robin had an odd thought. Where was Adam? Cirocco had been carrying him when they started out. Now she was carrying her, and it took both hands.

She didn't worry about it. She *did* trust Cirocco.

"She was also suspiciously tall. That didn't matter when we were riding high. Later on, there were whispers of acts better not described. And there was love."

"Love?"

"She loves me. She doesn't show it much these days, but she does."

"I could see that."

"She loves you, too. In a *quite* different way."

"I see that, too."

Cirocco finally set her down. Robin's senses were deliciously sharp. She felt soft, damp soil under her bare feet. (What had happened to her shoes? It didn't matter.) There was an aromatic vapor in the air. She felt a trickle of sweat run down her back. She stood there in the dark and waited. Cirocco's voice came from in front of her.

"You can sit down now, Robin, and open your eyes."

Robin did. She saw Cirocco kneeling in front of her. Her eyes were deep, fascinating pools. She glanced to her left and saw Chris, also kneeling, holding Adam wrapped in his pink blanket. He smiled at her, then Cirocco touched her chin with a fingertip and turned Robin's head forward.

"Don't look at him. Look at me."

"All right."

"I want you to go a little deeper. You can keep your eyes open if you want to, but don't pay any attention to what you see. The sound of my voice is the only important thing."

"All right."

"How deep are you?"

Robin thought it over earnestly.

"About three feet."

"Give it another foot."

Robin did. Her eyes were open. All she really noticed were swirling clouds of steam. Cirocco was no longer in front of her, but she couldn't have said just what *was* out there. She felt a light pressure on the top of her head. It was Cirocco's hand.

"Why did you let Adam live, Robin?"

She heard her own voice come from far away. She had a brief glimpse of the three of them, seen from above: a big, half-hairy man; a strong woman; a tiny, helpless, pitiful . . .

That thought was shut off quickly.

"I had a dream."

"What was the dream about?"

"Adam." Smiling. Pink. Delicate tiny toes. The smell of her own milk and his wet diaper. "Gaby." Black and peeling. Crispy skin. A ruined eye. A sweet smell.

"You dreamed of Gaby?"

"She sat with me. She helped deliver him. She held him up, all bloody and awful. Then she kissed me and I cried."

"In the dream?"

"Yes." Robin frowned. "No. She was better. Not burned."

"In the dream?"

"No. Yes...I don't remember waking up. I remember ...going to sleep after the dream. Adam was nursing."

"What did Gaby say?"

"She said I must find it in my heart to keep him. She said the world was going to be destroyed. The Earth, the Coven...maybe Gaea. She said he was important. I had to bring him here. She said Chris was his father. I said two virgin births was one too many. She said Gaea had done it, Gaea had used magic to...keep a part of Chris inside me. Tiny time capsules, she called them. Then she went away."

"She vanished?"

Robin was surprised. "No, she went out the door."

Cirocco didn't say anything for a while, and Robin didn't mind. She was waiting for more questions. Instead, the pressure of Cirocco's hand on her head went away, then came back. This time it wasn't her palm, but the heel of her fist. It touched lightly, but Robin felt she could almost read the ridges and whorls through her scalp. There was a tiny voice.

"Let go of me, you ancient cunt."

Robin had never heard anyone speak to Cirocco that way. The voice went on in that vein for a time. Robin felt the fist tense, and the little voice squealed.

"I'll report you to the fucking SPCA, you vomit bag. I'll fuck you in your big hairy ears, and I've got syphilis, I've got things they haven't even *named* yet, I'll—"

Again the squeeze, followed by a sharper scream.

"I command you to speak," Cirocco said. Robin said nothing. Somehow she knew the command wasn't for her.

"Gaea's gonna piss kerosene and shit napalm when she hears—"

"Speak!"

"I know my rights, I want a goddam *LAAAAAWYER!* I want—"

"Speak!"

"Aaaaaaah! Aaah! Okay, okay, okay, I'll speak!"

"Is the hand of Gaea on this child? I command you to answer."

"I can't, I can't, I can't see...see...I think maybe—"

"Speak!"

"No, no, no! Gaea touched her long ago. Gaea knows she is here. Gaea planned the child's family, but did not touch them. Gaea's hand is not on this child."

And suddenly, neither was Cirocco's. Robin sat, blinking, feeling somehow that a terrible weight had been lifted from her head.

"You can come up now, Robin. Slow and easy. Everything's all right."

Robin did come up. She felt refreshed, took a deep breath, blinked again, and turned around. Cirocco was stowing a bottle in a knapsack. In one hand she held a familiar object: an old Colt .45 automatic. Cirocco handed it to her. Robin turned it over in her hand. The safety was off. She put it back on, and looked up.

"This is my gun."

"I took it from you before Cirocco woke you up," Chris said.

"What was that?" Robin gestured to the pack.

"My demon." Her eyes bored into Robin's. "Can you keep a secret?"

Robin returned the gaze, and finally nodded.

"If that's the way you want it."

Cirocco nodded, and relaxed a little. "I can tell you only that it was something that had to be done. I used to have another method. It wasn't as reliable, and not nearly so easy." For a moment there was terrible pain in her eyes. She looked away, then back. "Ask Conal about it sometime. Wait till he's got a little wine in him."

"You thought I was a spy for Gaea?"

"I had to assume you *could* be. Could you be sure you weren't?"

Robin was about to deliver an indignant *of course I could,* but stopped herself. She thought about tiny time capsules, virgin births. *Gaea touched her long ago. Gaea planned her family.*

"She can do anything at all, can't she?"

"She'd like you to believe that. But, yes, just about. You have no idea yet just how bad that can be."

"Would you have killed me?"

"Yes."

Robin thought she should be angry about that, but she wasn't. She was oddly comforted. If Gaea *had* laid a slimy trap in her body, she would rather be dead.

"What about Nova?" she said, suddenly.

"Now you're starting to be properly paranoid," Cirocco said, nodding. "But you've got a long way to go to catch up with me. I examined Nova hours ago. I thought it wise . . . considering her temperament, that she not remember it. I told her to forget, and she will."

"And Adam?"

"Innocent as a baby," Chris said, and smiled at her. She smiled back, suddenly remembering how warmly she had liked him, many years ago. She was even willing to forgive him his hair, at least for now. Then she looked at her surroundings for the first time, and frowned.

"What *is* this place?" she asked.

"The fountain of youth," Cirocco said.

There had once been twelve fountains in Gaea. The one in Oceanus had been destroyed in the Rebellion. The one in Thea was deep beneath the ice and the ones in Mnemosyne and Tethys were buried in sand. Of the remaining eight, seven had been abruptly shut down one day twenty years ago, a day that had also seen the death of the first incarnation of Gaea and a rain of cathedrals from Heaven.

But Gaea did not control Dione, because the central brain of Dione was dead. She could not influence the land for good or evil. She could send her troops in and she could make Bellinzona a living hell, but the deeper functions beneath the surface were beyond her.

Dione did surprisingly well in spite of that. Cirocco thought the gremlins might have a hand in it. For whatever reason, plants continued to grow, water flowed, and air circulated.

And the fountain brewed.

The fountain was the primary reason Chris had built Tuxedo Junction where he had. He needed it as much as Cirocco did. It seemed a good idea to be close enough to keep an eye on it.

"How do I know it won't hurt me?" Robin asked.

"You don't have to do it," Cirocco said.

"I know that, you told me that, but...how do you know? Maybe it's a trick. Maybe Gaea's hand is on *you.*"

"If it is, you're sunk already," Cirocco pointed out. "You've already said you trust me. Either you do, or you don't."

"I do. Emotionally."

"That's the only way it works. Logic has nothing to do with it. There's no logical way to prove Gaea isn't controlling me."

"I know. I'm sorry. I'm just nervous."

"Don't be. Just get undressed."

Cirocco turned away, sensing that Robin was as nervous about getting undressed as about anything else. She thought about sending Chris away, letting him come back later for his own treatment. Then she turned and saw Robin stepping out of her pants and knew Chris had nothing to do with it. She hoped nothing showed in her face, but she felt heat in the back of her throat, the choking taste of sudden pity.

Robin looked very sad, standing there in the nude. She would have looked sad anyway, but to one who had seen her glory, it was heartbreaking.

All the tattoos had faded badly. Cirocco had already seen the Eye and the Pentasm on her head, and part of the snake on her arm. They had been multi-colored and bright when Robin was nineteen. Now they were muddy, with a hint of dull red or murky green in a design made up mostly of slate-gray. Her fourth tattoo—the snake around her leg—was in the same shape as the rest. But the fifth had been vandalized.

It was no great loss to the art world, Cirocco thought, but it was still butchery. Robin had known early in life that any children she bore would have the same disease she came to Gaea to eradicate. In a surge of youthful bravado, she had made a hideous design on her belly. It showed a shadowy monster tearing through her skin, trying to break free from her womb to the outside world with teeth and claws.

"Nova was so damn big," Robin said, ruefully, rubbing the scar that had made the tattoo even more ugly. "I had to have a

Calpurnian section." She stood with shoulders slumped, trying to make it look as if her hands just happened to be clasped over her abdomen. Her skin was pasty, and her hair lifeless. Her face was seamed and even her teeth didn't look good. Robin had been letting herself go for quite a time. Aging was one thing; this was something else.

"Never mind," Cirocco said. "This will put a stop to that."

She waded into the water, and held out her hand.

It was hotter than Robin had believed possible. She felt the heat in an odd way, aware of it, but not feeling burned.

They took it in easy steps. First out to the ankles, then the knees, then a pause before going in up to the hip. Chris was on one side of her, Cirocco on the other. They both held her hands.

The water—if water it was—had a sweet smell, and was the color and consistency of honey. No, she realized, that wasn't right. It wasn't syrupy. Maybe it was more like nectar.

She went in up to the waist, and she gasped. The fluid was oozing inside her. She could feel it, like a fine oil, as it filled her bowels and her vagina. It seemed that it ought to feel disgusting, but the plain fact was that it didn't. It felt wonderful. It felt better than anything she had ever known. She shuddered, and felt her knees grow weak. Cirocco supported her. Then the waters were covering her breasts.

She relaxed into Cirocco's arms, as the Wizard had told her to do. She closed her eyes, felt a hand pinch her nostrils, and she was lowered into the water.

It was a dreamy sensation. There was no reason ever to come out. The need to take a breath was building, but when it got strong she felt Cirocco's lips press against hers, and she inhaled the Wizard's breath. She let it dribble out slowly.

She did that for a long time. Robin didn't count, but she knew it was a long time. Then she stopped. Robin felt the urge to breathe building in her again. Cirocco had told her what to do, but she was still a little frightened. Did she really trust the Wizard that much?

Well, why not? She felt the hands release her nostrils. The hot nectar began to flow inside. She opened her mouth. Air bubbled out and the waters flowed in.

There were a few spasms as her lungs filled and she tried to cough away the last of the air. She struggled, but was held firm. Then she was at peace again.

Cirocco held her in the water for half a rev, then carried her to shore and put her beside Adam, who still slept. Chris produced a towel and Cirocco started to dry her. Golden fluid dribbled from Robin's mouth. Cirocco slapped her back, and she began to breathe again, after bringing up the last few pints in her throat. Her skin was brown and almost too hot to touch.

"You go ahead," Chris said, taking the towel. "I'll take care of her."

Cirocco nodded, and entered the pool. In a moment she was floating just below the surface. In half a rev she came out, and her long hair, soaking and plastered to her shoulders, was glossy black.

Chris stayed in the longest. When he came out he was almost an inch taller and his face had changed slightly.

Cirocco put Robin back into a light trance and Chris lifted her with Adam in her arms. With a glance over his shoulder at Cirocco, Chris set out to take Robin back to Tuxedo Junction, and to make his proposition.

FIVE

Luther stalked the docks of a Bellinzona as empty of people as the dusty streets of the western town in *High Noon*, with Gary Cooper. It is possible his mind made the connection, as he had recently seen the film at Pandemonium.

He didn't look like Gary Cooper. He looked like Frankenstein's monster after a three-day bender and a car wreck. Most of the left side of his face was gone, baring some jawbone and cracked teeth, part of a mastoid, and a hollow eye socket. Greenish brain tissue showed through a ragged crack in his skull, as if it had leaked out and been haphazardly stuffed back in. His remaining eye was a black pit in a red sea, blazing with righteous fury. Sutures encircled his neck; not scars, but actual thick threads piercing the skin. If they were removed, his head would have fallen off.

All of his body but his hands was concealed behind a filthy black cassock. The hands bore stigmata which wept blood and pus. One of his legs was shorter than the other. It was not a deformity, but a simple mechanical problem: the leg had once belonged to a nun. It did not slow him down.

There was no need to hide, and Luther made no attempt to. It wasn't easy for him and his band at the best of times. Luther was no delight to the nose, but his Apostles' aroma could stun a hog at fifty paces. Even humans, with their atrophied sense of smell, could usually detect Luther long before he hove into view. Sometimes a downwind stalk worked, but lately the Bellinzonans seemed to have developed a sixth sense where Priests were concerned.

His twelve Apostles shuffled along behind him. Compared to them, Luther was a beauty.

They were nothing but zombies, but Luther had once been Pastor Arthur Lundquist, of the American Unified Lutheran Church in Urbana, Illinois. Urbana had been destroyed long ago, and so had Pastor Lundquist, for the most part. Bits and pieces of him had once belonged to other people—Gaea assembled her Priests from the material at hand. But from time to time a stray thought of home passed through his murky brain, a thought of the wife and two children. It tortured him, and made him all the more zealous in God's work. A lot of air passed through his brain as well, the result of the gunshot wound which had given him his distinctive smile and manner of speech. That tortured him, too.

He marched up to the edge of the zone of death that led to the Free Female quarter. His eye scanned the fortifications ahead. He saw no one, but he knew they were there, watching him. He stood defiantly, contemptuous of them, his hands on his hips.

"Enemies of God!" he shouted, or at least tried to. With his left cheek missing he had trouble with any sound that required lips. Enemies came out sounding like "enaweesh."

"I auw Luther! I auw here on a wission of God!"

An arrow sizzled on a flat trajectory and hit him in the chest. All but the feathers went through him. Luther did not even bother to break it off, nor did he move his hands from his hips.

A Free Female hurried out to the bridge, a torch in her hand.

She threw it on the oil which had been spread at the first rumor of Luther's band in Bellinzona. A wall of fire sprang up between Luther and the Quarter. It began consuming the bridge. The woman hurried back to cover.

"A child was vrought to thish blace wany . . . sheveral revs ago. God hash need of thish child. God will schwile on she who tells we the whereavouts of thish child. Cuf forward, cuf forward, and resheive God's grashe!"

No one sprang forth to receive any grace. Luther had expected it, but it still enraged him. He began to howl. He shouted obscenities at the burning bridge, he turned in quick circles and stamped his long leg up and down on the planks of the dock. Soon blood was running from his eye and a mixture of spittle and black phlegm from the open side of his face. The front of his cassock darkened near his hips. The power was on him, the power was building. He flung himself to his knees, extended his arms to heaven, and began to sing.

> "A whitey for-or-tresh ish our God!
>   A sword and shield victorious;
> He vrakes the cruel offressor's rod
>   And wins salvation glorious!"

Verse after verse, the tone-deaf Priest shouted the hymn in a fractured, sibilant bass, bellowing when he forgot the words. It was not the words that mattered, anyway, but the Power, and he felt it on him as he had few times since his resurrection. He reached out, remembered the days when he had preached sermons from his pulpit. He had been something of a thunderer in those days, but nothing like he was today. God would be proud of him. Behind him, even the worm-eaten zombies were moved. They whimpered as if trying to sing, their slack tongues hanging from their horrible mouths and wagging as their bodies swayed.

And here she came, a single Free Female, standing and throwing aside her weapon. Her smile was a chaotic rictus, her eyes bright and empty as moonies.

The Free Females were screaming. They had started when Luther began his feculent hymn, and now they redoubled their efforts. They did not scream from fear—though they were all terrified to the depths of their souls—but as a tactic, to drown out the Power. It was a many-throated, astonishing warble, after the manner of Arab women in victory or mourning. Many had jammed cotton or wax into their ears, like Odysseus's crew, to protect themselves. Luther laughed at that. He knew it was a mistake. With their ears plugged they were more vulnerable, as they could not hear the communal shout, the sound of solidarity that was the only real defense against Luther and his kind.

She came forward. An arrow followed her, but the hand that loosed it had trembled too much for it to fly true. It missed, and so did a second. The third sank into her back. She shuddered, but kept walking.

The Free Females were not shooting out of contempt, or because they thought her a traitor. They knew too well the Power of Luther to cloud women's minds. They shot at her because death was the merciful alternative.

"The old evil foe, sworn to work us woe
    With dread and craft and wight he arms himself to fight.
On Earth he has no equal!"

She walked into the flames.

Two more arrows hit her. She fell to her hands and knees as her hair went up like dry tinder. She continued to crawl, blackening. She struggled to her feet, hearing nothing, blinded, and a burning board broke under her. She fell backwards and rolled off the bridge into the water.

Luther stopped singing and stood up. He watched, smiling as half a dozen Free Females broke from their hiding places and ran forward, shielding their faces from the heat of the flames and his own awful presence. Several of them made horns at him, which amused him even more. Did they really think sticking out pinkie and index finger would protect them?

They caught their sister's body with a rope and pulled it onto the deck. She still lived, but that was a minor point. Had she been dead, they would have gone for her with even more determination. Now she could die and have a chance to stay dead.

"God will funish you!" Luther shouted, then turned to his troops. "Andrew! John! Thaddeus! Phil...Judas!" Five zombies stepped forward, including Philip, whose dim awareness had been unable to decide if he, too, had been called. Luther waved him back impatiently. It was always these four when Luther wanted something done, and the reason was not mysterious. The other eight had a *b*, *m*, or *p* in their names. The names of two-thirds of his disciples were unpronounceable tongue-twisters to Luther.

"Advance uffon the unvelievers," he commanded them. "Swite the sinners! 'In flabing fire taking vengeance on they that know not God, and that ovey not the goshpel!' Firsht Thesshalonians! One! Eight through nine! Go, wy discifles!"

Luther watched them march into the flames. They were goners, but they would do some damage first. Already they bristled with arrows, which they utterly ignored, as they ignored the fact that they were burning. Since they were already dead, it hardly mattered.

The former Pastor Lundquist turned away from it. He could no longer feel pain, nor anything very much like doubt, but sometimes a feeling crept in that made him grope in the dark much as a man who had been blinded, deafened, and had all four limbs amputated might grope. For one thing, it was annoying to see Judas march away to destruction. This was possibly the twentieth "Judas" he had lost. Something always made him choose the biggest, strongest, least decomposed recruit to be Judas. He didn't know why.

And something else. Try as he might, he couldn't conjure the foggiest recollection of what a Thessalonian was.

It was habit that led Luther out of town on the path leading by the old graveyard. He didn't expect to find anything.

He got lucky.

There were six funeral pyres waiting to be lit, and there was even freshly turned soil. Luther's approach had apparently scared off the undertakers before they could torch the corpses. And could it be that someone had actually been buried?

The two things that almost everyone agreed on in Bellinzona were death and insanity. The insane were left alone as long as they were not violent. And the dead were promptly burned. A truce prevailed in the face of death, and the only example of community spirit Bellinzona had ever known showed itself. Everyone cooperated to get the dead to the graveyard, where they were disposed of in ceremonies taken from the Hindus of the Ganges.

It had not always been that way. In a town where ninety percent of the population had no relatives, bodies had been ignored. They might rot for days before someone got so disgusted as to kick them into the water and let them sink.

But then the bodies began to rise again, and climb over the sides of boats and lurk in dark corners. After that, the Vigilantes and Free Females organized burial details.

Burial proved no better. The dead clawed their way out of the graves. Cremation was the only sure answer.

"Vut you have to light the fire," Luther cackled. "Vring the vodies to we," he told his remaining Apostles.

Bartholomew and Simon Peter scrabbled in the dirt and came up with a dismembered body. Someone had thought they could beat the system, but Luther knew better. Even this was not beyond the power of almighty God.

The corpses were fairly fresh, except one that had been gone about two days. One was in a white winding cloth: a rich man, considering the price of fabric in Bellinzona. The rest were naked. Luther slit the cloth over the rich man's face and knew at once this was Judas Iscariot.

He worked himself into a minor frenzy. This was nothing compared to the holy-rolling toot he had thrown for the Free Females; resurrection was a routine matter, like handing out wafers. When he was in the proper state he knelt and kissed each pair of cold lips. He had to wait while Peter fit the pieces of the last one together.

In a few minutes they began opening their eyes. The Apostles helped them to their feet, while Luther studied them with a top sergeant's eye. That black female could be Thaddeus, he decided. And the Chinese would make a good John. He assigned names without regard to what sex they had been. After a few weeks, it was damn hard to tell, anyway.

The seven new zombies were weak and unsteady. It would take ten or twenty revs for them to attain their full strength. The dismembered one would take even longer. Luther would have it carried into the woods and left with the two others he would not be needing, to eventually make their way back to Pandemonium. Luther always traveled with just Twelve.

* * *

By the side of the river, Luther knelt in prayer.

Good, bad—there wasn't a lot of difference anymore. Luther could feel hatred, fury, and a religious ecstasy that was a great deal like both hatred *and* fury. The closest he ever came to feeling *good*, in the sense that Arthur Lundquist might have understood, was when he communed with God. When he prayed.

He didn't do it often. God was a very busy Woman, and didn't like to be bothered with trivia. Just to have Her not answer was stinging enough. To have Her deliver a rebuke could dash him to the ground like an insect. But today She heard, and She answered. Luther knew where the child was. He got to his feet and gathered his troops, gave them their marching orders.

He just hoped that spawn-of-a-whore Kali didn't get to Tuxedo Junction before he did.

SIX

Cirocco felt tired after her swim in the fountain. It hadn't always been that way. When she was younger, it had left her so full of energy it was almost painful. She had not needed to eat for two or three days. Chris said it was still that way for him. He was only forty-nine. It would probably be like that for Robin, too. But for the last fifty years or so, Cirocco needed to lie down for a few hours after a rejuvenation.

She did not do it at the fountain. It was the principle of the water hole. There were enemies who could come into Dione. They might come to the fountain, knowing Cirocco had to visit it once every three kilorevs.

So she went to a secluded lake she knew, about five miles from Tuxedo Junction. There was a beach of black sand, fine as powder, and warm from sub-Gaean heat.

She stretched, rested her head on her pack, and dozed.

Nova saw them when they reached the bridge. For a moment she didn't know who it was walking with the big hairy man, but there really could be little doubt. Robin wore only shorts, and the tattoos that made her body unique were visible. The snakes seemed almost alive. Robin glowed with vivid colors Nova knew only from photographs of her mother as a young woman. If anything, the colors were even brighter now. Patches of gold seemed to glitter, and reds and violets and greens and yellows shimmered like precious jewels. She looked like a little brown Hallowe'en egg.

Brown?

Nova looked again. Sure enough, Robin had managed to get a sun tan. It was a neat trick in this buttermilk sunlight. Even neater to do it in just two hours and not burn in the process.

She kept watching the other end of the bridge, but Cirocco did not appear. She sighed, and went down the stairs to meet them.

It was shocking to see the change up close. Robin had shed five years. Nova had begun to realize that Cirocco was a very powerful witch indeed, but this was almost beyond belief. It irked her in some way she wasn't proud of to see how fresh and happy her mother looked. She just didn't have the right to be that happy when Nova was so miserable.

A meal was served, and still Cirocco didn't show.

Robin and Chris went off together somewhere. Nova watched them go, then hurried up to her room. In a short time she came out again, and went to the kitchen. Serpent was alone in there, mixing something that smelled like cookie batter in a big bowl. He glanced at her, then looked back to his work.

She wandered over to the tremendous spice rack on the wall. Hundreds of blown-glass bottles contained leaves and powders and crystals and some items Nova thought best left un-named. Many were of Gaean ancestry. The problem was she *knew* there were many Earth spices in there, but they were all labeled in Titanide script, engraved on the glass.

By lifting the stoppers and sniffing a few likely candidates she managed to locate aristolochia root, then after more trial and error something that smelled like powdered extract of cubeb. It was the right color, and it tasted right. But after that she was stymied.

"Perhaps I can be of assistance."

She jumped in surprise—which was no small matter in the low gravity. She had been trying so hard to ignore the Titanide's existence that she had forgotten he was there.

"I doubt it," she said. For some reason, she was embarrassed when these outlandish animals talked. They pretended to be human, and did such a poor job of it.

"You could try," Serpent suggested.

"I was wondering if . . . if you had any cardamom."

"Great or small?"

"What?"

"We use two varieties: the Greater—"

"Yes, yes, I know. The small."

"Do you want the dried rind or the crushed seed?"

"The seed, the seed!" Nova regretted being drawn into the conversation in the first place. But Serpent handed her a jar, and she tapped a portion onto a slip of paper and twisted it shut. Then he helped her find the cinnamon. She could see he wondered what she might be cooking, and that whatever it might be, he didn't approve.

"Anything else?"

"Uh . . . would you have any benjamin?"

Serpent pursed his lips primly.

"You'd have to look in the medicine cabinet for that." It was clear his opinion of her recipe had dropped even lower. "It will be labeled in English, as 'benzoin.'" He paused, seemed about to ask a question, but Cirocco had warned him to tread on eggs when dealing with this human. "If it matters," he went on, "there won't be any potassium cyanide left in the solution, but there might be some alcohol."

Nova was going to say she meant the gum resin, not the crystal, but decided against it. She hurried away and upstairs to the infirmary, which she had already located and raided for other ingredients.

Back in her room, she shut the door, pulled the drapes, lit a candle, and stripped off her clothes. Sitting cross-legged on the floor, she tapped out portions of her new acquisitions into the small metal dish she was using as a crucible, added some water, and stirred it with her finger. She used a pin to draw blood from her thumb, and dripped it into the aromatic mess as it began to bubble from the heat of the candle. When it was going well, she plucked three pubic hairs, singed them in the candle flame, and added them to the crucible.

A dollop of vodka filched from the cabinet in the living room soon had the mixture sizzling with a blue flame. She continued to cook it until she had a few ounces of grayish powder. She sniffed it, and made a face. Well, she wouldn't use much. She fretted for a moment about the benjamin, and the fact that the recipe called for mushroom liqueur instead of vodka. But this was supposed to be sympathetic magic, not literal sorcery, so it ought to do.

She began plucking more hairs. She plucked until she was sore, and then wound them together and tied them up into a tiny, golden brush. Pulling on her shirt and pants, she peered out the door. When she was sure she was unobserved she hurried down the hall to Cirocco's room.

Inside, she used the brush to dab tiny spots of powder onto the bedposts and under the pillow. Under the bed she drew a five-sided figure and left a pubic hair in the middle. Then she retreated to the door, leaving an infinitesimal dab every three feet.

Down the hall she went, dabbing her brush in the pan and leaving little dots of powder in a trail to her doorway.

When she closed her door she had to lean against it for a moment. Her heart was pounding and her cheeks were hot. She tore off her clothes and jumped into bed. She used the brush to make a mark between her breasts, then thrust it down between her legs, muttering an invocation. Then she set the pan on the floor near the wall, where Robin would not see it. She pulled the bedclothes up to her neck and took a deep, shuddering breath.

Be still, heart. Your beloved will come.

Then she leaped out of bed and flung herself at the huge, wondrous vanity table with the wavy mirror. She dug into her cosmetics, heedless of the fact that some of them might be irreplaceable. She made up her face with infinite care, applied her best perfume, and jumped back into bed.

What if the perfume covered up the scent of the potion? What if Cirocco didn't care for lipstick? She wore none herself. She didn't wear *any* cosmetics, and was the most beautiful woman Nova had ever seen.

Sobbing, she flew down the hall to the bathroom. She scrubbed it all off, then was sick in the toilet. She cleaned it up, brushed her teeth, and hurried back to bed.

This must be love; what else could hurt so much?

She wept, she moaned, she thrashed the sheets to ribbons, and still Cirocco did not come.

Eventually, she cried herself to sleep.

SEVEN

In the dream, Cirocco opened her eyes.

She was on her back in the fine black sand. Her head rested on her pack. The sand was quite dry, and so was her body. She spread her arms and dug her fingers into the sand, pointed her toes and felt it shift under her heels, moved her shoulders and hips in a slow, sensuous circle that dug the Cirocco-shaped hole in the sand a few centimeters deeper. She let out a deep breath, and relaxed totally.

She was aware of every muscle and every bone. Her skin was stretched taut, each nerve ending waiting to feel the strange thing again.

It came after a timeless dream-time. A small hand was rubbing her left leg, from the top of her foot to her knee and back down again. She could feel it quite distinctly. Four fingers, a thumb, the heel of the hand. It was not pressing hard, not massaging, but neither was it the touch of a feather. She watched without alarm, in the way of some dreams. She could see the minute changes in texture on her skin where the hand moved.

Her nipples hardened. She closed her eyes (it was not completely dark beneath her eyelids), pressed her head back against the pack, raising her shoulders from the sand and arching her back. The hand moved up to her thigh, and another cupped her breast, moved light fingertips around the curve of it, brushed a thumb over the wrinkled nipple. She sighed, and relaxed back onto the accepting sand.

She opened her eyes again. In the dream.

The land was darker. In a land of unchanging light, dusk

seemed to be sweeping over the quiet lake. Cirocco moaned. Her legs were heavy, engorged; she opened them, offering herself to the darkening sky. Her hips seemed to grow from the ground; she thrust them out and up in the most primitive gesture of all, then relaxed again.

Two small footprints appeared in the sand between her legs, one at a time. Then there was the imprint of knees. The sand swarmed, taking on the shape of legs, hollowing out a space for a hip as the phantom knelt and shifted. Both hands were on her thighs now, moving gently up and down.

Cirocco closed her eyes again, and could immediately see better. Ghost images of the lake, the far shore, the sky pulsed against the inside of her eyelids. She lifted herself on her elbows and let her head fall back. Through the thin skin she saw trees converging on a point in the sky. The sky was the color of blood. She bent her legs, her knees up and open. She gasped as the hands explored her. Keeping her eyes closed, she lifted her head.

When she looked straight ahead she could see nothing but the throbbing of her own pulse, the fulgurant and amorphous ephemera of her own retinas. But when she looked to the side—careful to keep her eyes closed—a figure was revealed kneeling between her open legs. It was a Cubist conception, existing from all sides at once, a layered thing with depths her peripheral dream-vision could not reach. It was a thing of colored smoke bound together by moonbeams. Cirocco knew who it was, and she was not afraid.

In the dream, she opened her eyes to almost total darkness.

The shadow knelt there. She felt the hands descend her thighs and spread out over her belly, saw her hyaline lover's face moving down, felt the brush of long hair, felt the tickle of a warm breath, felt the tender kiss, the more insistent kiss, the eager opening of mouth and vulva, the entry of tongue, the hands sliding around to clutch her buttocks and raise her from the yielding sand.

For a moment she was transfixed. She threw her head back, mouth open but unable to make a sound. When finally she was able to sob, to release her breath, the breath became a moan that trailed off into a whispered word.

"...Gaby..."

It was utterly dark. Cirocco reached down and ran her hands

through thick hair, down to Gaby's neck, over her shoulders. She squeezed the smaller woman between her legs, and Gaby kissed Cirocco's belly, her breasts, her neck. Cirocco felt the familiar heavy breasts sliding over her, the wonderful weight pressing down on her. Her hands greedily explored the impossible solidity of Gaby's body. She heard Gaby's breathing next to her ear, smelled the special complex of scent she knew to be Gaby. She wept.

In her dream, Cirocco closed her eyes again.

She saw tears in Gaby's eyes, and a smile on her lips. They kissed. Gaby's black, black hair covered their faces.

She opened her eyes. It was getting light. Gabby still rested on her. They made meaningless noises at each other as a dim twilight stole over the land. Cirocco saw the beloved face. She kissed it. Gaby laughed quietly. Then she put her hands on the sand and lifted herself onto her knees, straddling Cirocco. She held out her hand and got to her feet, pulling Cirocco behind her. The ground clung like flypaper. She had to pull hard to get up. When she was finally standing, Gaby turned her and pointed down. Cirocco saw her own body reclined on the sand, unmoving.

"Am I dead?" she asked. It did not seem an important question.

"No, my beloved. I am not the angel of death. Walk with me." Gaby put her arm around Cirocco and they started up the beach.

In the dream, they spoke to each other. They did not use sentences. A word here and there was enough. Old hurts, old joys were brought out, held up to the yellow sky of Iapetus, cried over and laughed about, and tucked carefully away again. They spoke of things that had happened a century ago, but nothing of the last twenty years. The two decades didn't exist for the old friends.

At last it was time for Gaby to go. Cirocco saw that Gaby's feet no longer touched the sand. She tried to hold her, but the smaller woman kept drifting up into the sky and, in the manner of dreams, all Cirocco's movements were too slow and ineffectual to prevent it. It was a sad time. Cirocco cried for a while when Gaby was gone, standing there in the restored light.

Time to wake up, she thought.

When nothing happened, she looked down at the beach. Two sets of footprints led to where she stood, tired and discouraged.

She closed her eyes and slapped her cheeks. She opened them

to find no change in her situation. So she started back along the edge of the water.

She watched her bare feet as she walked. They made new imprints beside the two trails going the other way. Where the Woozle Wasn't, she thought, and could not remember where that came from. Getting senile, Cirocco.

Her body was a short distance from the water, up where the sand was dry and fine enough for filling hourglasses. It reclined with its head on the pack, its hands folded on its belly, and its legs straight out and crossed at the ankles. She knelt close to it. It breathed slowly and evenly.

She looked away from the body and down at . . . at her*self*. At the body she was living in. It was completely familiar to her. She touched herself, rubbed her hands together, held a hand up and tried to see things through it and failed to do so. She pinched her thigh and watched the skin turn red.

After a while she reached out and touched the body on the forearm. The body was *other*, not *self*. It was an everyday dichotomy, with a disturbing twist. What if the body sat up and wanted to talk?

It was definitely time to wake up, she decided.

Or to go to sleep.

She reached back into a century's experience of living from her gut as well as her mind, and found a non-verbal notion tickling the back of her head. There was no use in trying to think it out. Sometimes, in Gaea, this was the only way to deal with life. Things happened here. Not everything could be explained.

She allowed her instinct to take over. Without thought, she closed her eyes and toppled forward, turning as she fell. She felt the brief touch of the skin of the other, a singular but not unpleasant sensation of fullness—something like the sensations of pregnancy—and rolled along the sand. She opened her eyes and sat up, alone.

The tracks in the sand were still there. Two sets led away, one returned.

She moved on hands and knees to the harder, wetter sand nearer the water. Selecting one of the smaller prints—high-arched, five toes clearly visible and digging in—she ran her fingertips lightly through the depressions. She moved to the next print and lowered herself until her nose almost touched the print. She scented Gaby quite distinctly. The prints of the larger feet did not smell at all. Her own prints never did. Cirocco's sense of smell, though inhumanly keen, could not distinguish her own spoor from the ever-present odor of herself.

She might have thought about it longer, but suddenly she smelled something else, quite far away but unmistakable. She grabbed her pack and sprinted at top speed toward Tuxedo Junction.

EIGHT

Robin nattered on for almost a rev.

Chris had expected it, and didn't mind. The little witch was riding high on a wave of rejuvenation. Part of it was chemical, the result of mystic compounds still surging through her blood, entering every cell and working their changes there. Part of it was psychological, and entirely understandable. Robin looked five years younger, but she felt better than she had in ten years. The result was something like amphetamines, something like manic-depressive psychosis. The highs were Himalayan and almost unendurable, the lows sharp but mercifully brief. Chris remembered it well.

It was no longer so exhilarating for him. When he visited the fountain it felt just as good as it used to, but the feeling didn't last, and was replaced by pain within a few revs. He felt it beginning along his spine and on the sides of his head. He didn't mind that; it was simply growing pains.

Robin chirruped out most of her life story, unable to sit down, pacing the pentagonal room he had built and coppered with remembrances of her. Chris simply sat at the table in the center of the room, nodding at the right places, offering noncommittal responses when it seemed polite to do so, and contemplating the single candle before him.

Eventually she wound down. She took the high stool opposite him and rested her elbows on the table, looking at the candle with eyes brighter than the flame. Slowly her breathing quieted and she shifted her gaze from the candle to him.

It was as if she was noticing him for the first time. She made several attempts to speak, and was eventually successful.

"Sorry," she said.

"Don't be. It's refreshing to see somebody so exuberant. And since you tend to be close-mouthed, it saved me a lot of questioning."

"Great Mother, I sure babbled, didn't I? I just couldn't seem to stop, I had to tell you—"

"I know, I know."

"Chris, it's so...*miraculous!*" She looked at her arm, at the tattoo blazing forth on it. For the hundredth time she rubbed her skin in disbelief, her face showing that small remaining fear that it would rub off.

Chris reached for the fat candle, rolled it moodily around on its base, watching wax drip down the sides.

"It is wonderful," he agreed. "It's one of the few places Gaea can't touch. When you go there, you realize this must have been a pretty damn wonderful place to be, a long time ago."

She cocked her head and looked at him. He could not return her stare.

"Okay," she said. "You asked me out here to discuss something. A proposal, you said. You want to tell me what it is?"

He scowled at the candle again. He knew Robin valued directness and would be impatient if she sensed him stalling for more time, but he was unable to come out with it.

"What are your plans, Robin?"

"What do you mean?"

"Where are you going to stay? What are you going to do?"

She looked startled, then took another quick look around the crazy room he had built.

"I'm afraid I didn't think. That man, Conal, said it would be all right with you if we stayed here for a while, so—"

"That's no problem, Robin. This place belongs to all my friends. I'd be delighted if you made this your home. Forever."

She looked at him gratefully, but with a trace of suspicion.

"I appreciate it, Chris. It'll be good to spend a little time here and sort out the possibilities."

He sighed, and looked directly across the table at her. "I'm going to ask you right out. I hope you'll think about it before you answer. And I hope you'll be honest."

"All right. Shoot."

"I want Adam."

Her face froze. For a long time she did not move a muscle.

"What are you feeling right now?" Chris asked.

"Anger," she said, tonelessly.

"Just before that. Just before you clamped down on it."

"Joy," she said, and got up.

She went to the copper representation of herself on the far wall, and slowly ran her hand over it. She looked back at him.

"Do you think I'm a bad mother?"

"I haven't seen you in twenty years. I don't know. But I see Nova, and I know you are a good mother to her."

"Do you think I'm a good mother to Adam?"

"I think you're trying to be, and it's tearing you up."

She came back to the table, pulled the chair out, and climbed back up onto it. She folded her hands on the table, and looked at him.

"You're good, but you're not perfect, Chris. I told you I almost killed him when he was born. Maybe this will be hard for you to understand. If I *had* killed him . . . I would not feel like a murderer. It would have been the proper thing to do. Letting him live ruined me, politically, socially . . . just about every way there is. I'm asking you to believe those things didn't enter into my decision."

"I believe that. The opinions of other people were never very important to you."

She grinned at him, and for a moment looked nineteen years old.

"Thanks for that. For a while their opinions were *very* important. You wouldn't have known me. But when he came out of my body and into the air, I took a good look at myself. I'm still doing it."

"Do you love him?"

"No. I feel a lot of affection for him. And I'd die defending him. My feelings for him . . . Chris, ambivalent just doesn't say it. Maybe I *do* love him." She sighed again. "But Adam is not tearing me apart. I made my peace with him, and with our joint destiny, and I will be a good mother."

"I never doubted it."

She frowned at him, and rubbed her hand through her hair.

"I don't get it, then."

"Robin, I never intended to rescue him, because I never imagined he needed it." His face darkened for a moment. "I'll admit I worry about Nova."

"She almost killed him herself."

"That doesn't surprise me. She's a lot like you were at her age."

"I was meaner. The difference between me and her is I would have succeeded in killing him, and she didn't. And the reason she didn't is that she really didn't want to. She picked a time when I would have to catch her. She was acting out her pain, and seeing if I really would stop her."

"Do you think he is safe from her now?"

"Utterly. She gave her word. And you remember how important an oath was to me? Well, I was positively wishy-washy compared to her." She reached for the candle in the center of the table and moved it to one side. "Maybe you could tell me why you still want him."

"Because I'm his father." He took a deep breath. "I'm working from ignorance. I don't know what a family is like in the Coven. I don't know how it works with only women around. Do you marry? Does the child have two parents?"

Robin thought about it for a while, then grimaced.

"I talked to Gaby about some of this, a long time ago, and she told me about heterosexual customs. I finally decided the two lifestyles aren't that different. About thirty or forty percent of us pairbond and make it work. Most of the rest of us *try* to make a life commitment, but it falls apart in a few years. About ten percent separate sex life and family life completely, have casual or serial lovers and leave it at that."

"Single parents," Chris said. "The divorce rate where I grew up was about seventy-five percent. But I'm talking about *my* upbringing, my feelings of . . . what is right and wrong. And that tells me a father has a responsibility to his children."

"What about Nova? She's yours, too."

"I was afraid you'd ask me that. She's no longer a child. But she's still a part of me, and I will do right by her."

Robin laughed.

"You shouldn't grit your teeth so hard," she said. "It makes me wonder if you really mean it."

"It won't be easy, I'll admit that."

"Don't worry. She's a lot of things, but easy to like isn't one of them. But leaving that aside for a minute, and tabling the notion of you 'doing what's right' for Nova, whatever that may be . . . you still haven't told me why you want Adam. Just because you're his father?"

Chris spread his hands, looked at them there on the table— big, work-roughened, and ineffectual.

"I don't know if I can." He realized he was very close to tears. "I've been bothered . . . I have . . . doubts." He gestured toward his ears, half-hidden in his long hair. They were long and pointed. "I'm changing. I asked for it, and I want it . . . I think. It's a little late to go back. Me and Valiha . . . oh, God, I can't get into that now. I can't begin to tell you about that yet."

He put his face in his hands and wept. There seemed no way to make her understand.

He didn't know how long he cried. When he looked up, she was still looking at him curiously. She gave him a small smile that was probably meant to be reassuring. He wiped his eyes.

"I feel cheated. I had Serpent and I love him dearly. I love Titanides. I'm going to be one some day."

"When?"

"That's part of my doubts. The process is mysterious. It's taking a long time, and it's starting to be painful. I suppose I could stop now, and be forever stuck between human and Titanide.

"See, Robin. . . . Titanides are not human. They're better and they're worse, and they're similar and they're different, but they aren't human. Ninety-nine percent of me wants to be one so . . . so I can't hurt again the way I hurt for such a long time. So I can understand Valiha, so maybe I can explain to her why I did the things I did. But that nagging one percent is scared to death to stop being human."

"So *you're* the one who's being torn apart."

"I guess that sums it up."

"He's your link to being human."

"Yes. And I'm his father, no matter how roundabout it was."

Robin got up and walked once more to the wall. Chris took the candle and followed her. He held it high as she gently touched the hammered copper.

"I like this," she said.

"Thank you."

"I didn't think I would at first, but it grows on you." She gently traced the outline of the copper Robin, moving her finger along the line of the pregnant belly. She turned to him.

"Why did you make me pregnant in this?"

"I don't know. It wasn't a conscious decision."

"And you left off . . ." She put her hands on her own abdomen, over the place where there had been a hideous tattoo, a monstrous, defiant, and despairing graffito scrawled on her own body by a proud child. The fountain had taken it away. It was as though it had never existed.

"Take him, then," she said.

For a moment Chris could not believe he had heard her right.

"Thank you," he said.

"You look like you didn't expect to convince me."

"I didn't. What changed your mind?"

One corner of her mouth curled in amusement.

"You *have* forgotten a lot about me. I made up my mind about a half second after you asked me. Then I had to hear your reason before I knew if I was just trying to take the easy way out."

Chris was so elated that he picked her up as easily as if she were a child and kissed her, as she laughed and pretended to fight him off.

They were still laughing when the sound of the scream reached them. It went right past the conscious part of Chris's mind, directly to something so basic as to be a reflex action, and he was sprinting for the door long before he knew who had screamed.

NINE

Rocky and Valiha were two kilometers from Tuxedo Junction, in one of the few flat, open pieces of land in that neighborhood, pulling a plow like the draft animals they most definitely were not. The comparison would not have bothered them. A Titanide farmer simply walked in front of the plow, not behind it.

Titanides were unfailingly honest and square—in the sense of a square deal. They paid debts. They would not think of accepting shelter or food without doing something in return. They also knew how to combine the payment of a debt with legitimate self-interest. Rocky and Valiha liked to visit the Junction, liked to stay with Chris in his fanciful aerie, and liked to eat well. There were certain items that did not flourish in a Gaean jungle, that would do well only in light, on flat land, and in the absence of competition. Hence the plowing. Chris could not have done it himself, and when it was done he would be able to grow more crops and set a better table. Everything balanced out nicely.

They had done about two acres. The fresh-turned soil smelled good to Rocky. It was good to exert oneself, to feel ones hooves dig the ground, to hear the creaking of the harness, to see the rich brown dirt steaming from sub-Gaean heat. It was good to rub haunches with Valiha. Yellow had always been a favorite color to him, and the Madrigals were ever yellow.

He had not known her long. That is, he had known *about* her almost since his birth, as she had gone on that terrible journey with the Captain, famous in legend and song. He had known her son, Serpent, for many myriarevs. But he had begun to know Valiha as a friend only about seven kilorevs ago.

Over the last kilorev he had begun to love her. This was a surprise to him. Titanides could be as quirky as the next intelligent species, and Rocky had a thing about Aeolian Solos. He tended not to like them. He knew it was illogical, since it was the single parent of the Solo who had the egotism to wish to birth a genetically identical copy of herself without help from any other Titanide. The child was as blameless as any child . . . yet, if she was a copy, it stood to reason she would have her mother's egotism.

Valiha was an Aeolian Solo.

They came to the end of a row. Both were pleasantly sweaty, a little bit tired. Valiha reached for the buckles of her harness, so Rocky did the same. They shed the plow, and Valiha trotted forward a few paces, then turned, her tail high, and came back beside Rocky, facing the other way. She leaned over and reached beneath him to squeeze the bulge of flesh that sheathed his anterior penis.

"I'm horny," she sang. "Do you want to screw?"

"Sounds good to me," he sang, and trotted around behind her.

What they actually said in their song was much more than that, but Titanide song has never been readily translatable into English. Her four-note phrase was in an earthy mode, so "screw" and "horny" were close. But the way she walked was also a part of it, and the phrase included the idea that Rocky would mount her, not the other way around. Rocky's reply was more than simple assent. In a way, the entire exchange and their subsequent movements were as formalized as dressage.

She set her hind legs apart and lowered her hindquarters slightly. He walked his forelegs lightly up her back, straddled her, and entered her. He embraced her torso from behind and she reached back to hold his forelegs firmly. She reversed her head and they kissed, and humped merrily and lustily for a good two minutes before they reached their anterior orgasms—which, for sound Titanide neurological reasons, were always simultaneous. He rested in that position for a moment, his breasts squeezed firmly against her strong back, then backed down.

She asked if she might do him a similar service, and he declined, not because he didn't wish to be mounted—he wanted it very much—but because he had serious and intimate matters on his mind.

So he pranced out in front of her, lifting his forelegs high, and came to stand face-to-face, inches away from her. She smiled at him and put an arm over his shoulder and turned her head slightly to kiss him, then became aware of his frontal erection. She looked startled, but did not back away.

"Sir, I hardly know thee," she sang, in formal mode.

"It has been a short time," he agreed. "But a love as strong a mine sometimes grows quickly, in the manner of those-who-walk-on-two-legs. If she would permit, I would propose a union to m lady."

"Sing it, then."

"A trio. Myself the hindmother. I know not if I have spoke of it, but I have never been a hindmother."

"You are young."

"That is true."

"Mixolydian?"

"Lydian. And Serpent for the hindfather."

She lowered her eyes in thought.

"Sharped?" she sang.

"Yes."

What he had outlined was a Sharped Lydian Trio, one of th most common of the Twenty-nine Ways. He and Valiha would hav frontal intercourse to produce a semi-fertilized egg: Rocky th forefather, Valiha the foremother. The egg would be activated b Cirocco Jones, implanted in Rocky's womb, and quickened by Ser pent: Rocky the hindmother, Serpent the hindfather.

He could see her adding it up. Genetics was as instinctive i Titanides as it was imponderable to humans. He knew she woul find no flaw in his proposal, though the fact that Valiha was Serpent' hindmother might make it seem incestuous to a human. But inces was a genetic problem to Titanides only in special and limited cases and morally it was no problem at all.

"It is a good mating," she sang, finally. "It will require som thought."

"As she wills it."

"It is not thee, sir," she began, then dropped back into a les formal mode. "Dammit, Rocky, I'm beginning to love you, too, an you're an admirable fellow, but the times bother me."

"I know, Valiha. The world spins badly."

"I don't know if we should bring babies into a world like this."

"In your own hindmother's time, did we not war with th angels?"

She nodded, and wiped away a tear. She forced a smile.

"I know it. And Serpent will love it. Have you spoken of thi to him?"

"No other soul knows of it."

"Then I pray you, hold it within thy heart while the world spins another thousand times. Then thou shalt have thy answer."

They kissed, and heard Serpent come out of the jungle at a full gallop. His hooves sprayed dirt as he thundered across the plowed field.

"I thought you two were plowing!" he sang. "I felt so guilty, staying home and baking, my only burden that fierce human child, while you labored like common farm hands. So I hurried, only to find you—"

He stopped, digging in with all four hooves, and stood perfectly still for two long seconds. Then he reared on his hind legs, wheeled, and dashed off the way he came.

"Zombies!" he shouted, in English, but by then Rocky and Valiha had smelled them, too, and were in hot pursuit.

"Rescue a kid and what does it get you?" Conal asked himself. He glanced at Adam. There was spit dripping down his chin. "You get to be a babysitter, that's what."

He yawned, and settled deeper into the couch. He was in a corner room on the first floor of the main house at the Junction, one with a lot of windows and a good view of the waterfall. Nova was somewhere upstairs, doing something that had produced a strange smell for a while. Whatever it was, it had made her throw up. Before that, she had been running all over the house, acting like a spy. But there had been no sound out of her for over an hour.

"Too good to sit with her baby brother," he told Adam. The infant regarded him solemnly, and then threw a Titanide egg at him.

Actually, Conal didn't mind. He just got a lot of satisfaction out of feeling put-upon.

The kid was okay. Not a howler. Real smart, and real strong. He could probably start with the weights in another year or so, just as soon as he had his feet solidly under him. He had the bones for it. And in a way, Conal was proud that Robin had trusted him enough to leave the baby with him.

He had set the kid up in the middle of the floor with some toys he'd scrounged, and Adam seemed happy to sit there and throw them around, then crawl after them. His favorite was the rack of old Titanide eggs. They were round, about the size of a golf ball, and came in all colors. They were too big for him to put in his mouth, though that didn't prevent him from trying, and they wouldn't break. About their only drawback was a tendency to roll under furniture, so Conal had rigged a palisade of pillows all around Adam, four meters wide. He didn't manage to chunk too many that far. He stumped around in there, naked, not falling down much, and bouncing right back up when he did.

Conal watched Adam grow still, and start peeing on the floor. Conal laughed, and Adam turned awkwardly and started laughing, too.

"Ma!" Adam squeaked. "Tye-Nye! Ma!"

"Pee-pee," Conal told him, getting up. "Gotta learn that, kid. Say, 'Gotta go pee-pee.'" Adam laughed louder, nodding.

Conal got a towel out of the bathroom and mopped it up. It was a nuisance, but what could you expect? And it was better than diapers.

He sat down again and his thoughts turned, not for the first time, to Nova. Most likely she was sleeping up there. Hell of a problem, Nova. Hell of a problem. What to do about it? Where to start?

He couldn't think of a good place. At first he thought she hated all living beings equally. Lately he had come to believe he held a special place in her heart, just below rattlesnakes, pederasts, and spirochetes. Definitely a tough place to start from, but determination had always been Conal's strong point.

Unhappily, imagination was not. Nor was subtlety. Cirocco had told him he had an admirable directness, but that it took some getting used to.

So when his thoughts turned to Nova, they kept going around in the same unprofitable pattern. He knew it was ridiculous, he knew something radical had to happen before she could ever begin to see him as anything but a repulsive monster, but he kept having the same recurrent fantasy. It started with him getting out of the chair and going up the stairs. He would knock on her door.

"Come in," she would say. He would enter, smile winningly.

"Just wanted to see if you needed anything, Nova," he would say.

Then—he wasn't sure about the details of this part—he would

be sitting on the bed beside her, and he would lean over to kiss her, and her lips would part . . .

She screamed.

It was a dreadful, terrifying scream, torn from her throat. So deep had been his fantasy that for a confusing moment he tried to form an apology, and then his blood seemed to freeze as he understood this was real.

His feet touched the bottom stair, the ninth stair, and the top stair, and he was barreling down the hallway toward her room.

TEN

Nova came awake slowly, not knowing what had been bothering her. She lay there, waiting for the sound again, wondering why she had thought Cirocco was outside her door waiting to come in.

There it was again. A scratching sound. But they didn't scratch at doors here, they hit them with their fists. And this wasn't the door, it was the window.

She got up, yawning, padded to the window, and stuck her head out. She looked down.

What she saw was frozen in her memory for all time.

There was a thing climbing up the outside of the house. She saw its arms, which were made of bones and snakes, and the top of its head, which was covered with cracked parchment and scraps of long hair. But the true terror was in its hands. She could see the bare finger bones, pieces of rotting flesh, and mouths. Each finger ended in a little blind snake with a wide mouth and needle-teeth, and when the hand grasped the vertical wall the snakes bit into the wood with an audible crunch. The thing was coming up fast, hand over hand. She was fumbling for her gun, realizing belatedly that she had no clothes on, when the thing looked up. It had the face of a skull. Worms swarmed in the eye sockets.

Nova was not easily frightened. Even that horrific face was not enough to make her scream. But then she turned to get her gun and was face to face with the second thing, hanging from the wall beside the window, its face two feet away from her own. Above its eyebrows there was just jagged bone and a boiling mass of worms. It reached for her and she screamed.

It had her by the wrist. She pulled, still screaming, as the tiny snakes bit into her flesh. Then she tore free.

She did not remember how she got across the room. Time went very slowly, or racketed by leaving momentary gaps. She found her gun in her hand. The hand trembled, fumbling with the safety. She brought it around and up. The second thing was in the room coming right at her and she pulled the trigger and heard nothing because the blood had made the gun slip out of her hand, and the thing was still coming at her. She rolled over her bed and down into the gap between it and the wall as she heard the door splintering. The gun had to be down there somewhere. She fought an overpowering urge to take another look, heard something hit something else with a meaty sound, heard something else rattle the house as it hit the floor. She found the gun, steadied it with her good hand, and jerked her arms over the bed with the gun out in front of her.

Conal came within a tenth of a second of dying. The nerve impulse was already on the way to Nova's trigger finger when she realized he was grappling with one of the creatures and managed to jerk her hands up in time to put her first rocket-propelled bullet into the wall a foot below the ceiling.

There was no way she was going to get a safe shot at the one Conal was fighting, but the second monster was framed in the window, on its way in, so she gave it two explosive slugs, one in the head and the second in the chest, and paused one second to see what it thought about that.

The head exploded, pulverized, vanished. The chest wanted to fly apart, but the silvery snakes that threaded the thing's body somehow managed to hold it together.

And it kept coming.

You do that much longer, she thought, and I'm going to get scared.

The one on the floor had thrown Conal off. Nova put three bullets into it, with results not much better than before. The creature was thrown against the wall by the force of the explosions and its left arm was blown off at the shoulder. But it got up, one handed, and started toward Conal.

So did the arm. It pulled itself rapidly along with its fingers.

Nova swallowed the sour taste of vomit, and put her last three slugs into the one just inside the window. The headless one. It staggered back, hitting the sill, and tumbled out, backwards. She heard things scrabbling at the wall, receding, then a splash as it hit the water.

That's when the second zombie turned toward her.

Conal seemed stunned. He was getting to his feet, but he kept shaking his head. And the monster slumped toward her on a shattered leg, shedding bone splinters and pieces of jelly-like flesh and scuttling beetles and little fanged rodents as it came.

She threw the gun at it, wishing it was her mother's substantial Colt instead of the new, modern, lightweight type. It opened a gash on the zombie's cheek and worms poured out.

She picked up the bed and heaved that. The zombie batted it aside.

She was going down now, unable to stop herself from flinching away.

She threw a lamp, a vase, the bedside table, and still it was getting closer. Conal was coming up slowly behind it but it loomed over her now, she was crouched in the corner and it was going to get her. Her hand groped for a weapon. Anything. She found something and threw it.

And the thing collapsed just as Chris came through the door.

She saw Chris kick it as it fell, saw him attack the thing . . . and then stop. He frowned, and Nova wondered what was wrong, then realized he couldn't figure out why the thing wasn't fighting back. He kicked it hard again. The zombie was starting to fall apart. The silver snakes that had held it together, that had seemed to animate it, were limp and lifeless.

Chris knelt in front of her. She couldn't see him very well. He glanced at her arm and seemed satisfied that her wounds were not life-threatening, then put big hands on her shoulders and looked at her.

"Are you going to be all right?"

She managed to nod, and he was gone. She heard him say

something to Conal, something about Adam, and she heard him leave.

It seemed there was nothing in the room but the dead creature. She couldn't take her eyes off it. It was only about three feet away from her. Without conscious thought her feet began to push her away. Her back slid along the wall and her feet kept pushing until she hit something soft. That was no good, soft hadn't been what she'd had in mind at all, hard walls and hard floors were much better. She squeaked. It was a timid, frightened little squeak, and she regretted it, but there it was. She already knew she had bumped into Conal. The rough texture of his coat scratched against her shoulder, and that was okay. Anything warm was okay. The thing, when it grabbed her, had been terribly cold, and she was terribly cold now.

She sat there, shivering, as Conal put the coat over her shoulders. She heard shouting from the other rooms, sounds of fighting, and knew she should be helping them. But she sat quietly as Conal ripped his shirt and bound it around her bloody forearm and hand. While he did that she heard the pounding of Titanide hooves and what might have been war-cries.

Then he was getting up and she found herself clinging to his arm with her good hand. He stopped, waited for her to get up, and led her from the room. She never took her eyes off the thing on the floor.

It didn't make sense that the zombie was dead.

Dead? Well, hell, Chris thought. Of course, it's dead, it was dead to begin with, but that had never slowed them up in the past.

He wanted to kick the vile thing until what was left would have to be scraped off the walls, but he didn't have time for that. He didn't have time to figure out what had killed it, either. He really didn't have time to check on Nova, but he did.

Conal looked woozy. Blood ran from a scalp wound and he had a swelling the size of an egg on the side of his head.

"Where's Adam? Conal. Can you hear me?"

"... stairs," he muttered. "Downstairs. Hurry, Chris... zombies."

Out in the hall there was another dead—or unmoving—zombie. It had come from the direction of Cirocco's room. Chris ran down the stairs, around a corner, through the music room—and into the arms of another zombie.

This one fought him. It was not as far gone as the one in Nova's room; dead no more than a week or two, by the look of her. Chris lifted the zombie and threw it, hoping to gain some time. The only way to really deal with the things was with edged weapons. It also helped to have the steady rhythm of a lumberjack chopping wood, and the strong stomach of Conan the Barbarian. Hitting them or wrestling with them was a good way to get killed. They could soak it up almost forever, and even if you dismembered them they kept fighting. But severing enough of the deathsnakes that gave the zombies an obscene semblance of life would eventually do the trick.

They were incredibly strong. If they got in close, the deathsnakes would tear at your flesh.

As the zombie hit the wall he was already searching for an axe or a blade. There didn't seem to be anything. He picked up a chair, planning to use it to fend the zombie off while he made his way to the kitchen, when he noticed something. It wasn't getting up.

The zombie—it seemed ridiculous to use the female pronoun, though it had bloated and festering breasts—had collapsed on the floor, crushing a fine old silver trombone.

Once again Chris didn't pause to wonder or to question his luck. He had never intended to fight it; the zombie had simply been in his way. He hurried through the music room, made it to the kitchen, where he grabbed his biggest cleaver, and raced through the house in time to see Robin poised in a windowsill, her legs bent and her arms out in front of her.

He shouted at her, but she dived out.

Robin almost beat Chris to the doorway of the Copper Room—then almost got jammed with him, which would have hurt, as he had enough momentum by then to not really need a door; he could have just punched through the wall. She broke step enough to let him through, went through herself, and, running as fast as she could, gawked at the spectacle of Chris Major moving at full speed. She didn't get to watch long. He might have been flying.

Great Mother, but this was one *huge* tree.

It seemed to take forever, but finally she slammed in the back door and hurried through room after room, calling for Chris, Nova, Conal...anybody. She never stopped moving. Once, out of the corner of her eye, she caught a glimpse of some horror shambling through an empty room, but she didn't pause. Nothing was going to stop her until she found Nova, and the source of that scream. She knew her daughter well, knew it wasn't a mouse that had made her shout like that.

But something did make her stop. She looked into a room with a lot of pillows and toys on the floor. She heard Adam crying, and saw a man-shaped creature—there was something badly wrong with it, but she couldn't see what in the brief glimpse—diving through the window with Adam in its hands.

Stopping in one-quarter gravity is something that needs practice. Robin wasn't good at it yet, and had to bang into a wall, push off with her hands, and swing around into the room with her hand on the doorjamb. She ran to the window, looked out, and saw the creature swimming away, one-armed. The other arm was holding Adam out of the water.

She kicked off her boots, stepped up into the window, and jumped.

Later, she would deny that she had forgotten she didn't know how to swim. Once before she had been dumped into water over her head. Something had happened to her, and she managed to reach the shore. She was counting on that to work again. But it didn't.

She hit with a stunning splash, and then struggled toward the light.

Her head breached the surface and she took a deep breath, then tried to swim. The harder she worked at it the worse it got. Her head kept going under and she didn't know any better than to try to keep her nose high—an ambition she kept defeating with her windmilling stroke. The current was carrying her in the same direction as her goal, but that didn't help, as the kidnapper was swimming with the current, too, and in the brief glimpses she got he was always farther away. They were swirling through swift water now, with rocks here and there, but it was always deep, always cold, and before long she knew she was going to die in this river. She was getting her head above water less often, and for shorter periods, and more often than not taking in a lot of water when she gasped for air.

Then an arm went around her neck and she was pulled up, on

her back. She struggled for a moment but the arm tightened until she was nearly choking. She coughed up water, and relaxed. Chris pulled her strongly through the water toward the shore.

He got her to a rock in the middle of the stream where she could cling with her torso high and dry and not too much current tugging at her.

"Hang on!" he told her.

"Get him, Chris!" she shouted, hoarsely.

He was already away.

She pulled herself higher and looked over the top of the rock. The kidnapper was maybe a hundred feet ahead of Chris, and the gap was narrowing. But the water ahead was extremely rough.

A kind of frozen lethargy settled over her. She was exhausted, had been near death, and it was all she could do to hang onto the rock and watch events unfold before her eyes. They didn't seem to have much relation to her. She was able to wonder if the thief could make it through the rapids and keep Adam alive, but unable to connect his survival or death to herself. A scream kept bubbling up in her throat, but it didn't have anywhere to go.

She heard the Titanides crossing the bridge, making a sound like an avalanche. She turned, and saw Serpent pointing toward Chris, saw Rocky leap over the railing and float down, forelegs first, then hit with a splash that sent water fifty feet high. His head came up and he was swimming strongly as Serpent and Valiha went through the front door of Tuxedo Junction, not bothering to open it.

There were sounds of something crashing through the brush, and Robin turned in time to see Cirocco pounding along the edge of the river. She passed Robin's rock, passed Chris, reached a suitable place for take-off and leaped. Her body followed an almost flat trajectory and she was forty feet from shore before she hit the water.

And she didn't sink. She had arched her back and held her arms in a swept-back position, like a jetliner, and held her chin high as she hit, and she skipped twice, like a flat stone, then body-surfed another precious five feet before the water had her. She was thirty feet behind her objective and swimming strongly.

Robin found herself balanced on her knees, her fists tight and her teeth clenched, willing Cirocco onward. Dimly she was aware of the sounds of Valiha and Serpent diving into the water somewhere behind her, but her eyes never left the woman she would always think of as the Wizard. It looked like Cirocco would tear the bastard into tiny pieces when she got to him, and there was nothing in the world Robin wanted to see more than that.

She heard shouts behind her. A wide shadow swooped over her with breathtaking speed, then all she could see was the skimpy rear profile of an angel, twenty-foot wings at full extension, the tips skimming the water.

It folded its wings the tiniest bit, seemed to hesitate in its headlong rush. Then it snatched Adam with the effortless grace of an eagle hitting a steelhead. It soared up, converting forward momentum into altitude. At two hundred feet it began to flap its great wings, and in a little while it had vanished into the east.

ELEVEN

Luther had a Sight on the way to Tuxedo Junction. He knew it wasn't going to work out well for him. He thought Gaea might be goading him with this information. And sure enough, when he reached the high hill overlooking the lake, the tree, and the treehouse, he was just in time to see the ending.

The Sight was still with him. It didn't rely on his single eyeball; trees, walls, and distance were no hindrance to it. He could see Kali's troops in the house, the child playing alone in the room. He watched as the half-Titanide heathen raced up and down the stairs, saw Cirocco Jones come running into the scene, knew when the two humans and three Titanides hit the water.

For a moment he dared to hope, when the Demon dived into the water. Much as he hated Jones, he knew none of Kali's band was her match—nor, for that matter, were any of his own disciples. Nothing would please Luther more than to see the Demon rend Kali's slime-spawn into component parts. Then the child might be his. . . .

He watched in disbelief as the angel swooped down.

"Angels!" he shrieked. "Angels? Wy God, wy God, why hast thou forsaken we?"

His disciples shuffled nervously beside him, anxious to go.

Having no minds of their own, they were somehow attuned to his emotions. They received his towering frustration, his hatred of the Demon and of Kali . . . and his quick and virulent fear at the mortal sin he had just uttered.

Luther carried a special Cross in his belt, made of bronze, razor-sharp along all its edges. He pulled it out and began slashing at his own legs, feeling the arms biting deep, glorying in the mortification of the flesh.

He heard a gobbling sound above him.

When he looked up, there was Kali, climbing down from her perch in a tree. A pair of binoculars clattered against her improbable bosom. Her body-slave, a naked boy in his eighth year, scuttled after her, nimble as a monkey, with a golden collar attached to four feet of golden chain that bound him to Kali.

Kali was all gold and putrefaction. The slave chain was fourteen-carat, but the scores of rings she wore on fingers and toes were pure, soft, and fine. She wore a genuine brass bra, buttressed like a gothic cathedral to support the mammoth ochreus breasts. Her legs and her four arms were encircled by a hundred ornate bands and rings, each too small for the limb it squeezed, so that her flesh oozed around them. Her waist was constricted by a gold girdle ten inches in circumference, then her body swelled to a steatopygous abundance. The phrase "hourglass figure" might have been invented for her alone.

Her fingernails were six inches long, and made of bronze.

Her face . . . it was not completely accurate to speak of Kali's face, since she had three heads. But the right and left ones were simply tacked on. Each had a strangler's noose drawn tight. When one rotted off she would replace it from the supplies available to Gaea. At the time she dropped from the tree and walked toward Luther—in a grotesque, hip-sprung gait, a whore in a mortuary—one of the heads was pretty ripe, and another was a recent addition. The old one had been female and white. It was now extremely mortified, and purple, with red protruding eyeballs and black protruding tongue. It hung backwards by a scrap of flesh. The other head had belonged to a black man whose color had been changed very little by the act of strangulation. This one lolled drunkenly forward, swaying as Kali walked.

The central head had been—in the same sense that Luther had

once been the Reverend Arthur Lundquist—a priestess named Maya Chandraphrabha in her previous life. Of Maya, only the head remained. In life, hers had been a boyish, awkward and sterile body. She who now called herself Kali never suffered a moment's regret, never experienced even the brief torments that sometimes beset he who was now Luther. She gloried in her virulent fecundity. Her womb was prolific as a jellyfish; each kilorev she whelped a new squalling monstrosity for the greater glory of Gaea.

She wore a belt fashioned of human skulls.

Kali's face was dead. Her eyes could move, but she could not blink, smile, frown, or close her mouth. Her jaw hung, and her tongue sagged out of her mouth. The gobbling sound Luther had heard was Kali's laughter.

Kali was the avatar of atrocity.

She gobbled at Luther, and the fingers of two hands traced intricate patterns in the air.

"Shesez where the hell has you been, Luther," the boy droned.

The boy had been the heir to a large fortune. He was about a year older than the War. When he and his family had emerged from their shelter in the mountains of Mexico one of Gaea's mercy missions had picked him up. His mother had been deaf, which had given him a skill now useful to Kali. He had once been a bright, healthy, and alert six-year-old. Now his body was the sort a political cartoonist might draw, purposely exaggerated, and label World Hunger. His eyes never left Kali's hands. He was about eighty years older than he had been two years ago.

"Gaea gave *we* the right to take the child," Luther thundered.

Kali gobbled even louder, and her fingers flew.

"Shesez Gaea dint give you no right to get it lessen you got to it first," the boy chattered. "Shesez you was too fuckin late. Shesez you is a prodisint—" Kali slammed a hand across the boy's bruised face.

"—shesez you is a prod—"

Again he was slapped.

"—protisent—"

And again.

"—prot . . . is . . . tent . . . shesez you is a protestant muhfuckering ig . . . ig . . . ignor-a-mouse shitheaded buggerin christian.

Shesez you is too ugly to live. Shesez whyn't ya go suck on the Pope's prick."

"Whore of Vavylon! Harlot of Gomorrah!"

"Shesez damn straight. Shesez she gonna take on you and your whole asshole crew. Shesez lessen you tooken a vow of sebisiss—"

Kali hit him again.

"—sebila—sela—cellba—celili-li-li-li—celibin—celiba...cy."

The boy sighed his pleasure and relief when he got it right and Kali stopped hitting him.

"Celibacy, celibacy, celibacy," he muttered. He would get it right the next time, no question.

"Fofery!" Luther hissed, meaning *popery*. Arthur Lundquist, whose faint ghost informed the actions of the thing he had become, would not have known popery from plenary indulgences, being a thrice-Reformed Lutheran and a spiritual ally of most of the Catholic sects. But it amused Gaea for all her Priests to be fundamentalists, and she had a long memory, and so Luther was further enraged.

"Fofery!" he repeated, and his Apostles fuffed and fawed sympathetically in his wake. "Fofery! Vy what right do you take the child?"

"Shesez Gaea told her to. Shesez she did a hell of a lot better job than you and your fuckoffs did."

"Vut the *angels*. I..." Luther stopped, enraged but unable to do anything about it without the possibility of blasphemy.

Why had Gaea given her angels? Luther had no angels. He had *never* had any angels, had never been told he might even *get* angels.

"It won't work," he tried. "Your angel can't reach Fandewon-iuh."

The boy watched the hands again.

"Shesez it will too work. Shesez she's got a shitload of angels. Shesez she's got enough to relay the little muhfucker all the way to Pandemonium. Shesez howdja like to take a big juicy bite outta her big juicy—"

Luther shrieked, and hit the boy. The boy absorbed it, as he had absorbed everything for the last two years, never taking his eyes from Kali's hands, never pausing in his vile curses. He had learned that nothing that could come from anywhere else could ever rival the things that came from Kali.

He was wrong. Luther swung his cross and the boy was instantly dead. He turned on Kali and his Apostles followed. They all tore at her. She did not resist. She lay on her back and gobbled contentedly, and her laughter enraged Luther further...

Until he noticed that all his Apostles were dead.

TWELVE

They gathered in the room from which Adam had been taken.

Conal watched them come in, one after the other. His head still hurt something awful, but it was minor compared to the feeling of fear that was stealing over him.

The three Titanides were wet, and ignoring it. Cirocco was wet, and didn't seem to notice. Chris had a towel and was drying himself off. He seemed exhausted, and distant. Conal didn't know the special hell Chris was going through, but he could see some signs of it.

Robin was wet, and shivering. Chris handed her his towel when he was through.

Nova...

She still wore Conal's coat. She was holding it over her shoulders with one hand, shivering almost as badly as her mother. And, though she wore the coat, and though she was holding it in place, she was making no attempt to cover herself. It only reached to her waist, anyway, so it wouldn't have done her much good, but she held her injured arm out for Rocky to work on, and was unconcerned that one breast was revealed.

Nova seemed to have no body modesty. Conal was used to that in Cirocco, and saw it frequently in long-time residents of Bellinzona. But it was unusual in new arrivals.

He remembered her pressed against him up there in her bedroom. It was a moment he was not going to forget. And now he couldn't seem to take his eyes off her.

"This is going to hurt badly," Rocky said.

"Doctors don't say things like that," Nova said. "They promise you it isn't going to hurt much."

"I am not a doctor. I am a healer, and this is going to hurt a *lot*."

Rocky poured the antiseptic solution over Nova's cuts and started to clean them out. Her face froze, then turned very ugly, but she didn't scream.

Conal thought she was foolish. He had been treated for zombie wounds. Rocky had to probe deep to be sure he got out every particle of corruption. To have a zombie breathe on you was enough to put you in bed for a week. To be torn up like Nova . . .

He had to look away. He'd never had a strong stomach.

Cirocco had been waiting like stone for everyone to assemble. Now that they were all here, she wasted no time.

"Who was in the room with Adam when he was taken?" she asked.

Conal's heart froze.

He saw Chris looking around, frowning, trying to put it together.

"Me and Robin were out in the Witch room," he said. "When I got here—"

"I'm asking a simple question," Cirocco interrupted. "I just want to know who was in here. We need a place to start."

"Nobody was in here," Conal said, and swallowed hard.

Cirocco turned to face him.

"And how do you know that?"

"Because when I heard the scream, I ran upstairs . . ."

Cirocco kept looking at him. She was not in the mood to waste time, so her look couldn't have gone on much more than two seconds, and those seconds didn't take much more than twenty years to go by.

"I told you to protect him, at all costs," she said, tonelessly. For an instant the doors were open over the twin blast furnaces. Then she looked away and Conal could breathe again.

Chris spoke up.

"That's not fair, Cirocco. What was Conal supposed to do when he heard Nova scream? Ignore it? There's no way he—"

Then Cirocco was looking at Chris, and he didn't have anything more to say.

"Don't waste my time, Chris. We can debate fairness some other day."

That's right, Conal thought. Nobody told you it was going to be fair. You walk up to the oldest, meanest, most paranoid human in the solar system . . . and you try to make a man out of what is left.

"Cirocco, what about Nova?" Robin asked. "Chris couldn't have—"

"Shut up, Robin."

"Captain," Rocky began.

"Shut up, Rocky."

Several people tried to speak at once, including Nova.

"Shut up."

Cirocco didn't precisely raise her voice, but she put something into it that nobody could argue with. And she didn't wait for silence. It came, but she was already plunging ahead.

"I know how fast an angel can fly," she said. "I couldn't see this one well enough to know which clan it was. There are twenty-five species of angel and they all dislike each other, so it's possible we can get help from other flights. Their range is limited. We can assume it's headed for Pandemonium, so—"

"Why don't we just let him go?" Nova muttered.

Cirocco took two quick steps and slapped Nova's face so hard the young woman was thrown to the floor. She sat up, her mouth bleeding, and Cirocco pointed at her.

"Kid, I've taken all I'll take from you. This is your first and last warning. You will grow up, damn fast, and you will join the human race, or I'm likely to kill you accidentally, and I'd hate to do that because Robin is my friend. We will now discuss how to save the life of a human being who happens to be your brother, and you will speak only when spoken to."

Again, Cirocco had not raised her voice. There was scarcely a need to. Nova was lying on her side, stunned, in a place far beyond humiliation. Conal's coat had fallen from her shoulders as she went down. A few minutes ago Conal would have been quite interested, but now he could only spare her a glance as Rocky helped her up.

Cirocco needed him, and Nova had turned into just another broad, and a dumb one, at that.

"Gaea is behind this. Gaby warned me the child was important. I don't know why Gaea wants him. Possibly just to lure me to do battle with her, which she's been trying to do for years. But Gaea doesn't have him yet. She is in Hyperion, which is as far from here as you can get. There's something I need to know. Chris, when you entered Nova's room, was the zombie already dead?"

"That's right."

"And the one in the hall . . ."

"It wasn't there when I went in, and it was dead on the floor when I came out."

"Any of you kill it?" Cirocco swept them with her eyes, and everyone indicated they hadn't.

"The one in the music room. Tell me about that."

"I was getting ready to fight it, and it just keeled over."

"But the one with Adam got away." She turned to Nova. "What did you do to that first one?"

"I shot it," Nova whispered. "I shot it . . . three times."

"That wouldn't kill it. What did you do then?"

"I threw the gun at it."

Cirocco waited.

"I threw the bed. Then other things."

Nova shrugged, listlessly. She seemed to be in shock.

"The vase, the lamp, the cru— . . ." All the blood drained from her face.

"What?" Cirocco kept at her.

"Some-some-something I m-m-made."

"I'm not going to hit you again, Nova, but you *are* going to tell me what it was you made."

Nova's whisper was almost inaudible.

". . . a love potion . . ."

"She borrowed some ingredients from the kitchen," Serpent volunteered.

Cirocco turned away from them all and was quiet for several seconds. No one moved. At last she turned back.

"Chris," she said, pointing at him. "Radios. Three. Bring them back here, then meet me at the cave."

Chris hurried off without a word.

"Valiha. You take one radio and go, as fast as you can, to Bellinzona. Put out a general call to all Titanides who still have faith in their Wizard. I want live zombies, as many as you can take. Don't risk your life to get them, and stay in radio contact with me."

"Yes, Captain."

"Rocky, you will stay here. We may have further instructions when we find out how they plan to get Adam to Pandemonium."

"Yes, Captain."

"Serpent. As soon as you get your radio, you will head west, conserving your strength. You can't outrun an angel, but we will try to guide you from the air. Take weapons."

"Yes, Captain."

"Conal, you come with me. Robin, Nova, you can come with me or stay here, as you please."

She was already on her way out of the room when she kicked one of the loose Titanide eggs Adam had been playing with. She froze, then walked slowly to the wall where it lay, bent over, and picked it up.

Cirocco held the egg up to the light and stared at it, and for the first time in living memory, the Wizard looked stunned. The egg was transparent.

She dropped it and stood for a moment with her shoulders slumped.

"Rocky," she said. "Gather all these eggs. Be sure you get them all. Destroy all the furniture, rip up all the pillows, but don't miss any. I'll have Chris radio back a count after we get away.

"When you're sure you have them all, destroy them."

It took a huge effort, but Cirocco managed to get her mind off the Titanide eggs and back to the problem at hand.

Both Robin and Nova had elected to join her. She did not try to dissuade them, nor did she question their reasons. They followed her into the jungle and up the hill toward the cave.

It was funny how quickly it all came back. The habit of command. Starting with what she felt was no natural talent for it and in an era when there were still few female role models she could study, she had worked doggedly at learning how it was done. She had talked to a thousand old men, naval captains, some of whom had commanded ships as far back as the First Nuclear War. Then there had been the space captains, and whole new traditions, new ways of doing things . . . and yet with much in common. People were still people. Maybe they were a little more willing to let a woman command them than they had been in 1944, but the problems of insuring automatic obedience and earning the respect that would nurture a strong, united, and loyal crew were much the same as they had always been.

There were a thousand things you could learn, myriad ways of attaining that improbable position whereby men and women were willing to obey your orders. NASA had sponsored leadership courses and Cirocco had taken them all. She had read autobiographies of great leaders.

She knew, secretly, that she had no talent for command. It was all a false front, but if one kept it in place twenty-four hours a day no one was the wiser.

She lost her first command. Afterward, she had never been able to put the survivors back into a functioning team. They all went their own ways—all but Gaby and Bill—and she had lived for many years afterward with a deep feeling of failure.

NASA had been alarmed when only two of the seven people from *Ringmaster* could be convinced to return to Earth, and infuriated when they learned the Captain was among the five deserters. But NASA was a civilian organization, and after discharging what she saw as her responsibilities, telling everything she knew about what had happened and why, she felt justified in resigning her commission in a place of her own choosing.

NASA couldn't court-martial her, much as they would have liked to, even *in absentia*. But they did the civilian equivalent, which was to set up a dozen commissions and boards of enquiry.

She had had almost a century to think things over. In that time she had given a lot of thought to leadership. There were different kinds of leaders, she had concluded. Some were good, and some were bad. It was probably true that there were leaders who never suffered the doubts she had experienced, who were absolutely sure of themselves and everything they did. They were the egomaniacs, monomaniacs, megalomaniacs—Atilla, Alexander, Charlemagne, Mussolini, Patton, Suslov—men with obsessions, driven men, often psychotic or paranoid. It was even possible for them to be good leaders, but Cirocco felt that, by and large, the world was a worse place when they were through stamping their designs upon it.

For decades now Cirocco had been relieved of that kind of responsibility. She was most content when she had no one depending on her, and when she had to depend on no one. Her sole responsibility for the last two decades had been to keep herself alive, at almost any cost. Now maybe that was changing.

But when the need arose, it was satisfying to discover how quickly she could change gears.

Chris caught up with the rest of them just as they reached the cave.

It was high, wide, and deep: the perfect place for part of Cirocco's arsenal. The cave seemed to stand open, undefended. Actually, there were guardians so well-concealed that an intruder could walk over one without seeing it. Cirocco had gathered the creatures in Rhea, where they had once guarded an ancient idol, and had learned how to re-program their simple brains to suit her needs. They ignored Titanides. But any human not accompanied by Chris or Cirocco would have been dead before entering the cave.

Inside were the aircraft. There were six of them, but three had been cannibalized for parts to keep the others running. Twenty years ago, when Cirocco bought them and had them shipped to Gaea, they had been state-of-the-art. That state hadn't improved much in thirteen years, and not at all since the War. They were magnificent, incredible planes, bearing the same relation to the clumsy dinosaurs Cirocco had grown up piloting as the Wright Brothers Flyer did to a supersonic jet, though the differences would not have been obvious to the un-trained observer.

She started her walk-around.

"How long since you took them out, Chris?" she asked.

"About half a kilorev, Captain. According to your schedule. I observed no problems with the Two and the Four, but the Eight is going to need some work."

"No matter. We won't need it. Robin. Nova. Can either of you fly?"

"Fly an airplane?" Robin asked. "I'm sorry, Captain."

"No need to overdo the Captain bit."

"I've . . . back home, I fl-fl-flew a . . ."

"Speak up, child. I won't hurt you anymore, I promise."

"I've soared," Nova said, in a half-whisper. "We have these gliders, and we go out along the axis and—"

"I've heard of it," Cirocco said. She considered it, still going over the Dragonfly Two, which was the smaller of the available planes and the one already perched on the catapult. "It's better than nothing. Conal, you'll fly this one, and Nova will go with you. Familiarize her with the basics if you get any free time. Get in now and heat it up and start your check-out. Chris, assemble five sets of survival gear. The basic kit, extra rations, hand weapons, rifles, clothing. Anything else you can think of that might come in handy and doesn't weigh too damn much."

"Flak suits?" Chris asked.

Cirocco paused, started to say something, then listened to her gut.

"Yes. Nova can wear one of mine. Get the smallest size you can for Robin, and—"

"I got you," Chris said. He was watching her, his eyes narrowed. "What about the cannons? You want them loaded?"

Cirocco looked at the Two, which had heavy-caliber guns mounted in its transparent wings.

"Yes. I'll get that. Robin, you help him."

She got two cases of shells for the wing cannons and loaded them, hearing Conal conducting his radio check with the Titanides. She snapped the covers closed as Chris and Robin loaded the gear into the space behind the seats.

"Stand clear!" Conal called out. He fired a test round from each cannon. It was quite loud in the cave.

Cirocco dragged the fuel line over the cave floor and snapped it to the fuselage, then watched as the big, collapsible tank filled to capacity.

"Get in," she told Nova.

"Where can I step?"

"Anyplace. The thing's a hell of a lot stronger than it looks." She understood Nova's concern. When Cirocco first saw the Dragonflys she thought some horrible mistake had been made. They seemed to be made out of cellophane and coat hangers. Nova climbed in and Cirocco slammed the door behind her. She watched as Conal showed her how to work the straps.

"Clear!" Conal shouted again, barely audible in the enclosed cockpit.

The engine started up. It was clearly visible through the transparent fuselage: about a meter long with an eight-inch bore. To the casual eye it looked about as basic and uncomplicated as a Bunsen burner. That was partly true, but deceptive. There was almost no metal in it. It was built of ceramics and carbon-filament windings and plastic. Its turbine revolved at speeds that would have been impossible without zero-gee bearings, and at temperatures that would have vaporized anything in use when Cirocco was young.

The plane coughed one small cloud of smoke, and the engine went rapidly through red, to orange, to yellow-hot. Conal hit the catapult release, and it was launched into the air. After two hundred meters it turned and headed straight up into the sky.

"Give me a hand with this," Cirocco said, and Robin and Chris grabbed the other wingtip and the tail of the Dragonfly Four. They lifted it easily and carried it to the catapult. Chris fueled it while Robin loaded the supplies and Cirocco got in the pilot's seat for her checkout. The Four was unarmed. Cirocco fretted about that for a second, then put it out of her mind. She had been unable to imagine a use for the Two's armament, but worked on the principle that if you've got it, it's stupid not to have it ready.

"Conal, do you read me?"

"Loud and clear, Captain."

"Where are you?"

"Headed due east from the Junction, Captain."

"Call me Cirocco, and orbit your present location at five thousand until further notice."

"Roger, Cirocco."

"Valiha, Rocky, Serpent, do you read?"

They all replied in the affirmative, and Cirocco told Nova to radio the recipe and ingredients of her love potion back to Rocky. When the plane was fueled and loaded, Chris climbed into the two rear seats and Robin sat next to Cirocco, and she started the engines.

When the thrust was right, she turned to Robin.

"Put your head back against the rest," she said. "This thing has a bit of a kick."

And they were off.

THIRTEEN

Cirocco had taught Conal to fly not long after his arrival in Gaea. He was very good at it, and it gave him pleasure.

Not that a Dragonfly was tough to learn. On a point-to-point they were capable of taking off, navigating, and landing all by themselves. They didn't need runways, and could get by with no more ground support than the occasional re-fueling stop. Anyone who had ever flown a Piper Cub would have been right at home in a Dragonfly in a few minutes, though the lack of instrumentation might have bothered him. The Dragonfly had, in a sense, just one instrument: a computer screen. A single keypad to the pilot's right called up any information the pilot might want, or the ship's brain, reviewing data fifty thousand times each second, would make the pilot aware of any critical situation and recommend a course of action. It had ground radar and air radar and all the radio capability anyone could need. Cirocco had replaced the compasses with inertial trackers.

But the rudder pedals and the stick were the same type that had been in use on Earth for over a century and a half. Conal used the time waiting for Cirocco showing Nova the uses of these devices. She watched alertly, and did the right things when he handed control to her.

When the Four rose up to join him, Conal fell in with the larger plane and flew to the right and slightly behind it.

"Here's the plan," Cirocco said. "The radar is good for about thirty kilometers in all directions. An angel can do about seventy kilometers per hour, and can maintain that for maybe two hours. He's been gone slightly under one hour. We will assume he's headed for Pandemonium, which is currently in southern Hyperion. We're going up to twenty, that's two zero, kilometers, and we'll fly fifty kilometers apart, with the same heading. We will fly at one two zero kilometers per hour for another thirty minutes, and hope that puts us in his general area. We will then throttle back to sixty and attempt

149

to locate him by radar. If that doesn't work, we will move ahead at high speed until we're sure we're in front of him, and conduct a search pattern, diagonally across his project path, until we find him or one of us thinks of something better to do. Comments?"

Conal worked it out in his laborious but methodical way. Cirocco did not interrupt him. He realized that, aside from Chris, with whom she had already discussed this, he knew more about Gaea than anyone else.

"What if he goes higher?" Conal finally said. "Should the search pattern be vertical as well as horizontal?"

"I'm making the assumption that he's going to be fairly low."

Conal worked that out, too, and wasn't sure it was a valid assumption to make. Angels might not *like* clinging to the curved rim roof, but they could do it if they had to. Cirocco was obviously counting on some sort of relay maneuver, since no single angel could move Adam from Dione to Hyperion, and she must think the most likely place for the later carriers to hide was the outer rim of Gaea.

But Gaea was an unusual place for flying. You could climb a full hundred and fifty kilometers before running into the roof. And if you flew through a spoke, you could go even higher than that. If the angel went up to sixty kilometers, they could fly right under him and never see him.

"Hyperion is about halfway around," Conal pointed out. "He might just go up a spoke, through the hub, and down again."

"You're absolutely right, Conal," Cirocco came back. "But for now, I'm going to assume the rim route. If we don't find anything in two or three revs, we can reassess."

"You're the boss," Conal said.

"Yeah, but don't let that stop you from giving me ideas. And besides, I'm going to do my best to cheat, in just a few minutes."

Conal could tell from Nova's frown that she had no idea what the Captain was talking about. Conal could make a pretty good guess, but kept his mouth shut.

"Weather advisory," the computer said. "You are entering a region where severe turbulence has—" Conal hit the override and the computer shut up.

"What was that about?" Nova asked. Conal glanced at her. She seemed to be feeling better. She *must* be, he thought, if she was willing to talk to him. He had not been looking forward to a long trip in the small space with somebody who hated him.

"The brain carries a model of Gaea in its head," he told her, calling up a cut-away side view of the wheel-world. "This plane and all the others share the model, and they make a note of places where the storm probability is high, based on past experience. Mostly it's a nuisance."

"I'd think it would be helpful."

"Not too much. Look." He zoomed in on the segment of wheel rim that contained Dione, showing part of the spoke that loomed above it. Two blue dots winked on and off near the bottom of the picture, labeled 2 and 4. "That's us," he said, pointing to the 2. "We're moving toward Iapetus, and we're getting close to the twilight zone, which means warmer air coming up from the ground. When air rises in Gaea, it moves into masses of air that are traveling slower, because they're nearer the hub. So it sort of curls over, like a breaking wave. You get a lot of quick downdrafts in the transitional zone."

He glanced at her to see if she understood. It had taken him a while to get it straight, with his Earth-based thinking. The equivalent effect on Earth was the rotation of air masses caused by north-south currents, and depended on the fact that air at the equator was moving faster with the turning of the planet than air to the north or the south. When the effect was very intense, it was called a hurricane.

"Sure," she said. "The coriolis effect. We have to take that into account when we go soaring at home."

"It's not as bad here. Gaea's much bigger than the Coven. I don't have to think about it when I'm flying the plane, but the computer takes it into account for navigation." He pointed to the screen again. "The thing is, the weather's pretty regular in Gaea. Bad weather comes out of the spokes. Gaea sucks up a lot of air in one spoke, moves it through the hub into another one, and then lets it all fall out over a night region. It's all done by a schedule. So that's what the computer was telling me: I'm moving into a boundary line between day and night, which means I'm coming out from under a spoke, which means we can expect some bumps. The thing is," and he pointed up at the gargantuan mouth of the Dione Spoke looming above them, "I can see that easy enough."

She didn't say anything, but looked around her, studying the spoke, the curved roof ahead of them that arched over Iapetus, comparing them to the model on the screen. He knew the convoluted geometry of Gaea took some getting used to. It was one thing to look at a map of it, and something else to stand on the hurtling rim and get an ant's-eye view.

"I see what you mean about finding the angel," she finally said. "What's to prevent him from just going so high we'd never find him? It's shorter that way, too."

"All air distances in Gaea are shorter than ground distances," he said. "And if you wanted to go from Dione to Rhea, all the way around the wheel, the shortest way is straight up the spoke, through the hub, and down the Rhea spoke. It gets easier as you go, because you get lighter. And once you're in the hub, it's downhill all the way."

"Why does Cirocco think he won't do that?"

"A couple of reasons. Different flights of angels live in different spokes. They don't like each other and they're jealous of their territory. No matter which flight this one comes from, he'll have to go through unfriendly territory if he goes through two spokes. They might kill him, and he'd have a lot of trouble getting food. He'd do better foraging on the rim. It'd be easier for the others to hide on the rim, where no other flight has nesting rights."

"Why are you assuming he's going to Hyperion?"

Conal shrugged. "You'd have to ask the Captain about that. She has special knowledge which she doesn't always tell me about. Then again, that angel grabbing Adam was one hell of a surprise to her, I can tell you that."

They were in the west end of Iapetus when Cirocco gave the order to throttle back. Conal's plane was far to the north, invisible to the eye but making a strong steady blip when the computer displayed the ground map.

When the three-dimensional display was used, Robin found it hard not to be discouraged.

In that mode, Gaea's rim was a gently curved tube. The angel's possible locations made a hemisphere with Tuxedo Junction at the center. The search profile of the planes was a lengthening tube a hundred kilometers wide and fifty high. When compared with the region where the angel *might* be, it didn't seem enough. There was so much space above them where it could be, and a vast amount behind them.

"It's not as bad as it looks," Cirocco said. "I'm going to hang around here for a while and hope it shows up. But if we don't have it in an hour, I'll increase our speed and we'll start criss-crossing. We'll cover just about all the airspace."

"What if he's headed back toward Metis?"

"It's unlikely. But if we don't get results in four or five hours, I'll send Conal back in that direction."

"And the spoke?" Chris asked.

"That would be such a logistical nightmare I'm ruling it out."

Robin looked out at vast expanses of forest far below them.

"What if it just . . . settles down there in the bush?"

"Robin, if it does that, there's not much we can do."

She wished she hadn't asked.

"But," Cirocco went on, "it isn't going to do that."

Robin thought about asking Cirocco how she could be so sure, and found she didn't have the nerve to. She *wanted* the Wizard to be sure. Having somebody around who *seemed* to know what she was doing helped a little.

"Hand me my pack, Chris. It's time for the nasty part."

The pack had the unmistakable stamp of Titanide manufacture, and looked like an old friend. Robin watched as Cirocco set it on the transparent floor between her feet, opened it, and pulled out a small glass jar with a metal lid. Something white and slimy was curled up in the bottom. It lifted its head and blinked.

"What in the nine billion perversions of Christendom is that?" Robin asked.

Cirocco looked at her apologetically.

"It's what I didn't want to tell you about at the fountain. Things have gone a little far for us to keep secrets, though. It's a piece of the mind of Gaea. It's something Rocky took out of my head about five years ago. In a word, it's my own personal Demon."

Robin looked at it. The thing was uncoiling itself.

It was like a snake with two legs. When it stood up it balanced on those legs with its tail providing the third point of support. The legs were actually more like arms, with clawed hands. Its neck was an inch long, and its tail about three inches, with a stubby tip. There were two round, lizard-like eyes, and a surprisingly expressive mouth.

Robin leaned over and stared at it. The thing seemed to be shouting. She could almost distinguish words. Could it possibly speak English?

"Does it have a name?"

Cirocco cleared her throat, and Robin looked at her.

"Actually," she said, with a twitch of her lips, "if you look closely, you'll see it's a male."

Robin looked again. Great Mother save us, it *was* male.

"He claims not to have a name," Cirocco said. "When I want to call him anything but 'you lousy slimebag' I call him Snitch." Cirocco vigorously rubbed her upper lip with one finger, cleared her throat, and in general exhibited all the signs of nervousness Robin would have thought foreign to her nature. You learn something new every day, Robin thought.

"See," Cirocco went on, "...uh, from the position he was in when Rocky found him, uh...you might say he was sort of, well, fucking with my mind for about ninety years."

There could have been no possible reason for Gaea to make this thing male, since it had been meant to live out its days in Cirocco's head. Thus, its sex was one of Gaea's twisted jokes, and a special and ugly humiliation for Cirocco should it ever be found.

Cirocco twisted the lid off the jar and set it down on the flat surface just above the computer screen—what she had called the dashboard. Snitch jumped up and perched on the rim of the jar, looked around blearily, and yawned. He used one claw to scratch like a dog, then settled down like a tiny vulture with his head almost concealed by his shoulders.

"I could sure use a drink," he said. Robin remembered the voice.

"I'm talking to you, cuntface," he said.

Cirocco reached out and flicked a finger. The demon thumped hard against the windscreen and fell to the dashboard, howling. Cirocco reached out and mashed his head under her thumb. Robin heard crunching noises. *Great Mother,* she thought. *She's killed it.*

"Sorry," Cirocco said. "It's the only way to reach him."

"You're apologizing to *me?*" Robin squeaked. "Skin it alive and feed it to the worms. I was just surprised you kept him five years and killed him now."

"He's all right. I don't even know if he's killable." She removed her thumb, and Snitch rolled back onto his feet. His head was malformed and blood dripped from one eye. As Robin watched, the head returned to its former shape, like some weird plastic.

"Who do I have to blow to get a drink in this stinking place?" He hopped up and perched on the edge of the jar again.

Cirocco again reached into her pack and brought out a metal flask in a leather container. She took the top off and detached an eyedropper from the kit, inserted it in the neck, and drew out some clear fluid. Snitch was hopping from foot to foot in his eagerness, his head thrown back and his mouth open. Cirocco held the eyedropper over his mouth and let one fat drop fall into his mouth. He swallowed hugely, then opened his mouth again.

"That's it for now," Cirocco said. "If you're good, you can have more."

"What is that?" Robin asked. Snitch rolled his eyes toward her.

"It's grain alcohol. Snitch likes his liquor straight." She sighed. "He's an alcoholic, Robin. It's about all he consumes, along with a little blood once a day."

Snitch jerked his head toward Robin.

"Who's the bimbo?"

Cirocco flicked his face again, and he howled, then quickly shut up. "Maybe..." Robin began, then thought better of it.

"Go ahead," Cirocco said.

"Uh...maybe *he* was what was causing your...problem."

"There's no need to walk around it, Robin. Maybe it was him making me into a lush, right?" She sighed, and shook her head. "I tried my best to think that for a long time. But I knew I was just wishing my own weakness off on something else. If anything, *I'm* the cause of *his* problem. He sat there on top of an alcoholic brain for so long he got addicted." She straightened her shoulders and then leaned forward a little, staring at the demon.

"Now, Snitch," she said. "We're going to play a game."

"I *hate* games."

"You'll like this one. Gaea has done a terrible thing."

He cackled. "I *knew* something good was about to happen."

"But you'd never think of warning me, right? Well, maybe next time you will. What happened, you venomous pestilential chancre, is that somebody has kidnapped a child. Gaea is behind it, as surely as flies breed in shit, and you're going to tell me where the child is."

"Why don't you bite my ass?"

Robin was startled when Chris reached between them and grabbed the ugly little thing in a big fist. Only its head was visible, and its eyes rolled wildly.

"I want him, Captain," Chris said. His voice was low. "I've been thinking about him for the last hour, and maybe I've come up with some things you haven't thought of yet."

"Wait a minute, wait a minute!" the Snitch shrieked. "You know I do better work if you don't hurt me, you know that, you know that!"

"Hold on, Chris," Cirocco said. The tiny eyes moved from Chris to Cirocco and back again. He gulped, and then spoke in a wheedling tone.

"What do I care what Gaea's cooked up?" he said. "For a couple of drinks, I might be able to help you."

"Four drops is what I'm offering."

"Now be fair," he whined. "And be reasonable. You can't deny that I do my best work when I've had a few under my belt."

Cirocco seemed to consider it.

"All right. But you didn't let me tell you about the game. Put him down, Chris." He did, and Cirocco struck a match. She moved it toward the demon, held it about a foot away.

"I'm going to give you two drops right now. Then you are going to tell me where the child is. We will fly there. When we get there, if you were right, I'll give you three more drops. If you're wrong, I will wire one of these matches along your back and light it. They take about twenty seconds to burn. Then you'll try again. If you're wrong again, you get another match. I've got about..." she looked down into her pack, "...oh, about fifty matches. So we can play the game a long, long time. Or it can be over very quickly."

"Quick, quick, quickquickquickquick!" Snitch yammered, jumping up and down.

"Okay. Open your mouth."

Cirocco gave him his two drops, which seemed to calm him. And, oddly, to color him. He had been a rather sickly yellowish-white at first. He was turning ruddier.

He jumped down from the edge of the jar and began pacing up and down the dashboard. Robin watched, fascinated.

The demon paced for a few minutes. Eventually he began to stagger as the drinks hit him. But gradually he looked more and more toward one part of the sky. He lurched up to the windshield and pressed his repulsive face against it, as if to see better. At last he belched, and pointed with one leg.

"He's up thataway," he said, and fell over.

FOURTEEN

"Conal, turn left twenty degrees and climb to forty kilometers. Increase speed to two zero zero kilometers per hour."

"Twenty degrees left, forty, two hundred; Roger, Captain."

He executed the turn immediately, increased the thrust, and watched to make sure the plane did the rest as it was supposed to.

Like clockwork, he thought, with satisfaction. Outside, the wings were shrinking from their three-quarters deployed position and sweeping back slightly.

"Why do you suppose she decided to do that?" Nova asked.

"I don't know," Conal said. Actually, he had a good idea, but it would be too complicated to explain, and he had been instructed never to speak to anyone about the Snitch unless specifically authorized by Cirocco.

"I can't figure her out," Nova confessed.

"You aren't the first one."

"Conal, are you wearing your flak suits?"

"No, Cirocco. Should we?"

"I think so. We're putting ours on. I don't have any specific reason except my standard one."

"What's the use of having it if you don't use it, right, Captain?"

"That's it."

"Will do." He turned to Nova. "Can you reach them? Those blue outfits."

Nova fumbled with one of the suits until she had it unfolded.

It was a light, slightly stiff blue jumpsuit without arms or legs. The carbon-filaments woven through tough plastic would stop any handgun bullet, and give some protection against heavier weapons and bomb fragments.

"What if you get hit in the head?" Nova asked.

"If we get into something, we'll put on those helmets, and the leggings, and the sleeves. Do you need any help with that?"

"I can manage." She lifted herself off the seat, and shoved her pants down around her ankles. The plane lurched to the right, and she looked outside anxiously. "What happened? What's the matter?"

"Nothing," Conal said, and coughed nervously. "Ah, I thought you'd put that on *over* your pants."

"Does it matter?" She pulled her shirt over her head. The plane only jumped a little that time.

"No, it doesn't matter," he said, and pulled the privacy curtain down from its little niche overhead.

He heard her long-suffering sigh. Then she jerked the bottom of the curtain and let it roll back up. He glanced at her and saw she was holding her clothes over the front of her body. Her eyes were blazing.

"Can I talk to you a minute? Is this okay? Am I decent?"

He gulped. "It's . . . Nova, it's not enough."

She ran her fingers through her hair, then tugged at it in frustration.

"Okay. My mother told me about this but I just couldn't understand it, so maybe you can explain it. It's *not* that you don't like to look at me, is it."

"No, it's not that at all."

"That's what I can't understand. You make me feel ugly."

"I'm sorry." Jesus, where to start, how to explain? He wasn't even sure he could explain it to himself, much less to her. "Dammit, I get upset because I want you, and I can't have you. Seeing you gets me turned on, okay?"

"Okay! Okay! Great Mother, I don't know why you're so worried about getting turned on, but I'll go along with you. I'll cover up the places Robin told me to cover up. But I thought I was doing that *now*. So tell me, mister male man, what do I have to cover up?"

"You can throw all your clothes out the fucking window for

all I care," Conal said, through clenched teeth. "It's your business, not mine."

"Oh, no, I wouldn't want to *upset* you. I wouldn't want to make you lose your precarious *control* of yourself. Mother, *preserve* me." She slammed the curtain back in place, then, a few seconds later, pulled it back up enough to look under it.

"There's one more thing. I didn't have a chance to pee before we took off. Do I have to wait till we land?"

Conal opened a compartment in the dash and handed her the oddly-shaped cup, pulled the vacuum hose from its slot.

"You hook the hose to this thing, then . . . hold it to—"

"*I can figure it out!* I guess you'll want privacy for this, too."

"If you please."

Her reply was more growl than word, and she pulled the curtain down. Conal flew on, simmering, trying to ignore the sounds coming from the other side.

Seven years ago he might simply have gone mad. No telling what he might have done—what a temper he'd had! He'd learned a lot since then. The temper was still there. But it was tightly and permanently under control.

He went through the hard-learned routines to calm himself. When he was done, he felt foolish, as he usually did, for letting himself get so angry. She operated from her own logic, and by her lights he was being very silly.

Hell, he thought. By my own, too. He wished he hadn't allowed himself to get in a shouting match with her. She was right. Her nudity was no kind of assault on him.

He wished he could say those things as clearly as he could think them. But he knew from bitter experience that the words never quite came out right.

When she let the curtain back up she had her pants on over the flak suit. She had folded her shirt and stuffed it in back. She sat with her back straight and looked rigidly forward.

He made very sure he didn't laugh, though he wanted to. He felt a lot better. Now she was the foolish one. She didn't know how to turn off her anger, and that made him feel superior to her, which was a nice feeling. She was still so young.

So he solemnly pulled the curtain back down and quickly got

into his own flak suit, and pulled his clothes on over it.

"You watch the radar while I take care of this stuff," he told her, as he opened the curtain again. She nodded and he turned and secured the netting over the loose cargo in back. When he turned back there was still nothing in the empty sky. They flew on, in silence.

In the next hour Cirocco got two signals from the radar. They were all excited the first time, though she had warned them not to be. And they quickly saw it was a solitary blimp. Cirocco veered away. Blimps hated anything to do with fire, and had been quite cool toward her for years after she imported the jets. Which was unfair, as her reason for doing so was to destroy the buzz bombs that had made the skies unsafe for lighter-than-air beings. But you couldn't argue with a blimp.

The second blip proved to be a solitary angel. Spirits rose for a moment, until it was clearly established that this one's wings were the wrong color. She turned off her engine and glided beside him for a few minutes. He was of the Dione Supra Flight. He seemed genuinely shocked that an angel was working for Pandemonium, and swore that his flight, section, and wing remained loyal to the Wizard.

So she attached a match to Snitch and it inspired him wonderfully. After another drop of grain alcohol he was able to talk again, and said the angel was below them now, and slightly behind. She radioed the new heading to Conal.

"Can I ask you something?" Nova said.

"Go right ahead."

It had taken her a long time to get that much out. Now that she had, she found it hard to go on.

Somehow, she had to make sense of this insane world, because she was stuck here for the rest of her life with Titanides and males. She could still feel the impact of Cirocco's palm on her cheek. She loved Cirocco, and Cirocco had hit her, and those two things had to be reconciled somehow, had to be worked out so that Cirocco would never find reason to hit her again. For that to be possible, she had to understand some things.

"What do you think Cirocco Jones meant when she told me I had to join the human race?" Having asked it, she relaxed a little.

His answer wasn't going to mean much, she realized. It had been a silly idea to ask him in the first place. Perhaps her mother could explain it, when they had some time alone.

But he surprised her.

"I've been wondering the same thing," he said. "I guess she just didn't have time to say what she meant, so she said something to get your attention."

"So you don't know what she meant, either?"

"Oh, no, I didn't say that. I know what she meant." He frowned, and gave her a wry smile. "I just don't think I can explain it to you."

"Would you try?"

He looked at her for a long time. The look disturbed her.

"Why should I?" he finally said.

She sighed, and turned away. "I don't know," she said.

He shrugged. "I was asking myself. Why should I try to explain something to you, when every time I give you a friendly smile you look at me like I was a cootie bug? Don't you think I have feelings?"

It was just the sort of question Nova didn't want to think about. But not thinking about it had gotten her a slap in the face.

"You weren't thinking about *my* feelings a while ago."

"I admit I had an unfortunate lapse," he said. "You want to know what I'm going to do about that?" He looked at her again, and grinned. "I'm going to say I'm sorry, I apologize, and I'm going to do better from now on. How's *that* for a kick in the pants?"

She tried to meet his stare, but finally had to look away.

"It makes me feel uneasy," she admitted. "I don't know why."

"I do. Want to know?"

"Yes."

"Say please?"

What an infuriating person. But she took a deep, long-suffering breath, crossed her arms, and glared at him.

"Please."

"Jesus, that must have hurt."

"Not at all. It's just a word."

"It did hurt, and it's not just a word. It hurt for the same reason you didn't like me apologizing. Twice now you've had to look at me as a human being."

She thought that over for several minutes, and he didn't say anything.

"You're saying that's what Cirocco meant? That I have to become a herterosexual, make love to men?"

"Nothing so drastic, and nothing so simple." He rubbed his hand over his face and shook his head slowly. "Listen, I'm not the guy for this. I wish to hell Cirocco was here. Why don't you wait till you can talk it over with her?"

"No," she said, becoming more interested. "I'd like to hear it from you."

"I sure don't know why," he muttered. Then he took a deep breath.

"Look. With you, there's lines drawn all over the place. There's *us*, and there's *them*. Us seems to be a pretty small group. Okay, I can understand, I feel the same way. I don't like all human beings. And I know Cirocco ain't the biggest groupie the human race ever had, either. And she didn't even mean human, because Titanides aren't human but they're part of what she wants you to join. Are you with me so far?"

"I don't know. But go on."

"Shit. *Grow up!*" he thundered. "That's what she said. Stop making your decisions about people based on what they look like." He stopped, and shook his head sadly. "Nova, I could rattle on for half an hour, like a CBC public service spot, about how you're supposed to love the Qubeheads and the Normans and the Beecees and the Eeks and the niggers and the poor and little fuzzy animals and rattlesnakes. I hated some of those people when I was a kid, too. These days I keep my hate for slavers and babyleggers ... and like that. Every person I meet is on probation, because it's a no-kidding dangerous world out there, and you're *right* to be suspicious of new faces. But if they don't prove themselves to be villains, why, then you treat them as you'd like to be treated, like the old golden rule. If a friend of mine has a friend, then he's my friend, too, until he proves otherwise. I don't care if he's black, brown, yellow or white, male or female, young or old, two-legged or four-legged or sixteen-legged. And I'm a good friend to have, too. I'm loyal as hell, and I wash my own dishes."

"I'm loyal, too!" she protested.

"Sure. To anybody on your side of the line. Which is only two-legged females. Valiha can't be your friend because she looks like an animal, and I can't because I have a cock." He pointed out the windscreen at the empty sky. "That poor little brother of yours can't be your friend, either, because you don't see him as human. Nova, just looking at you—at the *good* part of you—I know you'd be a terrific person to have on my side. But I can't cross that line."

He sighed, and leaned back. Nova had watched in fascination, not getting a lot of it, such as the part about Qubeheads and niggers. She hadn't the vaguest notion of what either of those might be. And why did he bring skin color into it? What did that have to do with anything?

"How would you suggest I go about this? Should you and I make sex?"

He threw up his hands.

"I'm hurt. I really am. You think I said all that just to get in your pants?"

"I'm . . . sorry. I don't know what I said wrong, though."

He looked tired.

"I guess you don't, do you? All right. Can you take honesty and not get angry? I'd *love* to 'make sex' with you. I was offended because, where I grew up, guys will say just about anything to get girls to go to bed with them, and here I am being so stinking noble it makes me sick, so it hurt me you thought it was all a line. But you were serious, weren't you?"

"Yes. I'll do it, if it's what has to be done."

"Kinder words have never been spoken to me."

"Did I offend again? I'm sorry."

He grinned.

"You're getting better at that. I appreciate it. Shows you're trying. Listen, Nova, you ought to talk this over with your mother. *She* figured out how to do it. But if you want my opinion, you should do what I did when Cirocco started straightening *me* out. I was a right 'orrible stinking bigot when I got here. I'm not perfect, but I'm better. So when I thought 'Frog,' or Qubehead,' I changed it to 'Canadian.' When I thought 'black,' I changed it to 'white.' So when you hear 'man,' change it to 'woman.' When you look at a person and think 'Titanide,' change it to 'sister.' When you think about Adam, pretend he's your baby sister. Think how you'd feel."

She thought about it, and was amazed at her rage. It went away quickly—it was only a trick, after all—but it was interesting to think of how the world would be if those things were true.

"Can I check an impression I have?" he asked. She nodded. "You find me...physically repulsive, don't you."

And another amazing thing happened. She felt herself blushing.

"I don't wish to offend..."

"I'd prefer honesty."

She nodded, uncomfortably. "You have too much hair. Your chin is so rough, I think it would be painful to be kissed by you. Your arms and legs are...wrong. Do these things...attract Earth women?"

He grinned again.

"They have been known to."

"And you find me...attractive," she said.

"More than that. You are stunning. You're one of the most beautiful women I've ever seen."

Nova shook her head in wonder.

"It's a funny world," she said.

"What's wrong? Do lesbians have different ideas of beauty?"

"I don't know. In the Coven, I was freakishly tall. No one thought me beautiful." She looked at him again. "Is it true that men don't find extreme height unattractive?"

"Not in Artillery Lake," Conal chuckled. "Swear to God, after Cirocco Jones, I rate you number two."

"Now you're being ridiculous," she sniffed. She might have said more, but the radar alarm went off, and Cirocco was directing them on a new heading.

FIFTEEN

It was a shock to them all to discover that the thing which had Adam was not an angel. At least, if it was an angel, then a zombie was a human.

Cirocco cursed quietly as she studied it with her binoculars. Chris couldn't take his eyes off the thing. But when Cirocco handed him the binoculars he had to force himself to look.

His worst fears were not realized. Studying Adam, he couldn't see the bites of deathsnakes. Cradled in those repulsive arms, head hanging down, dark hair blowing in the wind, Adam was taking a snooze.

Chris had to lower the glasses and stop his trembling hands. He looked through them again and confirmed to a certainty what his heart already knew: the child was alive. Twice Chris saw Adam's mouth open and close, as though chomping, and he could see the tiny chest rise and fall.

Finally he was able to turn his attention to the zombie-angel.

It was a very old one. He couldn't see any skin remaining. There was just the skeletal framework, the feathers, and the networks of deathsnakes holding it together.

Robin was getting insistent, so he handed her the binoculars.

Cirocco let out a deep breath.

"Okay. That's why we didn't find it at first. It's flying faster than a live angel could. We're almost to Cronus."

Chris wanted to scream. He wanted to shout a thousand stupid questions, run in circles, bay at the moon. He swallowed it all. Remain calm, remain calm. Locate the fire exits. Move in an orderly manner. Don't lose your balance, put your head between your knees if you feel faint . . . and *think. Think!*

"Any ideas?" Cirocco said. Chris listened to the dead silence, both in the plane and over the radio.

"All right," Cirocco said. "Priorities. Number one, we do nothing to endanger him. Conal, we're going to drop back a little bit so there's no chance we'll disturb the air currents. How does two hundred meters sound?"

"It's okay with me, Cirocco," Conal's voice came back.

"Ideas?" she asked again.

"W-w-what if he, uh, drops him?" Chris managed to say.

"That's not an idea, that's a situation." She frowned, and thought about it for a while. "Okay. I'm going to drop down about a kilometer and stay slightly behind him. Conal, you stay where you are. If you see the baby fall, I want to hear about it a tenth of a second later. I'll jump out and get him."

Parachutes! Chris thought. Something was wrong with him, he should have thought of that. He turned around and scrambled along the gear in back, looking for them. Only it couldn't be Cirocco, that was crazy, it had to be—

"Sorry, Cirocco," Conal said.

Cirocco looked amazed for a moment.

"What the hell do you mean, 'Sorry, Cirocco'?"

"It won't work," Conal said. "For one thing, the Captain doesn't leave her ship. That must have slipped your mind. But even if you could, you have to fly it."

Chris can fly it!"

"Sorry again, Cirocco. He told me he's getting too big."

Bless him, Chris thought.

"He's right, Cirocco," Chris said, quickly. He was clipping his parachute—a fabric tube about the size of a tightly rolled umbrella—to the rings on his flak suit.

"That's crazy," Cirocco said. "You just move the lousy seat back and—"

He looked right at her.

"I've forgotten how to fly," he said. She kept staring at him, and he was able to return it calmly. Finally she sighed, and nodded.

"All right. Now—"

"I should be the one," Robin said.

"God *damn* it! Who's the—"

"I've done some free-falling," Robin said, raising her voice slightly. "Chris hasn't. I'd have a better chance of getting to him."

"He's my responsibility," Chris said, with a meaningful look at Robin.

"I'm better trained," Robin shot back.

Cirocco looked from one to the other with fire in her eye.

"Anybody else going to put their in their two-cent's worth?" she asked.

"I'll do it," came Nova's voice. "I've done twenty times as much parachuting as Robin. I was the Coven champion two years ago."

"Well blow me down," Cirocco muttered, then raised her voice. "All right, enough of this. We're all grandstanding and we're not getting anything done. Conal, you stay *right* where you are."

"You got it, Captain."

"Robin, Chris, if we get the word, you *both* go."

They got chutes rigged, and outlined the procedure for opening the plane and jumping. Robin worked the door latch a few times and pushed the door open just to make sure she could do it quickly.

"Right," Cirocco said. "Any more ideas?"

"I was thinking about the hand-off, Cirocco," Conal said.

"What about it?"

"Well, we're going to see the second one coming quite a while before it gets here. What if we shoot it down?"

No one spoke as everyone tried to work out all the implications of that. Chris began to think it might be a good idea.

"No," Cirocco finally said. "Not yet, anyway. First, I don't think they can make it with just one relay. I'm guessing four or five. So we should watch the first one and see how it's done, and be ready to catch him. If this one gets beyond the half-way point and *then* the relay shows up, we re-think it."

"I don't get it," Robin said. "If we shoot down the relay, this one's going to get tired and it'll have to land. Then we can take it, easy."

Cirocco nodded.

"That seems logical, doesn't it. But you can bet Gaea thought of that, and she's got some angle. We'll find out what it is on the first hand-off."

Chris agreed, though it was torture to wait.

"I'm just throwing this out for discussion," Conal said. "But could we try to take him? Is there any way I could maneuver closer and . . . well, I don't have the steps worked out."

"I don't think so, Conal," Cirocco said. "We have to stick to our first priority, which is not to endanger him."

"Okay, I'll say it," Conal said. "Why is he safer in the arms of that thing than falling through the air with Chris and Robin ready to catch him? And why do you think he'll be safe if those bastards get him to Gaea?"

Chris swallowed hard. He'd been keeping those thoughts in the back of his mind, but they hadn't been happy there. Now they scrabbled around in his brain, urging him to scream.

Cirocco looked very tired.

"I think he will be completely safe with Gaea," she said, heavily. "At least physically. I'm sure she wants him alive." She frowned. "Pretty sure. Hold on while I check it out."

She pounded her fist on the sprawled, sleeping form of the Snitch. He squalled, and leaped to his feet.

"No more matches, no more matches!" He stopped, stunned.

"My *head!*" He collapsed, chin on the dashboard, and covered his head with his feet. Cirocco pulled them away, one at a time.

"Relax, Snitch," she said. "You answer some questions and I won't hurt you anymore. And I'll give you three more drops."

One eye popped up on a slender stalk.

"No hurt Snitchy-baby?" he whined.

"No hurt."

"Drinky-winky?"

Cirocco got out the flask and let a drop fall into the demon's mouth.

"Answer the questions now?"

"Fire when ready, puss."

"We've found the child we were looking for."

"Tha's nice. Didn't do you lotsa good, did it?"

"No. He's going to Gaea, isn't he?"

Snitch nodded.

"Gaea loves the little shit. Gaea'll be real good to him. Star pris'ner. Nothin' too good for li'l ol' Adam. Stinkin' Priests out beatin' the bushes for *weeks* when the word came down the li'l bashtard's on his way."

"I don't understand how—" Robin began, but Cirocco silenced her with a gesture. She leaned over, and Chris could barely hear the whisper.

"When he's off his guard like this we can learn a lot."

He seemed to have gone back to sleep. Cirocco waved the eyedropper near him and his head came up, following it back and forth.

"More, Snitch."

The tiny demon began to weep.

"More, more, more, alla time it's more . . . *what do they want from me?* Why can't I get any peace? They keep after you, never any rest . . . and I tell ya, I'm innocent! I was framed! I didn't ask for any of this, I—"

"Where should I send the Oscar, Snitch?"

"My agent handles all that," he said, recovering instantly.

"The stinking priests were beating the bushes . . ." Cirocco prompted.

"—for *weeks!* Whoever found him's gonna be th' new Wiz, Gaea says. Da Wiz, da Wiz, da wunnerful, wunnerful Wiz!"

"And the child?"

"He be King! King o' da Wheel! She look after dat li'l basser real good, I guaran*tee!* Nothin' but da best."

"She doesn't want him dead?"

"No *way,* Jose! Don' hurt one hair on his li'l beanie, she say, or you wish you could die, only you can't, cause she gonna keep you alive least a *year* an' kill you in *pieces!* She got a palace all built to keep him in, all made o' gold and precious jools and pure plat'num, an' wet nurses running all around, an' flunkies to comb his hair and wash his pecker and butter his toes."

"And why is she doing all this?" Robin asked.

Snitch hiccuped, and turned one bleary eye to her. He looked her up and down, and one corner of his mouth turned up.

"Nice tits, sweetlips. How'd'ja like ta see where *I* got tattooed?"

Cirocco flicked his face. He belched.

"How about that snake? I see his tail, but where's his *head?*"

Again Cirocco flicked him. He blinked, shook his head, and began to sing.

"Hey, little snake, are you crazy, or what? Your butt's in the air and your head's up her—"

This time Robin flicked him, quite hard.

"That's it!" Snitch stormed, pacing angrily around the dashboard. "I gotta take that crap off *you,* douche-bag, but not from her. Nothing more, not word one, that's all I'm gonna say. My lips are *sealed!"*

Cirocco picked him up and shoved a match down his throat, end-first. It left a little of the shaft and the matchhead sticking out of the demon's mouth. His eyes bulged as she upended him and struck the match on the dashboard. Then she held him erect, arms pinned to his sides, and let him watch the match begin to burn down.

"I think these matches would burn practically down to your tail," she said, calmly. "What I'm wondering, do you think we'll be able to see it? You think you'd glow like a lantern? What was that? You'll have to speak a little louder, I can't hear you." She waited, as Snitch struggled vainly. "Sorry, Snitch, I can't understand a word you're saying. What's that? Oh, all right." She wet her fingertips and pinched the match-head, which sizzled and went out. She pulled the match out of him and he collapsed, wheezing.

"The trouble with you," he said, "is you can't take a joke. My lord, you're a mean one, Cirocco Jones."

"I'll take that as a professional compliment. Now, she asked you a question. And you will address her as 'Ms. Robin,' with suitable deference, and you will keep your filthy thoughts to yourself."

"Okay, okay." He lifted a weary eye toward Robin. "Would you please repeat the question, Ms. Robin?"

"I just asked why Gaea is doing all this? Why is she going to all this trouble to steal Adam?"

"No trouble at all, Ms. Robin. See, she wins whichever way it comes out. If she gets the kid, and Cirocco don't come, why that's fine. But she figures, if she *does* get the kid, well then, Cirocco is *sure* to come." He turned his head and leered at Cirocco. "And Cirocco knows why she has to come, too."

Cirocco picked him up and popped him back in his bottle. Chris could hear him screaming his protests—mostly having to do with the promised alcohol—as she twisted the lid tight. No one said anything for a while. The look on Cirocco's face precluded idle conversation. At last she relaxed a little, and looked at Robin, then Chris.

"You'll want to know what he was talking about. I don't know if I need to say it, but I will. I would be going after him with everything I've got, no matter what. If Gaea got him, I would not rest until we had him back."

"I don't know what you're talking about," Robin confessed, "but I never thought anything different."

"I do know," Chris said, "and I never thought it would have made any difference, either."

"Thanks. To both of you. Robin, I have a reason other than friendship for doing my best to see that he doesn't get into Gaea's hands, and if he does, to get him away from her." She punched numbers on her keypad. "Rocky, how many eggs did you find in that room?"

"Fifteen, Captain," came the voice over the radio. Cirocco turned to Chris.

"Does that sound right?"

"No. I'm sure I had a rack of sixteen in that room. It was full."

"Conal," Cirocco said, "what can you tell me about the rack of Titanide eggs you let Adam play with?"

"It was the standard keepsake rack, Captain. Two rows, eight above and eight below. It was full." Cirocco hit the keypad again.

"Rocky, it seems—"

"I've found the rack, Captain," Rocky said. "It held sixteen. I've been searching diligently, according to your orders."

"Rocky, so help me, if you—"

"Captain, permit me to interrupt before you say something that might insult me. I have the fifteen eggs here before me. I have not waited to find them all before destroying them. To be exact, I have split them in half, so you may count the pieces upon your return— as I anticipated the embarrassing situation which seems to have arisen. Now, I may still find the missing egg, or it could be that Adam was holding it when he was taken. But if it is not found, it would be rather incriminating if I were shortly to be pregnant, wouldn't you think?"

"I'm sorry, Rocky," Cirocco said. "It's just that I've seen the lengths a desperate Titanide will go to if—"

"No offense taken, Captain."

"Jesus." Conal's voice was awed. "I didn't see that, Cirocco."

"What are you talking about?" Robin asked.

"It's Adam," Cirocco said. "Suddenly he's more than just personally important to all of us."

"He's capable of fertilizing Titanide eggs," Chris told Robin. "The ones he chewed on turned transparent—they're activated."

"Yes," Cirocco said. "He can do the thing that only I could do for almost a century. So we *have* to get him back. We can't let Gaea have him, because if she has him the Titanides become her slaves. And if we can keep him free . . ." She looked up, out the windshield into nothing, and seemed surprised.

". . . then I can die."

"Settle down, settle down," Conal said. "She didn't mean it like that."

"How the hell else could she mean it?" Nova demanded.

"She didn't say she was going to kill herself, did she?" He let her think about that for a while. The truth was, Cirocco's words had rocked him, too, but he had soon been able to understand the meaning behind them.

"Then what *did* she mean? Explain it to me."

"First you have to understand what Gaea did to her," Conal said. "It was a long time ago, back when Cirocco and the rest of the original crew had just got here. Gaea offered her the job of Wizard. She took it. Part of it—and Gaea didn't mention this—was that the race of Titanides was changed. Gaea took out the built-in hatred of angels and stopped the war that had been going on for so long. She also changed them so...do you know how Titanides reproduce?"

"Only vaguely."

"Okay. They have frontal intercourse first. The female produces a semi-fertilized egg. You saw some of them in Adam's room. They have to be implanted in a rear vagina and fertilized again by a rear penis."

Nova's lips thinned, but she nodded.

"The step I left out is Cirocco. The egg will never be fully fertilized unless it's activated by Cirocco's saliva. Gaea planned it that way. They used to have big festivals, where Cirocco would pick who could have a baby. Population control. Cirocco got so tired of playing God to the Titanides that she became an alcoholic. But she couldn't get away from it, even these days, when Gaea's agents are after her all the time."

Conal saw compassion in Nova's eyes, and it touched him.

"It must be very hard," Nova said.

"Extremely. And in some ways you might not think of. Gaea has never given any sign that Cirocco would *ever* be let off the hook. What I mean is, if Cirocco died, then the Titanides would die, too. Her own survival had to take first place over everything. It meant that she had to do some things she wasn't proud of. Like with me, she had to..." He stopped himself just in time, and swallowed a bitter taste. There were some things Nova wasn't entitled to know.

"I know of two times in the last seven years when she has had to let a Titanide friend of hers go into a sticky situation where Cirocco *knew* he couldn't survive, because she couldn't risk her own life. One of those times...I know she feels she betrayed him. One day she might have to betray *me* so she can survive. I know that, and I accept it.

"That's not an easy way to live. You become the ultimate survivor, but you can't take any pride in it, because you know the lengths you'll go to. It doesn't leave much room for honor. And Cirocco laughs at honor, but I know it's important to her—not the way somebody else defines it, but the way she does."

Nova was giving him an entirely new look. It made him uncomfortable. None of the things he had said had come easy to him. It had taken him a long, painful time to work them out.

"What I'm trying to say," Conal went on, diffidently, "is that Cirocco would like the pressure to end. She'd like to go back to having only herself to worry about. And she'd still be a survivor, she'd still be awful tough to kill, but her death would just be . . . her death. What happens to us all."

"Yes," Nova said, still with that odd look. "I see that."

SIXTEEN

Robin watched through the binoculars as the first hand-off was made. She kept her hand on the door latch, ready to leap.

The second angel had been on their screens for half an hour, making its way up from the darkness of Cronus. In the last few minutes they had found it visually, then it had been swallowed up in the deeper darkness above. She could barely make out the two shapes at top magnification as she listened to Conal describe what was happening.

"The second angel is about fifty meters behind. He's coming up now . . . getting closer. The first one is turning over. He's handing the baby over . . . okay, the second one's got him. He's holding him the same way the first one did. Adam's awake. He's . . . uh, he's crying."

Robin swallowed hard. She heard a sound from Chris, but did not look back.

"The first one's dropping back now. He's . . . Jesus!"

"What?" Cirocco rapped out. "Report, Conal!"

"He, uh . . . the first angel just came apart. I mean, he goddamn well exploded. We just flew through his feathers. His bones and the deathsnakes are falling.... I can't see them anymore. If you're in the right spot to catch Adam, you ought to be flying through them in a minute."

They all waited. Robin watched the diffuse cloud that had been the angel growing. Soon she had to put the binoculars down, and could watch it with her unaided eyes. There was a patter, like hail. A limp deathsnake draped itself over the left wing for a moment, then was swept away.

"That's the trick, then," Cirocco said. "The angels aren't going to land at all. If we shoot the next relay, the one that's got Adam will just fly until it dies."

"But it wasn't alive to begin with..." Chris began.

"Don't be silly, Chris. A zombie is as alive as you or me. It is a group organism, a hive mentality that invades a corpse and lives in it. The deathsnakes slowly eat the dead flesh, and whatever else they can find. There's nothing supernatural about it."

"You don't think this one...just decided to die? I mean, all the deathsnakes went at once. Is that likely?"

Robin watched Cirocco think it over.

"You don't understand zombies. First, they have no instinct for survival as individuals, or as hives. They don't feel pain. I don't believe they are intelligent, but they can follow orders. Whoever is directing these probably gave them the general objective—which was to get the child, unharmed—and some specific tactics, and they pulled it off."

"This whole thing has the look of calculation to me," Robin said.

Cirocco nodded.

"I think she's right. Whoever set this up—Luther, Brigham, Marybaker, Moon; any of them—they figured out just how far a death-angel could fly, flat out. This one could probably have gone another couple kilometers, but it couldn't have made it to the ground. So when its mission was over, it died. Which means if we'd shot down its replacement, Adam would be falling toward Cronus, and you two would be doing your best to catch him."

Chris cleared his throat, and Cirocco glanced at him.

"I guess this is as good a time as any to bring this up."

"I agree," Conal said.

"Cirocco," Chris went on, "what do you think the chances are? If Adam is dropped, can me and Robin get him?"

Cirocco shook her head.

"What can I say, Chris? I've been thinking about it for hours. There are too many factors. To be truthful, I think the chances are pretty good. There are two of you, and you'll have a couple of shots at him. If you don't panic, if you learn how to control your fall . . . you should catch him. Robin says she's worked at it, so maybe she's got a better chance. I'd say your chances are better than ninety-five percent."

"Mine would be better," Nova said. "I should do it."

"You can't be two places at once," Cirocco replied. "My decision on that stands." She turned to Chris. "I'll spell it out. Your chances of catching him are excellent. If you were betting on a poker hand, I'd say go for it. But you've got a five percent chance of losing."

"I know, I know." Chris put his face in his big hands and was silent for a long time. When he looked up, his eyes were red. "What would you do, Captain?"

Cirocco leaned back in her seat and closed her eyes.

"Chris . . . I can't make that decision. I can't tell if I want him back because he's a human being in danger, or because he's my salvation. I feel like the professional they bring in when a child is kidnapped. I can tell you a few things about what might happen, but the decisions about the options are up to the parents." She looked from Chris to Robin, and back again. "I'll play it whichever way you two decide."

"What do you *want* to do?" Robin asked.

"Me? I want to steal him back, *right now,* so badly it's making me sick. But you know my ulterior motives."

"For what it's worth," Conal said, "I agree with Cirocco. I don't want Gaea to get her hands on him."

"I disagree," Nova said. "Sorry, Mother. There's too much risk, even if it was me going after him. I'm ninety-nine percent sure I'd get him. But one percent risk is too much."

"Tell me about Gaea," Chris said.

"Gaea?" Cirocco frowned. "You may not believe this, but I

feel on firmer ground there. What Snitch said is the gospel. She won't hurt him. Once she has him, he won't be in any physical danger. He'll be treated well."

"I worry about psychological damage," Chris said.

"I hate to say this, Chris, but all we can do is take our pick of the trauma he suffers. Falling, or having a fifty-foot woman as a loving grandma."

"That's going to hurt him. She'll take him over."

"That's her plan, of course. But don't under-rate her. She'll raise him to love her. But that will *insure* he'll be treated well."

There was silence from all for a time, and at last Chris sighed.

"I probably won't ever have a tougher decision. But I think we ought to try and take him now."

"I agree," Robin said, quietly. She reached back and took Chris's hand.

"Okay," Cirocco said. "We're about halfway across Cronus. In about a rev we'll have the light we're going to need to pull this off. I'd welcome any more ideas."

Both planes were very quiet for a long time as they moved through the silvery night of Cronus. There were a hundred things that could go wrong, and they all knew it.

At one point in the endless rev, Rocky called from Tuxedo Junction, and it was a relief to Cirocco to have something new to deal with.

"Captain," Rocky said. "I have located the sixteenth egg. It had rolled down the hallway outside the room. It is now destroyed."

"Good enough, Rocky."

"There is information I have held back, not wishing to distract you from the central problem."

"Now's probably a good time to give it to me."

"Very well. Valiha, on her way to Bellinzona, discovered twelve dead zombies on top of a hill about a kilometer and a half from here. There were no signs of struggle."

"Was this hill downwind of the Junction?"

"Yes, it was. I'm assuming it was Nova's love potion that killed them."

"Seems reasonable."

"Valiha believes two Priests were on that hilltop. She thinks they were Luther and Kali. The scent was too old to be sure. In addition, there was a dead human child, male, between five and fifteen years old. I have recovered his body, and cannot estimate more closely, though perhaps you could."

"He hadn't gone zombie?"

"No. Perhaps he won't."

"Maybe not, but we can't take that chance. Cremate him, please. Anything else?"

"Valiha spoke to me not long ago. She asked that, if you called, and if you had the time, would you call her back."

"Roger, will do." Cirocco switched channels. "Serpent, do you read?"

"I read you, Captain."

"Where are you, my friend?"

"I'm almost to the mid-point of Iapetus, Cirocco." They could all hear Serpent's exhaustion.

"You're making incredibly good time, Serpent, but I'm afraid it was for nothing. We're most of the way through Cronus, and we're sure he's on his way to Hyperion. I don't think it'll do any good for you to go on."

"I'd prefer to keep going, unless you have something better for me to do. But I'll soon have to stop for rest and food."

"Don't push yourself so hard. I don't think there's much you can do, either way."

"Then I'll go on until you turn back."

"All right." Cirocco once again pressed buttons. "Valiha, are you there?"

"I am at the outskirts of Bellinzona, Cirocco," Valiha said.

"What did you want to know?"

"You bade me catch live zombies," she said. "I have enlisted Hornpipe, Mbira, Cembalo, Sistrum, and Lyricon in this project. They tell me Luther was here a short time ago, but know of no other zombie band in the area. We can search for strays, but our noses tell us none are in the area. The citizens of this fair city have become cautious enough that few new zombies spring from their graveyards. What I wanted to know, Captain, is must these zombies be already dead?"

Cirocco thought it over for a while.

"Valiha, you are ruthless and practical."

"Captain, to me there are those who have been executed for their crimes, and those who, through an oversight, are still walking around. Do you wish me to read them their rights and arrange fair trials?"

"Follow the right path as you see it," Cirocco sang.

Valiha turned off the radio and stuffed it in her pouch. She sang a few notes to her five companions, and they trotted off down the broad pier that ran along the Grand Canal. When they came to the crossing waterway known as the Slough of Despond, they stopped, and looked around. It was here that much of Bellinzona's thriving business in slaves was done.

Soon a caravan came shambling down Edward Teller Boulevard.

There were twenty slaves in iron fetters: sixteen females and four males, many of them children. They were guarded by ten muscular men in rough armor, and at the head of the procession was the slavemaster, in a sedan chair carried by a pair of identical twins. The chair was a conspicuous indulgence in Gaea's low gravity, but it had nothing to do with utility and everything to do with showboating. The contingent of guards, on the other hand, might have proved too few, even if the caravan had been set upon by human bandits. But the slavemaster was counting on the unseen presence of the mafia to which he owed his allegiance.

The Titanides spread out along the edge of the pier. The guards looked at them nervously, as did the slavemaster.

"Are these for sale?" Valiha asked him.

The man was obviously surprised at the question. It was well-known that Titanides never bought slaves. But good business practice demanded steering clear of them, never offering offense—or at least treating them as the dangerous animals they were. So the man got up and made a perfunctory bow. His English was not great, but good enough.

"All for sale, sure. You in the market?"

"It so happens we are," Valiha said. She put her hand around his throat and squeezed. Long, long ago, she thought, someone was this man's mother. He was her darling baby boy. She felt a moment's regret as she heard his spine snap. I wonder what happened to him? she thought.

It was the only eulogy he would get from her.

When she looked up, the ten guards were dead. It had been done so quickly that many of the people on the crowded boulevard were only now becoming aware that it had happened at all. One moment there had been a slave caravan, and the next there were just slaves and Titanides lining bodies in a neat row. Some people hurried away. Others, noting that the Titanides made no more aggressive moves, watched warily, then went about their business. No one screamed. No one wept.

They stripped the corpses and piled weapons and clothing on the street, then removed the chains from the slaves. It took some time to convince them they were actually free. Valiha and her band held the scavengers off long enough for the freed slaves to take their pick of the booty. Cembalo volunteered to escort those women who wanted to go to the Free Female Quarter.

"Most of these will be enslaved again within ten revs," Horn-pipe sang.

"This I know," Valiha sang. "However, I did not come here to clean up the world. Just this part of it, and just for a moment." She reached into her pouch and took out the radio.

"Rocky, do you read me?" she said, in English. Titanide song was often garbled when put through these clumsy human devices.

"I'm here, Valiha."

"There are four Titanides on their way to you. They will build pens for these creatures. We have eleven in hand. Did the Captain give you instructions for their housing?"

"She did. Until we know if Nova's elixir remains potent in the house, they are to be kept some distance away. I have selected a site."

"We will be with you shortly."

There was no trouble on the way out of town.

Valiha paused at the graveyard and gathered a few bushels of dirt into a leather pouch. It was probably unnecessary—most corpses left un-burned eventually went zombie—but it was a certainty that the Bellinzona soil was thick with deathsnake spores.

They made good time to the Junction. When they got there, they arranged the corpses on the ground, back to back, belly to belly, and scattered the soil over them. As the zombies began to stir feebly they were put into the newly-built cages.

Valiha felt satisfaction when the job was done. She watched the monsters shuffling to and fro, bumping into the walls, directionless.

It would be very interesting to see what killed them.

SEVENTEEN

"I don't like this," Conal said, for the third time.

"I can't fly the plane," Nova said. She snapped the safety line to her harness, and looked at him.

"I still don't like it," he grumbled. "I don't know if you appreciate the danger to Adam."

"I guess I deserve that," Nova said, keeping her temper firmly under control. "But I'm playing your game. I'm going out there to rescue my little sister."

He looked at her for a long time, then nodded.

"Watch those feet," he warned again. "For chrissake, don't let that thing slash you up."

"I will watch, but not for the sake of Christ." She opened the door, latched it in place, and stepped out on the wing. Carefully, keeping herself turned so he couldn't see it, she unfastened the line and hooked it to a cloth loop on her shirt. If the deathangel dropped her bro...sister, Nova intended to jump after him. Her.

Great Mother, hear your daughter and grant her luck.

She looked down, and was pleased to note she felt only cautious, not afraid. Her concern was not of falling, but of falling at the wrong time.

She held on as Conal eased the plane closer. He edged around until Nova could almost touch him. She took a firm grip on the knife.

The deathangel turned its skull-face toward her, dipped one wing, and plunged straight for the ground.

Nova could hear Conal shouting into the radio. She stuck her head in closer and did some shouting of her own.

"Chase him, damn it! Follow him down! Get me in close enough so I can rip the christ-loving psalm-singing prick!"

Conal did as he was told, but not as quickly as Nova wanted. Even so, she had to hold on with both hands. Inertia, she told herself. You feel light, but your mass is the same.

He had the plane in a nose-dive, the throttle back all the way. Still the plane gained speed. They closed in again behind the death-angel—

—who turned away with a contemptuous flicker of his ratty tail feathers. Conal zoomed by, pulled up, turned left—

—and Nova found herself hanging by her fingernails, her feet having slid off the transparent wing surface.

Conal did a tricky little flip-flop that left her momentarily weightless, and she scrambled to get her boots down, felt weight returning, and looked up to see they were about to hit the angel.

This time, when Conal was through with his frantic maneuvers, she was holding on with only one hand. He leveled out and throttled back again, and she climbed up breathing hard.

"It's no good," Conal said. "I almost hit him."

"I know," she said, getting back in.

Conal was holding the loose end of the safety line and looking angry. He was about to say something, but Cirocco's voice came over the radio.

"He's still dropping, Conal. Why don't you level out and join us?"

He turned, spotted Cirocco's plane following the angel, which now descended at a more leisurely rate. He followed them down.

The deathangel went down for a long time. When it finally leveled out, it was at an altitude of one kilometer.

"Well," Cirocco said, dubiously, "it had to be tried. If we hadn't tried it, we'd all have been kicking ourselves forever."

"Is it over, then?" Robin asked.

"It might as well be," Cirocco said. "My dears, that thing has reduced our chances of catching Adam by a factor of ten."

"Worse," Nova said.

"Okay, worse. And worse than *that,* if it *does* drop Adam, it's our fault he's down so low."

"We had to try it," Chris said.

Cirocco nodded thoughtfully.

"Folks, we just got sent a message. Gaea will not hurt Adam. But she's willing to let *us* kill him, if we get too cute. So let's back off, like about a kilometer, and hope that son of a bitch gets up a little higher."

They did, and after a short time the deathangel rose to two kilometers and leveled out there. Then another appeared from the bright yellow sands of Mnemosyne and took Adam. They watched as the second one disintegrated just as the first had, and the third flew tirelessly on.

"Cirocco, I'm going to have a fuel problem," Conal said.

She watched as the figures from his computer filled her screen. Then she sat back and thought it out, going over it all three times, until she felt sure she had the right course of action.

"I'm going to give you some fuel now," she told Conal. "Leave myself enough to reach the base in the north wall. I'll leave the Four there, and come back in something bigger and meaner."

"Got you."

So Conal dropped down to the level Cirocco was maintaining, went below her, then put his plane on autopilot as he crawled out to catch the fuel hose dangling from the larger plane. He plugged it in and watched the fuel fill his own tank.

"Stay behind and below, as we discussed," Cirocco told Conal. "I won't be away long."

"Don't worry about us, Captain," she heard him say. She dipped her wings and turned to the north.

What followed was no more amazing than a mosquito turning into a hawk.

Airplanes are a series of trade offs. The designer has to pick which characteristic is most important, and work around that, knowing the other parameters will suffer for it. A slow-flying high-altitude plane needs a lot of wing surface to provide lift in thin air. A very fast plane doesn't need much wing, but must withstand atmospheric heating. Either way, there are problems of structural strength. The very fastest planes usually have a short range because they burn fuel extravagantly.

The Dragonfly series was the best attempt human engineers had yet made at planes that could do all things well. They had been designed for Earth conditions. Gaea's environment was different, but most of the differences worked to the advantage of the Dragonflys.

The powerplants were small, light, and almost one hundred percent fuel-efficient.

The airframes were very strong, light, heat-resistant, and of variable flight-geometry.

On Earth, a Dragonfly stalled at ten kilometers per hour. At Gaea's rim, where the air pressure was two atmospheres, a Dragonfly could stay in the air at walking speed. They could reach seventy thousand feet on the Earth; in Gaea that ability was wasted, as even in the hub the pressure was one atmosphere. They were aerobatic, able to pull more turning gees than a human pilot could withstand without blackout. They were ultra-light, idiot-proof, high-capacity, low-maintenance, fuel-efficient, high-altitude, long-range . . .

. . . and supersonic.

Cirocco had cracked the sound barrier a few times in Gaea, but there was not much point in it. At the rim the speed of sound was between thirteen and fourteen hundred kilometers per hour, depending on air temperature. The longest possible trip was about an hour and a quarter at that speed.

When Cirocco pushed the throttles forward in southern Mnemosyne she was about two hundred kilometers from her destination. The engines roared, the wings folded back and pulled in and the fuselage constricted at the waist, and in three minutes she was doing a thousand kilometers per hour. A few minutes after that she had to begin her deceleration.

Her destination was a cavern about a mile up the side of the sheer northern highlands cliff.

When she declared war on the buzz bombs, Cirocco had bought enough weaponry to arm a medium-sized banana republic. It had not been cheap, and the freight charges to Gaea had tripled the price, but it meant nothing to her. She had a great deal of money on Earth, earned mostly because she had lived so outlandishly long, and it was just paper—less than paper; you could use paper to start a fire. It had pleased her to at last find a use for the stuff.

Killing all the buzz bombs had not taken long. She could have used just the Dragonflys to do it, but she had bought a lot more than that. Most of it was still there, waiting to be used.

She let the plane's brain bring her in until the last hundred meters, then took control herself and harriered into the cave, directing the jet exhaust to bring the plane in vertically. They got out quickly, and she directed Chris and Robin to take out all the personal gear. Then she selected another plane.

It was a big cave. There were thirty aircraft in it.

She chose a Mantis Fifty. It was of the same generation as the Dragonfly, but its mission was not primarily transportation. Its name came from the fact that it could carry fifty people and a little armament. Or, it could carry twenty-five, and a lot of armament. Then again, it could carry ten, and enough firepower to shoot down a squadron of older planes and level a small city.

Counting Chris as two people, Cirocco was going to be taking off with four. She planned her payload accordingly.

The three of them spent the next half-hour attaching missiles to the wings, loading cannon, and stowing bombs. The lasers would take care of themselves.

The thing clinging to the vertical surface of the central Mnemosyne cable was not a buzz bomb, just as an alligator is not an iguana.

He was built along the lines of a 707. His wings were swept back, and four ramjet engines depended from them.

Gaea, who had dreamed of him three myriarevs ago and then seen her dream spring to life, as they so often did, had named him and his brothers and sisters Luftmorder. The name was visible, in English script, on his slim fuselage, which gurgled happily with a full load of kerosene. The name was in white, and the rest of him was the color of drying blood.

There were not many like him. In all of Gaea, only ten. All of them hung from cables, like barnacles.

His had been a dull life, so far, but he was patient. He had never tried his wings. But the day would come. He looked forward to it.

The Luftmorder was not a particularly bright being, but it would ave been wrong to call him stupid. He was single-minded, and quite canny in the pursuit of his goals. He had clung for three myriarevs, feeding on the kerosene drip from the cable. He could cling that long again, and more, but did not think he would have to. He sensed Gaea's excitement. Orders would come.

Clinging to him in turn, squabbling among the rows of cold nipples that lined the undersides of his wings, were scores of creatures called sidewinders and red-eyes. They were quite stupid; a necessary nuisance. Red-eyes were larger, sidewinders were faster—at least, that was the theory. Each would get only one chance to find out, as they were not reusable. Each was an organic creature built around a solid-fuel skeleton. Their brains rode on cores of explosive. They saw in the infra-red spectrum, and they loved bright things just like moths love flames.

The Luftmorder was not a buzz bomb, though he was related. The nine aeromorphs that clung to the cable quite near him, however, were much like buzz bombs, in the same way a greyhound or a Doberman is much like a Chihuahua.

The Luftmorder was undisputed flugelfuhrer of the squadron. He watched with infra-red-eyed concentration as the two planes dallied by far beneath him. He saw them come together for a time, saw the larger begin to burn much faster and pull away to the north. The buzz bombs wanted to go, but he counseled patience. When the larger plane was far away, when it had landed in that kerosene-source which his Gaean instincts told him must be there, he detached five of his underlings, one by one, and watched them fall toward the bright sand.

EIGHTEEN

"You'll have to take a close look at those one day," Conal said, when he saw Nova staring out at the south-central Mnemosyne cable. "I doubt you've ever seen anything quite like it."

"It looks so small from here," Nova said. "Just a thread."

"That thread is about five kilometers thick. It's made of hundreds of strands. There's animals and plants that live on them and never come down to the ground."

"My mother said Cirocco Jones climbed to the top of one once." She craned her neck and discovered the point where the cable joined the arched roof of Mnemosyne. "I don't see how she did it."

"She did it with Gaby. And it wasn't one of these. These go straight up. The one Cirocco climbed angled like those ahead of us. See how they bend up and go into the Oceanus spoke? You can't quite see into the spoke from here. She tells me they're what hold Gaea together.

"Why is everything so dead here?"

"It's because of the sandworm. He could pick his teeth with Mount Everest."

"Do you think..." She had to pause, and yawn hugely. "...you think we'll see him?"

"Say, why don't you get some sleep?"

"I'll be okay."

"No, really. You ought to. I'll wake you if anything important happens, and if nothing does, then you can spell me in a couple revs."

"How long is a rev?"

"Near enough to an hour."

"All right. I will. Thanks." She turned slightly in her seat.

"How's the hand? You want those bandages wrapped again?"

"It's okay. I banged it while I was hanging onto the wing." She gave him a sleepy, friendly smile, then seemed to catch herself at it. Conal suppressed his own grin; she was definitely improving. She had to remember to be surly. Maybe she'd forget entirely one of these days. Could happiness be too far behind?

She closed her eyes and fell asleep in no more than ten seconds. Conal envied her. It usually took him at least a minute.

Feeling a little guilty, he studied her as she slept. Her face was relaxed, and she looked even younger than her eighteen years.

She still had a little girl's face, with a lot of cheek and a protruding lower lip. Conal could see her mother's features in her upturned nose and large jaw. With her eyes closed that unsettling resemblance to Chris was hard to find.

He resolutely turned away when he found his eyes straying to the full curves of the breast, the round hips, the long legs. Suffice it to say she had a child's face on a woman's body.

"Advisory," the computer said. "Hostile aircraft have been known to—"

Conal hit the override, and glanced at Nova. Her eyes fluttered, then she made an un-ladylike sound and nestled deeper into the cushions.

Once again, a nuisance. The damn computer had a long memory. The results of Cirocco's air war with the buzz bombs had been fed into it, so now it tried to warn Conal of a base that had been empty for eighteen years. The buzzers had liked to congregate at central cables. They could hang for years, nose down, waiting their chance. They *had* to hang like that, as they couldn't start their engines without first having some forward motion. Primitive ramjets, that's all they had been, nothing like the ultra-refined torch that hummed quietly in the back of the Dragonfly.

He was glad they were all dead.

Still, wouldn't it be funny if . . .

He glanced at the central cable, and saw a tiny speck falling toward the sand. He blinked, rubbed his eyes, and it was gone. He kept looking at the cable, then shook his head. It was easy to forget how gigantic it was. What did he expect to see? Buzz bombs clinging to the side?

On the other hand, just what the hell could that speck have been?

He fiddled with the radar, but nothing came back. He glanced up at the angel carrying Adam. Nothing wrong there.

On impulse, he fed power to the engine and climbed rapidly to six kilometers.

And the radar pinged.

"Alert," the computer said. "Four—correction, five unidentified aircraft approaching. Correction, three unident—correction, four—"

Conal overrode the voice, which was just a distraction. The graphic display would tell him a lot more.

But it didn't. He saw two blips clearly, down on the deck, moving rapidly in his direction. Then there were three, then another

popped into being, "RADAR COUNTERMEASURES IN EF-
FECT," the computer printed on his screen.

That would seem to indicate Dragonflys, or Cirocco returning
in the Mantis. He supposed she could be flying three planes on
autopilot, but what for, and why hadn't she mentioned it to him?
But buzz bombs couldn't jam radar.

"Hold on there, Conal," he muttered to himself. The plain fact
was he had never seen a buzz bomb. He had never fought one. And
believing that things always stayed the same in Gaea was a quick
way to be dead.

"Wake up," he said, shaking Nova's shoulder. She was alert
very quickly.

"Cirocco, I have some unidentified blips on my screen. At
least four, probably five. They don't reply to transponders. They are
closing on me at about . . . five hundred kilometers per hour, and
they are employing radar countermeasures. I have climbed to six
kilometers in case . . . in case they take hostile action. I—" he paused,
and wiped sweat from his forehead with the back of his hand. "Hell,
Cirocco, what should I do?"

They both listened, and heard nothing but static. Nova was
searching the sky above them, but he doubted she would see anything.
Then, bless her, she turned quickly and began digging out the rest
of their flak suits.

"Cirocco, do you read?" Again, silence. She was probably out
of the plane, gathering weaponry, doing a check-out. Maybe she
could hear him, and was on her way to the radio.

"Cirocco, I'm going to lead them away from Adam, and then
I'm going to shoot them down. I'll leave this channel open." Nova
was handing him a helmet and leggings. He put the helmet on, then
waved the rest away. "Forget about that, we don't have time. Tighten
your straps and hold on." The instant she had the strap pulled tight
around her lap, Conal pulled back on the stick and pushed the throttle
forward. The little plane leaped forward and curved up like a rocket.

Nova was looking forward, and side to side.

"The ones on the radar were under us," Conal said. "They
were hugging the ground. So they'll be behind us now, and I don't
think—"

"Right there," Nova said, pointing forward and to the left.

It was heading straight for them, plunging like a hawk, growing bigger.

Conal turned right and pulled back, and they flipped over. The buzz bomb screeched by them, howling. Conal had a glimpse of a shark's mouth, gulping air, and of wings that arched high and then swept down and back. They were buffeted in the heated air from the buzz bomb's tailpipe, then Conal got them turned around and dipped a wing for a better view.

"Why didn't you shoot?" Nova asked.

"I...I forgot I had guns," he confessed. "You see them down there?"

"Yeah. The first one is pulling around, the other four—"

"I've got 'em." The four were climbing in tight formation. It took Conal back to a cold winter day. He had been ten, and the Snowbirds, Canada's precision flying team, had put on a show. They had flown wingtip to wingtip, turning as a unit. And they had climbed just like these were doing, and at the top of the climb—

—the buzz bombs spread out, trailing black plumes of exhaust, quartering the sky.

Conal had picked them all up on radar now. The images were clear; the computer, fooled at first, was learning the new radar signatures. And it was a damn good thing he had radar, he realized. It was amazing how quickly the devils flew out of sight.

He felt rather helpless. The two of them watched the radar blips twist and turn without apparent pattern. Conal felt he should be preparing some maneuver, as the buzz bombs so obviously were. But he didn't know anything about aerial combat.

He wiped his sweaty palms on his pants, and started to work it out.

What did he know about buzz bombs?

"They're big, clumsy, relatively slow, and they weren't equipped for air-to-air encounters." He could hear Cirocco's voice in his memory. She had not talked a lot about the creatures. "Their big tactic was ramming. I had to watch out for that, since they didn't seem to care whether they lived or died. One got me that way, once, and I was damn lucky to walk away from it."

That was all very well, and the one that had almost rammed them had certainly been big—possibly three times the length of the little Dragonfly. But clumsy, and slow? He looked again at the twisting trails in the sky. He thought he was faster than they were, and certainly more maneuverable, but these didn't look all *that* clumsy.

"There's one coming in behind us," Nova said.

"I see him." He tried a few things, feeling it out. All he could remember was dogfights in movies. There, they came out of the sun—but that wouldn't work well in Gaea. And they got on your tail and shot you down. Since buzz bombs didn't have guns, *that* wouldn't work.

He began to feel better. He slowed a little, let the pursuer move in closer, then went through a rapid series of turns and dives, all the time keeping his eyes open for the other four. The one behind him repeated his moves, but more slowly, overshooting. His confidence grew. Okay, the thing to do...

He put the thought into action, pulling back very hard on the stick, going up and up and over, feeling five gees press him into his seat. He kept going, through the loop, and the buzz bomb made a wide loop, falling back, and it was a little slow when Conal made an eight-gee right turn and a dive, and a sudden twist...and there it was, almost under him now, so he throttled back and the wings spread and shuddered as they dug into the air and lifted him but he kept the nose down firmly...

The thing was in his sights, and he found himself shouting as the wing cannons chattered. He kept shouting as he followed its frantic twists. Then it was spewing orange flame and he had to pull up and give it more throttle or he was going to fly up its tailpipe. He ripped through black smoke and saw the buzz bomb below him, one wing torn away, spiraling toward the ground ten kilometers below.

"Just like in the movies!" he roared. Nova was bouncing up and down in her seat, making a weird sound like nothing he'd ever heard, but you just *knew* it was jubilation even before you saw the eager light in her eyes. It was a fierce light, matched by the gleam of her teeth, and Conal loved her for it.

"Conal! Conal, do you read?"

"I'm here, Cirocco."

"We'll be taking off in about two minutes. What's your situation?

"I just splashed one buzz bomb, Captain." He was unable to

keep the pride out of his voice. "Four to go." He glanced at Nova and she had picked just that moment to glance at him. It couldn't have a second, but she wore a wicked grin that said *you're okay*, and, by God, he thought, we are, aren't we? It was the closest they had ever been. Then she was watching the sky again.

"We won't admire the scenery on the way there," Cirocco said.

"I think we're going to be okay, Captain."

"There's three pulling around behind us," Nova said.

"I see 'em." He had them on the radar screen, and visually. He wondered what they were up to, and where the fourth one was.

"I'm going to check with Snitch, see what he knows about this," Cirocco said. Conal didn't bother to answer. He pulled up again, did a wide loop, and almost had a shot at the trailing buzz bomb in the formation chasing him, but didn't take it as he knew he had better conserve his ammunition.

So he led them a merry chase through the skies until they were strung out all over hell, and they broke off and re-grouped as he gained altitude, still worrying about that last one. It wasn't on his screen. He had a thought.

"One may be headed your way, Captain," he said. "Maybe he'll try an ambush when you're taking off."

"I'll watch for it, thanks."

Once again they were behind him. He planned his moves, and figured he'd be able to pick off one this time, maybe two, before Cirocco arrived. They were in a line back there, weaving as they chased him. He pulled up, starting slow, and saw the last in line pull up quickly. He didn't like that. Then the Dragonfly lurched to the left and he had to fight the stick. He looked out his window and saw a ragged hole in the wing, just outside the cannon. As he watched, two more holes appeared, and something whined off the tougher canopy material over his head. He looked up at the deep gouge, then yanked back on the stick.

"They're shooting at us!" Nova shouted.

He didn't know quite what he did for the next twenty seconds. The ground was all over the place, off to the side one moment, then overhead, then twisting around them. It must have worked. For a moment one of them was in his sights and he fired, but missed. He looked back, and all three were far behind, but lining up again.

Maybe he should just outrun them. He didn't think they could match his top speed. Discretion being the better part of valor, and all that . . .

But he was worried about the damaged wing. Dragonflys were incredibly tough, but there were limits.

He shrugged, and pushed the throttle all the way forward.

"In front of you!"

She must have had incredible eyes. He never would have seen it until it was too late—did not see it, in fact, until it was almost filling his vision, just a gaping mouth shooting little gouts of flame at them. But he pushed down on the stick, and they shot under the fourth buzz bomb with about a meter to spare. He heard an explosion and risked a look back. The tactic had not paid off. It had just missed him, and collided head-on with the third one in the row behind him. What was falling toward Mnemosyne didn't even vaguely resemble airplanes.

"Conal," Cirocco's voice came, sounding concerned. "Snitch says they may be armed. I don't know how reliable that is."

"Thanks!" he shouted, and dived as he heard the bullets whipping by him. He aimed for the ground and twisted and turned all the way down. Then something smashed through the fuselage and seemed to ricochet around inside. The cabin filled with acrid smoke, and Nova was shouting and stamping her feet.

"It's alive, it's alive!" she was screaming, but he didn't have time for that. He kept turning, and once again they spread out behind him. When he thought he had a moment he looked to his right. Nova's face was contorted, and she was stamping at something black that wiggled and hopped and smoked. It had a mouth, and it kept biting at her legs. As he watched, she put one of the unused flak-suit leggings over it and tromped on it.

There was a bang like a firecracker, and Nova's leg was shoved up so hard her knee hit her chin. The whistling note he had heard since they were hit altered in pitch, and he saw the legging sucked through a four-inch hole in the floor.

He didn't have time to worry about it. He was almost on the deck. He pulled up, and streaked over the desert at seven hundred kilometers per hour, fifty meters above the dunes. The left wing was screaming its agony.

And *still* he didn't have time to think, because they were right behind him and still shooting.

"Well, *hell*," he said. "Now I'm mad." And it was true, he was furious, and he didn't give much of a damn. So, without thinking about it, he pulled up, still dodging for all he was worth, kept going up until he judged he had just about enough room, then he throttled back and pushed the stick forward as far as it would go.

For an instant they were weightless, then the gee forces pulled them, harder and harder, up against the straps. They were aimed at the ground, not very far below. Five gees, six, seven. Ten gees, and their faces were red as the ground, with agonizing sluggishness, rotated around them. Outside, the wing complained, and inside, Conal wondered if he had cut it too close. The outside loop was as tight as he could possibly make it. All he could do was hope the buzz bombs followed him, and hope he would soon see a slice of sky creeping over the nose.

He saw the sky appear through the floor, then grow. Dimly, he thought he heard two impacts behind them, and he managed a smile, but his thoughts were moving slowly. If he had worked it right, those buzz bombs had just flown into the ground.

Then he was flying level, upside-down. The sand was so close that if he lifted his hand, he could have touched it.

Gingerly he nursed the Dragonfly higher, until he had room to flip over again. He glanced at Nova, who looked green. He would have felt the same way if he'd had the time for it, but the wing was chattering at him now. He took it up slowly to one kilometer, having to throttle back three times as the left wing began to flap. The little plane felt like a car jolting over a rutted road. He glanced at the wing again, saw it was being held on by one thin strut, and cut the engine. They were crawling through the air in silence.

"Out!" he shouted, and watched her throw her door open. She had forgotten the harness release, so he hit it, shoved her, saw her push up and out, then leaped in the other direction and was falling.

He counted to ten—at seven his teeth started to chatter, when he realized he had never parachuted before—and pulled the cord. The chute billowed out, jerked him hard, and he let out a deep breath. He looked around, saw the twin columns of flame where his pursuers had crashed, and then spotted the bright orange blossom of Nova's chute.

He was five for five.

* * *

Gaea turned purple when she heard about it.

"He endangered my baby!" she roared, and began to stamp up and down the already churned grounds of Pandemonium. Everyone had to hustle to get out of her way. Many of them were successful.

"Who does he think he serves, anyway?" she thundered. "No chances, *no chances are to be taken with that child!* Didn't I make that clear?"

There were affirmative shouts. Bolexes jostled closer for the shot, climbing over each other like beetles in a jar.

She raised a hand into the air and there was silence but for the whirring of the cameras. She clenched it into a fist the size of a station wagon, and lightning crashed down from the sky to make a purple nimbus around her. Face contorted with rage, she drew her arm back like a javelin thrower and hurled something that might have been a bolt of hatred in the direction of Mnemosyne.

High on the central cable, the Luftmorder's fuel tanks exploded. Sidewinders and red-eyes caught fire and found themselves streaking in their death lunges, to explode when their fuel burned out. Four buzz bombs also caught fire. The event was noisy and bright, and looked very much like the traditional Japanese pyrotechnic shell known as Bouquet of Chrysanthemums. When it was over, there were only nine Luftmorder combat groups in Gaea.

Robin, Chris, and Cirocco saw the show, and Cirocco edged around it warily, but nothing came down from the cable to chase them. Cirocco laid the wings back almost flush to the fuselage, and headed for the place that was full of black smoke. She kept calling for Conal, and getting no answer.

She slowed down at the twin columns of smoke, and began to circle. They all dreaded to find that one of the pyres marked the graves of Conal and Nova.

A flare crawled up into the sky and burst, and three minutes later Cirocco was setting down lightly. She had no sooner cut the motors than Chris and Robin were out, hurrying toward the two figures.

Conal had somehow managed to twist his ankle. Cirocco would not have thought it possible in the soft sand—then she remembered she had never gotten around to the parachute training she kept meaning to give him.

He had an arm draped over Nova's shoulders and she had an arm around his waist, and they managed to move in the one-quarter gee about as quickly as one person could walk. Nova had four inches on him, and he was wearing a silly grin, and Cirocco wondered just how badly that ankle was really hurt.

"Do we have any time, Cirocco?" he asked.

"It depends. What's up?" She thought about Adam, and knew they'd have to hang well back if they might be attacked by buzz bombs again. Then she thought about buzz bombs, and her eyes went nervously to the skies. They made a hell of a target out here.

"There might be something in the fuselage we ought to take a look at. It's right over there."

"I'll get it," Nova said, and dropped him. He squawked, overbalanced, and sat down in the sand. They watched Nova running toward the wreckage of the Dragonfly.

"They were shooting at us," Conal said. "Snitch was right."

He told them about the attack, how he had shot down one and made two crash and lucked out on the other two. Cirocco told him about the explosion, which Conal and Nova had seen from a great distance.

"I haven't the faintest idea what caused it," Cirocco said. "But it was in the spot where the buzz bomb base used to be. And it wasn't just jet fuel, either. There was a lot of explosives, and maybe some solid rocket fuel."

Nova returned, breathing hard, and held out the remains of the thing that had tried to bite her.

It looked a little like an exploding cigar, after the explosion. It was about four inches of flexible, hollow tube. One end was scorched and the other was ragged, splayed out. Nova pointed to the ragged end.

"There was a head there," she said. "It must have been hard, because it clanged when it hit the floor. It was jerking around like . . ."

"Like a fish in the bottom of a boat," Conal said.

"It didn't have any eyes. But it had a mouth, and it kept snapping at me. I stomped on it and its head exploded."

Cirocco took it from Nova. She handled it gingerly, and sniffed the burnt end.

"It's sort of a rocket bullet," she said finally. "I guess it was supposed to explode when it hit. It must have had one hell of a hard head to get through the Dragonfly hull. But, see, if it twists it can aim itself a little after it's ignited." She grimaced, then looked at Nova. "You say it blew up under your foot?"

"Part of a flak suit was over it."

"Still, it wasn't enough of a charge to blow your foot off." She sighed, and tossed it away. "But it blew a hole in the floor. Friends, a buzz bomb could carry one hell of a lot of those little abominations. I don't like it one damn bit."

She couldn't think of anything to do but load them all back into the Mantis. She listened to Conal's description of the radar-jamming that had happened, and of the shape of the buzz bombs he had shot down. Most of the changes sounded to Cirocco like they were meant to confuse radar—that complex of characteristics known as "stealth."

Then they took off and headed east again. Soon they located the angel, and followed at a discrete two kilometers. Cirocco kept one eye on the radar and the other on the sky.

NINETEEN

During the long flight through Oceanus, Gaea sat still as stone in her monster chair, looking to the icy west, brooding. All the denizens of Pandemonium walked on eggs. They had never seen Gaea this way. Tons of fun, Gaea was, even if she did have a tendency to step on things. She was loads of laughs, the way she received all those preachers with big ceremonies, built the poor goons up till their heads were ready to bust, thinking Gaea had laid all this on for *them*, told them she had invited them to Pandemonium—them, personally, and nobody else, because nobody else quite had the *slant* on things, nobody else really understood the *true faith* quite as well as the schmuck-of-the-moment—and asked them would they pretty *please* let her in on the no-kidding Absolute Truth, and otherwise dispense their brilliant insights on theology? Then, when they were getting really wound up, she'd look at them like a pro gambler watching aces spill out of some poor dumb hick's sleeve, thunder *blasphemy!* and bite their fool heads off.

Then she'd spit the head into the Resurrect-O-Master and a dozen revs later some mewling abortion would come out the other end and she'd tell it *You're Rasputin,* or *You're Luther,* and solemnly intone the Gospel that one was supposed to believe in, and send it out into the world.

They lasted a while, the Priests did, not like the zombies, which had a half-life of about a kilorev. Still, even Priests reached a point where they were too mortified to do more than lie there and twitch, which was only funny for a short time, so Gaea had run through a lot of Luthers and a lot of Rasputins.

Everybody loved it.

But during the last part of the arrival of the King, Gaea was one goddamn scary fifty-foot special effect.

It was Oceanus that caused it, of course. Oceanus was the Enemy. Almost in the same league with Cirocco Jones herself. There's just no way she was going to feel good while the King was being flown over Oceanus's hyperborian precincts.

If the truth were told, not many of the Pandemonii felt good about being that close to Oceanus in the first place. Oceanus was a thing that ought to be comfortably far around the Great One's Curve, not looming frigidly like a gigantic breaking wave of icebergs. A lot of the most faithful sycophants were walking around with their shoulders hunched. You could have made a fortune on the gooseflesh concession.

But then the King was winging out of the twilight zone and over the Key of G—the most southwestern of Hyperion's eight regions, and only three hundred kilometers from the Key of D Minor, where Pandemonium had encamped. And maybe she did something with the sun panels out there in vacuum, constantly angling those rays down over fat and sassy Hyperion, or maybe it was just the enormous relief Gaea felt—and when a fifteen-meter goddess/starlet heaved a sigh of relief, brother, you felt it down to your *toenails* . . . but the day, the endless and unchanging day, was suddenly brighter.

Suddenly it was orders here and orders there, and everybody

falling all over themselves to see who could kiss ass the quickest.

"Wine!" Gaea trumpeted. "Let the land flow with wine!" And twenty baffled vintners were trotted out and upended and stuffed like Strasberg geese until the chablis spouted into a thousand flasks.

"Food!" she boomed. "Open the mighty cornucopia and let my abundance flow forth!" So butter was melted by the ton, and hard kernel corn shoveled by the bucketful into the rotating maws of thirty poppers big as cement mixers—which had, in fact, originally *been* cement mixers—and fires stoked beneath them until hot yellow puffs were exploding in every direction, littering the ground, being devoured there by legions of producers who momentarily forgot their taste for fresh film in their popcorn feeding frenzy. Ten thousand franks were soon sizzling on a hundred grills, and milk chocolate flowed from the crusty teats of the teamsters.

"Film!" Gaea roared. "Let it be a festival to the King, the most stupendous celluloid celebration of all time! Run it on three screens at once, suspend the pass list, and raise the price at the box office!"

Then she began to shout titles. *King of Kings. The Greatest Story Ever Told. Jesus Christ, Superstar. Jeez. Jeez II. Jeez III and IV. The Nazarene. The Gospel According to Saint Matthew. Life of Brian. Ben-Hur. Ben-Hur II. Bethlehem! The Story of Calvary.* There was some muttering among the Priests with Moslem or Jewish or Mormon heritage, but it was quiet muttering, and quickly forgotten in the general rejoicing.

For who could complain? The King was coming. There was wine, food, and film, and Gaea was happy. What more could Pandemonium ask?

But then there was more.

About ten minutes before the King was due to arrive, just as the party was getting into full swing, Gaea winched herself to her feet, took four disbelieving steps, then pointed into the air and grinned in cinerama.

"She's coming!" Gaea shrieked in a voice that shattered the eyes of ten bolexes and an arri, and sent real creepshow horripilations down the spines of everybody within ten kilometers who had a spine worth creeping on.

"She's coming, she's coming, she's coming!" Gaea was jumping up and down now, which was good for seven or eight on anybody's Richter scale. The commissary collapsed and a klieg tree toppled. "It's Cirocco Jones. After twenty years, I've lured her to do combat."

So everyone strained their eyes, and soon a lumpy, ridiculous little transparent plane hissed into view and started to circle about a kilometer over their heads.

"Come down!" Gaea taunted. "Come down and fight, you ball-less wonder! Come down and eat your liver, you stinking traitor, you killer . . . you of little faith! *Come to me.*"

The plane just circled.

Gaea drew a deep breath and bellowed.

"He'll learn to love me, Cirocco."

Still nothing. People began to wonder if maybe Gaea hadn't made a mistake. Gaea had been telling them about Cirocco Jones for years. Surely she couldn't be as unimpressive as that.

Gaea began running around Pandemonium, picking up and hurling whatever came to hand: a boulder, an elephant, a popcorn popper, Brigham and five of his Robbers. The plane easily dodged them all.

Then it waggled its wings, dipped one, and dived. It leveled out at a hundred meters or so, and now the crazy thing had a full-throated roar. Hard to believe it could do anything, but still, to a flock of people who had seen at least four war movies a week for years the scene had a certain nervous familiarity. It had some of the flavor of those passes the F-86's took in *The Bridges at Toko-Ri,* or maybe more like a Jap Zero skittering down toward that big scow the *Arizona* in *Tora! Tora! Tora!* Or a hundred other air combat pictures where the plane moves in fast and hot and starts shooting, only in those pictures you mostly saw the action from the *air,* where everything bloomed up toward you in terrific technicolor, not from the ground, where in a few short seconds things were beyond *belief.*

The entire row of temples went up almost simultaneously. There would be a hypersonic streak of fire and the smart missiles would go right through the front door and *boom,* nothing but splinters and a mushroom of flame. The plane was strafing, too, but instead of going *ka-chow ka-chow ka-chow* and making little fountains of dirt in neat rows, these damn things twisted and turned and *chased* you, and went off like hand grenades when they hit.

Then Cirocco was turning, a racing turn, all she needed was a pylon, she must have been pulling twelve gees and was so low that if there'd been a field out there, she could not only have *dusted* the damn thing, she could have *plowed* it with her wingtip. So here she came again, faster than ever, strafing, firing more missiles, but starting farther back so everybody had time to see the *sturm und drang* coming at them. And she pulled up, almost vertical, rising higher and higher, and released three fat bombs, one, two, three, that kept rising as she pulled away, that went up until they were almost invisible, hung there, and started falling. There was no *way* she could have aimed them. It was supernatural, they said, it just couldn't be done, but they plopped right through the roofs of sound stages one, two, and three, just like that. One, two, three, and all of them were history.

The humans and humanoids were understandably terrified by all this action, but the photofauns were ecstatic. What footage! Riots developed at the camera mounts of copters, which would rise with five or six panaflexes clinging to their legs, twisting to find the shot. Most of them got glorious footage of missiles from the target's point of view, shots that had never been done before. It was a shame none of the raw stock survived to reach the projector.

By then Pandemonium was so choked in smoke it was hard to tell where she was going to come from next. They listened to the sound of her engines protesting, heard it grow louder. Then she was on them again. Liquid fire was spilling from the belly of the plane. It twisted in the air . . . and, miraculously, fell a hundred meters from the carnage, in a semi-circle with Pandemonium at the center. Later, the survivors would agree it was impossible that had been a mistake. Jones had been too devilishly accurate for that. She had just been showing them she had it, and giving them something to think about for the next time. Most of them would spend a *lot* of time from then on, thinking about napalm.

Through it all Gaea stood. Solid as an oak. Great brows beetled as she watched the deadly gnat destroy everything around her. On the fourth pass she began to laugh. Somehow, it was more horrible than the sound of the bombs or the crackle of the flames.

Jones made a fifth pass—and for a moment Gaea stopped laughing as the Archives exploded. Twenty thousand film canisters became smoking debris. Ten thousand rare prints, many of them no longer replaceable. With one bomb Jones had wiped out two centuries of film history.

"Don't worry," Gaea shouted. "I have duplicates of most of them." The survivors, crouched under rubble and hearing Jones coming around for another pass, dimly realized that Gaea was reassuring them. She thought they felt the loss as acutely as she did, when in fact *all* of them would have traded every inch of film ever shot for the chance to get out of this nightmare. And again, Gaea laughed.

The plane was coming around one more time. Some of them sensed this would be the last run, and a few even managed to be curious enough to lift their heads and watch it.

Jones came in straight and level. She fired missiles in pairs, and each streaked for Gaea—and turned aside at the last moment, missing her by inches. More and more of them came screaming by, to explode a hundred meters behind her. It began to look like a circus knife-throwing act as the projectiles went by her ankles, her arms, her ears, her knees. And still the plane kept coming on, and Gaea kept laughing.

A line of bullet holes appeared along Gaea's chest. She laughed louder. It sounded like Jones had ten heavy guns on that plane, and all of them opened up as she got closer. Gaea was rocked, bloodied, marked from her legs to her massive head.

And anybody could see she was unhurt.

The plane pulled up, climbed . . . and kept climbing. At about three kilometers, when it was just a speck, it started circling again.

"I still won't hurt him, Cirocco!" Gaea shouted. Then she looked at herself, frowned, and turned to see a gaffer hanging on the back of her bullet-pocked chair.

"We'd better bring up the second unit," she told him. "And assemble my make-up crew. There's a lot of work to do."

The gaffer didn't move, and Gaea frowned, then tilted the chair and saw it was only half a gaffer.

So she strode off into the flames, shouting orders.

"Well," Cirocco finally said, much subdued. "It seemed like a good idea at the time."

There had been none of the wild jubilation Conal and Nova

had felt during their dogfight with the buzz bombs. Cirocco had more or less asked them all if she could do it, and they had all more or less agreed that she should. So she had gone about it with a cold intensity and thoroughness that left them all, including Cirocco, a bit shaken. Only during the last run, when she had fired on the monstrosity that called itself Gaea, had she felt the hatred boiling up inside her. The temptation to give it all she had, to pour firepower into the thing and hope against hope that she could blow it apart, had been tremendous. She wondered if the others understood why, in the end, she had settled for the show of force and the minor injuries.

Gaea would not be killed that way. She could sit on an atom bomb, be vaporized, and sprout again from the killing ground. Gaea was not immortal. She was over the hill, senile, growing madder every day. She couldn't last much longer... only about another hundred millennia.

And it was Cirocco's job to kill her.

They all looked down at the blazing ruin that had been Pandemonium. Only one structure was left standing. There could be no doubt it was the "palace" the Snitch had spoken of, made of gold and platinum. Adam would be installed there, probably in a solid-gold crib, with goose-egg diamonds for marbles.

"Why didn't you just take her out?" Conal asked, quietly,

"You still don't understand her," Cirocco said. "If I'd destroyed the palace, or killed Gaea, the deathangel would just have flown on, too low for us to catch Adam. He'd have kept flying until he fell apart, and Adam would die."

"I don't get it," Conal confessed. "She said come down and fight. Well, you gave her a fight. What does she expect? Does she want you to land and arm-wrestle with her?"

"Conal, my old friend... I don't know. That may be *exactly* what she wants. I have the feeling that..."

"What?" Conal prompted.

"She wants me to walk up to her with a sword in my hand."

"I don't buy it," Conal said. "I mean... jesus, this sounds completely crazy. I guess it's because I can't find the right words. 'Fair play' isn't it, but she has... *something*. Not all the time, and not in any sane way, but from what you've told me about her I'd think she'd even it out a little more than that. I just don't think that she wouldn't leave you *any* chance."

Cirocco sighed.

"I don't either. And Gaby says—" she cut herself off quickly when she saw Robin giving her an odd look. "Anyway, Gaea won't tell me what she wants, except to come and fight. I'm supposed to figure it out."

It got quiet again and they all looked out over the carnage. Human beings had died down there, and innnocent animals. The humans were in the service of evil, if not evil themselves, and Cirocco did not regret killing them, But she took no pleasure in it and did not feel proud of herself.

"I think I'm gonna be sick," Nova said.

"I'm sorry, kid," Cirocco said. "The head's all the way in back."

"Don't be sorry," Nova shouted, close to tears. "I *wanted* you to kill them, every last one! I *loved* it when you were killing them. I just...I just have a weak stomach, that's all." She sobbed, and looked imploringly at Cirocco.

"And don't call me kid," she whispered, and fled to the back of the plane.

There was a short, uncomfortable silence, which Chris broke.

"If you want my opinion," he said, "I sort of wish you hadn't done it." He got up and followed Nova.

"Well, *I'm* glad you did it," Robin said, hotly. "I only wish you'd spent more time shooting at Gaea. Great Mother, what a disgusting thing."

Cirocco barely heard her. Something was nagging at her, something that didn't feel right. Chris wasn't usually critical of her actions. He had a perfect right to be, of course, but he just usually wasn't.

Then, when she thought about it, he hadn't actually been critical....

"Chris," she began, turning in her seat. "What did you—"

"It's probably going to make things rough," he said. He waved a hand at them and shrugged apologetically. "Somebody's got to look after him," he said, and pulled the door open.

"*No!*" Cirocco shouted, and lunged at him. It was too late. He was out, and the door slammed shut. She could only watch in horrified fascination as his chute opened and he glided toward Pandemonium.

Chris and Adam touched the ground within a minute of each other.

SECOND FEATURE

I was always an independent,
even when I had partners.

> —Sam Goldwyn

ONE

The zombies were in separate pens, in a row, each about twenty meters from its nearest neighbor.

Cirocco didn't want to ask, but she knew she had to.

"Were these . . . already dead?"

"No, Captain," Valiha said.

"What were they doing?"

Valiha told her. It made her feel a little better. Slavery was an ancient evil from which the human race might never be free, in one form or another.

Still, Valiha's remark about reading them their rights and giving them fair trials hurt. It hurt because there were no such things in Gaea, and without some kind of rules the human animal seemed capable of anything—including killing eleven men at random. Cirocco was not so foolish as to mourn them. But she was very tired of killing, or of ordering men to be killed. She felt it could become too easy. She did not wish to play God.

She only wanted to be left alone. She wanted to be accountable to herself, and no one else. She longed for total privacy, for about twenty years all by herself to drag out her scarred soul and try to wash the sin from it. She no longer liked the smell of this being called Cirocco Jones.

The urge to jump out of the plane and follow Chris to what would be certain death had been overwhelming. Nova, Robin, and Conal had barely been able to restrain her.

She still didn't know if the urge had been toward suicide, or if she had been so consumed with rage she felt able to fight Gaea toe-to-toe. She had felt rage and despair in about equal portions. It would be so nice to lie down.

But now she had another battle to fight.

Maybe it would be the last.

The zombies shuffled aimlessly. She fought the sickness that came over her, and conquered it, but not before Valiha noticed.

"You shouldn't feel responsible," the Titanide sang. "This was not your deed."

"I know it."

"It is not your world. It is not ours, either, but we feel no compunction in ridding it of animals like these."

"I know, Valiha. I know. Say no more of this to me," she sang.

It was true these men had deserved death. But with a primitive and illogical certainty, Cirocco felt that no one deserved *this*. She had thought the buzz bombs the worst things ever created, until Gaea conceived the zombies. Suddenly, buzz bombs were like high-spirited kittens.

"What are you saying?" Nova asked. Cirocco glanced at her. The child looked a little green, but was holding up well. Cirocco didn't fault her; zombies were hard to take.

"Just discussing . . . capital punishment. Never mind. You don't have to be here, you know."

"I want to see them die."

Again, Cirocco was not surprised. Nova had demonstrated a talent for fighting, but little taste for blood. Cirocco approved of that. But zombies were something else entirely. She didn't know Nova's motives, though she suspected they had something to do with a creature that wouldn't die clumping inexorably toward her. As for Cirocco, she felt killing a zombie was a genuinely humane act.

"Let's get to it," she said. "Move the first one into the chamber."

Rocky and Hornpipe attached a rope to the cage and dragged it down a primitive road to a garage-like structure about a kilometer away. It had a few windows, a ladder leading to the roof and a trapdoor up there, and had been made reasonably air-tight. They loaded the cage into the structure and sealed the doors behind it. Hornpipe checked the wind and pronounced it to be within acceptable limits.

The problem was to find out what had killed the zombies with such startling efficiency. It seemed unlikely that all the ingredient's of Nova's love potion were necessary.

There were a lot of questions. She hoped some of them never had to be answered, but knew from bitter experience that Gaea often had practical jokes built into things that, at first, looked wonderful.

There was blood in the recipe. Did it have to be of a particular type? There was pubic hair in it. Would Nova's scalp hair have worked as well? Would only blonde pubic hair work, or any pubic hair?

It might be worse than that. Gaea planned ahead in some things. Nova was planned. She was the daughter of Chris and Robin, but not in the conventional way. Gaea could have planned even more finely. It might turn out that only Nova's blood and Nova's pubic hair would do the trick.

She hadn't gotten around to telling Nova that yet.

The first part was easy. Cirocco climbed the ladder, opened the hatch on top, and dumped in a measured amount of benzoin—what Nova had called "benjamin." She went back down and everyone clustered around the windows.

The zombie took no notice.

"Okay," Cirocco said. "Air it out, and then let's try the cubeb."

TWO

Conal stood in water up to his chest and watched Robin churning by with a lot more enthusiasm than grace. He grinned. Lord, but she was a worker. If she'd only relax a little, ease into it, forget about trying to set speed records and just let her powerful little body take over. . . .

The lessons had started soon after their return. Robin had said she would never again find herself in a tight spot because she couldn't swim, and Conal had found himself elected to teach.

It was okay with him. He was only an adequate swimmer himself, and no kind of teacher at all, but he could stand in the water and show her, and catch her when she started to sink, and that seemed to be enough.

He looked beyond Robin, out where the water was deep and swift, and saw Nova moving along with about as much effort as a seal. He wished he could take some pride in that, but the fact was that there are people born to the water, and she was one of them. It was funny it had taken her eighteen years to discover that. Now she was twice the swimmer he would ever be.

But she couldn't seem to impart any of it to her mother. Conal saw Robin floundering again, and pushed off. He was beside her in a few strokes. She was floating on her back, gasping.

"I'm okay," she said. "At least I've got this part down."

"You're getting better."

"No need to lie about it, Conal. I'm never going to be good at this."

He brought her in closer and they got their feet on the ground. Nova zipped by them and clambered across the narrow beach to stand, dripping, sleek and shiny, shaking the water from her short blonde hair. She bent to grab a towel and rubbed it vigorously over her head.

"I'll meet you back at the house," she said, and walked down the beach.

Conal looked away from her, to Robin, and saw she was looking at him.

"She's a hunk, isn't she," Robin said, quietly.

"I guess I was staring . . ."

"Don't be bashful. I may be her mother, but I can appreciate a hunk when I see it."

"The funny thing is," Conal admitted, "I wasn't really looking at her as a girl. I mean, not sexually. I've been swimming with you two almost every day, you know, so I'm used to looking at her. She's just such an incredibly healthy animal. She sort of glows."

Robin was giving him a skeptical eye, so he played the role she expected, acting abashed and shaking his head as if caught in a lie. But it *was* a funny thing, and it was true. He could be around a naked Nova all day long and never have a sexual thought about her. There were attainable dreams and there were impossible dreams, and Nova was always and forever the latter. It was too bad, but there it was. So now they were working cautiously toward a mutual respect that was still just shy of true friendship, and he liked that just fine.

And it didn't interfere at all with his appreciation of her stupendous beauty. A world couldn't be *all* bad if it contained such a creature.

So then wasn't it just like him, he thought, to be felled in the midst of his pride by suddenly and unaccountably becoming uncomfortably aware of Robin as a woman.

Well, it was her own falut. She shouldn't have brought it up.

They waded ashore and dried themselves on the fluffy white towels from the Junction. Conal kept stealing glances at her. She sat on a big smooth rock and carefully dried between her toes, fastidious as a cat.

She sure didn't look forty. She looked... thirtyish, he supposed, but at the low end. But age was a funny thing. You could be twenty-eight and a pasty, lumpy, draggle-tailed thing. Or you could be fifty-five with a firm, flat belly and the glow of health and laugh-wrinkles around your eyes.

Like the hair. Shaved off high and unnatural around one ear, the one that was centered in the odd pentagonal design. A real fright when you first saw it, but as time went by it was somehow right for her.

Like the snakes. Now there was something to put a guy off, those snakes coiling around one leg and one arm, one fat loop going under her breasts, and the heads facing each other. But when you'd seen it a few times, it was just Robin. More than that, it was a pretty thing in itself.

"Do you have a will?" he asked, rubbing his hair vigorously.

"A will? Oh, you mean for when I die. It wouldn't do much good in here, would it. No covens—or courts of law; whatever they have on Earth."

"I guess not. But when you die, those ought to be saved."

She grinned up at him.

"Like the snakes, do you? I wouldn't mind being skinned and tanned, when it's all over." She stood up, facing him. "Touch them, Conal."

"What do you—"

"Just touch them. Please." She held out her hand, and he took it.

Hesitantly, wondering if she was playing some kind of joke on him, he touched the end of the snake with his finger. It coiled three times around her pinky, so he traced that with a fingertip. It grew a little fatter as it crossed the back of her hand, then made three more loops around her forearm. He touched lightly along its length. Then three times around her upper arm. She turned and he drew his hand over her shoulder and down between her shoulder-blades, and she lifted her naked arm—the one without a tattoo—and kept turning beneath his hand until she faced him again, and he drew his fingertips up over her breast, down between the two of them, underneath, and then opened his palm and cupped the breast. She looked down at the hand. She was breathing deeply and evenly.

"Now the other," she said.

So he went down on one knee and touched her foot. The snake's tail started on the small toe. It made S-turns along the top of her foot, coiled around her ankle and looped twice around her calf. He traced it out, going slowly, feeling the firm, clever muscles beneath the skin, which was absolutely smooth. Her other leg, he noticed, had very fine hairs.

The snake swelled around her thigh. He traced it faithfully, reaching around her when it was out of sight. Then she turned again, and his hand went over her hip, across a buttock, and up her back once more. She lifted her arm and he reached under it and cupped her other breast from behind. He held it for a moment, then let go.

She turned and smiled sadly at him. Then she took his hand, lacing her fingers through his, and they walked side-by-side up the beach. For a long time he felt strangely content not to say anything. But the feeling couldn't last forever.

"Why?" he finally asked.

"I've been asking myself that question. I wonder if you've found a better answer than I did."

"Is it . . . was it a sex thing?" Conal, he told himself, you are the soul of subtlety. Just take all your little problems to Conal, girls. He'll stomp through them with his hob-nail boots.

"Maybe. Maybe not as simple as that. I think I just wanted to be touched. Deliberately. You've touched me while you teach me to swim, and it wasn't the same . . . but it disturbed me, how good it felt."

Conal thought it over.

"I'll rub your back for you. I know how."

She smiled at him. Her eyes were bright with tears, but she didn't look at all like she was about to cry. It was odd.

"Would you? I'd like that."

Again there was a time of silence. Conal could see the stairs leading up to the Junction, and was sorry they were there. He wished the beach were longer. He liked holding her hand.

"I've been . . . very unhappy most of my life," she said, quietly. He glanced at her. She was watching her own bare feet pad through the sand.

"I haven't had a lover for about two years now. When I was a girl I had a new lover every week, like girls do. But none of them could stand me for long. After I came back from Gaea, I wanted one woman to live my life with. I found three of them, and the longest one lasted a year. So I decided I just wasn't cut out for pair-bonding. In the last five years I didn't make love because it felt good—it felt awful, once the sweaty part was over—but because it felt so bad not to make love. I finally gave that up and just went without sex entirely."

"It sounds . . . awful," Conal said.

They were at the foot of the stairs. Conal started to go up, but Robin stopped, still holding his hand. He turned.

"Awful?" A tear went down her cheek, and she wiped it away with her free hand. "I don't miss the sex that much. What I miss is being touched. Being hugged. Holding somebody in my arms. Since Adam's been gone . . . there hasn't been anyone to touch me."

She kept looking up at him, and he felt more nervous than he had felt since his first month on the weights. Conal was not awkward around women, but this one and her daughter were different, and it went beyond the fact that they were lesbians.

She squeezed his hand tightly, so he thought *what the hell*, and put his arms around her and turned his head slightly to kiss her. He saw her lips parting, then she turned her head away so he started to let go of her, but she had her arms around him by then, so he put his hands on her back in what he hoped was a fatherly way, and she started to move her hips against him, slowly, and press dry lips to his neck. All in all, it was about as gracefully done as two ten-year-olds paying forfeits on a game of spin-the-bottle, but when all the adjustments were made they were pressed close together from knees to shoulders, and Conal could feel her tears trickling over his chest. She was holding him tightly, and he nuzzled the top of her head while running his hands up and down the smooth curves of her back.

Several times he tried to gently break away, but she kept holding him. After a while he didn't try anymore, and was beginning to entertain some wild notions. That was just in his mind; the rest of him was far ahead, to his consternation and embarrassment.

At last she wiped her eyes and moved a few inches away, keeping her hands lightly on his hips.

"Uh . . . Robin, I don't know how much you know—"

"Enough," she said, glancing down between them. "You don't need to apologize for him. I know your friend down there leads his own life, and that a touch is enough to excite him. And that he may respond in spite of your own feelings in the matter."

"Ah . . . actually, he and I are usually in pretty good agreement."

She laughed, and hugged him again, then looked up solemnly.

"You know it couldn't work, of course."

"Yeah. I know that."

"We're too different. I'm too old."

"You're not too old."

"Believe me, I am. Perhaps you shouldn't give me that back rub. It might be too difficult for you."

"Maybe I shouldn't."

She looked at him wistfully, then started up the stairs. She stopped, stood very still for a moment, then came back to stand on the last step. It put her on his level. She put her hands on his cheeks and kissed him. Her tongue darted around his lips, then she moved back and slowly dropped her hands.

"I'll be in my room for about an hour," she said. "If you're smart, you'll probably stay down here." She turned, and he watched the snakes play over her bare back as she mounted the steps, until she was out of sight. He turned and sat on the steps.

He spent a maddening ten minutes, getting up and sitting down again. No matter what, he couldn't go into the house in this condition. Rational thought was what was called for.

It was a situation that demanded cooling off. She was completely right. It could never work out. And once would be silly, she said that herself. Once wasn't enough with her, and once was all it could ever be with him. An experiment, and bound to turn out badly.

He looked up the stairs again. He could still see her trim backside.

"Well," he sighed, "it's been a long time since anybody accused me of being smart." He looked down at his lap.

"You knew it all along, didn't you?"

THREE

Valiha sat atop the hill overlooking Tuxedo Junction, near the wide scorch on the ground. Already, plants were sprouting in the ashes, growing around the white bones. Soon the place would be hard to find.

There were several human skulls. One was much smaller than the others.

Her hands were busy. She had begun with a broad, weathered plank and an assortment of carving tools. The thing was almost finished now, but she was only peripherally aware of it. Her hands worked, unguided. Her mind was far away. Titanides did not sleep except as infants, but they did go into a state of lessened awareness for periods of two or three revs. It was a dreamtime, a time when the mind could rove far and wide, into the past, into places it did not really want to go.

She relived her time with Chris. She tasted again the bitterness of him, the alien craving so deep in his soul that would deny her sharing her own body with those others she loved, the awful, extended goodbye-time when he had turned from wonderful-crazy to worms-in-the-head-crazy, the slow regaining of trust and the knowledge that it would probably never be the way it was. She touched once more her deep love for him, unchanged and unchangeable.

She thought of Bellinzona. The humans were sterilizing their home planet. To do this, they used weapons beyond her comprehension, weapons that could turn Hyperion into glowing glass. She had a thought she would not have entertained while awake. If she had one of those weapons, she would use it to sterilize Bellinzona. Many worthy people would die and that would be a shameful thing.

But surely the good of such a deed would outweigh the evil. The wheel was her home. These visitors were a cancer eating out the heart of the wheel. There were good humans, certainly. But it seemed that if you got enough together in one place, an evil thing grew.

She thought it over again, and knew the people on Earth must be thinking the same thought. "This is not a good thing I do, but the good outweighs the evil. It is regrettable that innocents are killed...."

Valiha reluctantly gave up all thought of sterilizing Bellinzona. She would have to continue as she and other Titanides had been doing for many kilorevs now, battling the cancer cell by cell.

With that thought, Valiha passed from dream-time into real time, and noticed she had finished her project. She held it up to the light and surveyed it critically.

It was not the first time she had made one of these things. She didn't have a name for them. Titanides had never buried their dead. They simply threw them into the river Ophion and let the waters take them. They raised no memorials.

Titanides had no god but Gaea. They did not love her, but believing in her was not an article of faith. Gaea was as real as syphilis.

Titanides did not expect an afterlife. Gaea had told them there was no such thing, and they had no reason to doubt her. So they had no rituals for it.

But Valiha knew it was different for humans. She had watched the burial rites in Bellinzona. Always pragmatic, she was not prepared to say the rites were worthless. And she had thirteen bodies, all unidentified, with no way of telling what any of them might have believed out of the Babel of Earthly cults. What was a conscientious being to do?

Her response was the carving. Each one had been different, a sort of free-association of Valiha's incomplete understanding of human totems. This one had a cross on it, and a crown of thorns. There was a hammer and sickle, a crescent moon, a star of David, and a mandala. There was also an image of Mickey Mouse, a television screen displaying the CBS eye, a swastika, a human hand, a pyramid, a bell, and the word SONY. Across the top was the most mystic-symbol of all, which had been written on *Ringmaster:* the NASA logo.

It seemed good to her. The television eye was centered over the pyramid. It reminded her of another symbol that might go well: the letter S with two vertical slashes through it.

She shrugged, stood, and placed the sharpened end of the plaque on the ground. With her left fore-hoof she hammered it until it was firmly planted. She kicked the skulls until they were grouped around the plaque, then glanced at the sky. That didn't work; Gaea was up there, and Gaea was not worth speaking to. So she looked around her at the world she loved.

"Whoever or whatever you may be," she sang, "you might want to take these departed human souls to your breast. I don't know anything about them except one was very young. The others were, for a time, zombies in the service of Luther, an evil thing, no longer human. No matter what they may have done in life, they must have started out innocent, as do we all, so don't be too hard on them. It was your fault for making them human, which was a dirty trick. If you are out there somewhere, you ought to be ashamed of yourself."

She had not expected an answer, and she didn't get one.

Valiha knelt again and picked up her woodworking tools, placing them in her pouch. She kicked at the wood shavings and took one last look around the peaceful scene. She wondered once more why she did it.

She was about to head back to the Junction, but saw Rocky coming up the path toward her, so she waited for him. Thinking back, she realized she had come to a decision about his proposal during her dream-time.

He joined her and looked at her handiwork without saying anything. He stood in solemn silence for a time, as he had seen humans do at graveyards, then faced Valiha.

"It has been one thousand revs," he sang.

One kilorev, Valiha thought. Forty-two Earth days with Adam and Chris captive in Pandemonium.

"I have decided," she sang. "I have concluded there is no good time to bring new life into the world."

His eyes fell, then he looked up again with a glimmer of hope. She smiled at him, and kissed his lips.

"There never will be a good time, so to do it anyway is a gesture that appeals to me. And to do it in this age, without Gaea's approval, appeals to me even more. May his life be long and interesting."

"The humans," Rocky sang, "sometimes use those very words as a curse."

"I know. They also say 'break a leg' to bring good luck. I don't believe in curses or in luck, and I can't imagine wanting life to be short and boring."

"Humans are crazy, it is well known."

"Speak not of humans. Speak to me with thy body."

She came into his arms and they pressed close together and began to kiss. It was interrupted by the clanking of Valiha's tools in her pouch. They laughed, and she put them aside, and resumed the kiss.

It was stage one of frontal intercourse. Though not as formalized as posterior intercourse, there was much of ritual about it. To warm up they would mount each other, and do it three or four more times during the course of their more serious lovemaking.

They had an interesting five revs ahead of them.

FOUR

Cirocco sat in the deep forest, twenty kilometers from the Junction. She had built a small fire five revs earlier. It was still burning brightly. The logs did not seem to be consumed.

Miracle.

One kilorev. One thousand hours since Adam had been taken.

"What have you learned?"

She looked up, saw Gaby's face beyond the dancing flames. She relaxed, letting her shoulders slump.

"We've learned to make a poisonous gas that kills zombies," she said. "But we learned that a long time ago."

It had turned out that any blood would do, even Titanide blood. But it had to be pubic hair, and it had to be from a human. The good news was that not much was needed. One hair could serve to make a pound of the stuff. Other than that, omitting even one ingredient from Nova's brew ruined the whole batch.

There were Titanides at work preparing bushels of it.

"What else have you learned?"

Cirocco thought about it.

"I have friends watching Pandemonium. From a safe distance. They told me about the latest move, to the base of the southern highlands. Nova and Robin have learned how to swim. They're teaching Conal some things he didn't know about fighting. I'm teaching them to fly."

She sighed, and rubbed her forehead with her hand.

"I know Chris and Adam are alive and are not being harmed. I know Robin is having strange thoughts about Conal. I know Nova still feels the same way about me, since she tried to follow me here. She's getting better at it. I know she's also coming around to the idea that Titanides are worth associating with. She's pretty much accepted Conal.

"And I know I need a drink worse than I have in twenty years."

Gaby reached out, through the flames. Her hand seemed to burn, and Cirocco gasped and shrank away from her. She stared at the indistinct face, and saw Gaby's bewilderment.

"Oh," Gaby said, and drew her hand back. "I guess that must have looked pretty awful to you. I didn't see the fire."

Didn't see the fire, Cirocco thought, and an image sprang into her mind. It was something she had never seen with her own eyes, but it had walked through her dreams for two decades. Gaby, one side of her face and most of her body blackened and cracking open . . .

"You didn't see the fire," Cirocco muttered, shaking her head.

"Don't ask too many questions," Gaby warned.

"I can't help it, Gaby. I can't make it fit around anything I believe in. You're like . . . the mysterious spirit in a fairy tale. You speak in riddles. I never understood *why* the spirits in those stories couldn't just come out with it. Why all the dire warnings, and the fragments and hints about things that are so dreadfully important?"

"Cirocco, my only love . . . nobody wants to help you more than I do. If I could, I'd tell you everything I know, from point A right through to point Z, just like a NASA debriefing. I can't do that. There is a very good reason why I can't . . . and I can't tell you that reason."

"Can't you hint at it?"

Gaby's eyes got very distant.

"Ask your questions quickly."

"Uh . . . Gaea watches you?"

"No. She watches *for* me."

Christ, Cirocco thought. It's all or nothing, but stop complaining.

"Does she know you . . . come to me?"

"No. Hurry, I can't do this much longer."

"Is there a way to . . ."

"To defeat her? Yes. Reject the obvious answers. You must . . ."

She stopped, and began to fade away. But her eyes were squeezed shut and her fists were clenched at her temples, and her image began to strengthen again. Cirocco felt the short hairs standing up on the back of her neck.

"It's better if you don't ask questions. Or not too many. Since she got Adam, her attention is with him most of the time."

Gaby rubbed her eyes with her knuckles, blinked, then leaned back on her arms and stretched her feet out. It was only then Cirocco saw the fire was out. Not only out, but long dead, nothing but crumbling ashes. Gaby moved her heels through the ashes.

"If not for her madness, Gaea would be invulnerable. There would be nothing you could do. But, because she is mad, she takes chances. Because she is mad, she approaches reality as a game.

"She operates by rules. The rule book came from her old movies, and from television, and from fairy stories and myths.

"The most important thing you must realize is that *she is not the good guy*. She knows this, and prefers it that way. Does that suggest anything to you?"

Cirocco was sure it ought to, but had been so intent on listening that the question surprised her. She frowned, chewed on her lips, and hoped she didn't sound like a fool.

". . . the good guys always win," she said.

"Exactly. Which doesn't mean *you* are going to win, because it hasn't yet been established, by her rules, that you are the good guys. If you lose, it would be at least two decades before another challenger could arise."

"Are you talking about Adam?" Cirocco asked.

"Yes. He is the next possible hero. Gaea has him waiting in

the wings, ready for you to stumble. But his task would be horribly difficult. She plans to make him love her. He would first have to fight that, before he could get around to fighting Gaea. That's why Chris was permitted to live. He will function as Adam's conscience. But Gaea will kill him when Adam is six or seven years old. That, too, is part of the game."

They were silent for a time, as Cirocco digested it all. She felt a deep urge to protest, but she swallowed it. She remembered her words to Conal. *You expected a fair fight?*

"So far, you're going at it the wrong way. You have been given powers that you don't seem to wish to acknowledge. You accept the physical powers easily enough, but the others are stronger."

Gaby began to list things on her fingers.

"You have many more allies than Gaea. There are those above, and those below. Some will come to your aid when you least expect it. You have a spy in the enemy camp. Use Snitch, and trust what he has to say.

"You have a guardian angel, of sorts." Gaby grinned, and jerked a thumb toward her chest. "Me. I will do all I can to stack the outcome in your favor. I'll tell you all I can...but don't expect timely warnings. Rely on me for deep background. Think of me as a mole."

Gaby waited while Cirocco absorbed that.

"Remember, it's better to wait until you feel right about it than to rush into something. Now. If you would...touch me—" Gaby coughed and looked away, and Cirocco realized she was close to tears. She started to get up.

"No, no, you stay there. Nothing sexy, nothing like that. But I can maintain contact with you a bit longer if we touch. Just move forward a little."

Cirocco did, until her bare feet were in the ashes with Gaby's. Gaby sat with her chin on her knees, and they held hands, and she told Cirocco a story.

FIVE

Robin watched Conal get up, open the door, and leave.

Rather abrupt, she thought, but she hadn't asked for anything else. They had used each other for their own purposes. Still, he could have said good-bye.

Then he was back, carrying the old jacket he had worn when they'd met him in Bellinzona, and which he had been wearing less and less in the days since the kidnapping of Adam. He rooted around in one of the pockets and came up with a long, fat cigar, the kind he had smoked constantly before and seldom did now. Come to think of it, he had gone through a lot of changes from the time she had first met him.

"Can I have one of those?" Robin asked.

Conal had clamped his in his teeth and now he gave her a sideways look. But he took another from his pocket and tossed it to her.

"You're not gonna like that," he said, as he sat on the bed and leaned back against the gigantic pillows heaped against the headboard.

"They smell good," Robin said. "I always liked the smell."

"Smelling 'em's one thing, smoking 'em's another." He bit the end off his, so she followed suit, then he struck a match and took a long time getting it going. The air filled with bluish, aromatic smoke. "Just whatever you do, don't inhale it," he said, and held a match for her.

She sucked on the bitten-off end, and in a few seconds she was coughing. He took the cigar from her and patted her on the back until her breath returned, then ground hers out in an ashtray.

"Pretty foul, huh?" he said.

"Maybe I can just take a few puffs on yours."

"Anything you want, Robin. You're calling the shots."

"Am I?"

He turned and looked at her, and she was surprised to see he was nervous and apologetic.

"Listen, I'm sorry I couldn't do better. I tried, honest, but after a while there's not much I can do but—"

"What are you talking about? You did fine."

His eyes narrowed.

"But you didn't come."

"Conal, Conal..." She turned and put an arm over his chest and a leg over his loins, and snuggled fiercely into the hollow of his neck. She spoke into his ear.

"I never expected to. Think back. Did I seem to be enjoying myself?"

"Yes," he admitted.

"Then you did fine. I didn't expect an orgasm. Frankly, I still don't see how it's possible, that way. The design of the bodies is all wrong. The act doesn't seem designed to satisfy the female."

"It can," he said. "Take my word for it. You just have to get used to it, that's all. And I have to learn..."

He trailed off, and they searched each other's eyes. He gave a fatalistic shrug and leaned back against the pillows. Robin did the same.

It was a hot day. Both of their bodies gleamed with sweat. Robin felt great. There was a boneless warmth in her that made her body hum. It had been so long since she had felt it. She put her hands behind her head and looked down at herself, and at him. Moving one of her bare feet to touch his leg, she compared her foot with his. So different, yet the same basic design. It was the same with the legs. Then the loins, so totally different. Her compact, tidy arrangement, his... flamboyant, exuberant, external softnesses, lying there smug and exhausted and damp from her.

She never had found it ugly, even when erect. It looked so vulnerable—and was, as she had learned long ago during an unfortunate episode with Chris.

She tried to imagine her head sitting where his was. What would it be like, to look at oneself and see that? Try as she might, she could go no further than the fear she thought he must always feel. She felt she would have to walk crouched over, eternally alert for an attack, pitifully exposed. His was a nakedness she could never feel. She thanked the Great Mother she had been blessed to be born a woman.

"You know what I liked?" she said, suddenly.

"What?"

"Your penis is so little. When I did it with Chris, it was uncomfortable, because he's so much bigger than you, but the first time I..."

She became aware that he was shaking, and glanced at him. His face was screwed up and he seemed to have trouble breathing, then he looked at her, tried to say something, and burst out laughing.

It was one of those laughs that are very hard to get under control. It was infectious, up to a point—Robin laughed with him for a while, but before long she felt that special insecurity that comes from not getting the joke, not knowing if you are being laughed at. Finally he settled down with a case of the hiccups.

"Did I say something wrong?" she asked, icily.

"Robin, all I'm going to say is thank you. I'll accept the compliment in the spirit it was offered."

"I'm afraid that's not going to be enough, Conal."

He sighed. "No, I guess it wouldn't be. I guess I'll have to explain it." He looked up at the ceiling. "Oh, Great Mother, give me strength."

It was so unexpected that Robin laughed.

"What in the world made you say that?"

"I don't know. I guess I've heard Nova say it enough times when she was up against this or that bit of cultural gap. And I had the feeling She was the only one who might understand."

Robin waited patiently as he wiped his eyes and held his breath, trying to banish the hiccups.

"It's stupid, Robin, okay? It's one of those things where you gotta laugh or cry. Not many years ago, I'd have been insulted. Thank god I've grown up a little bit since then."

So he explained it to her, and he was right, it *was* stupid. She was certainly no expert on the matter, but knew it was something that could only be important to a man. She wondered if it was tied up in their vulnerability, if they thought that, somehow, having a big penis would help. But he said logic had nothing to do with it. He wondered if there might be any parallels in Coven society. She couldn't think of any. He told her that, on Earth, breast size was often important in a woman's sense of herself.

"Not in the Coven," Robin said. "I'm sorry, but—"

"No, no, no. I told you, I knew it was an honest compliment. It just broke me up that . . . you know."

She thought she did, and it made her sad.

"It's just another example of why it couldn't work between us, Conal."

He sobered, looked at her, and nodded, reluctantly.

"I guess you're right."

She hugged him again, and it felt good to be held close in return.

"I want to thank you for . . . for the comfort," she said.

"It was entirely my pleasure, ma'am. Sorry to say."

She laughed, but knew he really was disturbed that he had failed to bring her to orgasm.

"I want you to know that I really like you, Conal."

"I like you, too, Robin."

He turned onto his back again. He puffed on his cigar, and Robin watched the blue clouds of smoke rising toward the ceiling. She lazily moved her bare foot up and down against his leg. He moved his leg so he could touch her foot with his, and they played a silly game with their toes, laughed quietly, and were still again.

Then Conal tossed his cigar out the window, raised himself on one elbow, and leaned over to kiss her nipple. He grinned at her.

"So. You ready to do it again?"

"I thought you'd never ask."

SIX

Nova had hated being in Gaea for a long time. The turning point had been quite recent; now she was having more fun than at a Black Sabbath.

Swimming had started it. Swimming was a sensual delight she

had never dreamed possible. It was better than all other sports put together; not even in the same league, really.

It would have been dreadful to have lived and never learned how to swim.

Then there was flying. She had soared in the Coven, but it was not the same thing. The raw power and infinite flexibility of the Dragonflys was a delight. She had taken to it quickly, though she doubted she would ever be as good as Conal.

And last but not least, there was Titanide riding.

At first they seemed dull as elevators. When you sat on one, you were hardly aware you were moving, so smooth was their gait. And while they walked along at a pretty good clip, it was not what you'd call speedy.

The important thing, she had found, was to find the right Titanide.

Now she clung to the broad back of the one called Virginal (Mixolydian Quartet) Mazurka, a two-year-old female, and out-raced the wind. It had been as simple as that, really. She had been under the mistaken impression that all Titanides were adults, since they were all about the same size. It had been a shock to learn Virginal was only two, and a pleasure to learn she still had a streak of recklessness. With Cirocco Jones gone so much of the time since Adam's kidnapping, Nova had spent every spare moment—when not swimming or learning to fly—on Virginal's back. Together, they had seen most of Dione south of the Ophion.

They were moving along the edge of the forest in the area where the trees thinned and the land rose slowly toward the towering ramparts of the southern highlands. Nova wore her riding clothes. Conal had called them Robin Hood clothes. They were made of supple green leather and covered her completely, leaving only her face bare. There were brown boots and gloves of the same material, and a green cocked hat with a white plume.

Virginal vaulted a fallen tree and for a moment Nova was weightless, holding on with her heels pressed to the Titanide's side and her hands clutching the swept-back arms. They came down, and Nova bounced up to stand lightly on the jouncing back, looking over Virginal's shoulder as they swept down a steep riverbank leading to one of four tributaries of the river Briareus. It was delicious; a controlled fall with the Titanide's hooves touching only here and there, with a noisy parade of small rocks, loose dirt, and boulders bouncing all around them but unable to keep up with Virginal's headlong plunge. The wind was raw and chilly and whipped at Nova's hair.

At the bottom, Virginal slowed when her hooves crashed into the water. There was a shower of spray, then only the slow clop-clop of her hooves on the rocky bank.

"Enough, golden one," Virginal gasped. Nova clapped the Titanide on her shoulder, and leaped to dry ground. She wouldn't have admitted it, but she needed a rest, too. Staying on the Titanide's back was almost as strenuous as running.

There would have been no hope of staying there at all without a lot of help from Virginal. A dozen times in a mile she would feel herself slipping from her bareback perch, only to be hauled back into place by a strong hand, or to feel the back shift beneath her just enough to nudge her back into precarious balance. A Titanide's sense of its load was almost supernatural. Nova suspected Virginal could run at a gallop with a dozen full wine glasses on her back, and never spill a drop.

She threw herself down on a broad, flat rock, rolled over, and looked up at the yellow sky.

Not such a bad place, after all. Of course, just to the left of the patch of sky was the incomprehensible depth of the Dione spoke, but there was too much haze to see it clearly. That was fine with Nova.

She looked at the Titanide, who had unbound her hair and was kneeling in the icy stream. Virginal ducked her head under the water, then whipped her torso erect, making a fine thick arc of crystalline water. Her hair was glossy brown, streaked with emerald green, and over a meter long. It hit her back with a slap, and Virginal shook her head vigoriously, producing a shower that left water streaming down her flanks. Her breath was making puffs of steam. Nova thought she was beautiful.

Virginal was one of the hairy Titanides. All of her body but the palms of her hands and her face was covered with the kind of hair found on horses. Only on her scalp did it grow long, just as on a human. The hair was zebra-striped in green and brown. Her face was brown. Standing still on the edge of a forest, Virginal was almost invisible.

Nova knew wildlife mostly from nature films, and from the Coven's small zoo. She had seen films of humans riding horses, including some stories of young girls who were crazy about them. The Coven zoo had five horses. Nova had never been much impressed by them, but now wondered if that was because no one was allowed to ride them.

The thought disturbed her. She was making progress in seeing Titanides as humans . . . or people, as Conal would put it. It was hard to reconcile with the image of a dumb animal. But she suspected that, had she been born on Earth, she would have been an avid horsewoman. And watching Virginal cooling off in the water inevitably brought to mind the nature films. When winded, Virginal snorted like a horse, her wide nostrils flaring. As Nova watched, Virginal did a startling Titanide trick. She inhaled water through her nose—as much as two or three gallons of it—and then turned to spray it explosively over her flanks.

There were three faint musical notes, and Nova saw Virginal reach into her pouch—another totally alien thing—and pull out something called a radio seed. The Titanide sang to it briefly, then listened. Nova heard it singing back. Virginal trotted out of the water and shook herself like a dog.

"What that Cirocco?" Nova asked.

"Yes. She wanted to know where we are."

"Is there anything wrong?"

"She did not say so. She wishes to know if you would accompany her on a short journey."

"Accompany . . . where's she going?"

"She did not say."

Nova jumped to her feet.

"I don't care. Great Mother! Tell her yes! Tell her I'll be there—"

"She will pick you up," Virginal said, and sang once more to the seed.

Cirocco arrived in a few minutes, flying an almost invisible Dragonfly One. The little craft was quick and spritely as a hummingbird. Cirocco landed it on a flat patch of ground ten meters long, stopping with the nose almost touching a house-sized boulder. She got out, picked the airplane up, and had it turned around by the time Nova and Virginal joined her.

"Hail, hinddaughter of Munyekera," Cirocco greeted Virginal formally, then looked at Nova, smiled with one side of her mouth, and touched two fingers to her eyebrow. "How you doing, Nova?"

"Hail, Captain," Virginal sang. It was the only fragment of Titanide song Nova could recognize. She said nothing. As usual, when first seeing Cirocco, her mouth was too dry for speech.

The Wizard, Nova thought. None of this Captain business for her. Wizard summed it up nicely.

Cirocco looked good in clothes. Nova had had few chances to see her that way. She wore black pants and blouse, and a broad-brimmed black hat. She was heavier than when Nova had first met her. Somehow, the clothes emphasized it. Even in this, Cirocco could not do things like a normal woman would. She had added flesh all over her body, but particularly in her breasts. It had to do with the mysterious expeditions into the forest. Three times now she and Robin had gone, returning each time more youthful, healthier, and, in Cirocco's case, heavier. It made her even more beautiful.

"I have this little expedition I have to make," Cirocco said, seeming a bit uncomfortable. "It's really not necessary that you go along, I could do it myself. But it's not very dangerous and I thought you might be interested."

Nova felt faint. Ask me to walk on broken glass, my darling. Ask me to tear my heart out and give it to you. Ask me to swim around the world, to out-run a Titanide, to wrestle a zombie. Ask me any of these things and I will do them gladly, or die in the attempt, for you. So now you ask me if I *might* be interested in going somewhere with you...

Trying to sound casual, she made a why-not shrug and said, "Sure, Cirocco."

"Good." Cirocco opened the door of the plane, and Nova saw the single seat had been taken out. The interior had been stripped. "It'll be cramped, but I wanted to take the smallest plane we have. I don't think it'll be too bad, but you'll practically be in my lap."

I'll find a way to endure it, Nova thought.

The plane was empty except for two tightly furled para-wings in the back. Cirocco handed one to Nova, and they both strapped them on.

"This will involve some jumping," Cirocco explained, and lowered herself into the cockpit. She squirmed over as far as she could go, and Nova wedged herself in. There was an awkward business with elbows for a moment, then they found the positions to sit.

"You think you can get us out of here?" Cirocco said.

"I believe so."

"Remember we're pretty heavy."

Nova was already roughing it out on the computer. Wouldn't it be just great to flub it, and have Cirocco take over to save both their necks? She put it out of her mind.

She sealed the door, looked around to see Virginal standing a safe distance away. She waved, and the Titanide waved back.

"Clear!" she shouted, feeling foolish. But in aviation, rules were for everybody, every time, as Conal had made clear in humiliating terms the day of her first lesson—backed up by Cirocco's cold glare.

She went over it mentally, then took a deep breath and pushed the throttle in. The plane leaped forward, came to the edge of the flat area . . . and started to sink slightly. Nova worked the controls, goosed the tiny engine, and generally came close to a nervous breakdown as, over a very long ten seconds, the plane seemed determined to crash into some treetops.

They skimmed over, and Nova risked a glance at Cirocco. The Wizard had not even been watching the trees. She was looking through the transparent roof, searching for something. Nova felt oddly proud. Cirocco had assumed Nova could do it. She also felt a little deflated. An approving "well done" would have gone down very well. Then she realized the compliment was implied in the confidence.

"Take it up to thirty kilometers and bear to the northeast," Cirocco said.

"Any particular heading?"

"I can't be more precise, since I don't know just where he is."

"He?"

"Whistlestop. He's somewhere over western Iapetus."

A blimp! Nova felt a surge of excitement, then bewilderment.

From what she knew of blimps, they would not appreciate an approach by a jet airplane.

"Does it matter how fast I climb?"

"Fuel-wise, we've got a big margin. You might as well scoot right along."

Nova calculated a rate of climb that was swift, without being profligate, doing it manually instead of just turning the whole thing over to the computer because she wanted the practice on emergency procedure. Cirocco watched, and said nothing.

"Do they usually cruise this high?" Nova asked, when they leveled out at the desired altitude. Cirocco was looking out and down.

"Very seldom. I want to be sure we get above him. Why don't you look out that side and see if you can spot him? It shouldn't be too hard. He's not much bigger than the State of Pennsylvania."

That was an exaggeration, but Nova was disappointed when they did locate him. She had seen several blimps from a distance—they never came too close to the ground in Dione—but Whistlestop didn't look all that big.

Then she noticed the numbers on the radar screen and realized that instead of being two or three kilometers away, he was twenty-five kilometers below them.

"Shut off the radar," Cirocco commanded. "It hurts his ears." Nova did as instructed, watched Cirocco checking her pack and her equipment belt and the attachments of her para-wing, so she did the same.

"Here's the plan. You program this crate to fly back to the cave by the Junction. Be sure it never gets closer than twenty kilometers to Whistlestop. After that, it's best for it to fly right down on the deck, two or three hundred meters." She looked at Nova. "Aren't you going to ask me why?"

"I didn't think I should."

"Relax, honey. We're not under military discipline here. The reason I want to fly low is I keep waiting for more buzz bombs to show up. They haven't yet, but one of these days they will. I don't want to lose this plane when it can't defend itself."

"That makes sense." She glanced nervously at the sky. Until that moment she had not thought of buzz bombs. She still remembered Conal's magnificent flying during the attack, and knew he had saved her life. She doubted her ability to handle a plane nearly so well.

So she started on the auto-pilot program while Cirocco waited calmly. Soon she was bogged down. She shook her head, and erased an impossible result.

"I don't know if I can handle all that," she admitted. "I'm sorry."

"Don't be. Here's what you're doing wrong." Her fingers flew over the keys, pausing only long enough to be sure Nova had seen and understood. "One of the most important things you can learn is when to admit you need to learn more."

Nova glanced at her, saw that Cirocco was smiling.

"Where would we both be right now," Cirocco said, "if you hadn't *known* you were up to a very hairy take-off situation?" For a fraction of a second her smile became a grin, then she was looking at the computer again. And Nova knew that, once again, the Wizard had been far ahead of her. She would have *sworn* that Cirocco had not been paying attention to the take-off, and had not noticed her nervousness.

"Okay," Cirocco went on, locking the program in. "You get out first. Go ahead and deploy as soon as you're clear of the plane, then follow me. If you see any buzz bombs, cut your lines and free-fall as far as you dare. There's a spare wing in that pack. Any questions?"

Nova had a dozen, but only asked one.

"Do you think we'll see buzz bombs?"

"No. But I can't rule it out."

They opened the door and Nova stepped out into the air. She got herself oriented, and pulled the rip cord. There was the familiar fluttering snap of the fabric, the singing of the lines, and she was tugged sharply. She glanced up....

For a horrible second she thought the para-wing had ripped loose. She had expected a colorful, traditional canopy. Instead, there was a thing of spiderwebs and air, almost invisible.

Well, it made sense. They would be hard to see.

She located Cirocco, who had both hands in the shrouds, swinging around to her right and losing altitude. With a few tugs on her own lines Nova fell in behind her. Follow me, the Wizard had said. *Anywhere*, Nova thought.

For several minutes Nova spent her time scanning the clear skies for the tell-tale contrails of buzz bombs. Twice she sighted their own abandoned jet. The first time it scared her; by the second she was already bored. She followed Cirocco sedately, on as fine a day for soaring as she had ever seen.

Then Cirocco began to gyrate wildly, swinging back and forth at the end of her lines. Nova was not worried at first, but the longer it went on the more she began to wonder what was wrong. She did not get alarmed until Cirocco went into a steep downward plunge. She had to work hard to follow her, and no sooner was she in her dive than Cirocco pulled up, and up, and up ... and almost over. A loop was difficult to do with a para-wing. The Wizard had not quite managed it. But she still couldn't figure out what the trouble was, until she heard the sound of laughter.

"I thought you were going to *follow* me," Cirocco shouted, and laughed again. "I thought you were All-Coven Girl Champeen, or something."

Oh, yeah?

Nova hauled on her lines with both hands and swept so close in front of Cirocco she could hear her startled gasp. Downward she plunged, faster and faster, swinging from side to side and building momentum until, with a hard jerk, she swooped up and around and poised for a moment, upside-down, the wing collapsing beneath her. She tumbled, expertly avoiding entanglement with the loose lines, was jerked to a stop amid the sharp cracking sound of the wing catching air, and came out in a glide, neat and sweet as ever it had been done in competition. She could see, in memory, the string of 10's flashing on the judges' scoreboards.

Cirocco eased in beside her, just far enough away to keep their wings out of trouble, and regarded her with a sour look which she couldn't maintain. She burst out laughing again.

"I yield to the better woman," Cirocco said. "You gave me a fright there, young lady."

"You scared *me*," Nova protested.

"Yeah, I guess I would have. So I probably shouldn't have done it."

"I didn't mind."

"Nova, I know I seem like a very cold, very sour old bitch.

Lately I can't afford much time to have fun. And I know I'm six times your age, and I know you've heard the tragic story of my life . . . but you know what? Adding it all up, the good and the bad, I've had a great time. The last thirty years have been hard, and they're about to get harder. But I wouldn't have liked any other life. The awful thing is . . . well, like now. When I want to cut up, it just seems out of character. That saddens me."

The last thirty years, Nova thought.

It was a long glide. They amused themselves with some more tricks, though nothing as extreme as the loops. And all the time, Whistlestop continued to grow larger beneath them.

Almost a century ago, when Cirocco and her crew had first seen him, Whistlestop had been just over one kilometer from nose to tail. The *Hindenburg,* the largest airship ever built on Earth, had been slightly less than a quarter the size of Whistlestop.

Since then, he had grown considerably.

Now he was two kilometers long. With the proportionate increase in his other dimensions, he was eight times as large as he had been. He contained half a billion cubic feet of hydrogen.

"Nobody knows why he grew so much," Cirocco told Nova as they made ready for landing on the broad back. "Blimps don't usually grow so quickly. I know he's about sixty thousand years old. His contemporaries only seem to grow a few inches every year. I know that Old Scout, who is at least twenty thousand years older than Whistlestop, is only about a kilometer and a half long."

There was more, and Nova listened to it all, but mere words could never do justice to Whistlestop. He had to be seen to be believed. She had thought making a landing on the back of a blimp would be a hazardous thing. It was going to be about as difficult as a mosquito landing on an elephant.

She touched down lightly, ran a few steps as she expertly reefed her chute, and was about to pull it in for folding when Cirocco touched her shoulder.

"Cut it loose," she said. "We'll get down another way."

"I don't have a knife," Nova said.

Cirocco looked surprised, then shook her head.

"I'm getting senile, I guess," she said, looking Nova up and down. Nova couldn't figure out what the problem was. Cirocco severed Nova's lines with a white-bladed knife. When she got a close look at it, Nova realized it was made of sharpened bone, intricately carved in the Titanide manner.

"You wearing anything under those clothes?" Cirocco asked.

"Just cotton shorts," Nova said.

"It's metal I'm looking for. It's not only impolite but extremely dangerous to take anything metal onto a blimp. Anything that can spark."

There were metal grommets on Nova's bootlaces, but after a close look Cirocco pronounced them acceptable. Nova was relieved; they had been a gift from Virginal.

Then Cirocco knelt and started feeling the tough hide of the blimp. Nova followed her. She knew she should be asking questions, but, despite the glimpse of a fun-loving Wizard she had had on the way down, her predominant reaction to Cirocco was awe, and her response was obedience.

She looked around. It might as well have been a flat, silvery saucer. She knew it curved downward, but she could have walked a long distance in any direction before it became a problem.

At last Cirocco seemed to have found her spot. She pressed the point of the bone knife to the blimp's skin and made a small hole. Nova watched her hold her hand over the puncture. She heard a hissing sound that soon subsided. Cirocco seemed satisfied, and, to Nova's amazement, she used the knife to make a large X in the blimp's hide. She pushed the flaps down into the hole, and the two of them looked into the incision.

It led down into blackness. On all sides of the narrow chimney the walls bulged inward, restrained by what looked like fishnet. Nova realized they were gasbags, and Cirocco had located a space between them.

"What if you'd punctured the bag?" Nova asked.

"Whistlestop has over a thousand gasbags. Three hundred of them could be holed at once and he'd still be okay. And if my first puncture had hit a bag, it would have healed in about ten seconds." She lowered her legs into the hole, found a footing, and grinned up at Nova.

"You follow me, okay?"

"He doesn't mind?"

"This hole will heal in five minutes. He won't even notice it, I promise."

Nova was dubious, but it had no effect on her willingness to follow. As soon as the Wizard's head was gone she stepped down, slipped, then grabbed onto some of the netting around her.

"Push the flaps back up," Cirocco called out, from below. "That'll make it heal faster."

Nova did as she was told, and it got darker inside the blimp.

"Now, just climb down. You'll see some things, but don't worry about them. There's nothing in here that can hurt you."

They descended a long time. At first it seemed utterly dark, then Nova's eyes adjusted and she could see a little.

It was easier to hold with her fingers, but it was tiring. From time to time her feet would find a larger cable she could perch on, but usually there was just the fine netting. Only the low gravity saved her.

After ten minutes there was a light below her. She stopped, and saw Cirocco taking a small, glowing orange globe from her pack. She handed it to Nova, and tied another around one of her wrists. It was a kind of bioluminescence, and it was sufficient to see by.

It was better at first. She could see where to put her hands and feet. Then, oddly, it began to make her feel more claustrophobic. It was like a nightmare where the walls were closing in on you, but it was real. The walls *did* bulge.

Then she thought about what she was doing. The things she grabbed and held were not ropes, not nets; they were the living muscles of a gargantuan being. She could feel them moving when she pulled on them. They were dry, thank the Great Mother and all her little demons, but it was still creepy.

They went by side passages. Some were no wider than her arm, but a few were big enough to walk in. Far away in the larger ones she could see eyes glittering.

"Cherubim," Cirocco said, after the first sighting. "They're the same relation to Angels as monkeys are to us. They nest in the greater blimps."

There were other denizens of the sky leviathan. Little things like mice kept skittering over her feet, and once Cirocco paused while something bigger scuttled out of her way. Nova never saw it, and didn't mind that at all.

"You're sure he doesn't mind us in here?" she asked, at one point.

"The more the merrier," Cirocco said. "If he didn't want us here we'd know it by now. All he has to do is seal this passage and flood it with hyrodgen. Don't sweat it, Nova. Blimps have their own internal ecology. There's a hundred animals that can't live anywhere else. And they take on transient passengers all the time."

At last they came to a broader passage, and Cirocco stepped into it. About twenty meters in diameter, it seemed to stretch to infinity in either direction.

"Central Park," Cirocco said. And indeed, there were tree-like organisms growing from the walls, pale and skeletal. They shrank from the light. Cirocco pointed forward. "Come on. It's only about a mile."

It was an odd mile. They were on top of a gasbag and the netting was much thicker, almost solid beneath their feet. And they bounced. It was like walking on a sea of pillows.

After a long time the corridor widened and there was light. They came into a vast, shapeless room. The floor sloped down to a transparent membrane cross-hatched with thin cables, bulging out from the internal pressure. It was cool in here, just as it had been everywhere inside the blimp.

"The B-24 Lounge," Cirocco said, and started scanning the piles of colorful cloth. Nova moved forward, almost to the giant window. She realized she was in the nose of the creature, and slightly on the underside. It was the view a bombardier would have had in an old military plane, and it was magnificent. Far below, the ground crawled by in a slow and stately parade that had been going on for sixty thousand years.

Her foot hit something solid in a pile of cloth. She looked down, and gasped. It was a human foot: brown, withered, attached to a scrawny leg. The toes wiggled. She looked up and saw the face of an old, old man, completely bald, brown as mahogany, showing strong white teeth in a satisfied smile.

"My name is Calvin, dear," the old man said. "And you're the prettiest thing I've seen in a long time."

She never did get to see much of Calvin. He moved around, but was always so swaddled in windings of cloth that only his head was visible.

"Only real problem with this life," he said at one point, "... only real problem's staying warm. Old Whistlestop, he likes to go where it's cold. So how's August doing, Rocky?"

Cirocco explained that August had been dead for a long, long time. Nova watched him, and wasn't sure the old man understood it. He then went on to ask about others, all of them dead. Each time he shook his head sadly. Only once did Cirocco seem upset, and that was when he asked her about Gaby.

"She's ... she's fine, Calvin. She's doing just fine."

"That's real nice."

Which was crazy, since Nova knew all about Gaby.

She finally realized Calvin was almost as old as Cirocco. He looked every year of it. And yet, he seemed spry enough, and quite happy and alert. It was only the business of inquiring about the dead that hinted of senility.

He bumbled around the chilly cave, rummaging in straw baskets, coming up with wooden bowls and bone knives and a cutting board. Cirocco sat next to Nova and spoke quietly to her.

"He's not crazy, Nova. I don't think he understands death. And I don't think he has any conception of time. He's lived up here for ninety-five years, and he's the happiest man I ever knew."

"Here it is!" Calvin crowed, coming up with a large wooden container. He came back to the flat surface where Cirocco and Nova were sitting cross-legged, and where he had already assembled bowls of salad and raw vegetables, and a huge jug of something he called mead.

"Just getting good," he said, then glanced at Nova. "Better bundle up some, girl, Get cozy."

Nova had been getting chilled, but was suspicious of the piles of rags. She had noticed some of the little blind, hairless mice crawling out of one pile. But the fabric didn't smell dirty.

"The blimp exudes this stuff," Cirocco said, pulling folds around her. "It makes good cold-weather gear. Go ahead, it's clean. Everything in here is clean."

"Always is, in a blimp," Calvin chuckled. He was using a wooden spoon to ladle thick and chunky soup into bowls. "Try this . . . Nova you said your name was? Nice name, I like that name. New and bright, and you look shiny as can be. This is my special gazpacho. Made from only the finest grown-in-Gaea ingredients." He chuckled again as he handed Nova a bowl. "Used to, I'd come down once a year for a hot meal. Then I realized it'd been a while since I'd done it, and I hadn't missed it any."

"I think you came down twice, you old fool," Cirocco said. Calvin had a good laugh at that.

"Oh, now, Rocky. That can't be right. Can it?" He looked thoughtful for a moment, started to count on his fingers, but got lost quickly. Nova was trying not to laugh because she thought he'd be offended. He was quite nice, if befuddled.

"Now don't you be afraid of that, honey," he told her. "You treat it with respect, though. I don't much care for heating my food, but I don't mind it *hot*, if you catch my meaning."

Nova did not, unfortunately. She sniffed, and liked the smell, so she took a big spoonful. It was based on tomato and celery and was good and spicy and cold. She took another mouthful . . . and then the first one hit her. She swallowed, gasped, and felt the stuff searing her nasal passages and burning behind her eyeballs. She lunged for the glass of mead and swallowed a whole beaker. It went down well. It had a honey taste.

Even the gazpacho was good, if taken in cautious sips. They all sat together and ate, and it was a fine meal, if a little noisy. All the raw vegetables crunched. They sounded like rabbits. Nova suspected she'd miss having meat after a while, but Calvin did well with his vegetarian, heatless cuisine.

And the mead was *terrific*. Not only did it cool down the spicier foods, it made her feel warm, loose, and nicely fuzzy around the edges.

"Time to wake up, Nova."

"Wha . . ." She sat up quickly. Her head was hurting and she had a hard time focusing on Cirocco. "What time is it?"

"It's a few hours later." Cirocco smiled at her. "My dear, I think you got a wee bit drunk."

"I *did?*" She was about to tell Cirocco it was the first time, then realized it would make her sound like a child, so she laughed. Then she thought she was going to be sick, but the feeling passed. "Well, what do we do now?"

"That's it," Cirocco said. "We'll get you sobered up a little, then we go back to the Junction. I'm ready to move."

SEVEN

The Titanides had labored eight revs to produce the feast. There was a whole roasted smiler, and eels and fish cooked, jellied, stuffed back into their skins, and suspended artfully in clear savory aspic. The fruit course was a towering edifice shaped like a Christmas tree, bulging with a hundred varieties of Gaean berries, melons, pomes, and citrines, garnished by leaves of spun green sugar and glowing internally from a myriad glowbes. There were ten pâtés, seven kinds of bread, three soup tureens, rickety pagodas of smiler ribs, clever pastries with crusts thin as soap bubbles . . . the mind reeled. Cirocco had not seen such a spread since the last Purple Carnival, twenty years ago.

There was enough food for a hundred humans or twenty Titanides. With just nine people to eat it all.

Cirocco took a little of this and a little of that, and sat back, chewing slowly, watching her companions. It was a shame, really, that she was not hungrier. Everything tasted very good.

She knew she was the luckiest of women. Long, long ago, when she might have worried about her weight, it had never been necessary. She could eat as much as she wanted and never put on a gram. Since becoming Wizard her mass had been as low as forty kilograms—after a sixty-day fast—and as high as seventy-five. It was largely a matter of conscious choice. Her body had no fixed metabolic set point.

Just now she was at the high end of that range. Three visit to the fountain of youth in less than a kilorev was an unprecedented frequency. She had an even layer of fat all over her body, and her breasts, buttocks, and thighs had become voluptuous. She smiled inwardly, remembering how the tall and gangly, slat-thin fifteen-year-old Cirocco Jones would have killed for breasts like this. The tredecenial Cirocco found them a minor but necessary nuisance. They would come in handy in the grueling days ahead. Eventually they would be consumed.

In the meantime, Conal was acting even more awe-struck than usual.

He was sitting to her left, having a good time. Robin sat next to him. They kept offering things to each other. Since no one could eat much of any one thing, it made sense to point out a special delicacy, but Cirocco suspected it was more than that with these two. She thought if the meal had been stale C-rations, they would still be giggling like kids.

I ought to be shocked, Cirocco thought.

She had a feeling it would end badly, that it probably should not have even started. Then she chided herself. That was the safe view. If you looked at life that way, your regrets for things undone and untried would forge an endless chain to rattle in your later years. She silently saluted their courage and wished them well.

The idiots thought no one knew of their clandestine affair. Possibly there were Titanides in Hyperion who didn't know about it, but certainly none here in Dione. Cirocco saw Valiha, Rocky, and Serpent—a threesome none of the other humans knew anything about—looking on with fond recognition. Hornpipe knew, but, as always, kept his own counsel. Virginal knew, but despite her growing closeness to Nova, would never mention it, mainly because the young Titanide realized her lack of knowledge of the ways of humans and would never risk hurting Nova inadvertently.

That left the ninth member of the party, Nova. She was coming along nicely, Cirocco judged, but was still far too much the self-centered youth to be aware of something her mother was taking pains to keep from her. She was blissfully ignorant of Robin's sin.

For sin it was. Cirocco wondered if Robin had recognized that yet, and how she would handle it when the guilty weight fell on her.

She hoped she would be able to offer some help. She loved the little witch dearly.

She looked around the table at her band. She loved them all. For a moment she felt tears threaten, and fought them back. This was not the time. She made herself smile, and made a polite comment on a pastry she was offered. Serpent glowed with pleasure. But she saw Hornpipe watching her.

But it was a surprise, as the glorious meal was ending in the small sounds of belches and satisfied pats on the tummy, when Hornpipe cleared his throat and waited until he had silence.

"Captain," he said, in English. "We were pleased when you made no objection to the preparation of this feast. You are aware this sort of thing is done only on a moment of great importance to all of us."

"'*We* are pleased,' Hornpipe?" Cirocco asked. She was disturbed to realize she did not know what he was talking about. And she looked at the other Titanides, saw them looking solemnly at their empty plates. Virginal glanced to the far end of the table, to the empty place setting which had been put out at every meal since Chris had jumped into Pandemonium.

"Who do you speak for, my friend?"

"I speak for all the Titanides here, and for many hundreds who could not come. I was elected to voice this . . ." Once more Cirocco was amazed, as Hornpipe seemed to be groping for a word. Then she realized it was something else.

"Is 'grievance' the word you're trying to say?"

"It's in the right neighborhood," Hornpipe said, with a wry shake of his head. He looked at her, appealingly. For an instant he was a stranger. For an instant he was the first Titanide she had ever seen—and he was, in fact, a direct descendant of the first. He could be mistaken for a truly stunning woman. His heaped-up masses of shining black hair, broad cheekbones, long lashes, wide mouth and baby-smooth cheeks. . . .

She returned to the moment, to a reality that seemed to be getting away from her.

"Go on, then," she said.

"It is simple," he said. "We want to know what you are doing toward the return of the child."

"What are *you* doing?"

"Probes have been made. The defenses of Pandemonium have been tested. Aerial reconnaisance by blimp has given us a map of the fortress. Plans have been advanced, in Titantown."

"What sort of plans?"

"An all-out assault. A siege. There are several options."

"Are any being put into effect?"

"No, Captain." He sighed, and looked at her again. "The child must be rescued. Forgive me if you can, but I must say this. You are our past. He is our future. We cannot allow Gaea to have him."

Cirocco let the silence grow, looking from one face to another. None of the Titanides would look at her. Robin, Conal, and Nova glanced away quickly when their eyes met hers.

"Conal," she said, finally. "Do you have a plan?"

"I wanted to talk it over with you," he said, apologetically. "I was thinking of a raid. Just the two of us, in and out real quick. I don't think the frontal assault would work."

Cirocco looked around again.

"Are there any other plans? Let's get 'em all lined up."

"Lure her out," Nova said.

"What's that?"

"Use yourself as bait. Get her to come out and fight. Set a trap for her. Dig a big hole or something . . . I don't know. I haven't worked out the details. Maybe some kind of ambush."

She looked at Nova with increased respect. It was a rotten idea, of couse, but in some ways it was better than the others.

"That's four ideas," Cirocco said. "Any more?"

The Titanides didn't have any. Cirocco was frankly astonished they had, among hundreds of them, come up with two. Titanides were many things, but they were not tacticians. Their minds didn't seem to work that way.

She stood up.

"All right. Hornpipe, there is no need for your apology. I've been remiss in not telling anyone what I've been doing. Naturally, you and all the Titanides are concerned about getting him back, and you don't see me doing anything. I've been gone a lot. I haven't been talking much. And, yes, he *is* your future, and I for one am thankful for it and sorry for him. I have been thinking of almost nothing else during the last kilorev. I expected to tell you my plans tonight, but you beat me to it.

"The first thing is Gaea. None of you understand her.

"You've given me four scripts. Four movies." She held up her fingers as she counted them out. "Hornpipe, you mentioned a frontal assault. We'll call that the World War Two movie. Then there was the siege; that's the Roman epic. Conal, your idea is a caper movie. Nova's idea is like a western. There are other approaches I've thought of. There's the monster movie, which I think Gaea would like, where we try to burn her up or roast her with electricity. There's the prison picture, where we get captured and make our escape. There's the aerial assault, which is probably a Viet Nam movie.

"What you have to remember is, she's thought of those, and of several more possibilities. My approach will borrow from several of them, but to defeat her, we have to move out of genre pictures altogether."

She looked from face to face, and was not surprised to see the bewilderment there. They probably thought she was going crazy, with all this talk about movies.

"I'm not crazy," she said, quietly. "I'm trying to think the way Gaea thinks. Gaea is obsessed with films from about 1930 to 1990. She has made herself in the image of a star who died in 1961. She wants to *live* movies, and she has a star system, and most of the ones she has selected to be the stars of her major epic are sitting right here. She has gone to great lengths to get some of you here. She has *built* some of you, in a sense, like the old studio moguls used to build images for their stars.

"She has cast me in the leading role. But this is a big production, with many important characters and a cast of billions.

"She can make mistakes. Gaby was one. Gaby was supposed to be alive at this point, as my faithful sidekick. Chris was another. He was supposed to be my leading man. There was supposed to be a love story between me and Chris, but Valiha got in the way. Their love wasn't planned.

"But Gaea is a smart director. She always has a fall-back subplot prepared, there is always an understudy ready to step in. The story department can always come up with some variation, some way to move things around and keep the plot going.

"Conal, you're a good example of that."

Conal had been looking mesmerized; now he jerked in surprise.

"You're descended from Eugene Springfield, one of the original players, one that Gaea chose to become the villain. That is certainly going to be important in upcoming events. I feel strongly—and Snitch backs me up on this—that you were manipulated into coming here."

"That's impossible," Conal protested. "I came here to kill you, and—" He stopped, and reddened. Cirocco knew he seldom spoke of their meeting.

"It felt like free will, Conal," she said, gently. "And it was. She didn't enter your mind way back there in Canada. But she owned the publishing company that put out that ridiculous comic book you brought with you. She was able to slant the story, and to be sure you knew of your ancestry, and probably nudge you into bodybuilding. The rest just worked out.

"Robin, you already know something of how you've been manipulated."

"I sure do," she said, bitterly.

"I'm sorry to have to tell you this . . . hell, there's worse coming up, and nobody's going to like any of it. She had a hand in your life before you were ever born. Do your people still speak of the Screamer?"

Robin looked wary, but nodded.

"It's what moved us into space. It was a big meteor. The Coven was in Australia. It hit, and killed about half of us. But it was on our land, and it was full of gold and uranium that could be easily mined. It made us rich enough to have the Coven built in orbit . . ."

Her eyes grew round with horror.

"The Screamer hit Australia in 2036," Cirocco said. "I'd been here eleven years. There is no doubt that Gaea sent it."

"That's crazy," Nova said.

"Of course it is. But not the way you mean, if you mean it couldn't have happened that way."

"But Gaea was being watched—"

"—and she was releasing eggs at the rate of one every ten revs all that time. The guardian ship tracked them out of range, and calculated if they could hit the Earth. None of them were ever seen as a threat, and there were too many to keep track of."

"It was awfully good shooting," Hornpipe said, dubiously.

"Gaea is very good at what she does. She hit the Earth once before, in 1908, getting the range, so to speak. That one landed in Siberia. The one that hit Australia had been launched nine years before, and appeared to come in from far out, like a long-period asteroid. It was steered on final approach. But all organic matter burned on re-entry, so there was no evidence it came from Gaea."

Robin was shaking her head, not in negation, but in incredulity.

"Why would she do that?"

Cirocco grimaced.

"'Why' is a tough question with Gaea. When I wrote my book about Gaea, one of the critics had a hard time with my analysis of her. He couldn't accept that such a mighty being would do such petty things. If there's any reason, it's for the fun of it. I suppose she heard of your group. She thought it would be a good joke to drop a fortune on your heads at 25,000 miles an hour.

"And she stayed interested in the Coven. She owned—through half a dozen dummy corporations—the facility on Earth where the Coven bought its sperm. She bred you all to be tough and small...and she threw in bad genes here and there, so sooner or later one of you would show up here for a cure. She was well pleased with you, Robin. You gave her a lot of laughs. Nothing like the uproar she got out of watching *me*, but funny enough."

Robin put her face in her hands. Nova touched her shoulder, but Robin shook her head and sat up straight again. Her eyes glittered with fury.

"Nova," Cirocco went on, "you already know what sort of fun Gaea had with you, and with Adam. You and Robin have both suffered the big reversal, the riches-to-rags script."

She looked at the Titanides.

"You all know how you've been used. Each of you is alive because of a decision I made. Each of your mothers and fathers had to come to me and beg for something that ought to be their right. You and your people have been so ground down that it took you a kilorev to nerve yourselves up to offer a very mild criticism of me...and I've become so used to that attitude that it shocked me. I believe your entire race is being stifled. I suspect you can be much better in almost all ways than humans can be, but unless we defeat Gaea you'll never get that chance."

She looked from face to face once more, taking her time with each one. They were all hurt, and angry ... and determined.

"She sounds ... infallible," Virginal said. "What I mean is, she set out to bring Chris and Conal and Robin here, and they are all here. She planned the births of Nova and Adam. Everything she set out to do, she did."

Cirocco shook her head.

"It only looks that way. I already mentioned some things that didn't work out. You can be sure there were other schemes that failed, and we don't know about them simply because no one ever showed up. For about a hundred years she was issuing ... think of it as a casting call, all over the Earth. She set up embassies, did things as direct as hitting the planet with an asteroid, and as sneaky as hiring a writer to make Gene look like the hero in Conal's comic book. Some of those projects didn't work, and the people never got here. But she has her cast now. It's possible we'll meet more, but I doubt it. This is going to sound awful, but there's no way to get around it. All the other people in Gaea are extras or bit players, in Gaea's mind. Most of the important roles are gathered in this room. Nine of us. Then there are Chris and Adam. Whistlestop and Calvin. Snitch. And ... two, possibly three others who I'll tell you about later."

"Snitch?" Robin asked, looking disgusted.

"Yes. He's important. Arrayed against us are Gaea and the might of Pandemonium. There are important players over there, too. I believe Luther may be one, Kali another. I don't know about the others. But it will eventually come to a showdown ... and the cameras will be rolling."

"What do you want us to do, Captain?" Conal asked.

"First ..." She reached out and took Conal's hand, and on her other side, Valiha's. "I want us to pledge our lives, our fortune, and our sacred honor. My goal is the return of Adam, and the death of Gaea."

"One for all, and all for one," Conal said, then looked embarrassed. Cirocco gave his hand a squeeze, as she saw him take Robin's hand.

"What about Chris? Aren't we going to get him, too?" Valiha asked.

"Chris is part of the pledge. His life is at risk, with ours. We will save him if we can, but if he must die, then he will, just like the rest of us."

Everyone joined hands now, except Nova and Serpent, who had no one beyond them but the empty chair meant for Chris. Cirocco looked at each of them in turn, measuring strengths and weaknesses. No one looked away from her. It was a good group. Their task was almost impossible, but she couldn't think of any others she would rather have at her side.

"There are two more things I have to tell you, and then we can get down to planning.

"I have seen Chris, and spoken with him briefly. He is not being harmed, and neither is Adam."

She waited for the murmurs to die down.

"I can't tell you any more just now. Maybe later. The second thing I have to tell you I've been putting off. It really has little bearing on what we have to do, but you should know it.

"I am almost certain that Gaea started the War. Even if she didn't, she has been instrumental in keeping it going for seven years."

There was the silence she had expected. There was shock, of course, but as she looked at the faces her estimate of the situation was confirmed: a lot of people had suspected something like that for a long time. Hornpipe was nodding sadly. Robin looked solemn. For a moment Cirocco thought Virginal was going to be sick.

"Forty billion people," Virginal said.

"Something like that."

"Murdered," Serpent said.

"Yes. In one way or another." Cirocco scowled. "Much as I hate her, I can't lay all the blame at her feet. The human race never did learn to live with the Bomb. It would have happened sooner or later."

"Did she drop the first bomb?" Conal asked. "The one on Australia?"

"No. She wouldn't have dared that. My . . . informant thinks it's likely Gaea engineered the accident.

"I saw a shark-feeding frenzy once, a long time ago. That's what Gaea did. She saw this immense tank full of hungry sharks, millions of them. So she let some blood into the water. So they murdered each other. They were ready to; Gaea simply goaded them. Later, when the sentinel ship out here had been withdrawn, when the War showed signs of letting up, she would drop one of her own bombs in the right place and it would start up again. So she directly murdered a few billion."

"You're not talking about eggs now," Robin said. "Real atomic bombs? I didn't know Gaea had any."

"Why shouldn't she? She's had a century to acquire them, and there are people willing to sell. But she didn't need to do that. She can make her own. For a long time Gaea has been vulnerable. One very large fusion bomb could destroy this world. It was never in the cards that she'd sit still for that. So the war was in her interest. The combatants by now are at the point where they have no hope of ever hitting her—and some attempts have been made. A couple dozen missiles have started out in this direction. None have made it any farther than the orbit of Mars. She takes care of them easily."

She settled back into her chair and waited for questions. There were none for a long time. At last Nova looked up.

"Where did you learn all this, Cirocco?"

Good question, kid. Cirocco rubbed slowly at her upper lip and studied Nova through slitted eyes until the girl looked away, uneasy.

"I can't tell you right now. You'll just have to take my word for it."

"Oh, I didn't mean I—"

"You have every right to wonder. All I can do is ask you to remember our oath, and take it on faith for now. I promise you'll know all I know before I ask you to lay your life on the line."

And I will, too, Gaby, she thought. Her biggest fear was that, in the end, Gaby would appear only to her.

"Can you tell us your plans?" Hornpipe asked.

"That I can do. In great and tedious detail. I suggest that beakers be filled, chairs pushed back, and cheese and crackers brought for those who can still find the odd corner of tummy to put them. This is going to take quite a while, and it's as crazy as anything that's gone before."

It did take a long time. After five revs they were still debating this or that point of the broad outline, but the plan itself had been sold.

By that time Nova was snoring in her chair. Cirocco envied her. She herself did not expect to sleep for a kilorev.

EIGHT

Cirocco left the table and climbed the main staircase of the big house, up to the third floor, which seldom saw use. Up here was a room Chris had set aside for her long ago. She did not know the impulse that had made him designate it "Cirocco's Room." He had been doing strange things at that time, like building the copper-clad shrine to Robin.

The room had bare wood floors and white walls and one window with a black shade which could be drawn. The only furnishing was a simple iron bed, painted white. The mattress was fat, bulging, stuffed with feathers. It was always made up neatly with bleached white sheets and one pillow, and it was so high she could see the springs beneath the mattress, and the floor under that. The only spot of color in the room was the brass doorknob.

It was a room where nothing could hide, or be hidden. It was a wonderful place to sit and think. With the shade drawn there were no distractions.

The light coming through the window reminded her of early morning. She remembered all-night sessions at college, returning to her room in light like this. There was the same pleasant weariness, the same ferment of ideas tossed back and forth, ideas still running around in her head.

It was not morning, of course. It was timeless afternoon.

Cirocco was used to that.

She missed little things. Sometimes she longed to see the stars again. Falling stars, making a wish.

She sat on the edge of the bed. What do you wish for, Cirocco? There's no falling star, but make a wish anyway, who's keeping track?

Well, someone to share this with would be nice.

She felt ungrateful as soon as she thought it. She had friends, the best in the world. She had always been lucky with friends. So the burden was shared.

But there was a special sharing she had missed. Many times she thought it might be possible, this might be the man. What is this thing called love? Maybe she didn't know. She had lived long enough that she had run out of fingers to count the almost-loves. The first one, when she was fourteen. The guy in college . . . what was his name?

Thinking back, she wondered if that was her last chance. As a Captain and a candidate for command, there hadn't been room for that. Plenty of lovers, in the physical sense, but falling in love would have endangered her plans. As a Wizard . . . something was always in the way.

She'd even been willing to stretch a point. When Mr. Right didn't show up, why not Ms. Right? She had been *so* close with Gaby. It might have worked. And all the dear Titanides. Twice she had borne children, once in the Titanide way, with another as the hindmother. Once in the human way, nurturing him in her own body. She had not thought of him in a long time. He went back to Earth, and he never wrote. Now he was dead.

All right, Cirocco, so much for that wish. That three wishes business doesn't work on stars—which you didn't even see anyway—but we'll stretch a point and give you two for the price of one.

She realized that just having a lover would help.

It would be so easy to do.

She wiped a tear from her cheek. Five Titanides down there. Any one of them would gladly be her lover—in the frontal mode, too, which they did not do lightly. But it had been decades since she had made love to a Titanide. It wasn't fair. All she had to do was put herself in their place and ask a simple question. Could they say no?

Conal. . . .

She went to her knees on the floor and sat there. Her face was wet with tears now.

Conal was and always had been hers for the asking. And she could never, never take him to bed. She had only to think of what she had done to him and she felt sick. No man should have his dignity stripped from him like that. To become his lover after such a thing was a grotesquerie she could not imagine.

Robin . . . was so sweet Cirocco could hardly believe it. What a cast-iron, short-fused, piss and vinegar *bitch* she had been twenty years ago! Any sane person would have said she should have been drowned at birth. That's probably why Cirocco had liked her so much. But with Robin there had never been that spark of attraction, not even as much as there had been with Gaby. Which was just as well. Robin was going to have enough trouble with Conal without an aging Wizard getting in her hair.

She put her hands on the cool, shiny, smooth boards of the floor and lowered herself until her cheek touched it. Her vision was blurred. She sniffed, and rubbed her nose, and wiped her eyes, and looked dully along the floor to the crack of light under the door. There was not a speck of dust to be seen. There was the smell of wood polish, sharp and lemony. She relaxed, and then her shoulders started to shake.

Nova...

Oh, god, she didn't want to be Nova's lover. She wanted to *be* Nova. Be eighteen years old, fresh and nubile and innocent and in love. In love with a tired old hag. It was bound to end in misery. But what a...*sweet* misery it seemed to be young and having one's heart broken for the first time.

She was sobbing aloud now, not making a lot of noise, but unable to stop.

She thought of Nova slicing through the blue water, seal-sleek, of the big, awkward girl swinging at the end of her chute cords and then soaring like an angel without wings. She saw Nova devouring the Titanide feast, bright-eyed and laughing, and thought of her alone in her room, mixing the potion that was to bring her love.

Cirocco gave herself over to her tears. She lay prone on the cool floor and wept for what had been and what was and what would be.

One tiny part of her mind said that she had better get it done with now.

There would be scant opportunity later.

Conal had been talking to Robin for what seemed like hours.

The talk had drifted away from Cirocco's plan—which still seemed slightly unreal to him—and into other things. Talking to her seemed easy, lately.

He noticed she seemed to be getting sleepy, and realized he

was, too. Nova still slept curled up in her big chair. But all the Titanides were gone. He hadn't seen them leave. Now, Titanides could certainly move quietly, but that was ridiculous. *Five* of them, and he hadn't seen them leave?

He saw Robin was smiling at him.

"Where have our minds been?" she said, and yawned. She leaned over and kissed him on the cheek. "I'm for bed."

"Me, too. See you later."

He sat for a time after Robin had left, amid the ruins of the meal. Then he got up and headed for the stairs.

Virginal was standing like a statue in the center of the next room. Her ears were pointing up and forward, and she looked at a spot on the ceiling with an awful intensity. Conal was about to say something, but Virginal noticed him, gave him a brief smile, and went outside. He shrugged, and went up the stairs to the second floor.

And there were Valiha and Hornpipe, just as still. Their ears were up, too. They looked like they were in pain.

Neither of them noticed him until he was walking by, then they just glanced at him with no word of greeting and began to move slowly toward the stairs he had just climbed.

He couldn't figure it out.

He shrugged, and went into his room. He thought about it, and opened the door, stuck his head out. The two of them were back in their listening posture. Rocky was on the stairs, also listening, also looking up.

Conal studied the ceiling that seemed so interesting to the Titanides. He could see nothing at all.

Were they listening to something, up there on the third floor? All those rooms were empty. He heard nothing.

Then Rocky started to sing, softly. Pretty soon Hornpipe and Valiha joined in, then Serpent came up quietly to join Virginal. It was a whispered song, and made no more sense to Conal than any of their songs did.

He yawned, and closed the door.

NINE

For five myriarevs, while Pandemonium continued its vagabond wanderings, the permanent site had been building in Hyperion.

The Iron Masters had been prime contractors. They had prepared the site, which encircled the south-central vertical cable. They had constructed a road to the vast forests of southwest Rhea. Bridges had been built over the placid Euterpe River, and over the violent Terpsichore. Two hundred square kilometers of wooded hills had been denuded, the lumber trucked to Pandemonium, where it was milled, sawed, cured, cut, stacked, joined, nailed, sanded, and carved by five thousand unions of carpenters. A railroad had been hammered through the difficult terrain from the mines, smelters, forges, and foundaries of Phoebe, through the Asteria mountains, bridging the mighty Ophion itself in the West Rhea twilight zone, and endless freight trains brought the metal bones of Pandemonium over the alien steel ribbons. To the west, the Calliope River had been dammed. The lake behind the dam was now twenty miles long, and its waters thundered through the turbines and generators, where electricity was fed into the lines and towers that marched over what had been Titanide herding land.

During the last myriarev, when construction was at its peak, Gaea had diverted more and more human refugees from Bellinzona for use as laborers at Pandemonium. At times the work force numbered seventy thousand. The work was hard, but the food was adequate. Workers who complained or died were turned into zombies, so labor unrest was never a problem.

It was to be Gaea's masterpiece.

At the time of the capture of Adam, work on the permanent site was almost complete. When Gaea saw the extent of the damage to her traveling show, she ordered the final move, though there was still a kilorev's work to be done.

The south-central cable was five kilometers in diameter and one hundred kilometers high at the point where it pierced the Hyperion roof and vanished into daylight. Five hundred kilometers beyond that point it joined the Gaean hub, where it became one strand of many in a monstrous basket-weave that composed the anchor at which Gaea's rim perpetually strained. The network of cables were fastened to Gaea's bones, deep beneath the rim, and it was their function to defeat centripetal force, to keep Gaea from flying apart. They had been doing this for three million years, and were showing certain signs of strain.

Each cable was composed of one hundred forty-four wound strands, each strand about two hundred meters in diameter. Over the aeons the strands had stretched. The process was called—though not by Gaea, who thought it crude—millennial sag. As a result, the base of the vertical cables was not a five-kilometer column but a narrow cone of unwinding strands about seven kilometers wide. There were gaps between the strands; it was possible to walk right through the cable, threading the titanic strand-forest. Inside, it was like a dark city made of round, brooding skyscrapers with no windows and no tops.

In addition to the sag, there were broken strands. There were one hundred and eight cables in Gaea, for a total of fifteen thousand five hundred fifty-two strands. Of those, two hundred could be seen to be broken because they were part of the outer layer. Each cable in Gaea had its visible wound, with the top part of the strand curling away like a stray split end, and the lower part lying on the ground, stretching for one kilometer or seventy, depending on how high the break had been.

All but one in south-central Hyperion. While other cables had two, three, or even five visible breaks, the one that rose from the center of New Pandemonium was pristine, climbing in smooth and breathtaking perspective.

Gaea absently patted the cable strand she had been standing near, took a last look up, and moved down into the heart of her domain. Only she knew of the internal broken strands, the ones that never saw daylight. There were four hundred of those. Six hundred failures out of fifteen thousand was a rate of around four percent. Not bad for three million years, she thought. She could tolerate twenty percent, but not easily. At that point she would have to start slowing her rotation. Of course, there were other dangers. The weakest cable was in Central Oceanus. Should several more strands give vay there the whole cable could fail under the added strain. Oceanus would bulge, a deep sea would be created as Ophion flowed into it from both directions and never flowed out, the imbalance would create a wobble which would weaken other strands in turn. . . .

But that didn't bear thinking about. For many thousands of years Gaea's motto had been Let Tomorrow Take Care of Itself.

She came to the areas of New Pandemonium still under construction, watched for a while as the carpenters and Iron Masters labored on a soundstage bigger than any ever built on Earth. Then she looked out over the Studio.

New Pandemonium was a two-kilometer ring encircling the seven-kilometer cable. That gave about twenty-five square kilometers of area—almost ten square miles.

Completely surrounding the studio grounds was a wall thirty kilometers in circumference, and thirty meters high. Or at least, that was the plan. Most of the wall was finished, but some sections had reached only two or three meters. The wall was made of basaltic stone quarried from the southern highlands, forty kilometers away, and brought to Pandemonium over a second Iron Master railway. It was built along the general lines of the Great Wall of China, but higher and wider. And it was adorned by a monorail track that ran along the inner rim.

Outside the wall was a moat filled with sharks.

The wall was pierced by twelve gates, like a clock face. The gates were arched, reached by sturdy causeways that ended in drawbridges, and were twenty meters tall—high enough for Gaea to walk through without lowering her head. Flanking each gate just inside the wall were temples, two at every gate, each presided over by a Priest and his or her troops. Gaea had put a lot of thought into the location of each temple. It was her belief that a certain amount of tension among her disciples made for both better discipline and interesting and unplanned events. Most of the events were bloody.

Thus, the Universal Gate, located at twelve o'clock, the northernmost of the New Pandemonium gates, was guarded by Brigham and his Boys to the east of the gate, and Joe Smith and the Gadianton Robbers to the west. Brigham and Joe thoroughly detested each other, as befitted the leaders of rival sects within the same overall belief system.

Over a mile away, in the one o'clock position, was the Gold-

wyn Gate. Luther's huge unadorned chapel, filled with his twelve
disciples and uncounted pastors, faced the Vatican of Pope Joan
teeming with Kardinals, Archbishops, bishops, statues, bleeding
hearts, virgins, rosaries, and other popery. Luther seethed when the
once-a-hectorev bingo games were held, and spat every time he
passed the booth which did a brisk business in indulgences.

Two o'clock was the Paramount Gate, where Kali and her
Thugs and Krishna and his Orangemen conducted endless stealthy
intrigues against each other.

Three was the RKO Radio Gate. Blessed Foster and Father
Brown gave virulent life to their respective fictional characters.

At four was Columbia Gate, where Marybaker had her reading
room and Elron his E-meters and engrams.

Near the First National Gate, the Ayatullah and Erasmus X
conducted a perpetual jihad from their dissimilar mosques.

The Fox Gate was relatively tranquil, the Gautama and Siddhartha only seldom resorting to violence, and that often directed at
themselves. The main diversion at Fox was an interloper Priest named
Gandhi, who kept trying to shoulder his way into the temples.

And so it went, around the huge clock of New Pandemonium.
The Warner Gate was the arena for Shinto and Sony in their ceaseless
battle of new and old. The MGM Gate was raucous with the perpetual
revivals of Billy Sunday and Aimee Semple McPherson. Keystone
was guarded by Confucius and Tze-Dong, Disney by The Guru Mary
and St. Claus, and United Artists by St. Torquemada and St. Val-
entine.

There were other, disenfranchised Priests, whose holy places
were far from the gates. Mumbo Jumbo of the Congo stalked the
Studio in a black rage, muttering of discrimination, which was just
as Gaea had intended. Wicca, Mensa, Trotsky, and I. C. grumbled
about the emphasis on tradition, and the Mahdi and many others
complained about the pro-Christian leanings of the entire New Pandemonium myth-system.

None of them voiced their complaints to Gaea, however. And
all felt deep and sincere allegiance to the Child.

Leading from each gate was a street paved with gold.

At least that had been in the original specifications. In practice,
Gaea did not contain and could not manufacture enough gold for
that many streets. So eleven of the streets had been paved for fifty

meters with bricks of pure gold, followed by a kilometer of gold-plated bricks, with the remainder of bricks covered with gold paint which was already flaking off.

Only the Universal street was pure gold from end to end. And at the far end was Tara, the Taj Mahal/Plantation-house/palace that housed Adam, the Child.

Yellow-brick road, indeed, Gaea thought, as she strode down the Twenty-four Carat Highway.

To her right and her left were the soundstages, barracks, commissaries, prop rooms, dressing rooms, equipment buildings, garages, executive offices, processing departments, cutting rooms, projection rooms, guild enclaves, and photofaun breeding pens of the greatest studio ever seen. And this, Gaea thought in vast satisfaction, is only one of twelve. Beyond the studio proper were the street sets—Manhattan 1930, Manhattan 1980, Paris, Teheran, Tokyo, Clavius, Westwood, London, Dodge City 1870—and beyond them were the back lots with their herds of cattle, sheep, buffalo, elephants, menageries of tropical birds and monkeys, riverboats, warships, Indians, and fog generators, stretching on each side to the next studio complexes: Goldwyn and United Artists.

She paused and moved to one side to let a truck laden with cocaine sputter by her. It was zombie-driven. The creature at the wheel probably had never realized the pillar he had driven around was his Goddess; the top of the truck was not much above Gaea's ankle. It turned into the cocaine warehouse, which was almost full now. Gaea frowned. The Iron Masters were good at many things, but had never gotten the hang of the internal combustion engine. They liked steam a lot better.

She reached the Universal Gate. The portcullis was up, the drawbridge down. Brigham stood on one side of the road, and Joe Smith on the other, glowering at each other. But both Priests and all their Mormons and Normans ceased their internecine squabbles when Gaea loomed over them.

Gaea scanned the scene, ignoring the whirring of the pana-flexes. Though the Studio was not yet complete, today's ceremony would finish the parts most important to her. Eleven of the twelve gates had been consecrated. Today was the final rite to complete the circle. Soon serious filming could begin.

The hapless fellow who had admitted to being a writer stood

in golden chains. Gaea took her seat—which creaked alarmingly beneath her, and caused several grips to come close to cardiac arrest. A seat had collapsed once...

"Begin," she muttered.

Brigham slit the writer's throat. He was hoisted on a boom, and his blood was smeared on the great turning globe above the Universal Gate.

Chris watched the ceremony from a high window of Tara. At that distance it was impossible to tell what was going on.

One thing he was sure of: whatever was happening was murderous, and obscene, and demented, and a waste of life....

He turned away and descended the stairs.

Chris had expected many things when he leaped from the plane, almost two kilorevs ago. None of them had been pleasant.

What had happened to him was not pleasant...but it was nothing like what he had expected.

At first he had wandered freely in the chaos of Pandemonium, avoiding the big fires, hoping against hope that he might locate Adam and flee into the countryside. That had not happened. He had been captured by humans and zombies, and by some things that seemed to be neither. He had killed a few of them, then been roughed up, bound, and knocked unconscious.

There had followed an uncertain time. He was kept in a large, windowless box, fed irregularly, given a pail for urination and defecation...and plenty of time to get used to the idea that this would be his lot for the rest of his life.

Then he had been freed in this new place, this vast, incredible, bustling insane asylum called New Pandemonium, shown to his quarters in Tara, and been brought in for an audience with Adam. Everyone called him the Child, with the capital letter implicit in their speech. He was unharmed, and seemed to be thriving. Chris was not sure Adam recognized him, but the infant was quite willing to play games with him. Adam had a king's ransom in toys. Wonderful, clever toys, made from the finest materials and all utterly safe, with no sharp edges and nothing that could be swallowed. He also had two nurses, a hundred servants, and, Chris soon realized...Chris. He was to become part of the household furnishings in Tara.

Not long afterward Gaea had paid a visit. Chris did not like to remember it. He thought himself as courageous as the next fellow, but to sit at the feet of this monstrous being and listen to her had almost taken the heart right out of him. She dominated him as a human might dominate a poodle.

"Sit down," she had said, and he had done so. It was like sitting at the feet of the Sphinx.

"Your friend Cirocco was very naughty," Gaea said. "I haven't completed the inventory yet, but it seems likely she destroyed three or four hundred films completely. By that, I mean they were films I only had one copy of. It's not likely any others exist on Earth. What do you think of that?"

It had taken more courage than he would have thought to make his reply.

"I think films don't mean anything compared to human life, or—"

"Human, is it?" Gaea had said, with a faint smile.

"I didn't mean that. I meant human and Titanide—"

"What about the Iron Masters? They're intelligent, surely you don't doubt that. What about whales and dolphins? What about dogs and cats, and cows, and pigs, and chickens? Is life really that sacred?"

Chris had found nothing to say.

"I'm toying with you, of course. Still, I have found no special virtue in life, intelligent or not. It exists, but it's foolish to think it has a *right* to exist. The manner of its death is of little importance, in the end. I don't expect you to agree with me."

"That's good, because I don't."

"Fine. Diversity of opinion is what makes life, such as it is, interesting. Myself, I find art to be the only thing that is really impressive. Art can live forever. It's a good question as to whether it *remains* art with no eye to see it, or ear to hear it, but it's one of those unanswerable ones, isn't it? A book or a painting or a piece of music ought to live forever. Whereas life can only wobble through its appointed moments, eating and shitting until it runs out of steam. It's all rather ugly, really.

"I happen to like film. And I think Cirocco did a great sin when she destroyed those four hundred films. What do you think?"

"Me? I would personally destroy every painting, film, record, and book that ever existed if it would save one human or Titanide left."

Gaea had frowned at him.

"Perhaps both our positions are extreme."

"Yours is."

"You have a sort of museum back home, at Tuxedo Junction."

"It's a luxury I would never miss. I won't deny the past is worth preserving, and it's a sad thing to see art—even bad art— pass out of the world forever. Destroying art is a bad thing and I don't applaud it, but Cirocco would not have done it unless she thought that by doing so she could save lives. So I don't think she sinned."

Gaea had thought that over for a while, then smiled at him. She stood up, startling Chris badly.

"Good," she said. "We're positioned perfectly, then. You on one side, I on the other. It's going to be interesting to see what Adam thinks."

"What do you mean?"

She laughed.

"Have you ever heard of Jiminy Cricket?"

He hadn't, then. He had since seen the film, and now understood his role. In fact, he had seen the film four times. It was one of Adam's favorites.

The shape of their days quickly became apparent.

Chris stayed at Tara. He could spend all the time he wanted with Adam, except for one rev during each of Adam's waking periods. During that time Adam was alone with the television set.

Every room in Tara had a television. Some had three or four. They could not be turned off. All of them showed the same program at the same time, so if Adam wandered from one room to another continuity was not lost.

It didn't matter much to Adam at this point. His attention span was not much more than a minute, usually, though if the program really caught his attention he might sit for five or ten minutes, giggling at things only he seemed to understand. During the times when Chris couldn't get to him and attempt to divert him from the set, he sometimes played with his toys, and sometimes spent most of the rev watching the screen. Often he went to sleep.

Chris was not impressed. In fact, he hardly noticed the television except as a constant, noisy nuisance.

He eventually noticed that some sort of neilson was in operation. The things that Adam liked most—measured in gpm, or giggles per minute—began to show up more often. Most of it was hardly objectionable. There were a lot of Walt Disney and Warner Brothers cartoons, a lot of Japanese computer animation from the 90's and the turn of the century, some old television shows. Here and there a western crept in, and there were kung fu films which Adam seemed to like because they were so noisy.

Chris actually laughed when the first obscure 20th Century Fox film showed up on the screens. It was called *A Ticket to Tomahawk*, and Gaea had a small part in it. Chris had watched it while Adam napped—there being little to do in his ornate prison when not actually occupied with Adam. It was a silly little western. Then he spotted Gaea in a chorus line.

It wasn't Gaea, of course, but an actress who looked very much like her. Chris looked in the end credits to find the long-dead woman's name, but couldn't pick it out.

Not long after that he spotted Gaea again in a film called *All About Eve*. She had a larger part in that one, and he was able to determine that the actress was named Marilyn Monroe. He wondered if she had been famous.

He soon decided she had been, as her films started appearing regularly on Tara Television. Adam took very little notice. *All About Eve* had rated zero on the gigglometer; Adam had hardly glanced at it. *The Asphalt Jungle* didn't fare much better. Neither did *Gentlemen Prefer Blondes*.

Then Chris started to see documentaries about the life and death of Marilyn Monroe. There were an astonishing number of them. Most of them talked about qualities Chris simply could not see. While she might have been one hell of a box-office draw during the twentieth century, when the documentaries were made, few of the films meant much to Chris.

But one thing eventually did. During one of the dull documentaries, Adam looked up from his toys, smiled, pointed at the television screen, and said, "Gay." He looked over to Chris, pointed again, and said, "Gya."

Chris began to be disturbed.

* * *

Gaea never came to Tara.

That is, she never entered it, though the place had been constructed with her monstrous frame in mind. All the doors were wide and high enough for her, and the stairs and second floor were reinforced enough to bear her weight.

But she did pay visits. When she came, she remained far away and Adam was brought to a second-floor balcony. Chris understood the logic of it. Someone so huge might alarm the child. Gaea would get Adam used to her gradually, coming a little closer every day.

When she visited she always had something interesting. One time it was fireworks, which Gaea held in her hand and then hurled up into the air. They were not too loud, but very pretty. Another time it was a herd of trained elephants. She made them jump through hoops and walk tightropes. She slung one uncomfortable-looking beast over her shoulders, then had one balance in the palm of each hand, and lifted them high in the air. Chris was impressed, and Adam giggled the whole time. Gaea kept up a running patter of baby talk, calling Adam by name, telling him she loved him, and mentioning her name as often as possible. And she always brought a marvelous gift.

"Gay, gay, gay," Adam would shout.

"Gay-*ah*," Gaea would call back.

Adam was about fifteen months old now. His vocabulary was expanding. It wasn't long before he could say Gaea.

Marilyn Monroe had made about thirty films. Chris had seen each of them at least once by the time of the dedication of the Universal Gate. He brooded about it as he walked down the stairs from the third floor. More and more often now, Adam would pause in his play to point to the television, laugh, and say the name of his gargantuan granny.

He was about to start down to the ground floor when he was startled by a loud bang, followed quickly by another. It took him a moment to identify the sounds as sonic booms.

He turned and hurried to the second-floor balcony.

Up in the sky were two medium-sized Dragonflys. They were turning, slowing, coming back after their startling pass over New Pandemonium. Chris was vaguely aware of shouting and scurrying on the ground. The planes were far too high for him to tell who was in them, or even how many people.

Cirocco, he thought. My god, Cirocco, you couldn't be that stupid. You can't think it will do any good to bomb this place....

He watched, open-mouthed, as the two planes, moving quite slowly now, went through an intricate series of turns and twists. They seemed to be lining up for something.

His heart almost stopped when both planes began to smoke. What could have happened to them?

One twisted quickly back and forth, while the other made a long, slow curve. Then they stopped smoking. Once more they were barely visible gnats turning around and moving into position again.

And he realized they had written the letters SU.

They curved up and over, and began to smoke again. This time they made two parallel lines, turned sharply, and added crescents to the tops of the lines. PP. SUPP. What the hell?

With precise, tight turns, two more lines were added.

SURR.

"Chris," someone whispered. He almost jumped out of his skin. Then he turned, and very nearly yelled aloud when he found Cirocco standing close enough to touch.

"Cirocco," he whispered, and found himself in her arms, which was a silly way to put it, he thought, since he towered over her. But the strength was all flowing in one direction; he was having a hard time fighting back his tears.

She pulled him back into the shadows within the building.

"Never mind that," she said, quietly, jerking her chin toward the sky. "An amusing diversion . . . with a punch line. Gaea's going to love it, right up to the end."

"What are you—"

"I don't have much time," Cirocco said. "Getting in here isn't easy. Can you listen for a while?"

Chris bit back the thousand questions he wanted to ask, and nodded.

"I wanted to . . ." Cirocco stopped, and looked away for a moment. Chris had time to notice two things. she was close to tears herself, and she was wearing an outlandish costume. He didn't have time to take it all in.

"How is Adam?" she asked.

"He's well."

"Tell me what's happened."

He did, as quickly and concisely as he could. She nodded from time to time, frowned twice, and once looked as if she might be sick. But at the end she nodded.

"It's about the way Gaby told me to expect," she said. "And don't give me any trouble about Gaby."

"I wasn't going to. Spooks don't bother me anymore."

"Good. You understand what you have to do, then?"

"Pretty much. I . . . I don't know if I'll do any good. She is a lot more subtle than I figured her for."

"You can do it," she said, with absolute assurance. "We will do our best to get you out of here. Like I told you last time, his soul isn't in danger yet, and won't be for quite a long time. But, Chris . . . it's going to *be* a long time Do you realize that?"

"I think so. Uh . . . have you any idea how long?"

"It can't be less than a year. It might be two."

He did his best to conceal his dismay, but knew she saw it. She said nothing. He took a deep breath, and tried for a smile.

"Whatever you think is best."

"Chris, it's not just best. It's the *only* way. I can't tell you much about it. If Gaea thought you knew, she could get it from you."

"I understand that. But . . ." He wiped at his forehead, and then looked directly at her. "Cirocco, why don't you just take him right now? Take him, and run like hell?"

"Chris, my old and dear friend, if I could do that, I *would* do it. And leave you to the tender mercies of Gaea . . . and probably die of shame as soon as I had him in a safe place. But I *would*. You know I'll save you if I can—"

"And if you can't, I accept that."

She hugged him again, and kissed his chin, which was as high as she could reach. Chris felt numb, but it felt good to be holding her.

"Gaea is . . . Chris, I don't know how to explain this. But her *will* is focused on Adam. I let him see me the last time I was here. She *knows* I was here, and getting in this time was much harder. I can't visit you again. And if I took Adam and ran, she would get both of us. I *know* that. Can you accept that?"

"I will if I have to."

"That's all I ask. Your job is to stay on good terms with Gaea, however distasteful that might be. And be careful of her. You might find yourself liking her. No, no, don't tell me that's impossible. I liked her at one time. All you can do is be yourself, love Adam, and . . . hell, Chris. Trust me."

"I do, Cirocco."

Her eyes were haunted. She kissed him again . . . and then left him. It was odd, how she left. She moved back into the shadows, into a place where she couldn't have moved away without him seeing her . . . and she was gone.

TEN

"Witch of the South, Witch of the South, this is Witch of the North. The bottom of that last E was pretty ragged, fellow."

Conal spoke into his mike as he sliced through a four-gee turn.

"Tend your own knitting, child," he said. "You got all the easy letters." He pulled back on the stick, looked rapidly to left and right at the vast, flat perspectives of the letters already drawn, and hit the smoke button again. He watched carefully until he was even with the base line, then killed the smoke and turned hard right.

They had practiced it for a week, starting with attempts that Cirocco, from the ground, had sworn looked like Chinese, gradually moving on to writing that was almost legible. By now Conal thought he could fly it in his sleep.

It was crazy, of course, but no more crazy than other things they had been doing. They were living on a new and unfamiliar plane, it seemed. An act, in and of itself, was no longer always enough. The way it was done was also important. Certain things had to be done with deliberation, others with something called panache. The skywriting could have been done letter-perfect, with no drill, simply by programming the maneuvers into the planes' autopilots. But Cirocco had vetoed that.

Conal didn't complain. He *liked* writing challenges in Gaea's clean sky.

"Witch of the North," he called. "You call that an R?"

"I'll stack it up against any R in the sky," Nova shot back.

"Knock it off, children," Robin called, from her vantage point high above. "Move down to the second line."

Cirocco stepped off the golden road just short of the point where it actually became pure gold, and slipped between two towering buildings. She found an alcove out of sight and quickly stripped off her costume.

She had been dressed as an Indian princess when she came through the Columbia gate, and had managed to pass herself off as an extra showing up for work in the horse opera currently shooting on that lot. Getting to Tara had been less a matter of costuming than sheer brass. There was a thing she could do. She didn't know how she did it, and thinking about it too hard could destroy what facility she had, but she thought of it as making herself small. People would glance at her and glance away. She wasn't worth looking at. It had worked long enough to get to Chris. She hadn't needed it much on her way out, as everyone's attention was on the skywriting.

But the exit had to be different, and called for a different brass.

She donned black pants, boots, shirt, and hat, clothing very much like what she had worn during her first meeting with Conal. She tied the short black cape around her neck, tucked a small automatic into the top of her boot and a large revolver into her waistband.

"Maybe I oughta wear a neon sign, too," she muttered to herself. "It couldn't be more incriminating than this get-up."

She stood for a moment, getting her breathing under control. On impulse—the sort of impulse she had learned to trust—she opened the top three buttons of her shirt and thrust her chest out. That would give them something to concentrate on other than her too-recognizable face. Then she stepped out onto the pavement and strode confidently up to the guard at the MGM Gate.

She had to nudge him with her elbow. He was staring up at the air show.

"What does S-U-R-R-E..." he began.

"Why do they have an illiterate on this gate?" Cirocco snarled. The man stood straight and jerked his clipboard protectively over his chest. She held out an empty, black-gloved hand.

"I'm the first vice-president for procurement," she said. "This is my identification. Gaea has ordered me to de-fusticate the thing-amabob *at once*." She thrust the non-existent identity card into a breast pocket, and the man's eyes followed the hand as far as the pocket, and then stuck. He gaped at her cleavage, and nodded.

"What did you say?"

"Uh ... go ahead, *sir!*"

"What about security? What about the record you're supposed to be keeping of who enters and exits through this gate? All the hounds of hell could come baying through here and you'd give them dog biscuits. *Aren't you going to ask me my name?*"

"Uh ... w-w-w-what is your n-n-name ... sir?"

"Guinness." She peered over the man's shoulder as he wrote on the clipboard. "Be sure to get that right, now. G-U-I-N-N-E-S-S. Alec Guinness. Gaea will want to know."

Cirocco turned on her heel and marched out the gate and over the drawbridge, glancing neither right nor left.

It was fifteen minutes before the man returned to full awareness. By then Cirocco was a hundred miles away.

Gaea had it figured out from the first SU.

She stood there at the Universal Gate, her huge feet planted firmly on more gold than Fort Knox ever had, her hands on her hips, and she smiled.

SURR.

SURREN.

She started to laugh. By that time some of the others, who had also seen a lot of films—more than they cared to remember, in many cases—were also getting it. It had been a nervous couple of minutes for most of them. Eyes moved constantly from Gaea's face to the writing in the sky. Then, when Gaea laughed, it was a signal for a massive eruption of laughter. The human population roared anew as each letter appeared, and each letter redoubled Gaea's own laughter.

By the time the message was complete the initial S was almost illegible. But it didn't spoil the fun.

SURRENDER GAEA.

"We must go see the Wizard!" Gaea howled. "He'll know what to do!"

The laughter got louder.

It's time for a festival, Gaea thought. Jones must be desperate to do a silly thing like that. Didn't she know it was the Wicked Witch of the *West* who did the skywriting? Didn't *wicked* mean anything to her? There were rules in this combat, and symbols were all-important.

Her mountainous laughter had dwindled to random chuckles. The letters were diffusing now, falling as a fine mist. The two planes were joined by a third which Gaea had been aware of all along. Most likely Cirocco herself had been up there, safely out of range, watching while her minions did the dirty and dangerous work. This contest wasn't even going to be worth it, she thought.

Oddly, that thought depressed her.

She shrugged it off. The three planes were flying lower now, in echelon, circumscribing the huge circle of New Pandemonium. They were still emitting smoke.

A fantasy film festival, she thought. What titles haven't been shown lately? Well, let's see, there was that...

She stopped, and looked up suspiciously.

"No!" she shouted, and began to run. "No, you bitch! I didn't *budget* for that!"

She stepped on a dead zombie, slipped, and very nearly fell. She saw another zombie keel over.

Within two minutes, every zombie in Pandemonium was dead.

"All you need is love," Robin said, then whistled it, then sang it.

"What's that?" she heard Conal say over the radio.

"Just a song we witches sing." She whistled it again as she banked her plane one last time over the strange scene below.

"*Mo*ther," Nova said, exasperated.

"My dear, it's time you stopped being embarrassed about the origin of our zombie-killer. Don't you think?"

"Yes, Mother." She heard Nova's radio click off.

"Turn left on my signal," Conal said. "That's the MGM Gate below. The one with the big stone lion on it."

"Roger," Robin said, still humming. She looked down once more at New Pandemonium.

Cirocco had described the place, so they had known the layout before they arrived. But seeing it was something else entirely. Robin had jittered during the whole crazy performance, circling high, her more powerful radar and heavy armaments ready for buzz bombs, a dozen contingency plans tumbling over each other in her mind—plans drilled into all of them mercilessly by General Jones.

She grinned, then laughed. It appealed to the practical jokester in her.

"What do you think Gaea will say?" she asked the others. "I wonder if she's figured out that we just dumped three tons of love potion on her?"

"Is that Robin of the Coven?" said a voice.

There was a moment of silence but for the high whine of the jet.

"Robin, what are you doing cluttering up my airwaves?"

"Jesus," Conal breathed. "Is that—"

"South Witch, remember your radio rules. I think we should—"

"I know it's Conal, my love," Gaea said. "And I know it's your dear daughter, Nova, in the other plane. What I don't understand is all this talk about a love potion."

Robin flew on in silence. The palms of her hands were moist.

"Ah, well," Gaea sighed. "You're going to be tiresome, I see. But there's no need to execute Plan X-98, or whatever you were about to say. I'm not sending anyone after you. No buzz bombs will hinder your flight back to Dione." There was a pause again. "I'm curious, though. Why didn't Cirocco Jones come along on this little escapade? Perhaps she didn't have the spine for it. She *does* have a knack for letting others fight her battles. Have you noticed that? How did you like her dramatic flying entrance back at the Junction, as my friends were rescuing your darling son from that awful place you'd taken him? Plenty of time for you all to see her heroic effort . . . which, sad to say, fell just short of actually having to *grapple* with the poor zombie. I wonder where she was? Did you ask her where she came from?"

Robin looked right and left, made hand signals to Nova and Conal to say nothing, and saw them both nod.

"Rather a dull conversation so far, I'd say," Gaea went on. "I just wanted to ask you how things have been. It's been a long time since last we met. I'd sort of hoped you would drop by when I saw you arrive."

"Just couldn't seem to find the time, I guess," Robin said.

"Ah, that's *much* better. You really should make the time. Chris has been asking about you."

Robin had to bite her lower lip. There was nothing worth saying. She couldn't treat it as a game for very long.

"Tell me," Gaea said, after a thoughtful pause. "Have you heard of the Geneva Conventions concerning warfare?"

"Vaguely," Robin said.

"Did you know it is considered immoral to use poisonous gases? I ask, because I'm sure Cirocco has filled your head with a lot of nonsense about good guys and bad guys. As if there were such a thing. But even if it were true, ask yourself this. Do good guys break the international rules of war?"

Robin frowned for a moment, then shook her head, and wondered if it might actually be dangerous to listen to Gaea. Could she cast some enchantment over the radio, cause the three of them to do crazy things?

But Cirocco had not mentioned it.

"You're a silly old biddy, Gaea," she said.

"Sticks and stones—"

"—wouldn't even put a dent in that ugly hide of yours. But words wound you to the core. Cirocco told me that. As to gas warfare, have you checked your human population? Have you looked in on the elephants and camels and horses?"

"They seem to be all right," Gaea admitted, dubiously.

"So there you are. Don't take it personally, Gaea, you old bitch. We found a way to exterminate a pest we used to call death-snakes. We're doing it as a public service. Pandemonium just happened to be on the spraying program. Hope it didn't inconvenience you too much."

"Not too . . . *used* to call them? What do you call them now?"

Hah! Walked right into that one, you abomination.

"We call them Gaea's tapeworms. I hope you have a large toilet."

Robin heard Nova laughing. That seemed to finally set Gaea

off. It started as an incoherent scream. Robin had to turn the volume down. It went on for an amazing time, then turned into a stream of vile language, horrible threats, and nearly incoherent ranting. During a brief pause, Nova spoke.

"That's really something," she said. "Maybe, when this is over, we can put her in a carnival sideshow."

"No," Conal said. "Nobody'd pay. Everybody's seen shit."

There was a short silence.

"Young man," Gaea said icily, "one day I will make you wish you had never been born. Nova, that was unkind, to say the least. But I suppose I can understand it. It must be hard for you. Tell me, how do you feel about that horrible fellow screwing your mother?"

There was an entirely different quality to the silence this time. Robin felt her stomach lurch.

"Mother, what—"

"Nova, maintain radio silence. And remember what I told you about propaganda. Gaea, this conversation is over."

But it didn't feel like having the last word. Propaganda was a fine term, but that didn't mean she was going to be able to lie any longer to Nova.

Gaea put down her radio and watched the planes vanish in the west, feeling thoroughly sour.

Though the logical and emotional parts of her mind no longer functioned as they used to—a fact she recognized and no longer worried about—the purely computational power was undiminished. She knew how many zombies had been lost. Some forty percent of the Pandemonium work force were undead—now doubly dead. That was bad enough, but a zombie was worth five human workers, maybe six. They were stronger, and they needed no sleep or even rest breaks. They could be fed garbage a hog would choke to look at. While they couldn't run something as complex as a tape recorder, they made excellent plumbers, electricians, painters, grips, carpenters . . . all the skilled trades so essential to the making of movies. With reasonable care they could be made to last six or seven kilorevs. They were economical even in death; when a zombie felt the final death approaching, its last act was to dig a grave and lie down in it.

Problems, problems. . . .

The unions of carpenters, used for her mobile festival, had

proven not versatile enough for the demands of New Pandemonium
Some of the buildings thrown up by them were already falling down
She could try to develop a master variety of carpenter...but knew
uneasily that her skills as a genetic manipulator were deteriorating
She could hope that, instead of more camels or dragons, her nex
birthing would be something more useful, and self-perpetuating, bu
she knew she couldn't count on it.

Such were the perils of being mortal. For mortal she was. Nc
just in the sense that, in a hundred thousand years, the giant whee
known as Gaea would wither and die, but in the giant Monroe-clon
in which she had elected to put so much of her vital force.

She sighed, then brightened a bit. Good cinema sprang fror
adversity, not an uninterrupted series of successes. She would spea
with the story department, incorporate this new setback in the vas
epic of her life, twenty years in the making. The final reels were b
no means in sight.

In the meantime, there must be a solution.

Once more she thought of Titanides. Hyperion was lousy wit
Titanides.

"Titanides!" Gaea shouted, startling all those within half
kilometer.

Titanides had to be her most recalcitrant invention. They ha
seemed a good idea at the time. They were still nice to look at. Sh
had made them in the early 1900's as a sort of first-draft human. I
turned out she had built better than she knew. They kept exceedin
specifications.

When labor had started to be a problem during the early day
of site preparation for the Studio, she had naturally thought of usin
Titanides. She sent Iron Masters out hiring—and they came bac
empty-handed. It was disconcerting. Didn't they know she was *God*

They were hard to capture alive, but she had caught a few.

Who wouldn't do a lick of work. Torture didn't help. As man
as were able committed suicide. As far as Gaea knew, there ha
never been a Titanide suicide before the construction of the Studio
They loved life too much.

She had asked one captive about it.

"We'd rather die than be enslaved," he had said.

A fine sentiment, Gaea supposed, but not one she had buil

into them. Damn it, humans took to slavery like ducks to water. Why couldn't Titanides?

All right, all right, Gaea was nothing if not flexible. If they wouldn't work alive, she'd make them work dead. A zombie Titanide ought to handle the work of a hundred humans.

But it didn't work out that way. The Titanide corpses that went zombie were weaker than the originals, badly coordinated, and tended to sag in the middle like a swaybacked horse. She did an engineering study and found it was the skeletal structure that was at fault. Taxonomically speaking, Titanides were not vertebrates. They had a cartilaginous spine that was much more flexible and much stronger than the rather precarious stacks that formed the backbones of humans and angels. The problem was that, in death, the cartilage rotted, and the deathsnakes ate it. So the Titanides cheated her even from beyond the grave.

Gaea would have thought it was a stinking world, had she not remembered that she had created it.

What better time for the messenger to arrive from the MGM Gate, hand her the clipboard, and kneel, quivering, knowing Gaea's usual reaction to bad news.

For once, the reaction was moderate. Gaea looked at the name on the clipboard, sighed, and scaled it negligently over the roofs of three soundstages.

She had been out-movied. Twice in one day, Cirocco Jones had used her favorite mythologies against her.

"I've been Ozzed, and Star-Warred," she muttered.

She needed a break. How about a new festival? she wondered. Movies about movies. That sounded nice. She looked around for her archivist, and saw him cowering behind the corner of a building. She beckoned.

"I'm going to Projection Room One," she told him. "Get me Truffaut's *Day For Night* to start off with."

He scribbled on a note pad.

"*Auteurs*," she muttered. "Pick out a couple films by Hitchcock. Any of them will do. *The Stunt Man*. And . . . what's that one about the collapse of the studio system?"

"*Lights, Camera, Auction!*" the archivist said.

"That's it. Be ready in ten minutes."

Gaea trudged down the golden road, more depressed than she had been in centuries. Jones had done a good job this day.

Part of her mind remained on the labor problem. She would just divert more refugees from Bellinzona. The terrible thing was, she was going to have to practically *coddle* her human labor from now on, because when they died, they were just gonna stay dead. Hell of a note.

And she wondered if she could pick up the slack from Bellinzona. The mercy flights to Earth were still going on, but the ships were coming back with a lot of empty seats.

She almost wished she hadn't started the War.

ELEVEN

The origins of the City of Bellinzona were, as so many other things in the wide wheel, mysterious.

The first human explorers to enter Dione had reported a large, empty city made of wood. It stood on sturdy pilings sunk deep in the rock below the waterline, and had freshly carved streets that wound up into the rocky hills on each side of Peppermint Bay. To the south were relatively flat lands, rising to a pass that led to an encircling forest. Dangerous creatures lived in that forest, but they were not as bad as the quicksands, fevers, and poisonous and carnivorous plants. It did not seem like a place where anyone would want to live.

Cirocco Jones had been there long before the "explorers." She simply never bothered to tell anyone about the ghost city which had appeared sometime during the fiftieth year of her Wizardship. She had been as puzzled by it as anyone else. It didn't seem to have any use.

But it was built to human scale. There were large buildings and small. The doorways were rather high, but Titanides usually had to duck to get through them.

After the start of the War and the beginnings of the stream of refugees, Cirocco had briefly cherished the notion that Gaea had simply caused a safe haven to be built, knowing that war would engulf the Earth sooner or later. But Gaea's influence in Dione was minimal, and her humanitarian impulses nonexistent. *Somebody* had built the core of Bellinzona, and built it rather well. Gaea's contribution had been simply to provide the populace.

Cirocco suspected it had been the gremlins. She had no evidence of this. There was no "gremlin style" of architecture. The creatures had put up structures as varied as the Glass Castle and Pharoah Mountain. She often wished she could contact them and ask them a few questions. But not even Titanides had ever seen a gremlin.

Humans had added to the central city in a haphazard and jerry-built fashion. The new piers usually rested on pontoons, and of course there were the jostling flotillas of boats. But despite neglect and misuse, some of the larger buildings of Bellinzona were quite impressive.

Cirocco had to raise an army to fight Gaea. Bellinzona was the only place able to provide that many people, but a rabble would not do for her purposes. She needed discipline, and to get it, she knew she had to civilize the place, to clean it up—and to utterly dominate it.

She chose a big, ornate, warehouse-sized structure on the Slough of Despond. The building was called the Loop by its tenant, a man by the name of Maleski, who came from Chicago. Cirocco had learned quite a bit about Maleski, who was one of the top four or five gang leaders in Bellinzona. It had the flavor of the unreal, but she decided it was just one of those odd things. She was going to go up against a real live gangster from Chicago.

When Cirocco and the five black-clad Titanides entered the building, almost everyone was clustered at the other end, looking out the windows there, staring up at the sky. That was not a coincidence. Cirocco stood there in the middle of the big room in the light of flickering torches, and waited to be noticed.

It did not take long. Surprise changed to consternation. No one was supposed to be able to just walk in to the Loop. It was heavily guarded on the outside. Maleski didn't know it yet, but all those guards were dead.

The ones in the room drew their swords and began to disperse around the walls. Some of them grabbed torches. A tight group of nine made a human shield around Maleski. For a moment, no one moved.

"I've heard of you," Maleski said, finally. "Aren't you Cirocco Jones?"

"Mayor Jones," Cirocco said.

"Mayor Jones," Maleski repeated. He moved forward, out of the group. His eyes went to the gun thrust in the waistband of her black pants, but it didn't seem to worry him. "That's news to me. Some of your people had a run-in with some of my boys a while back. Is this about that?"

"No. I'm taking over this building. I'm declaring a ten-hour amnesty. You're going to need every minute of it, so you'd better go now. All the rest of you, you're free to go as well. You have five minutes to take what you can carry."

For a moment they all seemed too bewildered to say anything. Maleski frowned, then laughed.

"The hell you say. This building is private property."

This time Cirocco laughed.

"Just what planet do you think you're living on, you idiot? Hornpipe, shoot this guy in the knee."

The gun had materialized in Hornpipe's hand when Cirocco said "shoot," and by the time she said "knee" the bullet was already coming out the other side of Maleski's leg.

As Maleski fell, and for a few seconds after he hit the floor, there was a flurry of noise and activity. None of the men who survived it were ever able to recount a sequence of events, except to note that a lot of men stepped forward and neat holes appeared perfectly centered in their foreheads and they fell down and did not move. The rest, some twenty men, stood very, very still, except for Maleski, who was howling and thrashing and ordering his men to kill the goddamn sons of bitches. But each Titanide held a gun in each hand, and most of the men were getting excellent views down the wide barrels. Finally Maleski stopped cursing and just lay there, breathing hard.

"Okay," he finally managed to croak. "Okay, you win. We'll get out." He rolled over heavily.

He was really quite good. The knife was concealed in his sleeve. He got it out as he rolled over, and his arm flicked it with the precision of long practice. It flashed in the air ... and Cirocco reached out and caught it. She just grabbed it, holding it with the point about six inches from her throat, where it was supposed to have been buried. Maleski stared as she flipped it up and got a new grip, and then it flashed again and he screamed as it buried itself up to the hilt in the torn flesh that had been his knee. A man standing to Maleski's left crumpled to the floor in a dead faint.

"Rocky," Cirocco said, "tie a tourniquet around his thigh. Then throw him out. You men, drop your weapons where you stand and walk slowly away from them. *All* your weapons. Then strip. Carry one pair of trousers to the door and hand them to Valiha—the yellow Titanide. If she finds a weapon in them she will break your neck. Otherwise, you can put them on and leave. You have four minutes left."

It didn't even take one minute. They were all feverishly anxious to leave, and no one tried to cheat.

"Tell your friends what happened here," she called to them, as her own people started arriving.

There were humans and Titanides in her crew. The Titanides were all calm, well-versed in their jobs. Most of the humans were nervous, having been drafted only hours before. There were Free Females among them, and Vigilantes, and others from other communities.

A desk was set up, and Cirocco took her place behind it as the lights were being arranged. She was suffering some reaction, both from the fight and from what she had done to Maleski—and from the close call. She felt she could do that knife trick six times out of ten, but that wasn't nearly enough. She couldn't let it get that close again.

But most of her nervousness was stage fright. Apparently, it wasn't something one could outgrow. She had suffered from it since childhood.

Two men from the Vigilantes who had worked in mass communications before the War were setting up cables and a tripod and a small camera. The lights came blazing on, and Cirocco blinked. A microphone was set before her.

"All this stuff must be a century old," one of the technicians grumbled.

"Just make it work for an hour," Cirocco told him. He didn't seem to be listening, but was studying her face from several angles. He reached out tentatively toward her forehead, and she backed away, alarmed.

"You really should have something there," he said. "There's a bad glare."

"Have *what* there?"

"Make-up."

"Is that really necessary?"

"Ms. Jones, you said you wanted a media consultant. I'm just telling you how I'd do this if I were running the show."

Cirocco sighed, and nodded. One of the Titanides had some cream that the man seemed satisfied with. He smeared her face with the greasy stuff.

"Picture's pretty good," the other man announced. "I don't know how long this tube will last, though."

"Then we'd best get to it," said the director. He picked up the mike and spoke into it. "Citizens of Bellinzona," he said, and was drowned out by a high feedback whine. The other man adjusted some knobs, and the man spoke again. This time it was clear. Cirocco could hear the words echoing off the hills outside.

"Citizens of Bellinzona," the director said again. "We have an important announcement from Cirocco Jones, the new Mayor of Bellinzona."

A Free Female was at the window, looking up.

"The picture's there!" she shouted.

Cirocco cleared her throat nervously, fought an impulse to smile brightly that *had* to have come from her NASA press conference days, a million years ago, and spoke.

"Citizens of Bellinzona. My name is Cirocco Jones. Many of you have heard of me; I was one of the first humans in Gaea, and for a time I was designated by Gaea to be her Wizard. Twenty years ago, I was fired from that job.

"It is important that you understand that, while Gaea fired me, the Titanides never accepted it. Every one of them will follow my orders. I have never taken full advantage of this fact. I am doing so now, and the results will change all your lives.

"As of this moment, you are all, as I said, 'Citizens of Bellinzona.' You'll be wondering what that entails. Essentially, it means you'll all take my orders. I have plans for democracy later, but as of now, you'd better do what I tell you.

"There are now some thousands of Titanides in your city. Each of them has been briefed on the new rules. Think of them as police. To underestimate their strength or their quickness would be a bad mistake.

"Since you are going to be living by rules, I'll give you some now. More will follow, after we have this thing going.

"Murder is not going to be tolerated.

"Slavery is prohibited. All human beings now in a state of slavery are freed. All humans who believe they own other humans had better free them at once. This includes any practice which may, through custom, deprive any other human of liberty. If you're in doubt—if, for instance, you are muslim and believe you own your wife—you had better ask a Titanide. There is a ten-hour amnesty for this purpose.

"Human meat will no longer be sold. Any human consorting with an Iron Master will be shot on sight.

"There is no private property. You may continue to sleep where you have been sleeping, but do not think you own anything but the clothes you wear.

"There shall be no edged weapons allowed in human hands for at least four decarevs. Surrender those weapons to any Titanide during the amnesty. As quickly as possible, I shall be returning the police function to humans. In the meantime, possession of a sword or a knife is a capital offense. I recognize the hardship this will pose to you who use knives for other purposes, but, I emphasize, you will be shot dead if you keep your knives.

"I . . . have little good to offer you in the short term. I believe that in the long term, most of you will appreciate what I am doing today. Only the exploiters, the slavers, the killers, will never regain their present positions. The rest of you will reap security and the benefits of an organized human society.

"I demand to see the following persons at the building known as the Loop within ten hours. Any who do not come will be shot in the eleventh hour."

Cirocco read a list of twenty-five names, compiled with Conal's help, of the most influential mafia, tong, and gang leaders.

When she had finished, she read the statement in French, and once more in her halting Russian. Then she relinquished her chair to a woman from the Free Females who read it in Chinese. There were a dozen other translators waiting, human and Titanide. Cirocco hoped to reach every new citizen of Bellinzona.

She felt drained when she was finally able to sit by herself. She had worked on the speech endlessly, it seemed, and was never able to make it sound good. It seemed to her there ought to be ringing declarations in there someplace. Life, liberty, and the Purfoot of Happinefs, maybe. But after a lot of thought, she realized there wasn't anything she believed in as a capital R "Right." Could any mortal claim a Right to Life?

So she had fallen back on pragmatism. It had served her fairly well through a long and pragmatic life. "This is the way it is, you poor silly suckers. Get in my way and you will be obliterated."

Even starting from the best of motives, that didn't taste so good in her mouth—and she was far from sure of her motives.

Life in Bellinzona was not what you could call dull. Violent death was all around and could happen at a moment's notice. For the well-connected, it was at best comfortable, and at worst nervous. One never knew when a particular Boss would be defeated and all one's careful preparations for the soft life come to nothing. Still, it was better than being down in the faceless masses. For them, Bellinzona was a special kind of hell. Not only were they constantly in peril of enslavement . . . most of them had nothing to do.

There were always the needs of survival, of course. That kept people busy. But it was not like having a job. It was not like farming one's own fields—or even the fields of a landlord. In most neighborhoods people owed allegiance to a Boss, a Shogun, a Landlord, a Capo . . . some local Mr. Big. For a woman it was even worse, unless she happened to have been taken in by the Free Females. Female slavery was rampant. It was more than the labor-slavery experienced by the men. It was old-fashioned sexual slavery. Women were bought and sold ten times as frequently as men.

And at the end of one's usefulness, there was the butcher's block.

Actually, there was relatively little killing for food. It happened, but with the manna and the bosses that sort of thing was fairly well under control. Still, with the meat shortage many of the corpses destined for the communal pyre were diverted to the hook, the knife, and the skillet.

Boredom was a big problem. It bred crime—senseless, random crime—as if Bellinzona needed any more reasons for violence.

It would be fair to say Bellinzona was ripe for a change. Any change.

So when the blimp drifted over the city, things ground to a halt.

Bellinzonans had seen blimps, from afar. They knew they were large. Many had no idea they were intelligent. Most knew the blimps never came near the city because of all the fires.

Whistlestop apparently didn't care. He mooched up to the city as if he did it every day, and spread his gargantuan shadow from the Slough of Despond clear out to the Terminal Wharves. He was almost as big as Peppermint Bay itself. Then he just hung there, by far the largest object anyone in town had ever seen. His titanic hind fins moved languidly, just enough to keep him positioned over the center of town.

That in itself would have been enough to stop traffic. Then a face appeared on his side, and began to say the most amazing things.

TWELVE

Twenty revs after usurping power, Cirocco was wishing she had left Bellinzona alone. She had anticipated the squabbles, but it didn't alter the fact that squabbles bored her. She sighed, and kept listening. It was best, at this point, if those she hoped would be her allies accepted the fact without the sort of demonstration that had been so useful with Maleski.

More demonstrations had been needed, but she had expected that. Of the twenty-five she had named, eighteen were now dead. Seven had come in, weaponless, to pledge their fealty to the new Boss. She knew damn well she couldn't trust any of them with a brass paper clip, but it was best to let them sink themselves through their own greed, let them hatch their conspiracies and hang them with due process of law. One could be perceived as fair, even when the fix was in.

So, in that sense, the bad guys were no problem. As usual, it was the good guys who gave endless headaches.

"We cannot and *will not* give up our separate enclave," Trini said. "You haven't been around here much, Cirocco. You don't know how it was. You can't understand how bad it was—and is!—for a woman to try to live in Bellinzona. Some of our women were subjected to...oh, Cirocco, it would make you *weep!* Rape was the *least* of it. We have to remain separate."

"And we won't give up our weapons," Stuart said. Stuart was the man who had come in response to Cirocco's demand for a representative of the Vigilantes, just as Trini had come as an elder of the Free Females. "You talked about law and order. For seven years, we've been just about the only group that has tried to maintain a degree of decency for *all* humans in Gaea"—and here he glared at Trini, who glared back. "We have been and remain willing to protect even those who don't belong to our organization, subject only to the availability of manpower and weapons. I won't claim we've made the streets safe. But our aim has been decency."

Cirocco looked from one to the other. Oddly, both of them had summed up their respective positions in two minutes. It was likely that neither of them remembered they had been arguing and embellishing for ten hours without saying a hell of a lot more than they had just said.

At any rate, they shut up for a moment, and looked anxiously at Cirocco.

"I like you both," Cirocco said, quietly. "It would bother me a lot to have either of you killed."

Neither of them flinched, but their eyes looked a little hollow.

"Stuart, you and I both know my weapons policy couldn't last long. I have been given one very large break, and I intend to use it for all it's worth. *I* control all the ammunition in Bellinzona. There are plenty of guns around. I intend to round them up, with house-to-house searches, if necessary. Making useful guns is beyond Bellinzona's industrial capacity, and will be for quite a while. But you can and will make knives, more swords, and bows and arrows and blackjacks...and so forth."

"I'm going to use this short time when *everybody* is disarmed to...to give the people a chance to breathe freely. There's going to be a *lot* of killing in the next few days, but it's going to be Titanides killing humans. If a human kills another human, execution will be swift and public. I want people to *see* that. My goal here is to get a social compact going, and I'm starting practically from zero. My advantages are superior force, and the knowledge that most of these people came from lawful societies before the war. They'll soon remember the ways of getting along."

"You're trying to make a paradise, is that it?" Stuart sneered.

"By no means. I have few illusions about what's going to happen here. It will be brutal and unfair. But it's *already* better than it was twenty revs ago."

"I felt *safe* twenty revs ago," Trini said.

"That's because you lived in a walled camp. I don't blame you; I'd have done the same thing, in your positions. But I have to tear down the walls. And I can't have a lot of sword-toting Vigilantes swaggering around until I know more about them." She turned to Trini.

"I have a couple things to offer you. After the disarmament, I'm going to have a period of time—possibly as long as a myriarev—during which only the police will be allowed to carry swords and clubs. And only women will be allowed to carry knives."

"That's not fair!" Stuart shouted.

"You're damn right it's not fair," Cirocco went on. "It also isn't fair that most of the women who arrived here after the war were knocked out and dragged away by some large hairy item and sold at public auction."

Trini was looking interested, but still dubious.

"Some women will die," Trini pointed out. "Most of them don't know how to handle a knife."

"Some women died yesterday because they didn't have one," Cirocco replied.

She was still looking dubious. Cirocco turned to Stuart.

"As for your Vigilantes...we are going to be needing human police after this initial period. I intend to give preference to the Vigilantes."

"Armed with sticks?" he asked.

"Don't underestimate the billy club."

"So my people will be going up to guys and searching them, right? What happens when the guy pulls a knife?"

"It depends on how good your man is. He may very well die."

She let them think it over again. It was a great temptation to come right out and say it: you don't have any choice. But they knew that. It would be better if they found a way to like it, or at least part of it.

"So there will be laws, and courts?" Stuart asked.

"Not just yet. I've already sketched out laws about slavery and killing. For now, they'll be enforced at the scene of the crime with Titanides acting as judges. Pretty soon we'll elaborate the laws and go through the formality of arrest and some sort of trial."

"I'd feel better with some laws and courts right now," Trini said.

Cirocco just looked at her. She did not mention that there was an even more brutal alternative which she had considered for some time—and had not totally ruled out even yet. She called it the Conal Solution. The Titanides could make judgment calls that Cirocco trusted utterly. If they said this or that human ought to be killed, she knew they were right. There was no denying it would make things quicker and easier.

She didn't even know if it was wrong. Cirocco believed in good and evil, but right and wrong were something else entirely. Trini craved the sanction of law because that's what she had grown up with. Cirocco had, too, and believed it was ultimately necessary if humans were to live together. But she didn't worship it. She had no doubt that a Titanide's innate knack of smelling out evil in humans was better than the judgment of, for instance, a jury of twelve humans.

But it didn't feel right. So she had elected the more arduous course.

"We'll have laws and courts eventually," Cirocco said. "We'll probably have lawyers, too, in time. But that's all up to you."

Trini and Stuart looked at each other.

"You mean the two of us?" Stuart asked. "Or all the citizens?"

"That'll be up to you, too. If you can get along with me for a while, you'll be in an excellent position to take over government when I leave."

"Leave?" Trini said. "When would that be?"

"As soon as I can. I'm not doing this because I want to. I'm doing it because I'm the only one who *can* do it, and . . . for reasons that don't concern you now. I've never had any urge to govern. I expect it's going to be a huge headache."

Stuart was looking more and more thoughtful. Cirocco thought her original assessment of the man was correct. He had the hunger for power. She wondered how high he had gotten in government before the war. She had no doubt he had been in government, though she had not asked him.

Trini had the same impulse, though in a different form. Cirocco had known Trini for twenty years. It was only in the last seven that Trini's hidden perversion had surfaced. All things considered, she had done rather well with it. She had been a founding mother and guiding force behind the Free Females. She was basically a good person. Cirocco didn't need a Titanide to tell her that.

So was Stuart. Cirocco didn't really *like* either of them. She felt that the urge to lead large groups of people was basically not very nice, but knew such people had to exist. She could deal with them when she had to.

"What sort of government did you envision?" Stuart asked, cautiously. "You abolished private property. Are you a communist?"

"I am, temporarily, an absolute dictator. I'm doing the things I believe need to be done, in an order I have worked out very carefully. I abolished private property because Bellinzona is a found object. The most powerful people live in the biggest buildings. The poorest don't even have clothes. That came about because there was no law here when they arrived. The solution I came up with was, first, to abolish slavery, and, second, to wipe out all the outsized gains the more ruthless citizens made simply because they were sons of bitches. Here's one of the headaches I mentioned. As of now, I *own* the city of Bellinzona. But I don't want or need it. I intend to return the buildings, rooms, and boats to the people . . . and I want to do it fairly. A lot of these people have worked hard. They built boats, for instance. I just stole them all. One of the things I hope you two will help me do is set up some sort of mechanism for sorting out claims to personal property and real estate and dwellings. So, yes, I'm sort of communist right now. But I expect that will change."

"Why not let the State keep everything?" Trini asked.

"Again, that will be up to you. I'd advise against it. I think you'll be more popular and sleep easier if you try to be fairer than that. But that may just be my own prejudice. I'll admit to a bias toward private property and democracy. It's the way I grew up. But I know there are other theories."

She again watched Stuart and Trini study each other. These two were going to be interesting, she decided.

"For now," she went on, "I need answers. Can you work with me, knowing my decisions are absolute?"

"If they're absolute, why do you need us?"

"For advice in making them. For criticism when you think I made a bad one. But don't think you'll have a vote."

"Do we really have a choice?" Trini asked.

"Yes. I'm not going to kill you. If you refuse, I'll send you home and get another Free Female, and keep doing that until I find one who'll work with me in getting the Free Females back into society. Somebody will, you know."

"Yes, I do know. It might as well be me."

Stuart looked up.

"Me? Sure. I'll start right now by telling you it's a bad mistake to have Titanides killing humans. It's going to foster race prejudice."

"That's a chance I'm willing to take. The Titanides can defend themselves. If anybody's in danger here, it's the *human* race, not the Titanides. If things can't be worked out peacefully in the end, they will simply kill every one of you, man, woman, and child."

Stuart looked startled, then thoughtful. Cirocco was not surprised. Even seven years of Bellinzona had not eroded the man's anthropocentric conviction that humans would eventually triumph over all other species, just as they had done on Earth. He had just now entertained the notion it might not be so. He didn't like it.

There were going to be plenty of things he didn't like.

THIRTEEN

Rocky didn't like police duty. He wasn't alone in this; none of the Titanides cared for it. But the Captain had promised them most solemnly that this was the way to get the Child back, so he patrolled diligently.

It had been an interesting time.

On the first day he had participated in a raid on a Boss's headquarters that had left three hundred dead, including one Titanide who had taken an arrow through the head. Rocky himself had received an arrow wound, not serious but painful, in the left hindquarter. He was still favoring that leg.

That had not been the worst raid. One Boss had held out for almost a hundred revs. The Titanides besieged the building and built fires all around it to make the interior as unpleasant as possible. At the end, the Boss's troops had thrown the man's head out the front door and surrendered. Three Titanides had died in that action.

Altogether, Rocky knew of a dozen Titanide deaths. The human deaths were in the thousands, but most of them had come in the first forty revs, with another brief spurt when the disarmament policy went into effect. Now all the gangs were dispersed. Humans eyed Rocky with suspicion and fear, but no one had taken any action against him in quite a while.

So he strolled his beat, his sheathed sword tapping against his left foreleg, and looked for trouble, hoping not to find any. From time to time he passed a human of the kind Cirocco called crazy, but who Rocky thought of as having worms in the head. *All* humans were crazy, it was well-known, but with most of them it was a glorious thing. A minority were something else. The English word for it was psychopath, but the word held no flavor for Rocky. They were the ones he knew should be killed on the spot, as the only question about them was not *if* they would have to be killed, but *when*.

287

But the Captain had said no one was to be killed unless caught "red-handed," to use her phrase, in a capital offense.

Actually, by now that was fine with Rocky. He had seen enough killing. Let the humans kill their own mistakes.

Rocky preferred to think of more pleasant things. He smiled, startling a human woman who, after a brief hesitation, smiled back. Rocky tipped his ridiculous hat in her direction, then scratched under his shirt. Clothes bothered the hell out of him. Sometimes even the Captain had to be humored in her craziness. Wear the uniforms, she said, so Rocky did, and scratched all the time.

He heard the vague, dark thoughts of Tambura in his mind, and smiled again.

Tambura was his daughter. She wasn't very old yet. Valiha had kept the semi-fertilized egg for a while, waiting for a good time to approach the Wizard. Cirocco had given her permission, and a decarev before the invasion of Bellinzona Serpent had quickened the egg in Rocky's womb. And there she nestled in her third decarev of life. She was just a microscopic smudge of dividing cells now, with a brain the size of a walnut—a brain that had once been Valiha's egg. Within the crystalline egg structure were molecular lattices organized quite differently from those of the human brain. The ability to sing was already programmed in. Many things Valiha had learned in her life were stored in there, too, including all of the English language. There were memories of Valiha's life, and of all her foremothers stretching back to the foremother of the Madrigal Chord, Violone. To a lesser extent, the forefathers and hindfathers were represented, in the only form of immortality that mattered to a Titanide.

Rocky tried not to be chauvinistic, but it seemed a more compassionate system than the mad brawl of human genetics. Humans evolved through horror and maladaption, through the cold mercilessness of chance, through endless defectives who, through no fault of their own, came squalling into the world with no chance of survival. At the best of times a human was a series of compromises between dominant and recessive genes. And the only programming in their infant brains, it seemed, was left over from ravenous animals who had lived in trees before Gaea began to spin.

This all explained, to Rocky, the cancer that was Bellinzona.

Titanides got a hard, basic, and practical education from their foremothers while they were still eggs, long before there was any awareness. The machine-like structures in the developing egg filtered the frontal semen for information and traits that would be useful, ran test simulations, rejected those that could not work, and then hardened into a potential. The egg did not take DNA helter-skelter, the good with the bad, but tore it apart, evaluated it, and used the bits that would be sensible.

If the embryonic Titanide got all things practical and much historical from the foremother, it got everything else from the hindmother. Rocky wondered if he wasn't prejudiced—being hind-pregnant himself—but it seemed to him this was the most important part.

Tambura was alive and aware and in communication with Rocky at all times. It was not verbal—though Tambura had words—nor was it musical—though Tambura spent much time singing the strange songs of the womb. As her outer brain grew into something quite similar to a human brain, but with a cybernetic egg at its core, Rocky filled the developing layers with his love, his song . . . his soul.

In many ways, for a Titanide, pregnancy was the best part of life.

Rocky broke off his communication with his daughter when he smelled violence. There was a change in the way the air felt. He had felt that change often lately.

Looking ahead along the causeway he saw the source. He felt tired, and wondered how human cops had handled their jobs. The situations were so predictable, and yet each one was dangerously different.

He took his hand-weapon out of his pouch and checked the magazine. It was a totally different type of weapon from the one he had carried, reluctantly, that day so many revs ago when he had come to Bellinzona to operate on his Captain. This was a twenty-second century weapon, and had been designed and ordered with Gaean conditions in mind. Most of the principles were the same, but the materials were different. Rocky's gun contained no metal. It looked like a long, narrow cardboard roll attached to a grip. There were short fins around the middle of the carbon-ceramic barrel; these glowed bright red for a second when the gun was fired.

The grip—which was too small for Rocky's hand—contained forty tiny rockets tipped with lead. The projectile was eased through the barrel at a relative snail's pace, then accelerated fiercely, cracking the sound barrier within one meter of the muzzle.

It was a marvelous weapon. Rocky hated it. From the way it felt in his pouch to the ugly results of its terrible accuracy, it was an evil thing through and through. He hoped the day would come when all such things could be erased from the land of Gaea.

In the meantime, he approached the shouting people.

A man had taken a woman by the upper arm and was pulling her along behind him as she shouted obscenities at him. He returned them, insult for insult. A crying child was following the two. A small group had formed to watch, but not to interfere. Rocky had seen the same events a dozen times, it seemed.

As he approached, the man—who must not have seen Rocky—finally stopped and hit the woman with his fist. He hit her again, and a third time . . . and then both of them noticed there was a Titanide standing very close with a gun pointed at them.

"Release her at once," Rocky said.

"Look, I didn't mean—"

Rocky tapped him lightly on the head in the place he had been taught would produce the fewest side-effects later, and the man crumpled. The woman, as Rocky had half-expected, quickly knelt beside the fallen man and began to cry as she held his head.

"Don't take him in!" she sobbed. "It was my fault."

"Stand up," Rocky ordered her. When she did not, he pulled her up. She wasn't wearing enough to conceal a weapon. He reached behind him, into his saddlebag, and came up with a short steel knife of the type already labeled "nutcutters" by the Bellinzonans.

"You are advised to carry this at all times," he told her.

"I *won't*. I don't need a knife."

"As you please." Rocky returned it to its place. "Today you're okay. In another hectorev you will be in violation of the law if you do not go armed. The penalty will be one kilorev in a labor camp for the first offense. Check the community bulletin boards for specifics, as ignorance is not acceptable as an excuse. If you cannot read, an interpreter will—"

She came at him, fists flying awkwardly. He had expected it.

He wanted witnesses, and he wanted her to hit him, mostly because he didn't like the idea of leaving the crying child with her. He let her land a few blows, then made her unconscious.

"Assault on a police officer," he informed the crowd, and no one had any objection. The child cried louder. He was about eight, Rocky thought, but he could have been wrong. Ages of human children were tough for Titanides.

"Is this woman your mother?" he asked the child, who was too upset to even hear the question. Rocky looked at the crowd again.

"Does anyone know if this is the child's mother?"

One man stepped forward.

"Yeah, he's hers, or that's what she says."

It was possible that she was his natural mother. Rocky suspected she was, because she didn't seem to him the sort of woman who would adopt one of Bellinzona's endless foundlings.

"Is there anyone who is willing to take responsibility for him in this community?" That was a laugh, Rocky thought. Community. Still, it was the prescribed procedure, and Cirocco maintained that communities would develop. "If not, I will take him to the community creche, where he will be cared for until his mother returns from the labor camp."

Surprisingly, a man stepped forward.

"I'll take him," he said.

"Sir," Rocky began. "Your responsibilities in this situation are—"

"I know what they are. I read the goddamn bulletin boards. *Very* carefully. You just run along with those two, and I'll see this fellow has a place to sleep."

There was some anger in the man's words, some defiance. Humans will take care of their own, was the implication. But there was a grudging respect. Either way was fine with Rocky. He had the authority to make field decisions of this nature, and judged the boy would be all right in the man's care.

So he bound the prisoners and slung them over his back and headed for the jail. On the way there Tambura intruded into his mind again.

Mother, what hurts? Tambura's question was both much simpler and much more complex than the English translation.

"Mother," for instance, was a gross oversimplification for the Titanide noun Tambura used. The question itself was more in the form of a wave of emotion.

Events. Interpersonal and interspecies relations. Life.
Mother, do I have to be born?
You will love life, my child. Most of the time.

FOURTEEN

Since the take-over, Nova had been busy as a witch with three holes in her spacesuit and only two patches.

Cirocco didn't seem to sleep at all. Nova had almost reached that state herself. It was now almost half a kilorev since the invasion. Nova had had little to do at first except record numbers of dead and wounded. But as laws were put into effect and the census got under way, her work load had increased. They were counting not only people, but dwellings, and an inventory of all formerly private property was contemplated.

Nova was in charge of the computers.

Can't run a revolution without computers, she thought.

Her title was Chief Bureaucrat. She didn't even know what it meant, except that it precluded her being out on the streets with a sword. That was okay with her. Now she fought only if it was unavoidable, and she was getting very good at avoiding it.

In that, she and Conal had a lot in common.

The thought of Conal irritated her for a moment. She looked away from her computer screen and went through some calming exercises.

There had been a fight upon their return from Pandemonium. Nova had demanded to know if Gaea's assertions were merely propaganda. Robin, reluctantly, had told the truth. Nova had informed her that from that day forward, she no longer considered herself Robin's daughter.

She sighed, and pushed her hair out of her eyes.

Cirocco, in the endless meetings at the Junction before the

invasion, had found out that Nova had a knack for running computers. Chris's ancient machines were brought out, dusted off, powered up, and readied for the big day. Since then, Nova had spent very few hours away from her console.

It was, she admitted to herself, an interesting way to view a revolution.

She was the first to spot the drop-off in summary executions. She knew before anyone else that the rate of admissions to the labor camps was declining. It was Nova who brought the first estimates of Bellinzona's population to the Wizard.

It turned out that Bellinzona had almost half a million humans living in it, a fact that surprised everyone but Conal. Nova's machines could line them up in any way that might be useful, from national origin to age and sex and languages and height and weight and eye color. It was a hell of a census. It was supposed to provide the basis for a system of identification in some hazy future time. Nova had a staff of one hundred constantly feeding information to her mainframe. She took the results to Cirocco and the Governing Council.

The Council still governed more in name than in fact. Cirocco was still the dictator, no one had any doubts about that.

The economics of Bellinzona had fascinated Nova as she learned more about them. There was one crucial factor that had caused Cirocco endless worry. Nova had dubbed it the Manna Factor.

Though Gaea did not control Dione, she owned the Spoke above it. When she had decided to discharge the human war refugees in the new town of Bellinzona she had apparently wanted to retain what control she could over them. So she had invented manna. As its name implied, it was food that fell out of the sky. It grew on a trillion plants up there in the darkness of the Dione spoke, and every few hectorevs it fell over Dione like a spilled cornucopia. Manna came in the form of coconut-sized balls floating on the ends of little parachutes. Even with the chutes, it was wise to get under cover when it was raining manna.

Like coconuts, manna modules had hard shells. They survived impact, but were not too hard to crack. Inside was one of a hundred varieties of nutritious meat. It came in a lot of flavors. It provided all the vitamins and minerals a human being needed to stay healthy. The manna was so good, in fact, that those who subsisted entirely on it—a large part of the population—were healthier than those who supplemented their diets with expensive and exotic Dionian meats and vegetables. Fat people lost weight on it, until they reached an optimum mass. People suffering vitamin deficiences recovered after a few kilorevs of eating manna. It also inhibited tooth decay, sweetened the breath, lessened menstrual cramps, and cured baldness. Naturally, it was a sign of status in Bellinzona never to have eaten the stuff.

Manna had a shelf-life of two kilorevs. All but the most inept were able to squirrel away enough of it to last until the next shower. Those few who either couldn't or didn't were ripe for slavery when they got hungry.

Of course, Gaea giveth and Gaea taketh away. The weather in Dione was awful. It never got *too* cold, but it was often cold enough so the homeless masses shivered through an endless afternoon sleep-time. And it rained a lot. So shelter was something worthwhile, something many people worked to obtain. It was not easy to come by, as the Bosses had grabbed every inch they could control and exacted harsh prices for the right to sleep under a roof.

But aside from seeking shelter and storing a supply of manna every kilorev or so . . . there was little one had to do to survive in Bellinzona. Cirocco had called it the ultimate welfare state.

And she had known that, not long after she moved to take control, the manna would stop falling from the sky. The question had been *how long?*

So the first and most important goal of her administration had been to feed the populace. It was a goal that came before everything else—even law and order. It had to be accomplished at all costs, because nothing could be worse than a subjugated but starving city.

Cirocco had been dismayed at Nova's population projections. She had envisioned feeding a city of two or three hundred thousand.

Still . . . Moros teemed with edible fish. The flatlands at the end of Peppermint Bay were fertile. Gaean crops grew quickly. It could be done, but not with a free population. Conscript labor was essential. Some of the laws had been designed with that in mind. Filling the prisons was essential to Cirocco's plans, as she had no illusions about legions of volunteers marching out to clear the jungle and tend the crops. Violent crimes were punishable by instant execution: one less mouth to feed. Other crimes earned the bewildered citizen a long term in the labor camp. Cirocco had been ready to go as far as necessary. She would have made sneezing in public a criminal offense if that's what it took to fill the camps. Luckily, the citizens of Bellinzona had obliged her by violating her entirely reasonable laws in sufficient numbers to guarantee a food supply.

So when the manna had stopped falling, Bellinzona was ready.

FIFTEEN

Without quite knowing how it had happened, Valiha and Virginal had become fisherfolk. Neither had ever netted a fish before.

Those humans who knew something about ships had, with the authority of the Mayor's decrees, taken command of all the Bellinzonan boats capable of doing more than rocking at anchor. For the last decarev the fleet had been putting out to sea, with Valiha and Virginal at the prow.

Their main function was to ward off the submarines.

There might have been a fishing industry in Bellinzona long before this, but for the fact that human-piloted boats that ventured more than ten kilometers from the environs of the city were promptly eaten. Submarines had huge appetites, and were not picky.

The Captain had made some sort of treaty with them. It worked so well that not only were the ships not eaten, but the fishing fleet could now rendezvous with the submarine flotillas and find the seas strewn with the disgorged and still living schools recently scooped up by the subs' vast mouths.

There was a submarine song. Valiha and Virginal sang it, though it was not one they were born to know. And the leviathans eased up from the depths to give much of their catch to the hungry city.

It was a miracle.

That's what they were doing now. Valiha stood at the prow of one of the largest boats in the Bellinzona fleet and sang the submarine song, while not far away the vast bulk of a submarine wallowed near the surface. Great gouts of water spurted up in the direction of the smaller ships and the nets rigged between them, stunned and bewildered fish vainly thrashing in the torrent, escaping from the jaws of the submarine only to be swallowed by the nets.

It was rather beautiful to watch. Lately, the fisherfolk had begun singing their own version of the submarine song as they hauled on their nets. Valiha listened critically. She knew it lacked the nuances of Titanide song, but like so much human music, it had a simple vitality that was attractive. Perhaps, one day, the submarines would respond to human song alone. That would be good, for Valiha had no wish to command the fleet for the rest of her life.

It had been turbulent seas, at first. With a hard core of dedicated sea-folk and a larger number of human police and a handful of Titanides, it had just been possible to put to sea with a cargo of recalcitrant prisoners. The first outings had produced little but blisters and aching backs. But the human police were zealous—maybe a little too much so, Valiha thought—and soon everyone was at least working as hard as possible. Then a spirit began to grow. It took root slowly at first. But now, when Valiha overheard conversations in the bustling fish markets, there was a clear sense that these people thought of themselves as a group—and what's more, as slightly better than the idlers ashore. It now took fewer police to keep them in line. When the fleet set sail, people hoisted the lines with a will, and when the fish were sighted there was cheering. There were songs for departure and songs for return, as well as the Titanide-inspired submarine chantey.

It was a good thing, Valiha knew. The last shower of manna had been many days late, and when it was opened, was too rancid to eat.

Bellinzona was now on its own.

SIXTEEN

"It's Gaea," Adam said.

"It sure is," Chris confirmed, as brightly as he could. Adam put down his toys and sat in front of the television screen.

Chris had been worried enough when Gaea only showed up in old Marilyn Monroe movies. He and Adam had seen them all a dozen times. Adam was quite bored with them.

But about a kilorev after the air show which had so badly upset Gaea, something new had happened. Gaea had showed up in an animated cartoon.

He should have expected it. It was an easy enough thing to do, and it wouldn't stop there. But Chris had been away from television for over twenty years, and had forgotten about that capability.

The first had been a Betty Boop cartoon, and had been simple image-substitution. Wherever Betty Boop had appeared in the original, Gaea had replaced her with a stylized but easily-recognizable cartoon of Marilyn Monroe. The sound track was un-altered.

If Earth computers could do it, it stood to reason that Gaea could.

Later, she began to appear in the movies Chris knew to be Adam's favorites. This was much more sophisticated stuff, with full-body replacement, facial enhancement, and the Monroe/Gaea voice. It was impossible to detect the fakery. It was seamless movie magic, special effects to the nth degree.

And it was distinctly odd to see Marilyn Monroe starring in *Fists of Fury*. She was a formidable figure, replacing Bruce Lee in every whirl, glower, and leap. All the Chinese actors spoke dubbed English, but Gaea/Lee was lip-synched. Of course, Lee had spent most of his time in those movies with his shirt off, so Gaea did, too. Then there were the love scenes....

After that there was no telling where Gaea might pop up. Chris saw her as Snow White, Charlie Chaplin, Cary Grant, and Indiana Jones. She appeared in old RKO serials, which Gaea broadcast at the rate of one episode per day. Pandemonium television had grown increasingly violent. Even the comedy tended sharply toward the slapstick.

There was little Chris could do about it. Having foreseen some of it didn't make it any easier. Gaea continued to make her regular visits. She came a bit closer each time, but was as yet still distant. There was no chance she would scare the boy.

Chris could only love the child.

Which, he reflected, was nothing to sneer at. He knew Adam

returned his love. But he knew a child's love can be quite fickle. One day it would come to a showdown. Nothing could be clearer than that. But the outcome was far from clear.

"Hi, Gaea," Adam said, waving at the screen.

"Hello, Adam, my lovely boy," said Gaea.

Chris looked up. The image of Gaea had stopped and turned away from the action still happening behind her. She was facing Adam, and smiling.

Adam still didn't get it. He giggled, and said hi again.

"How are you doing, Adam?" Gaea said. The action behind her was a fight scene. Gaea ducked as a chair was thrown. It sailed over her head. "Oops!! He almost got me!"

Adam laughed louder.

"Gotcha!" he shouted. "Gotcha!"

"They can't get me!" Gaea boasted, and turned skillfully to block a blow from a huge guy in a black hat. She hit him a quick one-two-three combination and he fell on the floor. Gaea dusted her palms together, and grinned at Adam again.

"How'd you like that, Adam?" she said.

"I *like* it, I *like* it!" Adam laughed.

Somebody save me, Chris thought, in a daze.

SEVENTEEN

Serpent thundered down the field, clods of turf flying from his hooves, his forelegs flirting nimbly with the black and white ball. He kicked it with the side of his hoof, and Mandolin reared on her hind legs to butt it with her head in the general direction of Zampogna, who couldn't take control and watched helplessly as Kekese of the Sharp team kicked it to Clavecin, who headed off toward the Flat's goal. Serpent kept a sharp eye from midfield, and when Tjelempang stole it away again and passed it off to Piano, he was in position to take it on the run. Then he was in control again, running like the wind, the Pele of the four-legged set, bearing down on the Sharp's goalie, who desperately tried to read Serpent's moves, dodged left, then right, left again—and was in the wrong place when Serpent kneed the ball up, thrust his head forward . . . deliberately missed the head-butt. The goalie went flying through the air toward the left side of the goal. . . .

—and watched helplessly as Serpent twisted around and kicked with a hind leg. The ball sizzled into the center of the opposing net.

Flats ahead, four to three.

That was still the score when, with only a centirev left to play, Mandolin scored her first goal of the game, to put it out of reach. Serpent gathered with the others to congratulate Mandolin, who was still a rookie at the glorious sport of football. It never occurred to him to point out that he, Serpent, had scored the winning goal. He had also scored two of the other points. He was, no doubt about it, the best football player in Gaea.

Breathing like steam engines, dripping sweat, the Titanides engaged in the sort of horseplay usual after a hard-fought game. Gradually, Serpent became aware of another sound. For one moment he was alarmed. It sounded a lot like the awful day of the riot.

But then he discovered a loose group of prisoners gathered near the sidelines, shouting and clapping.

They had been congregating there lately, watching the Titan-ides. This group was larger than before. In fact, the group had been getting bigger each day, Serpent realized. A few times, after the Titanide game was over, some of the human prisoners had taken the field to kick the ball around.

Serpent scooped up the football and kicked it high and long. It fell into the group of prisoners—all of these were males—and watched them toss it back and forth, waiting for the Titanides to leave.

He wondered if they might like to form teams themselves. He moved off to the sidelines and watched as they scrambled over the turf. They seemed to be playing twenty or thirty to a side on the over-sized Titanide field, cheerfully accepting the inconvenience caused by the rutted ground.

Serpent walked away thoughtfully. He joined the other Titan-ides on the hillside west of the valley, folded his legs under him, took his leather-bound sketch pad and a charcoal pencil from his pouch, stared out over the valley, and promptly fell into that mental state that was nothing like what humans called sleep, but was not quite like being awake.

He scanned the vista in front of him. Far to his right, to the north, was Peppermint Bay, with Moros just beyond it. Huddled at the near end under its usual blanket of haze was Bellinzona. Whistlestop was visible, stationed a prudent three kilometers above the firetrap city.

Sweeping in front of Serpent were the many kilometers of land reclaimed from the jungle.

It was not like Earth jungles, where the land, surprisingly, is fragile and not too fertile if cleared. Gaean land operated by different rules. Crops sank deep roots and thrived on the nutritious milk of Gaea, and from her underground heat. There was not much photosynthesis involved in the plants which could be raised in the dim light of Dione, so the fields were all colors. It was a huge patchwork quilt of crops. All the fields were square—except those right around the river, which were terraced and flooded to grow rice-like crops. Running between the squares were dirt paths where humans pulled hand-carts of harvested crops to the river docks, where barges floated the bounty down to the city. And dotted here and there among the fields were the neat rows of tents which housed the workers.

Cirocco insisted on calling them prisoners. Serpent thought slaves might be more accurate, but Cirocco insisted there was a difference. He supposed there was. Slavery was an alien concept to the Titanide mind, so he was ready to admit it would take a human to distinguish the gradations.

Once again, it was a matter of heirarchies, another concept Titanides had a lot of trouble with. They had elders, and were capable of obedience to the Captain, but anything more complex than that confused them terribly. The work camps, for instance, were ruled by a Warden, a former Vigilante Serpent didn't like very much but not a bad man. He was responsible to the Council back in town—specifically, to the Prisons Committee. The Council was ruled by Cirocco Jones and her advisors: Robin, Nova, and Conal.

In the other direction, the Warden commanded twenty Camp Bosses, who in turn gave orders to a dozen or so Overseers, each in charge of a number of work gangs supervised by a Trusty.

He glanced down at his sketch pad. He had been looking at it off and on as he sat there, but his eyes had sent no messages to his brain. Now he saw he had done a simple rendering of the scene before him. He looked at it critically. He had left out the humans on the road. There were some hesitant lines to suggest the tents of the nearest camp. Serpent frowned. This was not what his mind sought. He tore out the page, crumpled it, and tossed it away. Then he looked down at the camp.

The tents were green canvas. Each housed ten humans. The sexes were segregated for sleeping, but sexual abstinence was not enforced. The Overseers and Bosses were appointed by the Warden, but not reviewed by the Titanides. In practical terms this was a mistake, Serpent knew. Some of the Overseers and Bosses were worse than the prisoners. It had been possible to catch a few of these in acts of brutality, whereupon they found themselves toiling in a prisoner's loincloth. But these days such people were careful to commit their atrocities out of sight. The Titanides could not be everywhere.

It was impractical, it was inefficient . . . and it was the way the Captain said it must be done.

Serpent had fretted about it at first. Later he had seen the trap. Crazy as it was, it was the human way to do things. They couldn't detect lies or evil the way a Titanide could, so they had evolved these compromises which they usually called "justice," or, more accurately, "law." Serpent well knew that truth was a relative term, sometimes impossible to establish, but humans were almost totally blind to it. The trap—and it was a subtle one—was that if humans came to rely on Titanide perceptions of Truth and Evil, they would gain all the benefits of a sane society and Titanides would be enslaved to the humans' need.

Cirocco's solution made a lot more sense. She would use the Titanides as much as she had to. At first, this had been a lot, with Titanides acting as policeman, judge, jury, and hangman. The purpose was to galvanize the society into an understanding that evildoing *would* be punished.

But the humans had to be weaned away from this, back into their own way of doing things. Increasingly, it was so. The courts were taking more of the burden. That they were often inaccurate was simply the price humans had to pay for their freedom.

Once more he glanced down at his pad. There was a drawing

of three female prisoners. The one in the center was old and tired, her hands gnarled from the harvest. She stood there in her dirty loincloth. Her face had a wondrous beauty etched deeply. The youngest and—in human terms—prettiest of the bunch had been drawn with the face of a monster. Serpent remembered her. This was an evil one. Some day she would hang. Looking closer, Serpent realized he had drawn a gallows into her face. He tore it out and crumpled it and looked again toward the camp.

At the center of the community was the gallows. It had been used frequently in the early days of the conquest, less often now. There had been the one awful riot, but since that day the Titanide guards had been reduced. Now there were hardly enough to form six football teams.

Though prison life was hard work, it was better than most of the prisoners had known in Bellinzona. Food had never been a problem in the old days. But now the manna no longer fell, and new prisoners told of hunger and uncertainty. There was an economic system being born, social lines being drawn. There were jobs in plenty, but the wages would buy only enough food to feed oneself, and not well. Many of the jobs were harder and more dangerous than farm labor. And there were days when the fleet came back empty, or no barges arrived from the camps, and everyone went hungry.

Prison food was the best—the Warden was under orders to be sure that it was. It was plentiful. Prison was a secure place. Most of the people here didn't want to make trouble.

So Titanides only patrolled the strip of no-man's-land between the camps and the city. The seldom caught anybody, and few bunks turned up empty at roll-call.

Again Serpent looked at his sketch. Three men hung from ropes in the center of the camp. Two had been evil, Serpent remembered. One had only done something dumb. He had killed an Overseer in front of Titanide witnesses. The Overseer had certainly deserved it—Serpent recalled the man had been hanged in turn only a few hectorevs later—but the Law was the Law. Serpent would have let the man live. The human judge had felt differently.

Angrily, he tore that page out and threw it away. His mind kept returning to the thing he knew in his soul and hated to think about. This was a bad place, a place of suffering, a human place where no Titanide should be. Titanides *knew* how to behave. Humans spent their lives in an endless struggle to subdue their animal natures. It was quite possible that these laws, prisons, and gallows were the best solution they would ever find to that paradox. But it sickened the Titanide to be part of it.

He stared into the darkness of the Dione spoke and began to sing a song of sadness, and of longing for the Great Tree of home. Others joined him, their hands involved in simple tasks. The song went on for a long time.

There had to be something *good* to be done here. He didn't expect to change the world. He didn't expect to change human nature—and would not if he could. They had their own destiny. His aim was modest. He merely would like to make the world a slightly better place for his having lived in it. That seemed little enough to ask.

He looked down at his sketchpad. He had drawn a smiling human. The fellow was dressed in shorts and a striped shirt, and was wearing shoes. He was in violent motion, kicking a football.

EIGHTEEN

Robin took her seat to the right of the larger chair at the end of the huge Council table, in the Great Hall of The Loop. She opened her cunningly crafted leather briefcase—a gift from Valiha and Virginal—took out a stack of papers, and tapped them on the polished wood. Then, with a nervous glance around, she took out her wire-rimmed glasses and put them on.

She still felt funny wearing them. Back home, she had suffered from a recurring optical problem that had been easily correctible as she advanced in years. Here, without visits to the Fountain, her eyes kept getting worse. And, Great Mother, it was no wonder, since she spent her days staring at endless reports.

It should not have surprised her, she knew, but it still did. In every way but the final, most important one, she was the Mayor of Bellinzona. She suspected that, had she been born Christian, she would have been Pope by now.

Cirocco had been quite reasonable about it, that day six kilorevs ago. She had been reasonable . . . up to a point. Then she had been adamant.

"You have the experience of leading a large group of people," Cirocco had said. "I don't. For reasons you'll see, I will have to retain the final power in Bellinzona. But I will be relying on you and your judgment in a great many things. And I know you'll rise to the challenge."

Well, challenge it had been. But now it was more and more routine: the very thing she had hated about running the Coven.

She rubbed the table with her hand, and smiled. It was a wonderful table, made of the best wood, edged with more clever carvings than Robin could count. It had been made by Titanides, naturally. It was the second table to grace the Council Chamber.

The first one had been round. Cirocco had taken one look at it and told them to take it away.

"This isn't Camelot," she had said. "There'll be no meetings of equals here. Bring me a big, *long* table, with a *big* chair at this end."

Robin knew it had been a natural mistake for the Titanides. There was a human way and a Titanide way. They were ignorant of the psychological edge Cirocco sought by sitting at the head.

So they had brought a *big* chair. Sometimes Cirocco sat in it.

But more and more lately, it stood empty, and Robin conducted her business from her customary seat at the right of the throne.

Others were taking their seats now. Directly across the table, Nova thumped a huge stack of paper onto the table and slipped into her own chair. She glanced up at her mother, nodded, and then began penciling notes in the margins.

The older witch sighed. She wondered how much longer Nova could keep this up. She would speak to her mother. It was possible to conduct business with her. But it was all so careful. There was no laughter, no joking, not even any complaints except those couched in the reasoned, maddening language of the bureaucrat. Robin longed for a good old shouting match.

She looked at the still-empty chair. Cirocco Jones, flanked by her two chief advisors. The Bitch and Two Witches, she had overheard someone say. Most of the Council did not realize the rift between mother and daughter.

Stuart took his seat to Robin's right. She nodded at him and smiled politely, which was an effort. She didn't like the guy, but he was able, efficient, canny, and brilliant, when it suited him. He was also awfully ambitious. In another situation he would be doing his best to stab Robin in the back. Just now he was biding his time, waiting to see if Cirocco really would relinquish power at the end of one Earth year, as she had promised. If she did, the feathers would fly.

Trini sat down next to Nova, who leaned over and kissed the Elder Amazon on the lips. Robin squirmed in her chair. She didn't like Trini much more than she did Stuart. Maybe less. It was hard to believe they had once been lovers, briefly, twenty years ago. Now she and Nova were an item. Robin didn't know how genuine it was. Nova obviously retained her crush on Cirocco. Robin felt sure part of the reason for their public displays of affection was Nova's shrewd knowledge that it would irritate her mother.

She scowled, and looked away. O brave new world.

The other chairs were filling up. Conal took his eccentric seat, a few yards behind Cirocco's chair and slightly to one side, where he could watch the proceedings and smoke his cigars one after the other. He would say nothing, and hear everything. Most of the Council hadn't the slightest idea what to make of him. His position was a device, Robin knew. He had the look of an assassin about him when he cared to project it. He looked sinister, wreathed in smoke.

Cirocco slid into her throne, scooted down on the seat of her pants, and put her boots up on the table. She had an unlit cigar clenched in her teeth.

"Let's get going, folks," she said.

"So what's your gut reaction, Conal?" Cirocco asked.

"Gut?" He considered it. "Better, Captain. Not a lot, but better."

"Last time you didn't think it was going to work."

"So a guy can be wrong."

She studied him. Conal bore it, unperterbed.

At first he had felt left out. There was a job for everyone, it seemed, but Conal. Oh, sure, there was talk of him leading the air force, if and when, and he had organized the Bellinzona Air Reserve. They wore uniforms if they wanted to. But they didn't fly airplanes, and wouldn't for some time.

He had thought he was being left out, and had been hurt about it. But gradually he had realized that, if Robin was Cirocco's surrogate Mayor during those times when the Captain was out of the city on her mysterious errands, Conal was her eyes and ears.

His duties were amorphous, which suited him fine. What he did was drift around, in a variety of clothing. Nobody but Council members and a few of the top police knew he had anything to do with the governing of the city. He could come and go as he pleased, and people talked to him. Everything he heard went to Cirocco. He didn't have Nova's computer charts or Robin's experience and elaborate theories, but he knew the secrets.

"What about that black market crap?"

"I agree with Robin."

"Are you trying to needle me, or what? I agree with her, too, but I don't come to you for theories, Conal. I come to you for reality."

Conal was a little surprised at her reaction. Looking closely, he saw she was under a great deal of strain.

"The black market is not the problem Nova's building it up to be. There's not much stuff, and the prices are very high."

"Which means," Cirocco said, "that very little food is being diverted at the docks, and we've *still* got shortages. So the shortages are real."

"Nobody's going hungry. But a lot of folks wish the manna was still falling."

Cirocco brooded about that for a while.

"How about the Buck?"

Conal laughed.

"The word is, a Buck makes a good coffee filter. Use five or ten of them, and when you're done the brown stains might be worth something. They're also useful rolled up to snort coke with."

"Wastepaper, in other words."

"It's that law Nova was talking about. Robin said it meant bad money drove out good money."

"No," Cirocco said. "That's what's forcing the gold coins into mattresses and old socks. People save the stuff that has value and spend the stuff that inflates."

"Whatever. I don't think the school problem is as bad as they made out tonight. It's true there's some resentment. But most of the folks here were learning English, anyway, or enough to get by on. The thing that really jerks 'em off is having to learn *good* English."

"What do you suggest?"

"Lowering the literacy requirement. Let 'em out of class when they can read a campaign poster, and don't worry about teaching them the past perfect tense. Of course, coming from a guy who was illiterate when he got here and ain't much of a reader even yet, maybe—"

"Come off it, Conal." Cirocco chewed a knuckle. "You're right. We can let the non-English-speaking adults get by with pidgen. Their kids will learn more than they did. I shouldn't have pushed it so hard."

"Nobody's perfect."

"Don't remind me. What else do you know?"

"Most people prefer barter. I'd say sixty percent of the business done in town is barter. But there is another currency coming up fast, and that's alcohol. There's been beer for a long time. The wine is actually getting tolerable, but most of the time I can't tell what it's made from—and I probably don't want to know. But we're seeing more of the hard stuff."

"Distilled spirits. That scares me."

"Me, too. There's some methanol going the rounds. Some people have gone blind."

Cirocco sighed.

"Do we need another law?"

"Forbidding home-made hootch?" Conal frowned, and shook his head. "I'm applying your golden rule here. The minimum law to correct the problem. Instead of banning *good* liquor—which, believe me, is a contradiction in terms in Bellinzona—just ban the poison."

"Won't work. Not if it's being used as money. It gets passed back and forth so many times how do we know where it came from?"

"There's that problem," Conal conceded. "And even the good

distilleries use labels that are easy to counterfeit . . . and people water it. . . ."

"It's not a very good currency," Cirocco said. "I think the best thing is to start a public education campaign. I don't know much about methanol. Isn't it pretty easy to tell? Can't you smell it?"

"I'm never sure. First you have to get past the stink of the booze."

They brooded about it in silence for a time. Conal was inclined to let it go. He didn't believe in protecting people from themselves. His own solution was to drink only from sealed bottles he had received from the hands of a distiller he trusted. It seemed to him everyone else should do the same. But maybe a law was needed, after all.

He was ambivalent about the whole thing. It was not that he had loved Bellinzona before. He knew the place was vastly improved. You could walk the streets unarmed with reasonable safety.

But every time you turned around, you ran into a law. After living seven years without laws, it was hard to get your head back in gear to think about them.

Which brought him to the question he was sure Cirocco would ask next. She did not disappoint him.

"What about me? How's the Conal-meter rating?"

He held out a hand and rocked it back and forth.

"You're better. Ten or fifteen percent like you well enough. Maybe thirty percent tolerate you and will admit, with a few beers in them, that you've made things better. But the rest really don't like you at all. Either you upset their wagons, or they don't think you're doing *enough*. There's lots of folks out there who'd feel better if somebody told them what to do from the time they woke up to the time you put 'em to bed."

"Maybe they'll get their wish," Cirocco muttered.

Conal waited for her to go on, but she didn't. So he took another puff on his cigar and tried to pick his words carefully. "There's something else. It's . . . image, I guess. You're a face on the side of a blimp. Not really real."

"My media team has made that abundantly clear," she said, sourly. "I come across as a stiff-necked bitch on television."

"I don't know about normal TV," Conal said. "But on those big screens on Whistlestop they just don't *like* you. You're above them. You're not one of the people . . . and you're not *strong* enough, if that's the word, to inspire the kind of fear . . . or, I don't know, maybe it's respect . . ." He trailed off, unable to express what he felt.

"Once again, you're confirming my media studies. On the one hand, I'm Olympian and Draconian—and people *hate* that—and on the other, I'm insufficient as an authority-figure."

"People don't believe in you," Conal said. "They believe in Gaea more than in you."

"And they haven't even seen Gaea."

"Most of 'em haven't seen you, either."

Again she brooded. It was clear to Conal she was coming to a decision she found distasteful, but unavoidable. He waited, patiently, knowing that whatever she decided he would do his best to fulfill his part in it.

"Okay," she said, putting her feet up on the table. "Here's what we're going to do."

He listened. Pretty soon he was grinning.

NINETEEN

When the meeting was over, Conal went out into the unfailing light of Dione and turned left on the Oppenheimer Boulevard causeway.

Bellinzona was a city that never slept. There were three rush hours each "day," signaled by a massive toot from Whistlestop. During those times people would go from their jobs to their homes, or vice versa. Somebody was in charge of scheduling everything, Conal knew, so that about a third of the city was always relatively quiet, its residents sleeping, while another third hummed with the sounds of commerce, and yet another with the sounds of Bellinzona's meager amusements. Many people worked two shifts, or one and a half, to make ends meet. But there were taverns and casinos and whorehouses and meeting rooms to provide the necessary social life. All work and no play would have been a dismal way to run a city, in Conal's opinion.

The river docks and the wharves where the fishing fleet tied up were busy around the clock. The shipyards were always busy, as well. And others of the city's infant industries worked on three shifts. But the main reason for the staggered working hours was to keep the city from seeming too crowded. The plain fact was there was not enough housing if everyone tried to bed down at once. Cooperative living was the norm.

It worked fairly well. But the birth rate was rising and the infant-mortality rate falling and the carpenters were always busy at the Terminal Wharves and high in the hills building new housing.

Conal had decided he liked the city. It breathed new life. It was vital and alive, as he remembered Fort Reliance before the war. You heard a lot of gripes in the taprooms, but the very fact they felt free to gripe counted for something, he felt. It meant they had hope of improving those things they didn't like.

In quick succession he passed one of the new parks—a big square floating dock with horseshoe pitches, volleyball nets, basketball hoops, and trees and shrubs in pots—a hospital, and a school. All would have been unthinkable in Bellinzona just seven kilorevs ago. He got out of the way as a Titanide galloped by with a pregnant woman in his arms, heading for the emergency entrance of the hospital. Inside the school, children sat on the floor and waited for the class to end, as they had always done. The game equipment in the parks was always in use. All these things warmed Conal. He hadn't realized how much he had missed them.

Not that he wanted to live in the city. He thought, when this was all finished and turned over to locals, he would resume the life he had been leading, being a nomad known throughout the great Wheel, a friend of the Captain. But it was nice to know it was *here*.

He turned into a familiar building and walked up three flights of stairs. The door opened to his key and he went in.

The shades were drawn. Robin was in bed. He thought she was asleep. He went into the small bathroom and rinsed himself in the basin of water, using some of the hard, harsh soap that had recently become available on the black market. He brushed his teeth, and he shaved very carefully with an old razor. All these things were relatively new habits for Conal, but he had mostly forgotten those old days when a bath was something he took when his clothes got too stiff to bend easily.

He slipped into bed, careful not to wake her.

She turned to him, wide awake and hungry.

"This will never work," she said, as she often did. He nodded, and took her into his arms, and it worked wonderfully.

TWENTY

Cirocco Jones went from the meeting to the place where she knew she would find Hornpipe. She moved in the way she had learned, in the way that so befuddled Robin when she used it to show up at the meetings of the Council. No one took any notice of her.

She wondered if it might be the last time she could move that way. Not knowing where the power came from made it that much harder to believe it could last after what she planned to do.

She mounted Hornpipe and he galloped out of the city. Soon they were moving through the jungles of southern Dione, not far from Tuxedo Junction.

She reached the shores of the Fountain of Youth and dismounted.

"Stay close," she advised Hornpipe. "This will take some time."

The Titanide nodded, and faded back into the jungle. Cirocco stripped off her clothes and knelt on the sand. She opened her pack and took out the bottle containing Snitch. He blinked woozily. She dumped him on the ground and watched him stagger and curse. It would take him a little time to come around to any degree of intelligibility.

Cirocco felt her body, as she might explore an unfamiliar and possibly dangerous object. Her ribs stood out. She still had more breast tissue than she was accustomed to, and her thighs were firm and full, but the knees were getting bony. Her hair was once more streaked with gray. She could feel the fine wrinkles around her eyes and at the corners of her mouth.

She flicked Snitch in the face and he spat at her, but without any real heart in the gesture. Without having to be asked, Cirocco got the bottle from her pack and used the eyedropper to squeeze seven fat drops into his upturned and eager mouth.

Snitch smacked his lips, and used the expression that passed, in Snitch's limited facial repertoire, for a smile.

"The old hag is feeling generous today," he said.

"The old hag isn't in the mood for any games. You want to hear how I'll flay you alive if you don't talk? Or are you as tired of that as I am?"

Snitch balanced on one limb and used the other to scratch behind his ear.

"Why don't we skip all that?"

"Fine. How is Adam?"

"Adam is peachy keen. He likes his great big grandmaw. One day soon Gaea will have him—you should pardon the expression—in the palm of her hand."

"How is Chris?"

"Chris is blue. On his good days he still thinks he can win the heart and mind of the aforementioned Adam, his son. On his bad days, he thinks he's already lost. These days, most of his days are bad days. This isn't helped by the fact that Gaea is starring him in some of her television shows, and making him do some distasteful tasks to earn his...bread and butter."

Snitch blinked, and frowned. "Did I mix a metaphor?"

Cirocco ignored the question.

"What about...Gaby?"

Snitch cocked an eye at her.

"You've never asked me about her before."

"I'm asking you now."

"I could tell you she's a figment of your imagination."

"I could shove your head up your asshole."

"God," Snitch said, with a grimace. "Would that such a maneuver were the impossibility for me that it is for you."

"You know it's not."

"How well I remember." He sighed. "Gaby...is preparing her dirty trick. You know what I'm talking about. Gaby treads a thin line. You may never know just how thin. Leave her alone."

"But I haven't seen her in—"

"Leave her *alone*, Captain."

They stared at each other. Such a remark called for punishment. Cirocco wondered what it meant that she was prepared to let him get away with it this time. What was changing? Or was she just too tired to care?

She put it out of her mind, gave Snitch three more drops of pure grain alcohol, and put him back in his bottle. Then she moved carefully into the purifying heat of the Fountain, reclined in it, and took a deep breath of the waters.

She did not move for ten revs.

TWENTY-ONE

New Pandemonium was complete.

Gaea had personally inspected the outer wall, had scooped Great Whites from the moat with her own massive hands, checked all the preparations for siege.

The labor problem was still bad. It had taken some time to get her production supervisors to understand that humans could no longer be worked to death. Many people had died before that lesson was learned. There was now a small desertion problem, as well, with no zombie battalions to hunt down and torture runaways. The Priests were not happy with human acolytes, but knew better than to kick up too much fuss about it. Luckily, the zombie dust had no effect on the Priests.

All the preparations had been made. New Pandemonium could withstand any attack, any siege.

Content, she summoned her archivist and ordered up a triple feature. *The Man Who Would Be King. All the King's Men. Indira.*

Wonderful political films, all.

TWENTY-TWO

Gaby Plauget had been born in New Orleans in 1997, back when it had been a part of the United States of America.

Her childhood was tragic. Her father killed her mother and she was shuttled back and forth between relatives and agencies, learning never to care for anybody too much. Astronomy had been her salvation. She had become the best there was at planetary astronomy, so good that when the crew of *Ringmaster* was being chosen she managed a berth, though she hated to travel.

She had been more or less indifferent to sex.

Then the *Ringmaster* had been destroyed, and all the crew had spent a time in total sensory deprivation. It had driven Gene crazy. Bill had been left with gaps in his memory, so he didn't know Cirocco when he met her again. The Polo sisters, April and August, never the most stable of clone-geniuses, had been separated, April to become an Angel, August to gradually pine away for her lost sister. Calvin had emerged with the ability to speak to the blimps, and no desire to be around humans again. Cirocco had gained the ability to sing Titanide.

Gaby had lived an entire lifetime. Twenty years, she had said. When she woke up, it had been like one of those crazy dreams where, all at once, you know what it's all about. The Big Answers to Life are within your grasp, if only you can keep your head clear long enough to sort them out. All her experiences during that twenty years were right there, fresh in her mind, ready to change her life and the world...

...until, dream-like, they faded. Within a few minutes she knew only a few things. One was that it *had* been twenty years, full of the kind of detail only that amount of time could have provided. Another was a memory of walking up vast stairs, accompanied by organ music. Later, when she and Cirocco visited Gaea in the hub, Gaby had re-lived that moment. The third thing she retained was a hopeless and incurable love for Cirocco Jones, which was as big a surprise to Gaby as it was to Cirocco. Gaby had never thought of herself as a lesbian.

Everything else was gone.

Seventy-five years went by.

At the age of one hundred and three, Gaby Plauget died beneath the central cable of Tethys. She died horribly, painfully, of fluid building up in burned lung tissue.

Then came the biggest surprise of all. There really *was* a life after death. Gaea really *was* God.

She fought that notion all the way to the hub. She had seen her dead body lying there. She had become just a point of awareness, feeling nothing on a physical level. Disembodiment did not prevent her feeling emotions, though. The strongest one was fear. She regressed to her childhood, found herself reciting Hail Mary's and Our Father's and the Lord's Prayer, imagined herself in the huge, cool, forbidding, and yet comforting space of the old cathedral, kneeling beside her mother, saying the rosary.

But the only cathedral was the living body of Gaea.

She had been taken, or moved, or spirited, or in some way transported to the hub, to the movie-set staircase she and Cirocco had climbed so long ago. It was deep in dust, and adorned with movie-set cobwebs draped artfully. She herself felt like a camera on a very steady dolly, moving without volition or control through the little Oz door off to one side and into the Louis XVI room which was an exact duplicate of a set from the movie *2001: A Space Odyssey.* It was where she and Cirocco had first met the squat and dumpy old woman who called herself Gaea.

The gilt paint was peeling from the picture frames. Half the lights were out, or flickering. The furniture was frayed and sprung and musty. Sitting in a wobbly chair, her bare feet propped on a low table, staring at an ancient black-and-white television set and drinking beer from a bottle, was Gaea. She was shapeless as usual in a filthy gray shift.

Gaby, like everyone but the most fanatical, had envisioned a thousand possibilities for what life after death might be like, spanning the spectrum from heaven to hell. Somehow, this one had never come up.

Gaea turned slightly. It was like one of those arty films where the camera eye is supposed to represent a character, and the other players respond to it. She looked at Gaby, or at the locus of space where Gaby imagined herself to be.

"Do you have any idea the trouble you've caused me?" Gaea muttered.

No, I don't, Gaby said. Though, when she thought about it, "said" was a pretty concrete verb for what she actually did. There was no sound involved. She did not feel lips or tongue move. No breath was taken into the lungs which, so far as she knew, still lay in the darkness beneath Tethys, clotted with phlegm.

But the impulse was like speaking, and Gaea seemed to hear.

"Why couldn't you just leave it alone?" Gaea groused. "There are wheels within wheels, babe, to coin a phrase. Rocky was coming along nicely. What's wrong with being a little drunk every so often?"

Gaby "said" nothing. "Rocky" was, of course, Cirocco Jones. And she had been more than a little drunk almost all the time. As for leaving it alone...

Cirocco might have. There was no way to be sure. Possibly forty or fifty years down the line she would have bestirred herself and tried to *do* something about the impossible situation that had driven her to drink. On the other hand, maybe it was possible for even an immortal to drink herself to death.

At any rate, it had been Gaby who finally pushed Cirocco into the first, tentative step of surveying the regional brains of Gaea, looking for hints of useful subversion, hoping to locate somebody who could serve as focus for Gaby's planned Rebellion of the Gods.

It had earned her a nasty death.

"I had *plans* for that gal," Gaea was saying. "Two or three more centuries...who knows? It might have been possible to *tell* her a few things. It might have been possible to...to make her understand...to admit what..." Gaea trailed off in disconsolate mutterings. Again, Gaby did not respond. Gaea glanced irritably at her.

"You've pissed me off," she complained. "I never figured you for starting all this trouble. Tragic figure, that's you. Following Rocky around with your little pink tongue hanging out, like a bitch in heat. It was a *good role*, Gaby, one you could have built a *life* around. I ain't gonna forgive you for writing your own lines. Just where do you come off being the ..." At a loss for words, Gaea hurled her beer bottle at a huge stain on the wall. There was a lot of broken brown glass heaped beneath the stain.

Gaea looked up again, with a wicked leer.

"I'll bet you want some answers. I'm going to enjoy giving them to you. Here's one, right here." Gaea reached out—her hand blurring as it approached the Gaby/camera viewpoint—and came back holding a small, white, struggling thing with two legs and goggling eyes.

"Spies," Gaea said. "This was yours. Sitting in your head for seventy-five years. How'd'ya like that? This is Stoolie. Rocky's got one called Snitch. She doesn't know about it, any more than you did. Everything the two of you did, it came right back to me."

Gaby felt a bottomless despair. *This must be hell.*

"No, it isn't. That's all bunk, too." Gaea paused long enough to squeeze the life from the squalling obscenity in her hand, then wiped the bloody mess on the arm of her chair.

"Life and death aren't as important as you think. Consciousness is the real conundrum. Your awareness of yourself as a living being. You remember dying, you think you remember floating up through space till you got here, not so very long ago. But time is tricky on this level. So is memory. You aren't a spook, if that's any consolation to you.

"I *have* you," Gaea whispered, making a gesture much like the one she had used to crush the Stoolie. "I cloned you, I recorded you, I took everything there was of Gaby-ness about you when you first showed up here. Cirocco, too. Since then, I've been constantly updated by that little bastard in your head. I am not supernatural, I am *not* God, not in the way you think of God...but I am one *hell* of a magician. The question of whether *you,* Gaby Plauget, the little girl from New Orleans who loved the stars, really died down there in Tethys, is, in the end, philosophical hair-splitting. Not worth the effort. You know that the awareness I am now addressing is you. Deny it if you can."

Gaby could not.

"It's all done with mirrors," Gaea said, shrugging it off. "If you had a 'soul,' then I missed it, and it's floated off to your anthropomorphic-Catholic-Judeo-Christian 'heaven,' which I personally doubt, as I've never heard any radio stations broadcasting from there. Everything else of you, I *own*."

What are you going to do with me? Gaby asked.

"Shit. I wish there *was* a hell." She brooded in silence for a time. Gaby could do nothing but look on. Slowly, Gaea produced an expression that wan an awful hybrid of a grin and a sneer.

"Actually, though hell isn't available, I have a reasonable facsimile. I don't expect you'll survive it.

"But I didn't finish telling you *why*. Do you want to know?"

Gaby thought anything would probably be better than Gaea's substitute for hell.

"You can say that again," Gaea said. "Because you've *ruined* Rocky for me. Rocky was a genuine flawed heroine. I've been looking for one for *millennia*. Now, she's still flawed, but she's going to get some spine. Snitch can feel it building. She's just finding out you're dead. She isn't *sure* I killed you, but near enough. Robin and Valiha and Chris are in deep trouble. They may not survive it. Right now, Rocky's going to devote all her energy to saving their lives. Then . . . she's going to come up here and declare war. This"— Gaea thumped her chest—"this incarnation of Gaea won't survive it." She shrugged. "That's okay. I was getting tired of Mrs. Potatohead, anyway. I have some ideas for the next Gaea that might amuse you. But you won't care. I'm through with you. You're wasting my time."

With that, Gaea had reached out and . . . grabbed the dream/locus that was Gaby. Things went black, then she found herself rising within the curved emptiness of the hub, rising toward a red line of light at the very top of the hub, a line she and Cirocco had seen when they first stepped out. . . .

It's all a dream, she reminded herself. That conversation never happened, not on a physical level. Gaea had all Gaby's memories, and was capable of making new ones on the computer-program/memory-matrix that was all that was left of Gaby, who used to be flesh and blood. So this is all illusion. She is doing something to me, but I am *not* flying up into the air, I am *not* plunging into that swirling maelstrom which I have always known, in my heart, is the mind of this thing called Gaea. . . .

* * *

One thought protected her. One notion clutched tightly in the midst of chaos prevented her from slipping from mania into insanity.

This is the twenty years, Gaby thought. *I lived through it already.*

In the red line, the speed of light was a local ordinance, a quaint regional phenomenon which could be a nuisance—like a cop hiding behind a billboard in a rural Georgia town—but which, with the proper bribes or enough horses under the hood, need not cause concern.

Take it a piece at a time. "Speed" depends on space and time. Neither were very important concepts in the Line. "Light" was complex and unnecessary parcels of massless wavicles, a by-product of living in the line, like sweat and feces. "Speed of light" was a contradiction in terms. How heavy is that day in the mountains when you built a campfire and saw a shooting star? What is the mass of yesterday? How fast is love?

The line extended all around the inner rim of Gaea, which, considered from an Einsteinian perspective, was a circle. The line was not circular. Seen against the backdrop of the inner rim, the line was thin. The line was not thin.

The line seemed to exist within the Universe. None of it extended outside the physical boundaries of Gaea, and Gaea was contained by the Universe; therefore, the line existed within the Universe.

The line was much bigger than the Universe.

In the end, the word "Universe" was unsuitable for use in a definition of the line. The concept of a naked singularity most closely approached the true nature of the line . . . and had little to do with it.

Things lived in it. Most of them were insane, as Gaea had intended Gaby to go insane. But Gaby kept holding to that thought: *This is the twenty years.* And: *Cirocco will need me.*

Slowly, cautiously, Gaby learned the nature of reality. She became as a God. It was pitifully inadequate—she had a lot of the Answers now, and knew that the Questions had never been phrased properly—but it was something. She would have been a lot happier living out the sort of script she had thought of as Life, but it was too late for that now, and she would accept what she must.

* * *

Cautiously, staying away from that dominant presence she knew as Gaea, Gaby began to look out of the line.

She saw Cirocco arrive in the hub, saw the bullets tear into the thing that called itself "Gaea," felt the much more interesting series of changes pass through the entity she knew as Gaea, and grew thoughtful. There was a possibility there....

She thought about it for a moment that turned out to be five years long.

She realized she could not endure much longer in this place. Gaea had not made it here, though a part of her remained in the line. Gaby must do the same thing if she were to survive. Carefully, trying not to alert Gaea, she disengaged herself and moved her center of consciousness down to the rim. She saw Cirocco many times, and remained unseen.

She began to learn the ways of Magic.

TWENTY-THREE

"Maybe she's never coming," Gaea said.

"You could be right," Chris replied.

He dipped his scrubber into the soapy water, swished it around, and raised it again to the big, pink wall of flesh.

They were in the Bathhouse, which was simply one of the soundstages on the RKO lot which had been used for an Esther Williams spoof and then left idle for the task of Gaea's Bath. The light was dim. The walls and ceiling were wood, the huge sliding doors closed. Somewhere hot rocks had been heaved into hot water, producing clouds of steam. Sweat poured off Chris and Gaea alike.

The scrubber was simply a big pushbroom with stiff bristles. Gaea's hide, though soft to the touch, seemed unharmed by this implement, no matter how hard Chris used it. It was one of the minor mysteries.

A panaflex wandered by, scanned the scene, shot a few feet of film, and then drifted away.

"You don't really think that," Gaea said.

"You could be right," Chris said, again.

Gaea shifted. Chris stood back, as any movement of Gaea's bulk entailed hazards to normal folk who happened to be in the way.

She was reclining, face down, her head resting on her folded arms. She was in about two feet of water. When she settled down again her head was turned, and one massive eye tracked him. He was cleaning her right side, from the waist to the shoulder, working his way toward the upper arm. It would take him a while.

"It *has* been a long time," Gaea went on. "What . . . eight months now?"

"Something like that."

"Do you have any idea what she's doing?"

"You know she was here twice. You know I wouldn't tell you if I saw her again."

"You are impertinent, but I love you. Anyway, I know she hasn't been here."

Which was true. She had warned him that that was the way it would be, but it was still hard. Chris was badly in need of moral support.

On the other hand, this job as bath attendant was not as bad as he had feared it would be. It was obviously intended to demoralize him. He did his best to let Gaea think it was working, dragging his way to and from work on those days when she called for a bath. But it was just a job. Once you got over the bizarre nature of it, it wasn't much different than painting a house.

He worked his way along her side and down the outside of the arm, cleaned his scrubber again, and began rasping away at her elbow and upper arm.

"When she gets here . . ." he began, then trailed off.

"What?"

"What will you do to her?"

"Kill her. I've already told you that. Or try to, anyway."

"You really think she has a chance?"

"Not much of a chance. She's overmatched, wouldn't you think?"

"Anybody can see that. Why don't you just . . . go out and hunt her down? She couldn't escape you for long, could she?"

"She's very crafty. And my . . . sight doesn't include her anymore. She worked that part of it very well."

Gaea had made oblique references to blindness before. Chris didn't know for sure, but suspected that was Snitch.

"Why do you hate her so much?"

Gaea sighed. The clouds of steam swirled violently.

"I don't hate her, Chris. I love her dearly. That's why I'm going to give her the gift of death. It's all I have to give her, and it's what she needs. I love you, too."

"Are you going to kill me?"

"Yes. Unless Cirocco can save you. With you, death won't be a gift."

"I don't understand the difference."

"With you, it will be agony, because you'll miss Adam's love. You're young, and nothing so good as Adam has ever happened to you."

"I understand *that* part. I don't understand why it'd be a favor to Cirocco."

"I didn't say favor. Gift. She needs it. Death is her friend. Death is the only way left for her to grow. She will never find love. But she can learn to live without it. I did."

Chris thought about that, and decided to take a chance.

"You sure did. You substituted cruelty."

She raised one eyebrow. Chris did not like to look into her eyes, even from a distance. There was too much ancient pain inside them. Evil, too, much, much evil . . . but he had started to wonder where evil comes from. Did one just decide to become evil? He doubted it. It must be a slow thing.

"Of course I'm cruel," Gaea muttered, closing her eye again. "There is no possible way for you to get the *perspective* on my cruelty, though. I'm fifty thousand years old, Chris. Cirocco is just over a hundred, and already feels things eating away at her soul. Can you imagine what I must feel?"

"You mean three million, not—"

"Of course. What was I thinking of. You can do my back now, Chris."

So he got the stepladder and climbed up with his scrubber and a hose. Her back was soft and yielding under his bare feet. She purred like a cat when he scrubbed between her shoulderblades.

TWENTY-FOUR

Cirocco came out of the Fountain and stretched out on the sand. She closed her eyes for a moment.

When she opened them she was still on sand, but it was the fine black sand of the small lake where Gaby had made love to her on the day Adam was taken.

She turned her head, and saw Gaby standing beside her. She reached up and Gaby took her hand. Once more there was a feeling like being pulled away from a sticky surface, then she was on her feet. She hugged Gaby.

"You've been away so long," Cirocco said, on the edge of tears.

"I know, I know. Too long. And we don't have much time now, and there is much to see. Will you come?"

Cirocco nodded and, holding Gaby's hand, followed her into the lake. She knew the water was shallow, yet felt the bottom drop away quickly until they were floating with just their heads out of the water. Gaby made a movement with her head, and they dived.

It wasn't like swimming. They went straight down. Cirocco did not need to propel herself in any way; they simply moved. She could feel the water rushing past her.

And it wasn't water. It was more like mud, like warm earth. This must be what a worm feels moving along underground, she thought. She remembered, long ago, struggling through the damp soil of Gaea toward the light: hairless, disoriented, frightened as a new-born babe. This wasn't like that. There was no fear.

Then she was standing in a huge cave, with no memory of how she had come to be there. The cave stretched farther than she could see. She walked with Gaby beside the dry-docked, dormant, spidery forms of spaceships.

"I started saving these when the war started," Gaby said. "Captains would show up and refuse to go back to the war. They scuttled their ships. I brought them here and saved them."

There were hundreds of them. They looked very strange sitting there.

"It looks so . . . forlorn," Cirocco said.

"Most of the damage is easily fixable," Gaby assured her.

"I suppose. But . . . they weren't *meant* to be here. You know what it looks like? Jellyfish tossed up on the beach."

Gaby looked out over the silent armada and nodded. Spaceships did have a lot in common with the soft-bodied anatomical fantasies achieved by the more exotic marine invertebrates.

"*You* brought them here, you said. Not Gaea."

"I did. I thought they might come in handy one day. I brought a lot of other stuff, too, when I realized Gaea wanted the war to go on. Take a look over here." Gaby gently turned Cirocco . . .

. . . and the darkness closed in again. When it lifted, Cirocco realized they were in a different place entirely.

"How did you *do* that?"

"Honey, I could never possibly explain how. Just accept that I can."

Cirocco thought about it. She felt a little fuzzy-headed, something like being drunk, something like dreaming. It was an accepting state of mind.

"Okay," she said, placidly.

They were in an endless tunnel. It was perfectly round, seemed absolutely straight, and pulsed with multi-colored light.

"This isn't real time you're seeing," Gaby explained.

"I'm dreaming, right?"

"Something like that. This is The Alchemist's Ring. It's a four-thousand-kilometer circular colliding-beam atom smasher . . . and it uses some other techniques that soup it up way beyond anything we ever built on Earth. This is where Gaea makes heavy metals—mostly gold, lately. Before that, she stockpiled a lot of plutonium. I just wanted to show it to you."

Cirocco stared at the lights. They moved along the tunnel, like red-hot, yellow-hot, and white-hot bumblebees. Not very fast at all.

Not real time, Gaby had said. The lights had to be atomic nuclei, and they had to be pushing the speed of light. It's all a visual aid, she thought. Not a dream, but something like it. More like a film.

"There's no air in here, is there?"

"No, of course not. Does that bother you?"

Cirocco shook her head.

"Okay, take a look over here..."

...and she turned again....

This time Cirocco held her head and it was a little easier. She never closed her eyes, but it didn't do her any good. She was in another cave, much smaller than the spaceship hangar.

"It's very close to absolute zero in here. These are frozen samples from several hundred thousand Earth animal and plant species. Gaea collected some of them. I ordered others, just before the war started. I hope they might come in useful some day, like the ships. Now, take one step up...."

Cirocco did, and almost lost her balance. Gaby's hand steadied her, and her feet came down on the familiar black sand. She took a deep breath, one she could believe in.

"I don't like to go that way," she complained.

"Okay. But I have some other things to show you. You still want to go?"

"Yes."

"Then hold my hand and don't be afraid."

Cirocco did, and they rose into the air.

Cirocco had flown before, many times, in dreams. There were two ways of going about it, possibly having to do with some psychological weather report. Low visibility in the cerebrum; clear air in the medulla. One way was to sit and float, like on a Persian magic carpet. That way one could drift slowly over the world. The other was to swoop and soar—but never with quite the amount of control one had in an airplane.

This flying was like the second way, but very precise. She flew with her arms extended—holding Gaby's hand at first, but later letting go and flying on her own—and her feet together, legs outstretched.

It gave her a giddy feeling; it was wonderful. By sweeping her arms backward, she could go faster. The palms of her hands functioned as ailerons for banking and turning. Various movements of her feet put her into a climb or a dive. She experimented with it, doing some tight turns and loops. Something was very different from "normal" dream flying, and she quickly realized it was the kinesthetic sense. Though her vision was still oddly hazy and her mind very slightly drugged, she could smell and taste the air, feel it rushing over her body, and—most important of all—she had mass and inertia. She pulled gees at the bottom of her loops, having to strain to hold her arms out rigid, feeling the flesh of her cheeks and thighs and breasts pulled down.

She glanced over at Gaby, who was flying in the same way.

"Very nice," she said.

"I thought you'd like it. But we're running out of time. Follow me."

Gaby turned and started climbing over the dark terrain of Dione. Cirocco did as she had been told, falling in behind, finding herself accelerating without having intended to do so. She folded her arms back against her side, and the two of them streaked upward. *This* wasn't like flying in an airplane. There was no sense of strain, no laboring engines. They just went straight up, like rockets. Soon they were entering the mouth of the Dione Spoke. Cirocco no longer felt any air resistance, though they must have been moving hundreds of miles per hour. Experimentally, she extended her arms, and felt no wind. Turning her hands or feet did nothing. She just followed Gaby.

The Dione Spoke, like all of the six spokes of the great wheel, was oval in cross-section, about a hundred kilometers along one axis and fifty along the other. It joined the rim in a vast, bell-shaped flare of tissue that gradually became the arched rim-roof. At the top of the bell was a sphincter that could be completely closed. At the other end, near the hub, was another sphincter. By opening or closing these valves and by flexing the three-hundred-kilometer-high spoke walls, Gaea pumped air from one region to another, heating or cooling it as needed.

Except for the Oceanus Spoke, which was barren, the interiors of these towering cylinders supported life in abundance. Huge trees grew horizontally from the vertical walls. Complex eco-systems flourished in the labyrinth branches, in hollows of the trees, and in the walls of the spoke itself.

There were dozens of species of angel in Gaea, most of them

too dissimilar to inter-breed. The Dione Spoke supported three species—or Flights, as they called themselves. At the top, where gravity was almost nonexistent, were the spidery Air Flight: dwarves among angels, with translucent wings and skin, ephemeral, not too bright, more like bats than birds. They seldom landed anywhere except to lay eggs, which they abandoned to fate. They lived on a diet of leaves.

The middle part of the spoke belonged to the Dione Eagles, related to Eagle Flights in Rhea, Phoebe, and Cronus. Eagles did not form communities. In fact, when two Eagles met there was likely to be a bloody fight. Their young were born live, in mid-air, and had to learn to fly on the long fall to the rim. Many of them did.

But the Airs and the Eagles were in the minority. Most Gaean angels nested and nurtured their young. There were a lot of different ways to go about it. One species in Thea had three sexes: cocks, hens, and neuters. The hens were flightless and huge, the cocks small and savage. The neuters were the only intelligent ones, and they cared for the young, which were born alive.

The Dione Supra Flight—badly named, in Cirocco's opinion, as their territory was at the bottom of the spoke—were peaceful, community-oriented beings. They built big beehive-shaped nests in the trees out of branches, mud, and their own dried feces, which contained a bonding agent. As many as a thousand Supras might live in one nest. Their females gave birth to things called placentoids, a sort of mammalian egg containing an embryo which had to be attached to the living flesh of Gaea. In this way the females never grew too pregnant to fly and the young could grow quite large before being detached from the womb. Like humans, Supra infants were helpless for a long time. They learned to fly in six or seven years.

Cirocco liked the Supras. They were more approachable than most angels, had even been known to come trading in Bellinzona. They used tools more than most angels did. Cirocco knew it was illogical and prejudiced—it was not the fault of the Eagles that they were so heartless, it was simply their biology—but she couldn't help it. Over the years she had had many Supra friends.

Like most angels, Supras looked like very thin humans with giant chests. Their bodies were black and shiny. Their knees bent in either direction, and their feet were bird-claws. Their wings were mounted low on the back, below the shoulderblades. When folded, the wing "elbow" joints towered over their heads, and the tips of the long primary feathers trailed far below their feet.

Angels had one thing in common with Titanides. Both were relatively new creations, made by Gaea as variations on the human theme. Even with hollow bones, huge wings, giant muscles, and no fat at all, a flying human had taxed Gaea's design capability to the limit. The larger angels could lift little more than their own weight at the rim. They preferred to live in the lower-gravity regions of the spokes.

In addition to their nesting habits, two other things set the Supras apart. One was their coloration. Females had green wing feathers and males had red. The caudal empennage of both sexes was black, except in mating season, when the females grew peacock fans and put on glorious displays. They had no other external sexual differentiation.

And they didn't have names. Their language did not contain first-person singular pronouns. "We" was as near as they could come to it, and yet they were not communal minds. They existed as individuals.

This made communication with them somewhat difficult. But it was worth the effort.

The Supras did not seem at all startled to see Gaby and Cirocco fly up to the nest and land, light as a feather, near the big opening in the top. It was raining in the spoke, and the smiler-hide cover had been pulled across to keep the water out. Gaby ducked under it and Cirocco followed her into darkness.

Oddest damn dream, she thought. One minute she could fly, but as soon as she set down on the nest she was back to her normally awkward method of blundering through the Supra nest.

A Supra staircase was a series of rods embedded on the adobe-like nest wall. The angels grasped the rods with their feet; all Cirocco could do was hang on with both hands and try to pretend it was a ladder as she backed down it. In the same way, the Supra equivalent of a comfortable chair was a long horizontal pole. They perched on them effortlessly.

She and Gaby worked their way toward the back of the nest,

which was built against the spoke wall. Dotted along the wall were supra babies in little pockets of Gaea's flesh. Some were no bigger than ostrich eggs, while others were as big as human infants and needed a lot of tending so they wouldn't break their umbilical cords. Child care was done by all members of the flight, in rotation. Supras didn't imprint on a particular mother or father.

The base of the placentoid rookery was the only spot in the nest with a spot level and wide enough to be used as a floor. Gaby and Cirocco went there and sat, cross-legged. Cirocco remembered she should have brought a gift. Anything would do—Supras loved bright things. It was a polite way to begin a visit. But she didn't even have clothes.

Gaby didn't, either, but with a magician's flourish she opened her hand and produced an old plastic bicycle reflector that shifted colors when it was turned. The Supras loved it, passing it back and forth.

"It is a fabulous gift," one of them said.

"Most luminiferous," agreed another.

"Elegant and tricksy," one suggested.

"We are most brilliantly aghast," a fourth chimed in.

"It will be enshrined."

They chattered their appreciation for some time, and when Cirocco and Gaby could get a word in, they praised the beauty, wit, poise, wisdom, and elegant flight characteristics of their hosts in the most extravagant terms. They applauded the rookery, nest, branch, wing, squadron, and Flight of the inestimable Supras. One rutting female was so moved she spread her tail feathers in sexual display. Though Cirocco could barely see it in the dimness, she joined the others in praising the female's fertility and prowess in terms so explicit they might have made a whore blush.

"Would you take some...food?" one of them asked. The others looked away and kept a modest silence. It was a new thing for the Supras, something they were cautiously trying out in their dealings with humans. By custom, food was never asked for or offered outside of one's own nest. Food would not be refused a starving Supra from another nest, but most Supras would rather die than ask.

The invitation had been made by the lowest-status individual of the nest, a male who was old, scrawny, and probably near death.

"Couldn't possibly," Cirocco said, lightly, to another individual.

"Stuffed, we're absolutely stuffed," Gaby agreed.

"Flight would be impossible with another gram," Cirocco pointed out.

"Fat is perilous."

"Abstinence is a virtue."

They never looked at the one who had asked, thus spreading the load of embarrassment as equally as possible, which was the polite thing to do. The Supras clucked approvingly, and praised the prosperity of their guests.

Suddenly Cirocco remembered encountering that lone Supra in the air over Iapetus, while the deathangel was flying away with Adam.

"So, why have we come here to this nest?" Cirocco asked, addressing the group of angels, not Gaby, and inverting her question in a way calculated to cause the least confusion to the Supras.

"Yes, a most interesting thing," one said.

"Why have they come, why have they come?"

"One is of air, one is of dream."

"Dreams in the nest, how very strange."

"The one who burns. Why did they come?"

Gaby cleared her throat, and all looked at her.

"We have come for the same reason we came in the past," she said. "To prosecute the case against Gaea, and to further the preparations for war against her and all her estates and nests."

"Exactly!" Cirocco, who couldn't have been more confused, chimed in. "That is precisely our intention. To . . . engage in most brilliant stratagems and tacticalities."

"Most precise!" one angel said, enthusiastically.

"Oh, rue the day!"

"The nest of Gaea will be laid low."

"Mumble," said one angel, which is what they said when they had nothing to say but didn't want to be left out of the conversation.

"Mumble," another agreed.

It was easy to see the Dione Supras as amiable nitwits, idiot savants with large and fractured vocabularies. They were nothing of the kind. The English language was a delight to them, so illogical

nd fertile and well-suited to their natural desire to confuse, obfus-
ate, and generally side-step clear meaning whenever possible.

"Quite violent," Gaby suggested.

"Oh, so very violent. Much torment."

"And cautious, extremely cautious."

"The tactics," one said. "Such a lexicon of tactics." The way
e said it, Cirocco knew it was a question that might translate as
ow do we fight her?

Gaby made that same tricky pass with her hands. Nothing up
er sleeve, Cirocco decided. For a moment she knew how others
*ust feel when she worked her own meager magics.

She produced a red stick that was unmistakably dynamite—
*at was, in fact, labeled DYNAMITE: Product of Bellinzona. The
*ngels fell silent when they looked at it. Cirocco took it and turned
: around in her hands. The angels sighed in unison.

"Where did you get this?" Cirocco asked, momentarily for-
*etting the others. "There's nothing like this in Bellinzona."

"That's because you won't make it for another kilorev," Gaby
*aid.

"Ephemera!" a Supra crowed. "It's ephemera!"

"An insubstantial nullity," another opined.

"Not made yet? How farcical! We are keenly misinformed."

"It doesn't exist," one summarized. "Like this Cirocco one."

"Don't quibble," came an adjuration.

"Did you forget it's a dream?" one reminded Cirocco.

"Dynamite! Dynamite! Dynamite!"

"There will be dynamite," Gaby agreed. "When it comes time
* fight Gaea, there will have been dynamite for some time."

"Will have been! A truly stratospheric verb."

"Most sincerely."

"An . . . illusion?" a younger Supra said, with wrinkled brow,
*ill staring at the dynamite in Gaby's hand.

'A will-o'-the-wisp," one explained.

"A figurehead! A moonshine of farragos, a pre-pentimentoized,
*fra-extinct, fleeting mockery! A vacuity!" shouted another, effec-
*vely shutting off debate.

They stared at it again, in a feather-rustling quiet. Gaby made
* vanish back to where it had come from—the future, Cirocco
*esumed.

"Ah," one of them sighed, at last.

"Indeed," affirmed another. "My goodness, the things we will do with such a lump of power!" he asked.

"Yes, you will," Gaby agreed. "And right now, you're going to tell us all about it."

Which Gaby did, at great length.

When she was through, there was the customary offer of sex. Both Cirocco and Gaby accepted, which was the polite thing to do.

They went through the courting ritual, which had always reminded Cirocco of a square dance, while the others sang and clapped in rhythm. Cirocco's partner was a sterling specimen of the species. His bright red wings enfolded her warmly as the act was "consummated."

And that was another thing she found attractive about the Supras. They didn't have an ounce of xenophobia. A tribal people, their culture was laced with ritual, custom, and tradition—but they had flexibility. With visiting Supras the offer of sex would have been in complete earnest, and the act would not have been simulated. They had formalized this ritual solely for the purpose of dealing with human visitors. Real sex with the Supra would have been grotesque for both of them. As it was, the male simply gave her the lightest possible touch with his tiny penis, never seen, and everybody was happy. It made Cirocco feel good. In a way, it made her feel loved.

She had almost forgotten it was a dream until they landed lightly on the black sandy beach and she saw her sleeping body. Nearby was Hornpipe, resting on folded legs, making a carving during his own dream-time. He looked up and nodded at them both.

Cirocco kissed Gaby good-by and watched her fly away. Then she yawned, stretched, and looked down at herself. Time to wake up, she thought, wryly.

Once more she was impressed with how easily the fantastic could become commonplace. She knelt beside her sleeping body, remembering how it had been the last time, and rolled over onto it.

She gasped when she hit warm, muscular flesh instead of the sand she had expected. For a moment she lay sprawled across the sleeping body, then she leaped into the air as if she had landed on an ant-hill. She stood, horrified, as the other Cirocco stirred, raised a hand to her face . . . then turned slightly on her side and went back to sleep.

She turned her head and saw Hornpipe looking at her. *What is he seeing?* She wondered if she would ever ask him that.

"I'm not ready for this," she said aloud. But she sighed, knelt on the sand, and hesitantly touched the body. Again, it was *other*. It was a big, strong-looking, brown-skinned, and not very pretty woman.

She took the other Cirocco's hand. The other stirred slightly, muttering something. Then she opened her eyes and sat up quickly.

There was a moment of vertigo, and then there was just Cirocco. She looked around quickly, saw no one else.

"Just you and me, kid," she said to herself, and went to join Hornpipe.

TWENTY-FIVE

Historians, when Bellinzona eventually produced some, were never quite sure when the change happened. The city had been born in chaos, had grown in confusion, been conquered in disarray. There was a brief time when there were almost as many inmates in the work camps as free citizens walking the streets.

Conal, with his informal polls of the citizens, detected no dramatic jump in morale, or in the approval rating of Cirocco Jones, not even after the aerial attack. He suspected it was the result of a combination of things.

But for whatever reason, at some point between the sixth and the ninth kilorev after Cirocco's invasion, Bellinzona stopped being a brawling collection of fractious individuals and became a community—within the human-defined limits of that term. It was nothing so dramatic as all men suddenly deciding they were brothers. Deep and persistent differences still existed, nowhere more strongly than in the Council. But at the end of the ninth kilorev Bellinzona was a city with an identity, and a purpose.

Football had a surprising amount to do with it.

Serpent's obsession, combined with strong help from Robin's organizational abilities and the willing work of the parks commissioner, soon had two leagues formed, ten teams to a league, and that was just for the adults. There were intermediate and junior teams, too. A second stadium had to be built to accommodate the number of games, which were strongly contested and heavily attended. It was something to cheer for. Local heroes were born, intra-city rivalries established. It was something to talk about in the taprooms after a long hard shift. For some, it was something to fight about. Titanide police were instructed not to interfere as long as only fists were used. When word spread about this unprecedented instance of the law looking the other way, some mad brawls developed, some people were hurt . . . and the Mayor did nothing. Even this seemed to improve the community spirit. Cooler heads began to move in and stop the fights as the emerging citizens learned how better to tolerate each other.

Which is not to say no more noses got broken.

Whistlestop's departure played a part. One day he simply drifted away and did not come back. People seemed to breathe easier. He was too visible a symbol of oppression. He was just an old bag of wind, completely harmless, but the people didn't like him up there and were glad to see him go.

Titanides became less numerous, and less visible. The occupying force was in fact halved on the day of Cirocco's return from the fountain, and halved again a kilorev later. Human police took up the slack, and Titanides intervened in only the worst violence. They were monumentally uninterested in civil crime.

Both the quality and quantity of food deliveries improved as more acreage was put under cultivation, and as the ones who grew it learned better methods. Smiler meat began to appear in markets, at gradually reducing prices. Independent farmers were created under land-grant schemes, and proved, to no one's surprise, more efficient than forced laborers.

Inflation remained a problem, but—in the immortal words of one of Nova's economic reports—"The rate of increase of the rate of increase is slowing."

Most people thought the biggest reason for the lift in morale was the most obvious one: the cowardly and unprovoked attack by what was later learned to be the Sixth Fighter/Bomber Wing of the Gaean Air Force, based in Iapetus. The Sixth was composed of one Luftmorder and nine buzz bombs, which came screaming in from the east on the first bright day following many decarevs of rain, catching people out of doors enjoying the unaccustomed warmth.

The "cowardly and unprovoked" line was used by Trini in a speech twenty revs later, as the pieces were still being picked up. She had been even more intemperate than that; in an illogical but heart-felt rage, she had called the attack a day that would live in infamy.

Aside from the word "day," the phrase was amazingly accurate.

"It's Gaea, giving me help, damn her miserable hide," Cirocco told the Council at the next meeting. "She's handing me a Pearl Harbor on a silver platter—and a victory to boot. She must be desperate to have it out with me. She knows I'll have to come soon now, with patriotism building like it is."

The Sixth Fighter/Bomber Wing inflicted heavy damage on the city with bombs and missiles. Had the attack continued, or had they been joined by the Eighth, which Cirocco knew to be in Metis, the city might have turned into an inferno.

But the Bellinzona Air Force arrived in the nick of time.

The fact that there *was* a Bellinzona Air Force was news to the Bellinzonans, and those who dared emerge from cover had watched in awe as the Dragonflys, Mantises, Skeeters, and Gnats engaged the marauding aeromorphs in deadly combat. What they didn't know was that the Sixth was overmatched at the start. It certainly didn't *look* that way. The buzz bombs were huge and fast and loud, they trailed great clouds of black smoke, and spouted fire when they attacked. The Bellinzona planes seemed to be made of wire and cellophane. But they would turn and twist with a ghastly ease, and though their armament didn't make a lot of noise getting out, it certainly had the desired result when it hit the target. Three Mantises harried the big, galumphing Luftmorder from the air, followed it as it shrieked in agony before bursting in flame on a hillside. From the frightened Bellinzonans there arose a ragged cheer.

It would have been a rout but for the lack of experience of some of the Bellinzonan pilots. One managed to run afoul of an especially cunning buzz bomb, lost a wing, and crashed into the sea.

His body was recovered, and a spontaneous cortege carried it down Oppenheimer Boulevard. A monument was later erected to this first hero of the Gaean War.

So the victory in the Battle of Bellinzona was certainly an important part of the change that came over the city. But the crucial element of the change began upon Cirocco's return from the Fountain.

She became a public figure.

Within a hectorev, the by-ways of Bellinzona were festooned with posters showing her face. They were heroic posters, modeled after those big banners of Lenin and Suslov carried through Moscow on Mayday. Looking at them, you just *knew* Cirocco Jones stood for brotherhood, solidarity, three square meals a day, and the welfare of the proletariat.

The community bulletin boards had developed into news centers, into big walls covered with messages and stories and football scores. A fledgling newspaper industry had developed; just four or five intermittent and scarce parchment sheets. The industry was quietly taken over. Editors were reasoned with, and one was jailed. Stories began to appear about Gaea, about New Pandemonium, about rumors of preparation for war in the east. That the stories were true did not change the fact that the Bellinzona media were State-run. A lot of people in government didn't like it. About the same number thought it was a fine idea. Libertarians and fascists existed in about equal numbers everywhere, Cirocco had found.

Stuart and Trini *hated* it, though not from any moral foundation of civil liberties. They watched helplessly as Cirocco consolidated a stranglehold on Bellinzonan public opinion. And they knew that, as long as she could keep delivering security and stifling opposing opinion, she could remain Mayor until she died. Which, in her case, might very well be a thousand years hence.

On the other hand, there was the chance she would not live another kilorev.

She had started making public appearances. There were meetings, rallies, parades. She waded into groups of people, shaking hands, kissing babies, being seen with community leaders. She cut ceremonial ribbons on new development projects.

She gave speeches. They were *good* speeches. They were good for the same reason the posters were stirring: Cirocco found the people who knew how to paint posters and how to write speeches, and set them to work.

It was all very slick. Even Trini and Stuart had to admit it. When they were in her presence, they could *feel* it: a force that seemed to emanate from the woman, a power that made you feel good to be around her, and to think good thoughts about her when she was gone. She could be whatever the situation demanded. In a crowd she had the common touch. On a podium she was rousing, uplifting . . . or alarming, when speaking about the threat of Gaea.

Trini began calling her Charisma Jones, at least when the Mayor wasn't around. Luckily, it was now possible to *know* when she was around. There were no more of those mysterious appearances. Cirocco seemed ubiquitous.

And that was the big hazard to her, Trini knew. All the good feeling aside, there were still those who hated her. There were two assassination attempts in three kilorevs. There would certainly have been many more in the early days of her administration had she been more accessible. Now, out in the crowds, she made a nice target. Had guns been available, she would not have stood a chance. As it was, those who came at her with knives had died in seconds. Cirocco was too good to need much in the way of bodyguards.

So far. One day a very good archer would stand far away and make a try.

In the meantime, it was good to live in Bellinzona.

When Cirocco began raising an army, it seemed the most natural thing in the world.

TWENTY-SIX

"I don't like all that army stuff," Robin said.

"Why not? It's equal opportunity. Men's regiments and women's regiments. The pay's good, the food's terrific—"

"I never know when you're kidding anymore."

"Robin, when it comes to the army, I'm kidding just about all the time. It's the only way I can cope with it."

Robin looked at Cirocco Jones, who sat astride Hornpipe, as she was sitting on Valiha. Nearby, the infant Tambura cantered in the gawky and amiable way of all young Titanides, enjoying the educational outing with her foremother, Hornpipe, and the two humans.

The Wizard, the Captain, the Mayor...the Demon. Cirocco Jones was all of them, and she was also an old friend. But sometimes lately she scared Robin. Seeing her at the big rallies in the stadium, watching the throngs cheer her every word...it reminded her too much of the historical footage of demagogues of the past, the silver-tongued rascals who led their people into disaster. She was a stranger, standing up there, arms raised, drinking the vast approval of the crowds.

Yet, on those rare occasions when she could be alone with her, she was just Cirocco. Of course, that had always been slightly overwhelming in itself, but in a quite different way.

Cirocco seemed to sense Robin's mood. She turned to her, and shook her head.

"Remember what I told you, way back at the Junction," Cirocco said. "Way back when we planned all this. I told you you wouldn't like all of it. But I told you to remember it isn't all what it seems."

"Putting that editor in jail...that made me sick. He was a good man."

"I know he is. I admire him. When this is over I'll use whatever influence I have left—if I'm still alive—to see that he is properly honored. Make him the head of the school of journalism, maybe...and he'll hate me the rest of his life. With good reason."

Robin sighed.

"Hell. As soon as she's sure you're gone, Trini will just stick him back in jail. Or Stuart."

They were heading almost due west, into the heart of the Dione darkness. The Titanides had already brought them through the "impenetrable" jungle and up over the "unscalable" mountains about as easily as a pair of tanks moving over paved road. They had swum the Ophion, and were now nearing the Dione central vertical cable. It was like an Earth night with a full moon in the sky. Behind them, Iapetus curved up the inside of the wheel, and in front was Metis. Both regions reflected enough light into Dione for the Titanides to see by. Tambura scampered to the left and right of the main trail, but always returned at a gentle admonition from Valiha, and never got into trouble. Titanide children never did.

Cirocco had not mentioned the purpose of the trip. Robin had thought the central cable was just a landmark on the way to their final destination, but when they reached it, the Titanides stopped.

"We'll be happy to accompany you, Captain," Valiha said. "This place holds no horrors for us."

She was referring to the instinctive fear Titanides held for the central cables, and for the beings which lived at the bottom. Twenty years ago, trapped under a rockfall beneath the central Tethys cable, Robin and Chris had faced the nightmare task of herding Valiha down the five-kilometer spiral stairway that ended in the lair of Tethys himself—a cranky, obsessed, terrifying, and, luckily for them, myopic Lesser God. Valiha's I.Q. had decreased with every step down, until at the bottom she was no brighter than a horse and twice as skittish. The encounter had ended in two broken forelegs for Valiha, and an endless nightmare for Robin.

It was not a fear the Titanides could do anything about. It had been programmed into them by Gaea.

But Dione was dead, and that apparently made a difference.

"Thanks for the offer, my friends, but I would prefer it if you awaited us here. Our business will not take us long. You might use the opportunity to teach this useless one something of the good grace and dignity your race is known for, and which she so sorely lacks."

"Hey!" Tambura protested, and leaped at Cirocco, who dodged to the side, grabbed her, and wrestled in mock ferocity until the young Titanide was laughing too hard to continue the game. Cirocco mussed her hair, and took Robin's arm. They started into the forest of cable strands.

At twenty-five centimeters per step, there were twenty thousand steps leading down to Dione. Even in one-quarter gee, it was one hell of a lot of steps.

Cirocco had brought a powerful battery light. Robin was grateful for it. There was natural light from creatures called glowbes which clung to the high, arched ceiling, but it was dim and orange, and there were long stretches where the animals didn't nest. They marched in silence for a long time.

Robin realized she would probably never get a better chance

to talk to Cirocco about something that had been causing her a lot of agony. The new, improved, glorious Mayor had little time these days to spend talking with her friends.

"I don't suppose it's possible you don't know about me and Conal."

"You're right. It's not possible."

"He wants to move in with me again."

"Why did you throw him out?"

"I didn't—" But she had. She might as well admit it, she decided. It had been almost a kilorev now, and she wasn't getting much sleep. Not used to sleeping alone anymore, she told herself, and knew it was more than that.

"Nova was part of it, I guess," she said. "Every time I looked at her I saw the accusation, and I felt guilty. I wanted to get close to her again."

"Worked pretty good, didn't it?"

"That cold-ass, sanctimonious, snot-nosed little—" She bit it off before the rage could build.

"She's all I have," Robin said helplessly.

"That's not true. And it's not fair to her."

"But I—"

"Listen for a minute," Cirocco cut in. "I've given this some thought. I've been thinking about it since the feast, since we made the Pledge and started planning to take over Bellinzona. I—"

"You knew *then*?"

"I hate to see friends in such a mess. I've stayed out, because people don't really want advice about things like that. But I have some. If you want it."

Robin didn't want it. She had learned that the observations and plans made by the Mayor were usually the right thing to do—and quite often not what you would *like* to do at all.

"I want it," she said.

Robin counted three hundred steps before Cirocco spoke again. Great Mother, she thought. It must be really awful if she's taking this much time to choose her words. Who does she think I am?

"Nova hasn't learned the difference between evil and sin."

Robin counted fifty more steps.

"Maybe I haven't, either," she finally said.

"Naturally, I'm implying that I *have*," Cirocco said, with a chuckle. "Let me tell you what I *think,* and you can make of it what you will."

Ten more steps.

"Sin is a violation of the laws of the tribe," Cirocco said. "On Earth, in most societies, what you practice in the Coven was a sin. There's another word, too. Perversion. Historically, most humans have seen homosexuality as a perversion. Now, I've heard about a hundred theories as to why people are homosexual. Doctors say it happened in childhood. Biochemists say it's all chemicals in the brain. Militant gays say being gay is good for you, and so forth. In the Coven, you say men are evil beings, and only an evil woman could mate with one.

"I don't have a theory. I don't *care.* It just isn't important to me if somebody's heterosexual or homosexual.

"But it's important to you. In your mind, you have sinned by having carnal knowledge with a man. You're a pervert."

Another fifty steps went by as Robin thought this over. It wasn't a new thought to her.

"I don't know if this helps me," she said, at last.

"I didn't promise to help. I think your only hope is to look at it objectively. I've tried to. What I've concluded is that, for reasons I don't understand, some people are one way and some people are the other. On Earth, with *overwhelming* societal reasons to be heterosexual, there have always been those who are not. In the Coven, it's like a mirror image. I suspect there might have been a fair number of unhappy women in the Coven. They probably didn't even know what was making them unhappy. Maybe they dreamed about it. Sinful dreams. But their problem was that—for whatever reason, biological, behavioral, hormonal—they were ... well, for want of a better word, they were gay. They'd have been happier with male sex partners. I don't know if you're born gay or are made gay—on Earth, or in the Coven. But I think you're a pervert."

Robin felt the blood rushing to her face, but did not break stride on the long descent. It was best to have it out.

"You think I have to have a man."

"It's not that simple. But something in your personality meshes with something in Conal's. If he'd been a woman, you'd be the happiest person in Gaea right now. Since he's a man, you're one of the most miserable. It's because you've bought the Coven's big lie, even though you think you're too adult for all that. There were millions of Earth men and women who bought the Earth cultures' big lies, and they died just as unhappy as you are now. And I suggest to you that it's a foolish thing."

"Yeah, but . . . damn it, Cirocco, I can see that. I've had those thoughts—"

"But you haven't fought them hard enough."

"But what about Nova?"

"What about her? If she can't accept you the way you are, then she isn't the person you hoped she would be."

Robin thought about it for many hundred steps.

"She's grown up," Cirocco said. "She can make her own decisions."

"I know that. But—"

"She represents the unforgiving weight of Coven morality."

"But . . . can't I make her get over it?"

"No. I'm not even sure you can help her. But . . . maybe I shouldn't say this, but I think time is going to cure your problem. Time, and a Titanide."

Robin questioned her about that, but Cirocco would say no more.

"So you think I should let Conal move back in?"

"Do you love him?"

"Sometimes I think I do."

"I don't know a lot of things for sure, but one thing I'm pretty sure about is that love is the only thing that's worth much."

"He makes me happy," Robin admitted.

"All the better."

"We're . . . very good in bed."

"Then you're a fool to be anywhere else. It was good enough for your great-great-great grandmaw. You are descended from a long line of lesbians, but there's a touch of perversion in your blood."

Another hundred steps went by, then still another.

"Okay. I'll think about it," Robin said. "You told me what sin is. What's evil?"

"Robin . . . I know it when I see it."

That was all there was time for, as, to Robin's surprise, she found herself at the bottom of the Dione stairs.

It was nothing like the other regional brains. Robin had seen three of them: Crius, still loyal to Gaea; Tethys, an enemy; and Thea, one of Gaea's strongest allies. The twelve regional brains had chosen sides long ago, during the Oceanic Rebellion, when the land itself had become disloyal to Gaea.

It had been Dione's misfortune to be located between Metis and Iapetus, two of Oceanus' strongest and most effective supporters. When war came, she was squeezed between the two and mortally wounded. It had taken her a long time to die, but she had been dead now for at least five hundred years.

It was dark at the bottom of the staircase. Their footsteps echoed. The moat surrounding the huge conical tower that had once been Dione was dry. Where Tethys had glowed with a red inner light and had seemed alert and aware even in his utter immobility, Dione was obviously a corpse. Parts of the tower had collapsed. Robin could glimpse a lattice-like internal structure through the gaping holes. When Cirocco's flashlight fell on it, it threw back a million shattered reflections.

When the flashlight turned the other way, the reflections were only two. The twin gleams were about two meters apart, and came from inside a big, arched tunnel entrance. It looked like a train was sitting just inside.

"Come on out, Nasu," Cirocco whispered.

Robin's heart turned over. She fell back through the years, twenty and more . . .

. . . to the day when, as a young girl, she had been given the tiny snake, a South American anaconda, *Eunectes murinus,* and selected it as her demon. No cats or crows for Robin; she would have a serpent. She named it Nasu, which someone told her meant "little pig" in some Earth language, after watching it devour six terrified mice in one meal.

. . . to arriving in Gaea, Nasu in her handbag, terrified and confused by Customs, and by the low gravity. Nasu had bitten her three times that day.

. . . to losing the snake somewhere in the depths of Gaea between Tethys and Thea. She and Chris had looked for a long time, had set out bait, called endlessly, to no avail. Chris had tried to convince her the snake would find prey down there in the darkness, that she could survive. Robin had tried to believe it was so, and had failed.

She had meant to keep the snake all her life. She had intended to grow old with this reptile. She knew they could grow to ten meters in length and outweigh a mere python, inch for inch, by a factor of two. A truly remarkable snake, the anaconda....

Nasu made a hissing sound that raised the hairs on the back of Robin's neck. There must have been sounds like that, though not so deep or so loud, in the swamps of the Cretaceous Period. A remarkable snake, but they didn't grow *that* big.

"Sh-sh-sh . . . Cirocco . . . let's get—"

Nasu moved. Surely there could never have been a slither like that since the dawn of time. It was a slither to make tyrannosaurs run squealing into the brush, to loosen the bowels of a wolverine, to give lions and tigers cardiac arrest.

To stop Robin's heart.

The anaconda's head came out of the tunnel and it stopped. Her *tongue* was twice the girth of a full-grown anaconda, and it slid out and flicked this way and that. Her head was completely white. It was about the size of the locomotive Robin had first visualized in the darkness. The eyes were golden, with narrow black slits.

"Talk to her, Robin," Cirocco whispered.

"Cirocco!" Robin hissed, urgently. "I don't think you understand! An anaconda isn't a puppy dog or a kitty cat."

"I know that."

"You *don't!* You can care for them, but you never own them. They tolerate you because you're too big to eat. If she's *hungry* . . ."

"She's not. I know a little about this, babe. There's big game down here. You don't think she grew that big eating chickens and rabbits, do you?"

"I don't believe she grew that big at *all!* In twenty years? That's impossible."

There was that awful slithering sound again, and twenty more meters of Nasu entered the dark chamber. She paused, and tasted the air again.

"She won't remember me. She's not a *pet,* damn it. I had to handle her carefully, and even then I got bites."

"I promise you, Robin, she's not hungry. And even if she was, she wouldn't bother with anything as small as us."

"I don't understand what you want me to do."

"Just stand your ground and talk to her. Say the things you

used to say to her twenty years ago. Get her used to you...and don't run away."

So Robin did. They were three or four hundred meters from the snake. Every few minutes there would be more slithering, and another fifty meters would emerge from the tunnel. There was no sign Nasu was about to run out of meters.

There came a time when the head was no more than two meters away. Robin knew what came next, and braced herself for it.

The great tongue came out. It touched her lightly on her forearms, flirted briefly with the textures of her clothing, flicked over her hair.

And it was all right.

The tongue was moist and cool, but not unpleasant. And in that moment of touching, Robin somehow knew the snake remembered her. The touch of the tongue seemed to pass some sign of recognition from Nasu to Robin. *I know you.*

Nasu moved again, the great head lifted slightly off the floor, and Robin found herself in a semi-circle of white snake higher than her head. One fearful yellow eye regarded her with reptilian speculation, yet she was not afraid. The head tilted a little....

Robin remembered something Nasu had liked. She had sometimes rubbed Nasu on the top of the head, with her forefinger. The snake would rise to it, coil around her arm, and present herself for more.

She reached up and, with both fists, rubbed the smooth skin on top of Nasu's head. The snake made a relatively small hissing sound—no worse than an ocean liner coming into port—and retreated. The tongue touched her again, and Nasu moved around her from the other side and tilted her head the other way for more rubbing.

Cirocco moved slowly up to join them. Nasu watched placidly.

"Okay," Robin said, quietly. "I've talked to her. Now what?"

"Obviously, this is more than an anaconda," Cirocco began.

"Obviously."

"I don't know what changed her. Diet? Low gravity? Something, anyway. She's adapted to living underground. I've spotted her two or three times, bigger each time, and she's stayed out of my way. I have reason to believe she's a lot more intelligent than she was."

"Why?"

"A friend told me she might be. The next time I saw Nasu, I told her to meet me here in Dione if she wanted to be with her old friend again. And here she is."

Robin was impressed, but beginning to be suspicious.

"So what's the purpose?"

Cirocco sighed.

"You asked me what evil is. Maybe this is. I've thought about it a long time, but I'm afraid I can't get much of a handle on what might seem an evil thing to a snake. I don't think she loves Gaea. And anyway, all I can do is suggest. The rest is up to you, and her."

"Suggest what?"

"That you ask her to follow us to Hyperion, to slay Gaea."

TWENTY-SEVEN

Nova looked up at Virginal and tried to conceal her disappointment.

"Are you tired? Is that it?"

"No," Virginal said. "I . . . just don't feel like running today."

"Not feeling good?" Nova couldn't remember any Titanide complaining of so much as a headache. They were disgustingly healthy. Short of broken bones or major internal injuries, not much could keep a Titanide down.

It was her right, of course. Nova had no illusions of owning Virginal, or even of having a claim on the Titanide's time. But it had been a thing they did regularly since coming to Bellinzona. Nova would pack a huge picnic lunch and they would gallop off to some remote, scary, mountainous place, Nova clinging for her life yet knowing she was in little danger. They would eat, talk of this and that, Nova would nap while Virginal had her dream-time.

At first, they had done it faithfully, once every hectorev. As Nova's responsibilities grew she had found less and less time for the outings. But it was her only real recreation, her only escape from the eternal, dreary numbers. Football bored her. She didn't drink.

"Well, maybe tomorrow then," she said, using the common Bellinzona term for "after my next sleep period."

To her surprise, Virginal hesitated, then looked away from her.

"I don't think so," she said, reluctantly.

Nova dropped the heavy pack on the wooden causeway and put her hands on her hips.

"Okay. There's something on your mind. I think I have a right to hear about it."

"I'm not sure you do," Virginal said. She looked pained. "Perhaps Tambura would like to go riding with you. I can ask her."

"Tambura? Why her? Because she's a baby?"

"She can bear you with no trouble."

"That's not the *point,* Virginal!" She pulled herself back from the edge of anger and tried again.

"Are you saying . . . you don't want to ride with me today, tomorrow . . . forever?"

"Yes," Virginal said, gratefully.

"But . . . why?"

"It is not a 'why' thing," Virginal said, uncomfortably.

Nova tumbled the sentence around in her mind, trying to make sense of it. Not a 'why' thing. But there's always a why. Titanides were honest folk, but they did not always tell the whole truth.

"Don't you like me anymore?" Nova asked.

"I still like you."

"Then . . . if you can't tell me why, you can tell me what . . . what's different. What's changed?"

Virginal nodded reluctantly.

"There is a thing," Virginal finally said. "Growing in your head."

Nova involuntarily put her hand to her forehead. She immediately thought of Snitch, and felt ice and spiders sliding on her skin.

But she couldn't have meant that.

"I thought it would quickly die," Virginal said. "But you are nourishing it now, and it will soon be too big to kill. I weep for this. I wish to say good-by to you now, before the thing consumes the Nova I have loved."

Once again, Nova tried very hard, and this time she came up with something.

"Does this have to do with my mother?"

Virginal smiled, pleased to have gotten through.

"Yes. Of course. That is the seed of it."

Nova felt the anger building again. She wondered if she would be able to restrain it this time.

"Listen, damn you, if Robin put you up to this—"

Virginal slapped her. It was quite a light slap for a Titanide. It didn't quite knock her over.

"It was Cirocco, wasn't it? She told you what I—"

Virginal slapped her again. She tasted blood. And she was crying.

"I'm very sorry," Virginal said. "I have my pride, too. No one is playing a trick on you. I would not allow myself to be the instrument of anyone's schemes for your reunion with your mother."

"It's none of your *business!*"

"That's exactly right. It's none of my business at all. You have your own life to lead, and you must do as you think best." She turned and started off.

Nova chased after her, grabbed her arm.

"Wait. Please wait, Virginal. Listen, I . . . what can I do?"

Virginal stopped, and sighed.

"I know you don't intend to be impolite, but offering advice in a situation like this is considered rude by my people. I cannot chart a course for you."

"Make up with my mother, right?" Nova said, bitterly. "Tell her it's *okay* for her to . . . to break every solemn vow . . . to *consort* with that . . ."

"I don't know if that would help you. I . . . have said too much. Go to Tambura. She is young, and will not see the thing for a time. You can go for rides in the country with her."

"For a . . . you mean other Titanides can—"

The enormity of the idea overwhelmed her. She felt naked. Were all her secret thoughts on display to every Titanide?

What do they see?

Virginal reached into her pouch and came up with a small flat piece of wood, the kind she often used for her carving.

It showed a girl, easily recognizable as Nova, sitting in a box with a stony expression on her face. Outside the box were others— Robin? Conal? Virginal?—not as distinct, but in attitudes of sorrow. Nova realized the box might be a coffin. But the girl inside was not dead. It made her feel sick, and she tried to hand it back.

"Look more closely at the face," Virginal commanded.

She did. It had seemed expressionless. On closer examination, she saw a smug, cat-like twist of the lips. Self-satisfied? The eyes were empty holes.

She thrust it away. Virginal took it, glanced sadly at it, then scaled it out over the water of Moros.

"Shouldn't you keep that?" Nova asked, bitterly. "It might be worth something someday. But maybe it's a bit over-done. A little too overtly symbolic. If you try again, I'm sure you could get it just right."

"That was the fifth in a series, Nova. I made them during my last five dream-times. I have tried to ignore them, I have thrown them away. But I can no longer ignore what my dreams are telling me. You are rejecting those who love you. This is sad. You are enjoying it. This is something which—as you say—is not my business, but something I cannot be around. Good-by."

"Wait. Please don't go yet. I'll...I'll go tell her it's okay. I'll tell her I'm sorry."

Virginal hesitated, then slowly shook her head.

"I don't know if it will be enough."

"What can I *do?*"

"Open yourself again," Virginal said, without hesitation. "You have sealed off the possibility of love. Not only from your mother. There is a girl in your office. You hardly see her. She admires you. She might be your friend. She might be your lover. I don't know. But there is no possibility for either thing as you are now."

Once again Nova was bewildered.

"Who are you talking about?"

"I don't know her name. You would see her, if you looked."

"I don't know how."

Virginal sighed.

"Nova, if you were a Titanide I would tell you to go away for a time. If this disease of the soul infected me, I would go into the wilderness and fast until I could see things clearly again. I don't know if it works for humans."

"But I can't. My *job*...Cirocco needs me..."

"Yes," Virginal said, sadly. "You're right, of course. So good-by."

TWENTY-EIGHT

Cirocco found Conal sitting on a hillside, overlooking Boot Camp.

It was located on a big, long island in the middle of Moros. Tents had been set up. There was a big mess hall and a parade ground. The air was filled with the shouts of sergeants, and the tiny figures of new recruits marched in lines or scrambled over obstacle courses. He looked up as she sat beside him.

"Some place, huh?" she said.

"Not my favorite," Conal confessed. "But you're sure getting the recruits."

"Thirty thousand, last time I checked. I thought I'd have to offer bonuses in pay and food rations to get so many, but they keep coming. Isn't patriotism a wonderful thing?"

"I never thought about it much."

"You been thinking about it now?"

"Sure have." He gestured out over the fledgling Bellinzona Army. "You say they aren't going to have to fight. But I wonder. They look like they *want* to. Even..."

"After all they've seen on Earth," Cirocco finished. "I know. I thought it would be hard to raise a volunteer army here. But I don't think some...deep, basic taste for warfare will ever be gone from the human race. One of these days Bellinzona will grow too big. We'll establish another city somewhere nearby, maybe in Iapetus. Not too long after that they'll start trading back and forth. And pretty soon they'll be fighting each other."

"Do they *like* running around and taking orders?"

Cirocco shrugged.

"A few. The rest...lots would go back home if they could. We didn't tell 'em enlistment's for the duration, and a medical discharge is the only way out. Half the people down there are thinking they made a mistake." She pointed to a fenced area. "That's the stockade. It's a *lot* worse than the work camps. When they get out, they soldier very hard."

350

Conal knew that; he knew a lot of the things she had just said. He had spent some time here, trying to understand it. He had been born much too late for the days of large armies. Military discipline was foreign and frightening to him. The soldiers he talked to seemed ... different.

"They're sure getting *ready* to fight," Conal observed. It was true. The drilling below was in earnest. Sword production was way up. Each soldier was to be provided with a short sword, a hardened-leather chestplate or—for the officers—one of bronze, an iron helmet, good boots and trousers ... the basic infantry equipment. They were organized into legions and cohorts, and had learned Roman tactics. There were legions of archers. There were combat engineers learning how to construct siege towers and catapults, which would be built on the site from native materials. Some units had already departed, and were busy in Iapetus and Cronus repairing the bridges of the old Circum-Gaea Highway.

"They *have* to be ready," Cirocco said. "If the big fight, the one between me and Gaea ... if I lose that, the war won't be over for those soldiers. They'll be stuck a long way from home, and Gaea won't call it off. She's got maybe a hundred thousand people in Pandemonium, and they'll *all* fight. They won't be trained—Gaea's too slipshod. But our people will be outnumbered four to one. I owe it to them to see they're ready to fight."

Conal took a moment to add this up in his head.

"But we've already got thirty thousand, and more coming ..."

"Some will die along the way, Conal." He turned to look at her, and saw she was watching for his reaction.

"That many?"

"No. I intend to do some weeding out. But there will be casualties. How many is up to you, in part."

He understood that, too. These "Roman" legions would march under the constant threat of air attack. It would be his job to fight off the Gean Air Force.

"How many planes? Do you know that yet?"

"Buzz bombs? I'm pretty sure there are eight combat groups left. That's eighty planes. How's the training going, by the way?"

"Very well. I've got more good pilots now than I have planes."

"Well, in planes, what you've got is all you'll ever have. Don't waste any."

Conal was momentarily annoyed. It wasn't like Cirocco to say something like that. He looked at her, and was frightened to see, just for a moment, that she almost looked her age. It must be a hell of a burden.

"Conal . . . maybe this is a bad time to bring this up. I just got back from a trip with Robin, and I detected a . . . nervousness about her."

"What do you mean? What kind of nervousness?"

"Oh . . . I got the feeling that . . . maybe she was afraid I was enjoying all this too much." She gestured with her head out toward the camp, but the gesture implied a lot more.

Conal had had the same thought.

"It did occur to me," he said, "that nobody's going to *take* your job away from you. Not even if you stood for election."

"You're right."

"It's a great deal of power."

"It is, indeed. I told you something of what it would be like when we all first discussed this. But hearing about it and seeing it are two different things."

Conal felt a coldness creeping over him. It hadn't happened in a long time. The hub of his universe was this enigma called Cirocco Jones. Their relationship had begun in blood and agony. It had moved slowly through the politics of terror and submission, into acceptance, to something close to worship . . . and finally to friendship.

But there was always a tiny chip of dry ice down there in his soul.

There had been a time, up in that cave, when he thought he was going to die. Cirocco and Hornpipe had not been back in over a kilorev. What little food had been stored for him was long gone. He existed in a half-waking state appropriate to the unchanging light. He watched the meat melt off his bones, and knew they had abandoned him.

That didn't seem right. He hadn't expected Cirocco to do that.

But it made him feel oddly superior. He had learned some lessons about himself, and the fellow who starved to death in a few more weeks would be a better man than the one who walked up to the black-clad stranger in the Titanide bar. If she let him die, it would be her loss.

Then Hornpipe had clambered into the cave one "day," and

Conal's new-built world crashed around him. They were testing me, he thought. Let him get hungry, see what he thinks about that. So what if he goes a little crazy? It'll make him more manageable.

It lasted only a fraction of a second. Then he saw that Hornpipe was badly injured, bleeding from a dozen wounds, one arm in a sling. How he had made it up here in such a state...

"I am deeply shamed," Hornpipe had said, in a weary voice. "Had it been within the realm of possibility, I would have been here long since. But we have been unable to move. Cirocco bade me bring you her word that, should she survive, she will apologize to you personally. But live or die, she now grants you your freedom from this place. You should never have been left here."

Conal had been filled with a thousand questions, none of which seemed important when he saw the food. Hornpipe prepared a meal of broth, and stayed with him a short time to be sure he was going to be all right. He would not answer any questions, when Conal got around to asking them, except to say Cirocco had been badly injured but was in a moderately safe place.

Then the Titanide had left again, leaving a cache of food in glass jars, a stove and some fuel, and a parachute. He explained its operation, assuring him his chances of survival were excellent if he were forced to use it—at least until he was on the ground. But Hornpipe emphasized that the cave was, at that moment, the safest place in Gaea, and that he was going to bring Cirocco there for that very reason. Terrible things were abroad in the land, Hornpipe told him, and he would do well to stay until the food ran out. Hornpipe swore that nothing but his own death would prevent him from returning to the cave. If Hornpipe didn't show up before the food was gone, Conal was to jump.

But Hornpipe was not gone long. He returned with Cirocco, whose injuries were too numerous to count. She had lost blood and weight—and two fingers, which later grew back. She was feverish and semiconscious.

A Titanide named Rocky had come with them. He was a healer, and gradually nursed her back to health.

But it took a while, and during that period an opportunity had come, as Conal had known it would. Both Titanides were at the mouth of the cave, doing that half-sleep, half-waking thing. Their backs were to him. Cirocco slept on a pallet a few feet away.

He had worked the gun free of her pack. He had pulled the hammer back with his thumb. He had pressed the barrel against her temple. And he had waited to see what he was going to do next.

A few ounces of pressure against the trigger and she would be dead.

He remembered glancing to see if the Titanides were watching him. They were not. Another suspicion came, and he looked quickly to see if the gun was loaded. It was.

So he moved it away from her head, carefully lowered the hammer, and put it away. When he looked up, both Titanides were standing a few feet away from him. They had odd expressions, but did not seem angry. He knew they had seen him put the gun away. Later, he understood they had known everything he did, and his belief in the judgment of a Titanide was complete from that moment.

It was shortly after this that Rocky had put his ear to Cirocco's head and proclaimed he heard something in there. . . .

"Conal?"

He looked up, startled.

"You looked like you were a million miles away."

"I guess I was. You were asking me if I was worried you would become permanent dictator of Bellinzona."

Cirocco stared.

"I didn't actually come out and *ask* it . . . but I guess that was the idea."

"The answer is, I don't care. If you did, I think you'd do it better than anyone else, except maybe Robin, who I'm planning to convince to get out of government and go live in a little cabin in Metis with me and maybe have a couple more babies, and you and Nova and Chris and all the Titanides can come visit us on their birthdays. And I think you know what you're doing. And I don't think you'll stay on in the job . . . if only because you're too damn smart for that."

"Whew." Cirocco shook her head, then laughed. "You're right. It's seductive, even to a confirmed old solitary bitch like me. But you're right again when you say it isn't *that* seductive."

"So what did you come up here for?" Conal asked.

"To get an honest opinion, I think. These days, I get so paranoid I think even the Titanides are just telling me what I want to hear."

"And I didn't?"

Cirocco grinned.

"Sure you did, Conal. It's just that from you, I believe it."

TWENTY-NINE

It was to be the last meeting before the Great March began, only one hectorev away. Plans for the big parade were being finalized. It was a nuisance—the troops would have to be barged into Bellinzona, landed, paraded through the city to the cheers of multitudes, re-loaded, and barged to the south end of Moros, where the overland trek to the highway was flat and easy. But it couldn't be helped. The city needed to see its army. The army needed to know the people were behind them as they moved into harm's way. It was deadly to underestimate the importance of morale.

The meeting was a nuisance, too. Cirocco sat quietly and listened to the usual complaints, suggestions, and displays of ego, and waited her turn.

The big tent easily held the four Generals, twenty Colonels, and one hundred Majors who formed the top brass of the army. She knew all of them by name—part of being a politician was to remember *everyone's* name, and she had been meticulous about it— but privately she liked to think of them by the names of their commands.

There were four Divisions, each led by a General. Thus, there was a General Two, Three, Eight, and One Hundred and One, leading the Second, Third, Eighth, and One Hundred First Divisions. That there were no First, Fourth, etc. Divisions did not bother Cirocco. She had picked the numbers for historical reasons that would appeal to Gaea.

Each General presided over five Legions, commanded by Colonels. The Legions had two thousand soldiers each, and were numbered consecutively.

There were five Cohorts in a Legion, ten Companies in a Cohort, two sections in a Company. Companies were commanded by Sergeants, of which there were sixteen hundred in the Bellinzona Army.

These numbers had resulted from endless wrangling, and were still the cause of debate. Most of the senior staff agreed the officer/enlisted ratio was hopelessly small. Forty thousand soldiers *needed* more officers, in the view of these professional military people.

The second major complaint was lack of weaponry and equipment. Procurement had fallen short of expected goals. Cirocco listened to General One Hundred and One expounding the numbers: a shortfall of X in swords, Y in shields, Z in breastplates.

The third was lack of training. The brass complained bitterly of having no one to practice on. As a result, there were no blooded troops except a handful who had fought on Earth.

Cirocco listened to it all, and finally stood up.

"First," she said, and pointed to General Two, "you're fired. You have contempt for human life, and ought to be back on Earth pushing buttons and creating deserts. I'd send you back if I could. As it is, I'm sending you to the prison camp for two kilorevs. Your bags are packed. Go home and write your memoirs."

She waited in the thick silence as the red-faced man marched from the tent. She pointed to Colonel Six.

"You're promoted to take his place. There's a star sitting on your bunk. Pin it on when you get there. Pick your successor for the Sixth Legion—and it doesn't have to be one of your Majors." She pointed three more times. "You, you, and you. You're not Colonels anymore. You're not good enough to run a Legion." The three got up and left. If anything, the silence was even thicker.

"I don't know the Majors well enough to make reasoned judgments on their performance, so you can breathe easier. But I urge all of you here to do whatever is necessary in the way of discharges and demotions to make this a more efficient outfit.

"And now . . . I'm going to solve all your problems. I am going to decimate your troops."

She waited for the buzz of conversation to die down, then addressed the Generals.

"I want the orders to go out to the Sergeants. Each of them is in charge of twenty soldiers. I want them to pick the two worst they have, and send them home. I want them to choose the rawest recruits, the guy who keeps tripping over his bootlaces or stabbing himself with his sword, the girl who can't keep her head down or remember which end of the arrow fits over the string. . . . I want all the fuck-ups and misfits and weaklings and idiots weeded out. Muster them out within twenty revs, honorable discharges, no stigma attached." She waved a hand negligently. "It doesn't have to be two from each Section. Some sections are going to be solid all the way through, and others will have four or five rejects. Have it worked out on the Company and Cohort level . . . but *work it out*. In twenty revs, I want this army to be ten percent smaller."

There was more conversation, as she had expected. She repressed a smile. It damn sure improved the officer/enlisted ratio, but it wasn't what they'd had in mind at *all*.

"Next step," she went on. She pointed at General Three. He cringed slightly. "Yours is the newest Division, with the highest percentage of recruits. I believe you to be a good General, with a genuine concern for the welfare of your troops. It isn't your fault that your Division is the weakest of the four. Nevertheless, it is the weakest. So you become the Home Division."

"Now just a—"

Cirocco did not have to glare very hard to silence him. The man realized he had overstepped his bounds, and shut up.

"As I was saying, your Division will stay behind. This will solve the equipment problem, and help with the training problem, since you will be leaving all your equipment behind and continuing to train your troops while the rest of us are marching on Pandemonium."

The General swallowed hard, but remained silent.

"You will be receiving new equipment as it is manufactured. The rest of us will have to make do with what we bring along . . . which will now be adequate. Your mission is to set up two garrisons, one at the east road leading to Iapetus, and one at the western pass into the mountains. These garrisons should be defensible if Gaea sends armies into Dione. You will also establish outposts on the northern rim of Moros. In consultation with the civil authorities, you are to establish a Navy to patrol Moros. I am leaving tactical decisions up to you, but I recommend some degree of fortification of the city, and a certain number of troops—possibly one Legion—stationed nearby. If we fail, the defense of Bellinzona will be up to you."

The General was looking a lot more interested, though Cirocco knew there was no way to make him like the assignment.

"One more thing, General. When we leave here, we will be leaving the worst Division behind. When we return, I want it to be the best, or you should look for another job."

"It will be," he said.

"Good. Go get started on it now."

He looked surprised, then stood up quickly and marched out, followed by his Colonels and Majors. When they were gone, the number of empty chairs was impressive. Cirocco had just cut the size of her Army by more than one fourth, and was well pleased with her work. She looked from face to face, taking her time, and when she was done, she smiled.

"Ladies and Gentlemen," she said, "we are ready to march on Pandemonium."

THIRD FEATURE

You've got to take the
bull by the teeth.

— Sam Goldwyn

ONE

Maybe Gaea heard about the parade.

It was a mistake to blame *all* unpleasant events on Gaea's malign intervention, but the rain that drenched the parade through Bellinzona was the sort of thing she would have loved. It didn't affect the citizens' enthusiasm; it seemed every Bellinzonan stood on a street corner or hung from a window to watch the troops march through. The troops, of course, *hated* it, just as soldiers have hated parades since the dawn of warfare. Their boots got wet, and a hardened-leather breastplate that hadn't yet been broken in by sweat and oil and use was like an economy-size Iron Maiden.

But the Army slogged through it. They endured the crossing of an unusually rough Moros. A predictable number got seasick. They disembarked on Moros' western shore in a sea of mud, joining up with a thousand massive goods wagons—half of which were already bogged down to the axles.

The Quartermaster Corps—a separate, non-combatant group which had been assembling equipment and training drivers on the Dione Road—had become proficient in the care and handling of Gaea's only draft animal. These were beasts called Jeeps, native to Metis. Until recently they had had no names at all, except in Titanide song. Cirocco had caused fifteen hundred of them to be rounded up and trained to harness. This was not too difficult. Jeeps were amiable, bovine omnivores. They were built along the lines of those early ancestors of the rhinoceros which had once thrived in prehistoric Persia and stood almost twice as tall as modern elephants. Jeeps were not quite that big. They had bear-like claws, heads like camels' heads, and their forelegs were twice as long as their hind legs. This gave them a comical gait. They ate anything that was handy. With Jeeps around, garbage disposal was never a problem. Their worst characteristic was a tendency to stumble over their own feet and overturn the wagon they were carrying. But they were clean, smelled pretty good, and responded to affection. Most of their handlers had learned to appreciate them.

And they could haul monstrous loads long distances, with just little water. They had big, floppy humps atop their shoulders which ould store fat for lean times.

The Jeeps soon had the columns moving.

. . . and as the army started into Iapetus, the clouds rolled away nd a warm breeze began to blow. Soon the air sparkled and the oad dried. You could see all the way to Mnemosyne. It seemed a ine day to be setting out on a trip—no matter what might lie at the nd of the road.

The wind whipped the brightly colored pennants at the head f each Legion, Cohort, and Company. The banners had numbers r letters on them, but no other symbols. And at the head of the rocession, there was no flag. There had been a lot of pressure to dopt a Bellinzona flag, but Cirocco had resisted it to the end. She vould accept being Mayor, she would raise, train, and equip an army nd lead them out to do battle . . . but she drew the line at flags. Let Gaea raise her flag, and fight for it.

The sunshine of Iapetus gleamed off the breastplates of the fficers. The air was full of the sound of creaking wooden wheels, nd the slap of leather boots, and the peculiar honking noises made y the Jeeps, who were about as excited as they ever got.

The human legions marched together. Between them marched ontingents of fifty Titanides, pulling their own wagons, which seemed tronger and better-built—and were certainly a lot prettier than the uman wagons. The Titanides, though colorful enough in them- elves, wore their finest jewels and had festooned their bodies and vagons with the most colorful flowers. They carried no flags. There vere a thousand of them formed into battle groups, and it was lebatable whether they or the almost thirty thousand humans were he stronger force.

In addition to these regular troops, scout Titanides ranged far head of the column, and twenty kilometers on each side. There vould be no ambush the Titanides could not detect. The only peril n this day of beginning was from the air. Some of the soldiers spent lot of time looking at the clear sky, wishing for clouds.

Majors marched at the head of Cohorts. Each Legion was led y a Colonel, also on foot. Three Titanides of an unusually easy- oing nature had been persuaded to bear the Generals at the heads f their Division. The Titanides didn't like it—they barely knew the

Generals in question, and were not accustomed to allow any human but a dear friend to ride on their backs. They saw to it that the ride was as rough as possible. The Generals seethed in their own discontent. Not from the rough ride—none of them knew the uncanny smoothness of the Titanides' usual gait—but because it was impossible to sit astride the creatures and see around their broad backs. Dignity forbade the practical carriage Cirocco had worked out long ago: to ride facing backwards. The whole purpose of these steeds, after all, was to set the Generals above the common foot soldier. So they endured the bumps and the lack of visibility, and tried to look as dignified as possible.

And at the head of the column, several hundred meters from the One Hundred First Division, were nine individuals. In front was Cirocco Jones, in her unadorned black clothes and hat, astride Hornpipe. Following her in no particular order were Conal astride Rocky Robin on Serpent... and Nova riding Virginal. Valiha trotted along without a human burden.

None of them had much to say. There was no festive air. This would be the only day Conal would ride with the army, so Rocky and Serpent saw to it that he was often quite close to Robin. Whatever they had to say to each other had apparently already been said. After the first bivouac, Conal would be heading to the northern highlands to take command of the air force.

Virginal held back from the two, at Nova's request. The young witch and former bureaucrat—she had resigned after a shouting match with Cirocco, and been replaced by someone from Trini's faction—wanted to give her mother and her mother's lover all the time together they could get. There was a new, more mature relationship between witch and Titanide. Nova was not yet perfect, according to Virginal, but she was getting there. She had said that many times, and each time they would laugh harder. Virginal, for her part, was ashamed of her own behavior. The lecture from her hindmother when she heard of the scene with Nova still stung.

Every so often Nova would reach down to her waist and finger the spell bag that hung from her belt. It was beautifully embroidered with an ancient Yin-Yang symbol, and contained the Zombie-dust she had inadvertently discovered and which must, by law, be carried at all times by every Bellinzonan. The bags had quickly become general-purpose good luck charms. This one had been given to her

y a shy Korean girl named Li, who still had a lot of trouble with
nglish but spoke the universal language of love very well indeed.
here had been a steamy send-off. Nova found it hard to believe she
ad overlooked such beauty and sensitivity for so long. Li had worked
n her Statistics Bureau. Could this be love? Nova wondered. Well,
aybe. It was too early to tell. But Li was someone to write home
o, someone to keep the home fires burning.

At the head of the column, Cirocco Jones sat very straight,
ware that the Army could see her out there, and kept her own
ounsel.

The Generals had warned her the first day's march was too
ong for unseasoned troops. The camp had been prepared deep in
apetus a hectorev before, with tents that would be struck and added
o the burden of the goods wagons.

Cirocco knew it was too far, and had intended that it be. She
as decimating again.

So she marched her troops mercilessly through the increasing
eat and unending light of Iapetus. They began passing out. As they
id, they were loaded onto the wagons. When they finally reached
amp most of the army was in a state of exhaustion. Not a few
fficers had fallen by the wayside.

"Here's what we do," she told the assembled top brass—before
ey had a chance at the mess tent. "Those soldiers who fainted or
ho have a medical problem as a result of today's march will remain
ere. At this site they will build Pontus Camp with materials at hand.
hey will keep their weapons and other equipment, but the wagons
ill go with us. Pontus will be fortified, and be the permanent home
f two Cohorts of one Legion. The other three Cohorts will establish
imilar but smaller outposts to the north, south, and east. The job
f these detachments will be to improve the highway and keep it
pen, and to fight a delaying action should an attack come from
yperion. They will be under the command of the General of the
hird Division, in Bellinzona. Send a messenger to inform him of
is. And requisition what wagons are needed to carry back the most
erious medical cases, those that go beyond mere exhaustion. All
lear?"

No one had the strength to argue with her.

TWO

Four hundred fifty kilometers to the west, and five kilometers beneath the ground, Nasu slithered through the darkness until she came to a long, narrow tunnel that smelled very bad.

She knew these places, and hated them, in her cool and ponderous reptilian brain. She did not want to go into the tunnel. It was a place of hurt. She remembered it dimly, beneath Iapetus only a kilorev ago, and other times in the past.

She probed it with her tongue, and tasted hatred. Almost a kilometer away, great coils of her mid-section writhed in indecision and eagerness to go. Her tail actually started to crawl away. It took some time for impulses to get from the gallon of gray matter she used as a brain down to the nethermost extension, which increasingly was not in agreement with headquarters.

The immense bodily conflict caused acids to squirt into her monstrous digestive cavity, which would have been painful enough, but the acid set up a great galumphing uproar that caused her sides to bulge out unpredictably. The reason for this was simple: she had recently devoured seventy-eight of the slow-moving, blind, and elephantine creatures, called Heffalumps, who resided in this darkness, and they did not die easy. Twenty-six of them were still alive, and they didn't like acid any more than Nasu did.

Acid. Hyperion. The Robin-thing. Go to Hyperion. Acid. Robin.

These concepts floated through her mind like disconnected wraiths, a hundred times, two hundred, and finally were imprinted again. She must go to Hyperion. She must meet the Robin-warm protector there. She must go into the tunnel, where there was acid.

Once in motion, Nasu was impossible to stop. She barreled through the tunnel like history's worst Freudian nightmare.

She encountered the acid far later than she had expected to. By then there was no question of stopping. She plowed up a great wake of it, shutting her eyes tight. But she could see through the

364

translucent lids as she entered the deep sanctum of Cronus, faithful friend of Gaea.

Cronus howled his rage, humiliation, and pain. It didn't stop the snake. She selected the easternmost of three tunnels leading out of the chamber, and thrust her head into it. At that moment, the end of her tail was just inside the west end of the tunnel.

It hurt like hell. Doing this was what had turned her white. She would be shedding her skin again soon, and that helped, but only a little. It burned her eyelids away. They would grow back, but the pain would be intense.

And it was still hurting, of course, way back there, but the signals were slow to arrive. She burst forth into the cavernous darkness of the East Cronus maze and kept going until she was sure she was out. Then she began to writhe, thumping monstrous coils of herself against the rock. The twenty-six surviving heffalumps were quickly killed. Had anyone been standing directly above, on Gaea's inner rim, it might have felt like an earth tremor.

But the pain didn't stop for a while. Nasu curled herself into a tight ball with her head somewhere near the center, and waited for healing to come.

Only one more to go, she thought.

THREE

Cronus was royally pissed.

When you are the lord and master of a hundred thousand square kilometers of land area—*plus* the endless caverns beneath them, and, in a sense, the air above them—and you get maybe one visitor in ten myriarevs and aren't even very enthused about getting *that* one . . . well, it just really *narks* you to have some frigging nightmare reptile come barreling through your home like a runaway freight train. It just confirmed his bitter opinion. The goddamn wheel was going in the toilet. Nothing worked anymore. *Everything* sucked.

He'd been faithful to Gaea for millennia—for *aeons!* When this Oceanus business came up, who was it stood behind Gaea a thousand percent? *Cronus,* that's who. When the dust had settled and old Iapetus sat over there dry-washing his nonexistent hands like a comic-book commie spy and whispering sweet nothings in Cronus's ears, had he listened? No *way.* Cronus had a direct line to heaven, and Gaea was on her throne, and all was well with the wheel.

When that schizo Mnemosyne slipped off the deep end and started blubbering in her beer, boo-hoo-hoo, about what that lousy sandworm was doing to her stinking forests, did he lose faith in Gaea? He did not.

And even when she foisted that back-stabbing Cirocco Jones bitch on him, told him Jones was now the Wizard and he had to make nice to her, did he make trouble? No, not good old Cronus. Served her right when Jones...

He backed away from that thought. Gaea was in poor health, anybody could see that, but some thoughts are best left un-thought. No telling who might be listening.

But this was too much. It really was.

It's not like he hadn't seen it coming, either. He'd had his requisition in for *eleven myriarevs!* Three hundred thousand gallons of ninety-nine percent pure hydrochloric, that's all he needed to bring his reservoir up to capacity. There's this *thing,* he had told her. Snake-like, but awful big. It ain't one of mine; maybe it's one of yours. But it lives down here, and it's been through here *twice,* and the fucker gets bigger every time. Not only that, but this chronically low acid level is drying out my upper synapses. Gives me a perpetual pain...

She hadn't believed him. Not one of hers, she said. Don't worry about it. And it's Iapetus stealing your HCL, and I can't do a bloody thing about it. So shut up and let me get back to my films.

Well.

This time he was damn well going to report it. He called for Gaea. What he got was the new assistant, as had been happening more and more often. Their conversation was not in words, but it had a certain flavor that, if translated, would have been much like this:

"Hello, Gaean Productions."

"Let me speak to Gaea, please."

"I'm sorry, Gaea is on location."

"Well, put me through to Pandemonium, then. This is important."

"Who shall I say is calling, sir?"

"Cronus."

"Beg pardon? How do you spell that?"

"Cronus, dammit! The Lord of that region of Gaea—exactly one-twelfth of her total rim land area, by the way—known as Cronus."

"Oh, of course. That's spelled C-H-R-O——"

"*Cronus!* Put me through to Gaea, at once!"

"I'm sorry, sir, but she is in a screening. *Spartacus,* I believe. You really ought to see it. One of the best Roman epics ever——"

"Will you just put me through?"

"I'm sorry. Listen, if you'll leave your number, I'll have her get right back to you."

"This is an emergency. She should know about it, because it's headed her way. And you *have* my number."

"...oh, yes, here it is. It slipped behind the...are you still at——"

"I'm going to report this whole conversation to Gaea."

"Whatever you wish."

Click.

Cronus tried again later. Once again he got the smart-ass assistant, who told him Gaea was in a production meeting and couldn't be disturbed.

Well, screw her, then.

FOUR

There had been no beer in Tara most of the time Chris was there. It was available in the commissaries, to those who could prove they had finished their work shifts. Chris had not imbibed. It was not very good stuff.

Now there was excellent beer in the iceboxes of Tara. The weather was hot. Adam didn't seem to mind it, and it didn't bother

Chris a lot, but a cool beer or two was just what he needed after a long day spent trying to keep Adam's attention away from the television sets without being too obvious about it.

Two or three beers were just what he needed.

The hard thing was to never admit that the games he structured were mostly to keep Adam from looking at the television programs. Without the TV he certainly would have spent a lot of time with Adam, but would have been content to let him play alone more often. As it was, he feared he was spending *too* much time with the child. It got more difficult to interest him. Adam often tired of the games, and playing with the toys. Sometimes, when he was at his lowest, Chris thought Adam was humoring him.

Very paranoid thought, Chris. Three or four beers might soothe it.

But the worst thing, the most awful thing...

He sometimes caught himself about to strike the child.

He spent every waking hour near Adam, and as many as he could manage actively engaged with him. An adult human being can take only so much of childish things, of baby-talk and games and silly laughter. Chris could take a lot, but there was a limit. He ached for intelligent company...no, no, *no*—that wasn't the right word at all, that was completely wrong. He ached for *adult* company.

So when Adam was asleep and he felt so horribly alone, four or five beers was just the ticket to calm his shattered nerves.

He needed adults around. What he had was a sharp, intelligent, delightful two-year-old...and Amparo, and Sushi. Other household help came and went, and never talked to Chris. He assumed they were under orders from Gaea to treat him as the man-who-isn't-there. Only Amparo and Sushi were constant.

Both had been wet-nurses when Chris arrived. Amparo seemed to be an intelligent woman, but she had no English, and no urge to learn any. Chris had picked up enough rag-tag Spanish to communicate with her, but it would never be very satisfactory.

As for Sushi...

He didn't know if that was really her name. She was an idiot. She might have been a super-genius before coming to Gaea, but Gaea had done something to her. The mark was on her forehead. It was a swelling below the skin in the shape of an inverted cross. When Chris had finally realized that Sushi's mind was really as blank is her eyes, he had touched the swelling one day, and been astonished to see her fall on the floor and writhe as if in the throes of a seizure. Upon more careful examination—and queasy experimentation—he had learned it was not a seizure. It was the old pleasure principle. Gaea had put something like Snitch in Sushi's head, and wired it into her pleasure center. Now she would do *anything* for a jolt. Touching it herself did no good. Someone else had to. She seemed to need it about three times a day. If she didn't get it from Chris, she would nuzzle up to Adam, who thought it was very funny when Sushi writhed on the floor and moaned and masturbated.

So Chris had to keep Sushi content several times a day.

Luckily, he could drink five or six beers to settle down afterward.

They called her Sushi for a very simple reason. She subsisted on a diet of raw fish. The fish didn't have to be fresh. They didn't even have to be scaled, and the heads didn't bother her.

Her breath was *horrible*.

It took Chris some time to put it together. Eating the fish was a conditioned reflex. Eat a fish, get a jolt. Before long, she wouldn't eat anything else.

The television was fifty percent interactive these days. And now he was appearing in it, though he had never gone before Gaea's cameras. At first, like many things in Tara, it had seemed harmless. He had first appeared in an Abbott and Costello feature. He had been substituted for Costello. Subtle changes had been made in him. He was short and dumpy, but it was definitely him. His voice was a blend of his real voice and the voice of Costello. Adam had loved it. Even Chris found himself grinning from time to time. Costello was a dunce, no question, but he was an amiable one. It could have been worse.

It got worse.

Next it was Laurel and Hardy. Gaea was Ollie, and Chris was Stan. Chris studied the movies carefully, weighing the pro's and con's. The two comedians had an affection for each other. That worried him. At first glance Stan seemed an idiot, but it was actually more complex than that. And Ollie was a blowhard, took a great many of the pratfalls . . . but in the end was the dominant personality. Again, Gaea was working up to something.

Lately he had begun to appear in some questionable roles. Not the villain *per se*, but someone rather unsavory. In one role, from a movie whose title he couldn't remember, he saw himself beating Gaea. And he saw that it disturbed Adam, though he wouldn't talk about it. Adam drew a line between fantasy and reality . . . but it was a fuzzy line. Gaea was that amazing, funny, huge, and harmless lady who came to the third floor window of Tara and handed him pretty toys. Why would Chris be beating her up? The plot wasn't important, nor was the fact that Chris, at just over seven feet tall, was hardly a worthy opponent for the fifty-foot Monroe.

He was now sure he would lose, in the long run. It was all very well to be set up as Adam's conscience, but television had always had a louder voice than a child's conscience—which didn't even exist until someone nurtured it. Chris wasn't being given a chance.

A year had gone by. Cirocco had said it might be as long as two years before she came again.

He was pretty sure it would be too late by then.

It would have cheered him considerably to know Cirocco and her army were already on the march to Hyperion. But Gaea had not seen fit to tell him, and he had no other way of knowing. He might have gotten a clue from Gaean television. Adam was asleep, and Chris was sitting slumped in front of a set. The movie was the 1995 version of *Napoleon*, un-altered, and on the screen vast armies marched toward Waterloo.

But by then Chris was too drunk to notice.

FIVE

The second day's march saw even more soldiers pass out than on the previous trek, though this one was shorter.

Cirocco had expected that, too. It probably looked like an easy discharge. She told her medics to examine everyone carefully and send back only the most serious cases. Those turned out to be sixteen in number. Everyone else shouldered packs when camp was broken and marched on into Iapetus.

They crossed the two small, nameless rivers that flowed south
from the Tyche Mountains into the great sea of Pontus that dominated
Iapetus. The bridges were in good repair. The terrain was easy.
Iapetus, an enemy of Gaea, would not hinder their progress through
his domain, Cirocco knew. Their problems would begin in Cronus.

For several "days" the army camped by the lovely sea. The
weather held clear and warm. Cirocco gradually picked up the pace
as the soldiers grew more accustomed to the rhythm of the march.
But she did not push it too hard. She wanted them tough, not exhausted, when they reached the hard parts.

At the confluence of Pluto and Ophion, very near the border
of Cronus, Cirocco had her Generals pick the garrison of her extreme
eastern line of defense. This time she did not go for the weak ones.
She wanted veterans, the toughest men and women she could find.
They would set up a fort just west of the Pluto ford, and north of
Ophion. She left them Titanide canoes for crossing the big river.
They were to patrol north and south, traveling light and fast. Their
position was not defensible against a determined attack, but that was
not the point. It was her hope that, if attacked, the troops could send
messengers back to Bellinzona and fight a delaying, guerilla action,
giving the city as much time as possible to prepare for the assault.

All this depressed her. Almost everything she had done in
Iapetus was preparation for defeat. If the Bellinzona Air Force still
existed, this outpost of its swift messengers would be superfluous.
Even the slowest Dragonfly could get to Bellinzona from here in
twenty minutes and sound the alarm.

But the Air Force might not make it through Cronus.

And of course, if her army was victorious in the coming fight,
no one would be returning from Hyperion but her own soldiers and
the refugees and prisoners of war from Pandemonium.

But she owed the city every precaution she could think of. She
had conned it into producing not just a bunch of foot soldiers, but
a dedicated and motivated fighting force.

She knew that, if it came to it, these troops would fight.

The Circum-Gaea had crossed the Ophion at a point just within
the invisible boundary between Iapetus and Cronus.

Back when Gaby was building the Highway, Ophion crossings

were her biggest challenges. The river was very broad and fairly deep in the flatlands, and in those places where it ran swift, it did so through unforgiving mountains. So she had kept the crossings to a minimum.

But some had been necessary. Cronus was a good example. There was no really easy way through Cronus, but the northern route was five times as hard as the southern. So a big bridge had been necessary.

Cirocco's engineers, who had scouted the route as far as Mnemosyne and done what repairs were feasible to the roadway and bridges in Iapetus and, to a lesser extent, in Cronus, had reported that the Ophion Bridge was hopeless. The entire south end had collapsed. It had taken Gaby's crews five years to build it, almost seventy years ago. There was no way it could be repaired in time for the march to Pandemonium.

So they encamped on the northern shore and hundreds of rafts were built. This was hard and slow work, as that part of Cronus had few trees large enough to provide the lumber.

Cirocco and the Generals scanned the skies nervously throughout this operation. She expected an attack to come in Cronus or Hyperion—possibly in both places, if the first battle was not decisive. And the army, divided by the river and strung out on vulnerable barges, were sitting ducks during the Ophion crossing.

She had explained her reasoning to Conal, his pilots, and the Generals shortly before the beginning of the campaign. Using a clockface analogy she had mapped the twelve regions of Gaea in a great circle, starting with Crius at twelve o'clock.

"That puts Hyperion, our destination, here, at two o'clock," she had said, writing in the name. "The central Hyperion cable is the base for the Second Fighter/Bomber Wing of the Gaean Air Force. Next door, at three, is Oceanus. There is no Third wing; Gaea has no control in Oceanus." She put a large X by the name of Oceanus.

"The Fourth, based in Mnemosyne, was wiped out by an explosion just over a year ago. My sources tell me it has not been replaced." She made another X. "The Sixth, from Iapetus, attacked Bellinzona and was wiped out. There is no Seventh, in Dione, for the same reasons that apply to Oceanus. The next viable unit is the Eighth, here in Metis." She made the two more X's, and stepped back to admire her work.

"You can see that Cronus exists in the middle of a large gap in Gaea's air power. From Metis, here at eight o'clock, all the way around to Hyperion, at two, there are seven fully armed bomber wings. Metis is being watched closely. If an attack originates from there, we'll get some warning over the radio. The same with Hyperion. But if the Fifth drops down on us while we're in Cronus, we'll have very little warning.

"I've worked out a couple possible scenarios. Say the Metis Eighth starts its attack. It takes them some time to get here, and we get some warning. The more logical thing for Gaea to do, I would think, is to begin with the Cronus wing to surprise us and pin us down. At the same time, the Eighth or the Second, or both, take off and get here in time to relieve the Fifth.

"The second option is to let us go right through Cronus. Frankly, I'd rather be attacked here. Because if Gaea waits until we get to Hyperion, she can bring in *all* these groups—Phoebe, Crius, Rhea, Hyperion, Cronus...maybe even Tethys, pretty much simultaneously and with little or no warning."

Everyone had studied Cirocco's big Gaean clock solemnly. Ideas had been advanced, some of them useful. The consensus was that the smart thing for Gaea to do was wait until they were in Hyperion and bring her full strength to bear.

Cirocco agreed... and thought glumly that Gaea would probably do just the opposite. All logic aside, Cirocco dreaded an attack in the hostile night of Cronus.

SIX

The Luftmorder in Tethys did not know he was the flugelfuhrer of the Tenth Fighter/Bomber Wing of the Gaean Air Force. It was not a designation given to him by Gaea. He only knew he was the leader of the squadron. He had a vague awareness there were other squadrons, but it was of no importance to him. His mission was well-defined—and he didn't work well with other Luftmorders. It was not in his nature to do so. *He* was the flugelfuhrer.

Orders had been coming through. They would involve re-fueling at bases under the command of other Luftmorders. The thought was distasteful to him, but Orders were Orders.

He knew there was an army, now marching through Cronus.

He knew that, at some point, Orders would come telling him to attack that army.

He knew there were enemies in the sky. This did not frighten him.

It all made him feel warm and contented.

About the only nuisance in his life were all the angels that had been coming around lately.

They flew quite close, chittering curiously. Green ones and red ones. He was contemptuous of them. Their jelly-bodies would make amusing targets for his red-eyes and sidewinders . . . but there were no Orders. He was contemptuous of the angels. They had so little power. They were so inefficient as flying machines.

They had begun building nests that hung, as he did, from the cable. There were three of them below him, great bulging structures that seemed to be made of mud and wattle. He considered them eyesores.

There had been four. He had loosed a red-eye at one, to test its strength. It had come apart like rice paper. The red and green feathers that drifted out of it and the alarmed squawks of the survivors had amused him.

But he had tried no more shots.

He awaited his mission.

SEVEN

Conal had wanted to lead an attack on the base in Cronus. He had argued his point long and well, until all Cirocco could do was let him in on her top secret plan, the one that might or might not work. There was just no other way Conal was going to sit still while Robin—and the rest of his friends, of course—marched helplessly under those bloodthirsty monsters perched on that loathsome cable.

When he heard the plan he agreed, reluctantly. It still put Robin in danger, but there was no way to get completely around that.

"It has to be this way, Conal," Cirocco said. "I suspect an attack on the Cronus base will bring in reinforcements from all around the wheel, before we've had a chance to pull our surprise. If enough of them show up, you and your people could be wiped out. Then we'll be vulnerable to air attack all the way to Hyperion."

So Conal sat at his base now, well-concealed in the northern highlands of Iapetus, and brooded. It seemed an eternity. He didn't sleep well. He never went more than two hundred meters from his plane, which was always fueled and ready.

The other pilots played cards, told jokes, and generally tried to pass the time. These were mostly men and women who had flown military aircraft back on Earth. Conal didn't have much in common with them. College kids, most of them. They looked down on him, resented the fact Cirocco had placed him in command . . . but admired his skills in aviation. He was a natural, they said. That was true, but the biggest factor that made them listen to him was that he had more air time in Gaea than all the rest of them put together. He knew the special conditions of Gaea, knew what the tough little planes could endure in the high pressure and low gravity, understood the coriolis storms that so confused many of the other pilots.

They tolerated him, and learned from him.

He sat by the radio every waking hour.

The base itself maintained radio silence. It was their hope that Gaea did not know its location, and their suspicion that the buzz bombs could hear radio communications. So they listened to the forward observers in Metis, and to the terse communications from the advancing army.

At last the alert came.

"Bandits at eight o'clock," said the voice on the radio. ". . . six, seven . . . there's the eighth, nine . . . and Big Daddy makes ten."

The crews scrambled. Conal was already in the air when the rest of the message came.

"They're dropping down to the deck. Can't see them anymore. Station one signing off. Come in station two, station three."

Station one was in the southern highlands of Metis. The people there had the biggest telescope in Gaea—requisitioned, as so many other high-tech things had been, from Chris's improbable base-ments—and it was constantly trained on the Metis central cable.

Two and three were to the east and west of the cable. No matter which direction the Eighth went, Conal would know soon. He expected them to turn east, toward Bellinzona and the army; still, it was always possible this was a diversion or a trick.

But he was pretty sure of one thing. The Fifth Wing was dropping down toward Cronus, and they didn't have far to go.

"Station three reporting. We have all ten bandits in sight. Heading...due east, within the limits of our radar."

Three squadrons of five planes had scrambled at the initial alarm. Conal didn't like to think of how few planes were in reserve.

"This is the Big Canuck," Conal said. "Squad Leader Three, turn east and execute plan three."

"Roger, Canuck."

"And good luck to you."

"Roger," came the laconic reply. They would need it, Conal knew. The Eighth would head due east for as long as possible before disclosing their final destination by either turning sharp left for Bellinzona, or continuing toward Cronus and the army. Either way, the Third Squadron would take them on, outnumbered two to one.

Conal watched the five planes peel off, neat and sweet as an air show. He wished that was all it was.

They had been heading due south. Now he gave the order to turn to the east. Squads one and two would angle away from each other and then converge over the army from the north and south.

Just as they were completing the turn his radio gave him the message he had been dreading.

"This is Rocky Road. We are under attack from the air. No ground troops reported. Attackers are believed to be the Cronus Fifth, but unable to confirm at this time." There was the sound of an explosion. "Hurry up, you guys! We're getting chewed to pieces out here!"

At the first word from station one, the army executed their defense plan, meager as it was.

They had pushed on into Cronus from Ophion, over gently rolling land that left them hideously exposed from the air. They were moving into a narrowing neck of grassland that would eventually be squeezed out by the jungle to the south, and the sea of Hestia to the north.

There was no offensive action open to them. Nothing in the arsenal had any hope of hitting a buzz bomb. Attempts had been made to convert the Air Force's weaponry to ground-launched control, and they had been dismal failures. Cirocco had given it up, knowing she had already wasted too much of the Air Force's dwindling supplies in her self-indulgent display over Pandemonium. She would pay for it now, and so would everyone around her.

Bellinzona had recently begun the manufacture of gunpowder and nitroglycerine. The army had gunpowder, in the form of big rockets, but almost all the nitro—in the form of dynamite—had been diverted to to a destination Cirocco would not disclose, which infuriated the Generals. But even if they had access to dynamite it would not have made much difference in fighting off an aerial attack. The rockets and their warheads were useful only as diversions. It was hoped the red-eyes and sidewinders would be attracted to their meat.

The bonfires had been constructed with the same principle in mind. Several dozen wagons were filled with dry wood and kerosene. As the attack was announced, these wagons were driven forward, backward, and out to each side as far as they could get before the planes were sighted, then set afire. In the middle of the Cronusian night, it was hoped these bright lights would confuse the attackers as to the size of the army, and provide them with easy and expendable targets.

The main body of the army extinguished all lights, spread out, and set to work with their Personnel Entrenching Tools—shovels, to a civilian—something high-tech had done little to improve. An infantryman from the Argonne would have known how to use them instantly. The ground was hard, but it was amazing how quickly one could dig when the bombs began to fall.

Cirocco found herself doing an amazing thing. As the blue-white dots of the Fifth Fighter/Bomber Wing began circling above them, getting into position for their runs, she ran back down the highway, shouting and waving her sword.

"Get down! Take cover! Get down, get down! The Air Force is on the way. Keep your goddamn heads down!"

She saw the first deadly orange blossom ahead of her and to

one side, still quite far away, and she was grabbed by the arm, lifted, and tossed onto Hornpipe's broad back. She landed on her feet, and held his shoulders, then yelled into his ear.

"Take cover, you crazy bastard!" she told him.

"I will when you do."

So they thundered down the highway, startling the troops, waving their swords, shouting warnings that were entirely unnecessary as the landscape began to thunder and burn beneath the pounding of the Ferocious Fifth. She knew it was insane. She had never understood how commanders could do crazy things like that, and wasn't quite sure how she was managing it herself. She had no illusions about being immune to bombs and bullets, did not think the mad force of her personality could somehow protect her—a theory she had actually seen propounded in some of the more fanciful military texts.

She only knew it wasn't right for her to take cover now. Better to chance being killed. The troops had to see her and perceive her as unafraid, even though she was shaking so badly she almost dropped her sword. There was no other way to convince them to risk their own lives when she demanded it of them.

God, she thought. Ain't warfare wonderful?

Most of the Titanides took the course Cirocco and the Generals had agreed was the logical thing for them to do. It would take them forever to dig trenches big enough to protect their huge bulk. Their great advantage was speed.

So they ran away.

They scattered in all directions, got as far from the center of the action as they could, and watched, horror-struck, as the malignant beauty of the battle unfolded in the air and on the ground.

Skyrockets screamed into the air from the pyrotechnics wagons, trailing orange sparks, glowing bright red, then exploded. Redeyes and sidewinders burst like coveys of incandescent birds from beneath the wings of the buzz bombs, trailing red or blue or green fire, accelerated at a frightening rate, screaming in bloodthirsty joy as they suicidally dived into the bonfire wagons or chased skyrockets or, all too often, were not fooled and raced along a few meters above the ground to spread liquid fire over the pock-marked landscape. The aeromorphs themselves were visible only by their blue-white exhaust. The bombs were not visible at all until they reached the ground, and then they made everything else seem insignificant.

A few Titanides, moved beyond endurance, started back, but were stopped by their more sensible comrades.

Only the Titanide healers did not run. Like the human medics, they did what doctors have always done in war. They gathered the wounded, tended them . . . and died beside them.

"Oh Great Mother if you let me live through this I'll never leave my computer again, never again, never again, never again. . . ."

Nova was not aware she was shouting. She was scrunched up in a trench that seemed about a quarter of an inch deep—and she was sharing it with two foot soldiers she had never seen before.

It was actually quite a bit deeper than that, and when a relative lull came all three of them scrambled out and dug like maniacs. Then the monsters made another pass and they piled in again, a mess of harp elbows, boots, sheathed swords, askew helmets, and the stink of fear. They held their shields above them and heard dirt clods rattle against the dull bronze.

A bomb hit very close. Nova wondered if she would ever hear again. There was nothing but ringing for a long time. Shards of hot metal fell on them, and steaming soil.

"Never again, never again, never again . . ."

Part of Conal's mind knew that the Metis invaders had turned north, were headed for Bellinzona. That part of his mind wept for the outnumbered Third Squad.

The rest of him was concentrated on the dark air ahead that, minute by creeping minute, grew lighter. They could see the battle long before they arrived there.

Then they engaged the enemy, and there was no time to think of anything but flying.

He had to let his computer do a lot. There were too many blips on the screen, too much confusion, too much darkness. He twisted and turned, got lined up on something promising . . . and was overruled by the firecontrol computer, who had identified his target as friendly. Then he splashed a buzz bomb. The whole encounter between them was over in less than three seconds. He did not bother to watch the wreckage fall down into the night, but immediately slammed into a ten-gee turn toward the next target of opportunity.

The battle was actually anticlimactic. He knew it hadn't been for those who had sat it out on the ground for the twenty minutes it had taken his squadrons to arrive. But by the time they got there the Fifth Wing had foolishly used up much of its air-to-air capacity. Their guns were running out of the little bullet-creatures. They still had some bombs left, and that was gratifying, as it made a much healthier explosion when Conal's missiles hit them. Each airburst meant one less parcel of death for those in the trenches below.

At last there was only the Luftmorder. Conal and two of his pilots closed in on it from behind. He shot off most of its left wing. A Gnat seemed to be trying to fly right up its tailpipes, then delivered a missile, and they all throttled back and watched it fall. The air was full of smoke, and there were a frightening number of fires on the ground.

"This is Big Canuck, calling Rocky Road."

There was a pause longer than Conal would have liked. Somebody had been separated from his radio, he realized.

"Rocky Road here, Canuck. I don't see any more enemies."

"That's right. They're all dead. The Fifth is no more. I haven't heard from my Third Squadron yet, but I know they engaged the Eighth somewhere over Dione, and you people have at least a half-rev breathing space before any survivors could get here."

"Roger, Canuck. We'll be digging in."

Conal was moving at dead slow, just over stall speed, while the computers formed up the First and Second Squadrons. Glancing around, he saw one hole in the Second, and one in his own, the First. He looked at his screen and saw one emergency beacon, stationary, on the ground, just short of Hestia. He dispatched one of his pilots to fly over and see if it was a survivor.

Two planes lost. One pilot lost, possibly two. Two other planes with minor damage.

Conal realized he was soaking wet. He put his plane on complete automatic, sat back, and shook for a few minutes. Then he wiped the sweat from his face.

"Big Canuck, Big Canuck, this is Squad Three."

Conal recognized the voice. It was Gratiana Gomez, the youngest and least experienced pilot in Third Squadron.

"I read you, Gomez."

"Canuck, Third Squadron engaged the enemy ten klicks south of Peppermint Bay. Ten aircraft were reported, and ten were destroyed. One got through to Bellinzona, and I have just destroyed it. It dropped three, maybe four bombs on the city."

There was something in her voice that disturbed Conal.

"Gomez, where is your squadron leader?"

"Conal...I am the squadron leader. In fact...I'm the Third Squadron." Her voice broke at the end, and he heard a dead mike.

"Gratiana, go back to Iapetus North and park it."

There was a long pause. When she spoke again her voice was under control.

"I can't, Canuck. The aircraft is pretty shot up. I think it might be salvageable. I'm gonna try to put it down on the football field up by the labor camps. I think I can—"

"Negative, Gomez." Conal knew exactly what she was thinking. Pilots were easy to come by, but airplanes were at a premium. The equation offended him.

"Well...then I'll ditch it up close to the wharves, where the water isn't too deep. They can pull it out and—"

"Gomez, you head that thing out toward Moros, and when you're right over the biggest, flattest piece of land you can find, you punch out of it."

"Canuck, I think I can—"

"Punch out, Gomez! That's an order."

"Roger, Conal."

Later, when things were sorted out, Conal learned that Gomez had made it safely to the ground. She died an hour later of blood loss from the shrapnel wounds she had not told him about.

Nova slowly realized that things had quieted down.

She lifted her head a little. There were fires in the night. She could hear people moaning not too far way. Some were screaming. She moved cautiously around on her elbows, straightened her helmet, and found herself face to face with one of her trench-mates. He gave her a foolish grin. She heard herself giggling. Great Mother, what a terrible thing to do. But she could not shut it off for a long time. The man laughed with her, glad to be alive. Then they turned to the third person in the trench to let him share in the joy.

But there was a little hole under the man's left arm, and a big one in the center of his chest. Nova held the bloody corpse for a long time, and could not cry, though she wanted to.

Though they never spoke a word to each other, they had shoveled together like mad animals, and huddled together in the dark and the fire, shivering, sharing warmth. And she hadn't known when the warmth leaked out of him in a flood of red.

Cirocco and Hornpipe had been knocked over by the blast wave of a near-miss. Though unhurt, they had decided to stay down. Enough was enough.

Now she strode through the battlefield, limping slightly. Her ears were still ringing. The ends of her hair and her eyebrows on the right side were singed. There was a little blood on her right hand.

She took it all in. There were many dead and injured, but they were being attended to. Sergeants were shouting like it was just another drill on the obstacle course. Dirt was flying everywhere. Many of the trenches were already eight feet deep. Cirocco couldn't find a single slacker. The Fifth Wing had made believers of them all.

The infirmary was a large tent set up as far away from the trenches as Cirocco had dared. She had debated a long time about whether to mark it with a big white cross. In the end, she decided not to. Gaea had cast herself in the role of the bad guy. She might very well have told her buzz bombs to seek out white crosses.

She entered the radio shack and grabbed a hand mike.

"Big Canuck, are you still up there?"

"I'm not going anywhere. Captain, have you seen Robin?"

"I have no information on that, Canuck."

"...Okay. Sorry. I shouldn't have asked."

Cirocco glanced around, saw no one was watching her.

"Conal, I'll let you know as soon as I know anything."

"Right. What do I do now?"

They discussed it, using code words Gaea and her troops would not understand if they happened to be listening in. Conal was the only other person who knew about Cirocco's plan for the Gaean Air Force.

"I think," Conal said, "if you're gonna do it, you ought to do it as quickly as possible."

"I agree. Give us...two more revs to get as solidly dug in

here as we can. You and your people go back to Iapetus and re-arm and re-fuel. I'll take it up with the Generals."

Robin had spent most of the battle half-buried under a dead Titanide.

She and four others had dug a foxhole, the bombs had started to fall... and the Titanide had fallen right at the edge of it. Its body slipped slowly down, not quite covering Robin. She thought it had probably saved her life. When everything was over and she was able to struggle out, she saw the amount of debris the huge, dead hunk of meat had soaked up. One of her companions in the foxhole had a chunk of metal in her leg, but the others were unharmed.

She managed to locate Cirocco, who had time for a brief embrace before hurrying off toward the Generals' tent.

Robin and Nova were oddities out here, and Robin was acutely aware of it. They were not in the army, as everyone else was. They had no assigned duties. Nova was not even in the city government anymore. In a sane war, one fought entirely by strategy and tactics of masses of soldiers and airplanes, Robin would never have been brought along. But her presence here was necessary.

The trouble was, she couldn't tell anybody *why*. She didn't even entirely understand it herself.

So now she wandered through the carnage, looking for her daughter. A few other people were wandering as aimlessly as she was, but they had that shell-shocked look. Robin was shaken, but in control of herself. She had come to terms with her fear twenty years ago, when she first allowed herself to feel it. She had been very afraid while the attack was happening, shocked and sorrowful at all the casualties, but now that it was over she felt only disgust at the atrocity of the attack... and worry for her daughter.

She found her digging a trench. She had to call three times before Nova looked up. Then the girl's lower lip quivered, she climbed out of the hole, and went to Robin's arms.

Robin felt only tears of happiness. And she felt a little silly, as she always did, putting her arms around a daughter almost a foot taller than she was. Nova wept uncontrollably.

"Oh, Mother," she said, "I want to go *home*."

EIGHT

Cirocco spread her clock-face map on the rickety table. A Captain held a lantern over it as she drew in two more *X*s.

"The Cronus and Metis wings of the Gaean Air Force are wiped out. That means this whole half of the wheel, with us right in the middle, no longer contains any enemy air power. The nearest threat to us is all the way over here, in Hyperion. Bellinzona is still threatened by the Thea Wing. Now, if you were Gaea, what would you do?"

General Two studied the layout, and spoke.

"She must know by now that one of our groups outmatches one of hers."

"But I don't think she knows our total strength," Cirocco said.

"Good. That might make her wait. An attack on Bellinzona from Thea is a possibility. But you say her main objective is the army."

"It is."

"Then...we'll get a good deal of warning if the Hyperion Wing takes flight. You said our spies in Hyperion are excellent."

"They are."

"If I were her," General Eight said, "I would start massing my planes. Shift the Hyperion group into the empty base in Mnemosyne, for instance, if that base is still usable."

"It isn't."

"All right. And the Hyperion couldn't make it to the Cronus base without being attacked by our Air Force. So I'd tell them to sit tight. I'd move the Thea wing to the base in Metis. Iapetus is out of the question, for the same reason as Cronus. How many buzz bombs can use one base?"

"That I don't know."

"Hm. Well, if more than one wing can land at one base, I'd start moving those more remote ones in closer. Phoebe, Crius, Tethys, into Metis and Hyperion. We don't know the range, either, do we?"

384

"No. I suspect we're at the outer limits of the Hyperion group's range. But we'll get closer. I thought she might launch them at us now, while we're still recovering, and move Rhea up to take their place. But I *think* what she'll do right now...is nothing. So far, I've been right." She pointed at the map again. "We have to defend the army, the city . . . and the base in Mnemosyne. The base in Iapetus is expendable—in fact, I've given orders to blow it up if they try to take it."

"Why would they try that?"

"Because they're going to be hungry. I propose a surprise attack. If it works, it might give us total air superiority."

She watched the effect of that magical phrase. In large army engagements for two centuries, those words had been the key to victory.

Naturally, they wanted to know how she planned to do it. She told them.

NINE

"Begin Operation Hotfoot. Begin Operation Hotfoot."

Perched on central cables from Hyperion to Mnemosyne, those Dione Supras who were gathered around the little radios began to chitter excitedly.

The dream-demon had said the radios would speak, and my, didn't they ever? The Supras had sat entranced as the pristine gibberish issued from the clever machines. Mentioning exotic bafflers like Canuck, poesy like Rocky Road, speaking of metal Squadrons, Luftmorders, and a fellow named Roger, the radios had become a great source of fun to the Supras. They played rhyming games.

"Big Canuck, are you in position?"

"Intromission."

"Inquisition."

"Pig and puck."

"Rig a duck."

It was great fun.

The dream-demon and her insubstantial companion had explained what a hotfoot was. It appealed to the Supras. Not the mission—to which they were already committed—but the code name, and the practical joke. Supras had a rather rough sense of humor.

They had been setting up for it for kilorevs. It was unpleasant. They did not like the stink of kerosene. But they did it, for the Demon.

And now the code word had been spoken by the radio. The plan had to be executed instantly, so it would be simultaneous all over Gaea. Any other way would be perilous to the Supras, Gaby had been quite emphatic about that.

"Oh, such dynamite there will have been," one of them said.

"Bouquets of Chrysanthemums," one gasped, a bit previously.

"Showers of flowers."

"Break out the soothing salves," one worried.

"Casualties are to be expected," another encouraged, referring to the dastardly attack on the nest in Tethys.

"The sword cuts both ways."

"That's a pyrotechnicality."

"Is there film in the camera?"

They dropped away from the cable and plunged toward the nest of vipers clinging below them.

The Luftmorder was only peripherally aware of the angels until they got within fifty meters. They had been around so much, his perceptions had simply edited them out, like smart radar erasing the signatures of birds.

Then they were among the squadron, chittering and chattering, actually coming close enough to touch his vassal aeromorphs. He saw one put something against the side of a buzz bomb. He heard something rattle down the exhaust pipe of another.

With a screech, he launched himself into the air, fell to ignition speed, and lit up all four engines. Behind him his squadron was following. . . .

One exploded. The limpet mine attached to its side tore a hole down to the combustion chamber, and the buzz bomb lurched to the side and went spinning endlessly down, trailing flame and smoke.

Another never made it away from base. As its engine turned

on, the dynamite bomb lodged in its afterburner burst it apart. Only pieces were left to flutter toward the ground.

The Luftmorder banked hard and began to climb. He felt no hatred, only an overpowering urge to explode every angel in Gaea.

He worked at it for a time. He loosed a few sidewinders, managed to score one hit on an angel in flight. He send a missile into their nest. From the look of the explosion, it was already empty.

And the angels were impossible to hit. He watched as his underlings twisted through the air, trying to get them. Before long there were no angels to be seen. They had flown to the cable and crawled into tiny spaces there. It would be futile to shoot at them, and it might endanger ...

So great had been his concentration that only then did he notice the base was on fire. Great gouts of fuel flowed from the attachments he had so recently abandoned. It spilled down the side of the cable. He knew it would continue to burn until the Source—whatever that might be—ran dry.

His brain clicked this piece of information into place, and he formed his next tactic around it.

He had no fire extinguishing capability. He had not been informed of any other being in Gaea equipped to fight such an inaccessible blaze. Therefore, the base was lost. Therefore, he must defend the upper base. He climbed ...

Soon he could see that it, too, was on fire.

Click. Another bit of information filed.

He called upon his squadron to form up around him. There was a base in Thea. He would take them there, provisionally. He radioed a terse description of the engagement to Gaea, and awaited her Orders, confident that a flight to Thea was the only logical choice.

He was not worried.

In the six remaining regions of Gaea that supported air groups, Luftmorders and buzz bombs fell away from burning bases. The Tethys squadron got off with the lightest losses: only two buzz bombs. Crius lost three buzz bombs and their Luftmorder, and milled aimlessly around the flaming cable, unable to think where to go. Hyperion was hit hardest, with six of the nine buzz bombs crashed or disabled in the initial attack.

The Dione Supras suffered casualties, as they had known they would. In a few decarevs they would gather to mourn them, after ~~enough time had passed to cherish their memories.~~

In the meantime, they put their own losses out of their minds.

It had certainly been a delicious joke.

"Big Canuck, all the bases are burning. Repeat, all. Every survivor is in the air. Right now there is a great deal of confusion."

Conal swallowed hard. He knew they'd get it sorted out eventually. Some of them would get here. Perhaps a lot of them.

He listened as Cirocco relayed the reports of damages, added them up in his mind, and matched them mentally against his own forces. Allowing for the unknown variables—maximum range, and the possibility of fueling stations the Supras didn't know about—it came out pretty good.

Rhea and Hyperion squads would head for Cronus, and the army. It was their only possible target. His fliers were waiting for them in Mnemosyne. There was the possibility of an ambush there, though he wasn't counting on it.

Crius could go either way—though if their estimates of maximum range were right, it would do them no good.

The Thean squadron could probably reach Cronus. Tethys might make it, too. Phoebe couldn't, but would have a shot at Bellinzona.

Conal's big advantage, tactically, was that he'd be able to take them on in waves. He thought it highly unlikely that the closer ones would orbit in place, wasting fuel, waiting for the stragglers to catch up. He didn't think Luftmorder minds worked that way, for one thing. They seemed to fixate on a target and then go to suicidal lengths to reach it and destroy it.

He deployed his squads accordingly.

Orders came. The Luftmorder had guessed correctly . . . up to a point. He had expected to be assigned the city as his target. But the Orders, relayed through the Thea Luftmorder, were short and explicit. He and his squadron were to fly to Cronus and attack the army. He was to fight until there was not an enemy plane in the sky, and not a bomb left to drop on the army. Only then was he to consider his further survival.

This was no surprise, at least the last part wasn't. It hardly needed saying, as it was part of the standing Orders. What failed to click properly into his tactical computer was what had not been said. He had not been told to re-fuel at the Thea base.

He came as close as a Luftmorder could come to disobeying Orders. He decided that, as he neared the base in Thea, he would request permission to re-fuel. This could not in any way be seen as disobedience. All proprieties were satisfied by this decision.

Then he reached the Thea central cable and saw the base was burning. It explained everything.

Once again, he was not worried. He pressed on toward Cronus.

Conal's Fifth and Sixth squads stayed in the radar shadow of the Mnemosyne cable. When the Hyperion Second came streaking by, intent on Cronus and the army four hundred kilometers away, the smaller planes fell on them like hawks swooping from a great height, and tore them to pieces.

The Hyperion Luftmorder, before dying, managed to warn the Rhea squadron about the trap in Mnemosyne. They would arrive in about twenty minutes.

The Second and Fourth squads of the Bellinzona Air Force tried a similar trick in Dione, but had to wait to be sure the enemy was not heading for the city. The Thea squadron had a little more warning, and gave a good account of itself. Conal, back at the base in Iapetus, ready to bring the First Squad up in relief, listened as three of his pilots died and a fourth was forced to eject. One of his squad leaders was among the dead, so he combined the six remaining planes of the Second and Fourth into one squad and ordered them back to Iapetus for re-fueling.

He took off for Dione at the head of the First squad—five of his eleven remaining planes in the East.

Tethys was going to make a try for Bellinzona, that seemed certain. It would be insane for them to push on into Cronus.

The First squad, from Rhea, was already getting low on fuel when they met Conal's Sixth and Seventh—the Seventh consisting of only two planes which had been assigned to guard the Mnemosyne base while the Hyperion squadron was being attacked. Now the Fifth was re-fueling, and would not come to help out. There was still the chance of a last wave arriving from Crius, and the base had to be defended.

Thea began firing missiles from a great distance. Flights of sidewinders came streaking out of the west before the squadron was even in sight.

It turned out to be a good tactic. Three Bellinzona planes were hit and downed. Two pilots managed to bail out over the sands. Then the dogfight began, and within ten minutes the sky was cleared of buzz bombs.

The Mnemosyne detachment didn't know it yet, but the war was over for them.

In Crius, the surviving buzz bombs still orbited the remains of their Luftmorder, burning on the ground. From time to time one would send a red-eye into the wreckage, as if hoping to stir it back to life.

With pitiful keening sounds, they stayed over their fallen leader until, one by one, they ran out of gas and crashed.

The Phoebe Luftmorder and his attendant buzz bombs cruised into Metis. He noted that, like in Tethys and Thea, the base on the central cable was burning.

The Luftmorder had a tactical problem. He had been assigned to attack the Bellinzona Army in Cronus, two thousand kilometers away. He had a range of eighteen hundred kilometers.

He saw now he could have made it had he flown up the Phoebe Spoke, through the hub, and down over Cronus. It would have made a nice surprise, too.

He had counted on re-fueling in Metis. Nobody told him there would be no fuel stops along the way, and standing Orders had been to proceed along the rim for all engagements unless specifically instructed. Something about noise abatement procedures in the hub. Gaea was up there—or part of her was—and perhaps Luftmorders gave her a headache.

But there was no such word as hopeless in the Luftmorder's vocabulary. He cruised on through Metis, into Dione—seeing the burning corpses of the ones who had gone before him, supremely confident that the mission would be accomplished. His buzz bombs, with only one engine each, had a range of twenty-one hundred kilometers. They would live to fight.

Over Iapetus he ran out of fuel—and into a dilemma.

Buzz bombs were not bright. There was a small repertoire of commands he could give them. "Follow me," "Attack," "Set up for bombing run," "Take defensive action," "Engage the enemy" . . . things like that. He searched through the list. There was no Order for "Go on without me."

It was an interesting problem. He considered it all the way down to the ground, flying as a big glider, surrounded by the low roars of his troops in echelon behind him.

About two meters above the ground, he entertained the first doubt of his life. *Maybe this isn't going to work,* he thought, and he hit, and began to roll end over end.

Behind him, the buzz bombs flew into the ground, one after the other.

Above him, Conal's Second squad watched incredulously.

Just about twenty minutes before the death of the Phoebe Eleventh, Conal had watched in horror as the Tethys Tenth ignored Bellinzona and arrowed into the west.

He and the other planes of the First had been hiding near the Dione central cable, in perfect position to ambush the Tenth and demolish them. Now the enemy had a good head start on him—and his other squads were at base re-fueling, with even less chance of getting the jump on them. He gave his orders to his squad, and they quickly went supersonic. It wouldn't leave them much fuel for dogfights when they caught up. Then, his hand trembling, he punched in the code for Cirocco's army.

"Rocky Road, this is Big Canuck,"

"Go ahead, Canuck."

"Rocky . . . Cirocco, the Tenth has gone through Dione. I'm afraid you may be seeing them in a few minutes."

"We're as ready for them as we'll ever be."

"Captain . . . I'm sorry. I misjudged them. I thought they'd—"

"Conal, don't flog yourself. We thought we'd get three squads at us, *minimum.* So far, we haven't even seen a contrail."

"Yeah, but there's still Crius, which I haven't heard from, and Phoebe, which has been spotted twenty minutes behind me."

"Crius is splashed, Conal. As for Phoebe . . . a little bird told me they're going to run into trouble that has nothing to do with you. Tell your people to hang back, don't engage them, and report on what happens."

". . . well, if you're *sure* . . ."

"I'm sure. Now do what you can about Tethys, and let me tell everybody to get their heads down here."

"Roger, Rocky Road."

TEN

The Luftmorder was aware of the enemies closing in behind him. They had come out of nowhere, and they would reach him before he and his squadron could engage the enemy in Cronus.

There had been an overpowering urge to turn north toward the juicy, helpless target of Bellinzona. The city had seemed almost like a magnet. He wanted to turn north. . . .

And then the tiny, contemptible planes had appeared, and he realized they had been in hiding all along. Gaea was great. Gaea was good. Gaea was wise, and had surely known he would be flying into a trap had he turned north.

Supremely confident, he flew on toward Cronus.

When the enemy fleet began to get within missile range, he detached four of his seven buzz bombs to go back and do battle. They peeled off quickly. He flew on, and with his hind-looking radar senses, watched them die, one after the other. He felt as much emotion as a rifleman who sees four bullets miss the target. It was annoying to have *missed,* but he never gave a thought to the bullets themselves.

Then he saw that one of the five enemy planes was going down. What was even better, three of the others were now far behind him, having wasted time and fuel downing the four buzz bombs. Only one still came on with a chance to overtake his reduced squadron before they spread death over the army.

Hesitating only a moment, he detached another buzz bomb to

ow this enemy plane. He had no illusions it would shoot down the
nemy.

The buzz bomb made a head-on run at the attacker... and
issed. It was turning, but now would be taken by the three other
ursuers. And still the other came on.

Click. So be it. He was almost in Cronus now. This plane
ehind him would take one, maybe two of the three remaining fliers
f the squadron. He would not take three. Even if the Luftmorder
imself was shot down, the buzz bombs had their Orders. They
ould attack until they ran out of fuel, and then kamikaze into the
rgest target of opportunity.

Just like an air show, Conal told himself, as the buzz bomb
rew larger in his windshield, heading straight for him. The planes
ould fly right at each other and you thought there was just no way
ley weren't going to hit, and then at the last minute one of them
ould flip one way and one the other and they'd go by a couple
iches apart.

Only at an air show, the planes weren't shooting at each other.
treaks of light came from the approaching buzz bombs, going by
n all sides. Conal felt two of them slash through his wings, but he
dn't look away.

From the time he saw it until he made his move couldn't have
een more than two seconds, at the speeds they were traveling. It
eemed like an hour. It grew and grew and he waited and waited,
en he turned so hard he blacked out.

It was only momentary. When he lifted his head he was still
the air, and almost behind the remaining three, though they were
ill distant. Far behind him the attacker was screaming into a turn,
it he could forget about that one. It would never catch him.

He tested the controls gingerly. The plane hadn't been hurt
idly. The right wing cannon wasn't working, and some of the
sponse was a bit sluggish, but he decided it would bear up. He
osed in behind the three attackers.

It began to seem almost too easy. He picked off one buzz
mb, which didn't even try to dodge. He zeroed in on the Luft-
order, but it twisted up and away. That left him with the other
izz bomb, which also took no evasive action. He almost hated to
ke the time, but he gave the computer its scent, the computer

instructed a missile, and it screamed away to bury itself in the buz
bomb's tailpipe.

Conal looked up and saw the Luftmorder. He turned, sho
another missile—then was turning even harder as he saw the side
winder coming at him. He was still turning when it went off, takin
a meter from the end of his left wingtip.

The little Dragonfly coughed, and he was pulled forward agains
his straps. He lost three hundred meters of altitude very quickly a
the transparent wings strained and groaned, finding a new shape t
compensate for the damage. At last—four, maybe five seconds later—
he knew he was still airworthy, though not as fast as he had been

He spied the Luftmorder. One of its four engines was missing
and black smoke trailed from that spot. But it didn't seem to bothe
the Luftmorder. It was descending, and Conal knew that was pur
poseful, as he could see the scattered fires of the army not too fa
ahead.

He moved in above and behind.

Carefully, he lined it up in his sights and told the computer t
blow it to hell.

Nothing happened.

Cursing, he switched to manual control and tried to shoot
down with his remaining wing cannon.

Nothing happened.

The computer was still running, but no messages were gettin
through to his armaments.

Shouting his outrage, he moved in even closer.

The Luftmorder was not worried.

He couldn't shut off the flow to the missing engine, so the fir
would not go out, and that hurt some, but pain would not dive
him. A quick check of consumption assured him he was losing n
more fuel than if the engine had still been in place. He would mak
it.

He would make it, so long as that little . . .

Where the hell was it? He'd had it on his radar just a secon
ago. It had been descending. He would have seen it if it crashed
He scanned the skies with radar and visual senses, and found nothing

Finally, he began to worry.

* * *

Conal was ten meters beneath the Luftmorder.

He felt like he could almost reach out and touch its great bulk. ed-eyes and sidewinders hung in clusters, squirming eagerly in the gh wind.

He saw the trailing edges of the great wings bend down and te air, and had to move quickly getting his own flaps down or he ould have shot out ahead of the monster.

Slowing down. Getting ready for the bomb run. It would want make it accurate, drop as many bombs as possible during its one d only pass. It probably knew there were no ground guns that uld hurt it.

Guns.

Conal had been thinking about ramming. If the Luftmorder dn't slowed down, that would have been his only option.

He looked up at the belly. There were sphincter-like puckerings along it. He had wondered where the bombs came from. Might ve known, he thought. That would certainly appeal to Gaea's sense humor.

He blew his canopy. The wind hit him like a fist. But he and e creature were still slowing, and it got a little better. He dug in s flak jacket and came up with his flare pistol. The wind snatched e first shot and pushed it off to the Luftmorder's left, just missing e fuselage. He had two more. Was the creature starting to turn? ever mind. He took aim again, giving it a lot of windage. He saw e flare embed itself in what was, surprisingly, soft flesh a few ches away from one of the sphincters. It was magnesium, and too ight to look at.

Conal dropped and turned—and so did the Luftmorder. He ard a screaming sound, looked up, got a glimpse of a loathsome, blinking eye protected behind a hard plastic-like material. The eye ared its hate at him, and the Luftmorder fell helplessly away, its nards on fire.

Conal thought of all those bombs and kerosene fumes and ssiles, and turned his plane as hard as he dared.

Then it was like the Chinese New Year. Things were flying all around him, trailing fire. The Dragonfly was buffeted by shock ves, rattled by schrapnel, for a moment engulfed in flames as a mb went off close by.

He was in clear air again.

The Dragonfly shifted gears.

It shifted again, and again, trying out one shape after another, slowing, beginning a slow roll to the left. *Somewhere* among its vast array of possible airframes there must be a configuration that would make further flight possible.

But there wasn't.

Sorry, the brave little plane seemed to say, as it nosed over and dropped like a stone.

Conal pushed himself away from it, popped his chute, and saw the Luftmorder hit the ground a hundred meters short of the army.

And to think, he was the guy who had to be convinced that life never came out as well as it did in comic books.

He looked up, and saw his chute had a big hole in it. In his present state of mind, it didn't worry him in the slightest. This, too, I will survive, he told himself, with a big grin.

And he did survive it.

When he tried to get up he howled in pain. He had broken his ankle.

"Never *did* get that parachute practice," he told his rescuers.

ELEVEN

It might have gone differently.

Gaea did not have much of a military staff, but she had a few, and when the first reports of the defeat of the Cronus and Metis air forces came in, one of the staff found her and informed her. He recommended moving other units up from the far side of the wheel, getting them in positions more favorable for a massed attack. It was generally agreed that was the best way to defeat the tricky little Bellinzona planes.

Gaea was in a screening of *War and Peace,* the long, Mosfilm version. She agreed that was probably a good idea, and to ask her again when she got out and had a chance to think it over.

When she came, blinking, out into the light again, she was

informed that all her air bases had been destroyed and her air force was in the final stages of being obliterated.

The news had produced a petulant frown on her huge face.

"See if you can scare up that copy of *Strategic Air Command*," she told her advisors, and went back into the screening room.

TWELVE

The dead were counted, and gathered together. Just over six hundred humans, twenty-two Titanides. Their bodies were stacked with wood and set afire as all the Division stood at attention.

The wounded were treated. There were fifteen hundred human and thirty-five Titanide injuries, many of them serious. Wagons were loaded with the less serious casualties, and moved out toward the city, with three Cohorts to guard them.

So it was one Legion of dead and wounded, and half a Legion who would not go on to Hyperion. Similar numbers applied to the Titanides. It was, in effect, another decimation.

It could have been much worse. Everyone kept telling themselves that. Nobody mentioned it while the pyre was burning, or as blinded, burned, and dismembered survivors were loaded into the wagons.

In the remorseless logic of warfare, Cirocco knew it could not have been better if she had planned every second of it.

The Air Force was much more badly hurt than the army, both in planes and pilots—but the Gaean Air Force no longer existed. The survivors were heroes. The tale of their fight would be told in many a Bellinzona taproom.

The Army was damaged—but was probably stronger now than it had been before. It had been, in that horribly exact word, "blooded." Soldiers had seen comrades die. They blamed Gaea for it, and they hated her. They had learned something about fear. They were veterans now.

Her Generals knew better than to bring up any of these points.

They remembered the ex-General who had talked of "acceptable losses." But they all knew it was the truth, and they knew Cirocco realized it.

It could hardly have been any better.

Cirocco was so happy she wanted to throw up.

The only thing that made it even marginally tolerable was that, so far, they had been fighting monsters. She could accept and approve of this hatred, this spirit of bloodthirsty vengeance that would have repulsed her so had it been directed at another group of humans. So far, they had been fighting true evil.

But in Hyperion, at the gates of Pandemonium, it might all change. If Cirocco's plans for Gaea did not work out, these people would soon be fighting other human beings.

A very few of those people had chosen to be there, and were as evil as Gaea herself. But the great majority in Pandemonium had been tossed on its shores as randomly as the Bellinzonans had been washed up in Dione. It was the luck of the draw, and Gaea was using a stacked deck.

Cirocco found herself raising silent prayers to Saint Gaby. Please don't let me fail. Please don't let this army—this army I raised only when you promised me Adam could be saved without human beings ever warring against each other—please don't let them learn to love killing other humans.

One other thing kept her going. If she died, and the army had to fight, it was better to die a bloody death than live in slavery.

The army pressed on.

As the road vanished into the jungle, the Titanide groups moved to the front.

There had been grumbling about the Titanides. It wasn't logical, but those things never are. No matter that the pinned-down humans had nothing to fight back with—had not really fought a battle at all. No matter that, had it been possible, the humans would have run from the field of battle, too. The plain fact was, the Titanides had left and the humans had stayed behind to soak up the bullets.

The jungle changed all that.

Progress was slow through the jungle. As the troops moved through a long, dark tunnel of foliage, they would pass groups of exhausted, bleeding Titanides sitting at the side of the trail. Sitting with them would be the Legion that had been marching in the point position. When the end of the line passed them, the Legion and the Titanides would fall in at the back. This happened about every two revs.

When a Legion got to the front, they saw what was happening. The groups of fifty Titanides were hacking through the jungle with the speed and energy of a large, continuous buzz saw. It was awesome to watch. Little creatures that bit and clawed attacked them. Poisonous plants scored their colorful hides. It didn't take long to see that humans could have moved the army at about a tenth its present speed, and only with heavy casualties.

It was bad enough in the middle of the column, with things jumping out of the underbrush all the time. The troops got very jittery. Some just died, for no reason anyone could see, victims of contact poisons.

When they camped, the jungle closed in. Creatures better suited to drugged nightmare than reality came blundering through the darkness and briefly into the light, fighting off four or five Titanides.

They had to camp twice in the jungle. Nobody slept much.

There was another constant tension. Word had come down that an attack in force might be made against them while they were in Cronus, who was an ally of Gaea. Nobody knew the nature of the possible enemies, but from what they had seen, it would be awful.

But for some reason, Cronus did not attack. The army came out the other end and breathed a sigh of relief—all but fifty-two Titanides and sixteen humans who would never breathe again.

They made a more elaborate camp by the river Ophion, on the verge of the great desert of Mnemosyne, not too far from where the river plunged underground and ran for two hundred kilometers before emerging.

Cirocco let them rest, recover from the jungle, and gather strength for the desert crossing. Football games were organized. Men and women soldiers retired to the conjugal tents and forgot about fear for a while.

Every available water container was topped off. There would be no oasis, no spring, no water of any kind until they reached the snows of Oceanus.

THIRTEEN

There was a universal mystic dread of the sandworm.

Many a tale had been told of it, though of the humans there only Cirocco had ever seen it.

It was ten kilometers long and had a mouth two hundred meters wide, some said. It thirsted for human blood, according to others. It liked to stay under the sand, where it could move faster than a Titanide could run, then come bursting to the surface to devour whole armies.

Well... sort of.

A lot of the tale-tellers were remembering the beast who had first appeared in a movie long ago—one of Gaea's favorites. She had liked it so much she had *built* the beast, and let it loose in Mnemosyne, which, according to Titanide legend, had once been the Jewel of the Wheel.

The truth was a lot more, and a lot less.

They passed one great loop of the worm midway through their crossing. The worm was three *hundred* kilometers long and four kilometers in diameter. It preferred to stay below the surface, but where the bedrock was less than four kilometers down it had no choice, so loops of it were visible far into the distance. It was gradually crunching the rock into finer and finer sand, and somehow living on the minerals it ingested.

As to its speed...

Three hundred kilometers of sand creates a great deal of friction. The sandworm was made of huge ring-segments, each about a hundred meters long. What happened was, one of the visible segments would hitch itself forward six or seven meters, then the next one in line would pull itself back up against the first, then the next, and so on down. Two or three minutes later the segments would hitch along another six or seven meters.

The relief of seeing it, awesome as it was and so utterly harmless, was so great that a fad developed which Cirocco did nothing to stop. The army began covering it with graffiti.

As each Legion passed the two or three kilometers of visible worm, their commanders gave them a short break, and they crowded around to write on the biggest damn living wall any of them had ever seen, and to laugh at the messages left by those who had gone before. Names and hometowns were sentimental favorites. "Marian Pappadapolis, Djarkarta." "Carl Kingsley, Buenos Aires." "Fahd Fong, the GREAT Texas Free State!"

You could carve the surprisingly soft hide of the thing with sword or sheath-knife; it didn't give a damn.

There was poetry: "Those who write on a sandworm's balls..."

Urgent messages: "Sammy, call home!"

Advertising: "For a good time, see George, Fifth Legion, Tent Twelve."

Criticism: "Sonja Kolskaya gives great head!"

Philosophy: "Screw the Army."

Helpful suggestions: "Blow it out your ass!"

And patriotism: "DEATH TO GAEA!!!!!"

That message was repeated up and down the length of the worm. There were touching eulogies to dead friends, homesick laments common to soldiers everywhere. Even a bit of history: "Kilroy Was Here."

It was a good thing the sandworm was there, Cirocco knew. The army was in need of some comic relief. The crossing of Mnemosyne was hellish.

The temperature soared as high as one hundred and forty Fahrenheit, and seldom went below one-ten. The humidity was very low, which helped. Nothing else did. There was no relief of night, no cooling breeze.

The strategies of dealing with Gaean desert were quite different from those useful on the Sahara. The sunshine was weak as diluted tea. You couldn't even tan in it, much less burn. So hats were not worn, nor any sort of protective garment. Many preferred to strip right down to the buff so the sweat could evaporate at the maximum rate. Others wore the lightest possible garments to trap some of the water.

Neither strategy was very good. They had enough water to

make it across without rationing, so Cirocco made no decrees. The problem was saving one's feet, and getting some sleep.

Odd devices, carried all the way from Dione, were broken out and passed around. They looked like snowshoes, and were woven of tough reeds. It took some practice to walk in them, but it was worth the effort. All the heat came from below, up through the sand, which in some places was hot enough to cook on. The sand shoes spread the weight so one didn't sink in. And, most of the time, they kept the soles of the boots away from contact with the ground.

Titanides had their own, heavy duty versions. But the jeeps had an awful time of it. They honked almost continuously.

The encampments were nightmares.

People slept standing up, leaning against wagons. It was possible to heap folded tents, clothes, and anything else that came to hand in a pallet that would insulate to some degree. People crowded onto them—and awoke gasping, drenched in sweat, from nightmares of burning.

It was better to sleep during the march. Troops did it in rotation, climbing atop the wagons and grabbing a few hours of sleep until roused by the next shift. Still, many fell asleep while marching, fell down, and jumped up screaming.

There were cases of exhaustion, and dehydration. The Air Force flew in and out constantly, taking the worst cases ahead to the edge of Oceanus. Even so, there were deaths, though not as many as Cirocco had feared.

At the twilight zone between Mnemosyne and Oceanus, on the shores of the warm lake where Ophion emerged from his subgaean journey, Cirocco allowed a brief encampment. It was possible to sleep on the ground. Then she hurried them on to the shores of the biggest sea in Gaea, the one that took up sixty percent of the land surface of Oceanus and was called, simply, Oceanus.

The water was cool. Plants grew along the shore. The Legions stripped off what little they had been wearing and plunged into the sea. Jeeps clambered into the water with joyous hoots. Titanides swam out where it was deep, looking like improbable Loch Ness monsters with their human torsos just out of the water.

Cirocco gathered her Generals once more to discuss the arrangements for troops too weakened by Mnemosyne. She tried to conceal her fear from them, and didn't think she succeeded. To Cirocco, Oceanus was the great unknown. She had crossed it many times, but always with a deep fear. It was hard to explain, since nothing really bad had ever happened to her there. But Gaby had refused to talk about it, and that worried her.

It was decided that those soldiers certified by the Medical Corps as too debilitated to stand the Oceanus crossing would stay here at the west shore of the lake. No troops would guard them. They would have to take care of themselves, if it came to fighting.

Cirocco showed them what they could eat and what to stay away from, and, having put it off as long as she could, led her army into Oceanus.

FOURTEEN

The wagons were as light as they would ever be. Gear brought along for the jungle had been left at the west edge of the desert. Desert gear was with the convalescents on the eastern edge. There was no need to carry water into Oceanus, and the cold-weather gear, carried so long and so far, was now on the backs of the troops. If the jeeps appreciated their lighter burdens, they didn't let on.

Their route through Oceanus took them along the southern shore of the sea, past the point where the great ice sheet began forming, and to the edge of one of the three major glaciers that inched their way from the southern highlands. At that point the ice sheet was more than a hundred meters thick, plenty of safety margin to bear the weight of the army.

There was no Circum-Gaea Highway in Oceanus, just as there had not been in Mnemosyne. It would have been silly to try to carve a permanent route. The easiest way was across the frozen sea. While it was not flat—pressure from the glaciers fractured the ice and pushed huge sheets of it up and over other sheets—it was possible to find a reasonably level route. Now that the angels had used all the dynamite they would ever need, regular flights by Conal's remaining plaines brought in tons of the stuff, which was used by the scouts to blast passages.

As they moved into the ice-bright night of Oceanus toward their first encampment, a familiar shape grew in the east. It was Whistlestop, once again doing the inexplicable. Blimps always went through Oceanus at high altitude. But here he came, as if he had a down payment on the place.

He stopped short of the army, and what looked like fine dust began to fall from his belly. It kept falling for a long time. At intervals they would hear the eerie foghorn bellow as he valved away excess hydrogen. Even so, he gradually rose higher as the dust kept falling.

When he was done he moved a few kilometers away, turning again toward the east, and dropped a torrent of ballast water that froze to sleet before it reached the surface.

The payload turned out to be firewood. It was scattered all over the site Cirocco had picked for the first encampment, cut to lengths convenient to the burners which could be set up inside the troops' tents. It was dry and almost smokeless.

Cirocco told the officers to pass the word through the ranks that the wood was a present from the Hyperion Titanides. The general opinion of Titanides, already high among the jungle veterans, went up another notch as they wolfed down hot meals and crawled into their bedrolls in the warm tents.

It was during their second encampment in Oceanus that Gaby came to Cirocco again.

She was in her tent. Her feet were stretched out toward the fire, which had been laid in a thing like a big oil drum. There was a cot in the tent. She had thought she might sleep. She hadn't done so since...when was it? Somewhere in Cronus. But she wasn't having much luck.

Still, she knew she needed it, so she stretched out again, yawned, closed her eyes...and Gaby came through the tent flap. Cirocco heard her, and sat up. She didn't have time to think. Gaby took her by the hand and hurried her toward the outside.

"Come on," Gaby said. "I've got something important to show you."

They went outside into the swirling snow.

It wasn't a blizzard. It wasn't even really a storm, but any sort of wind was unpleasant when it was ten below. The two guards outside her tent were alert, standing with their backs to their fire so they wouldn't be blinded...and they didn't see Gaby and Cirocco. They looked right through them.

Which was natural enough in a dream, Cirocco thought.

They plodded through the snow toward another tent, and Gaby led Cirocco inside. There were two bedrolls, both occupied. Robin was asleep in one of them. In the other, Conal sat up, rubbing his eyes.

"Captain? Is that..."

Conal apparently had no trouble seeing Gaby. He must be dreaming, too.

"Who's that?" he said.

"I'm Gaby Plauget," Gaby said.

Cirocco really had to admire Conal then. He looked at Gaby for a time, saying nothing, apparently fitting the reality to the endless stories he had heard during his time in Gaea. The idea of a ghost didn't seem to give him a lot of trouble. Finally, he nodded.

"Your spy, Captain...right?"

"That's right, Conal. That's very good."

"It couldn't have been anybody else, I figured." He started to stand up, winced, then swung his legs around so he could lever himself up with his crutch.

Conal should have been sent back to the city with his broken ankle. He had been prepared to put up a fuss if anybody suggested it, but it didn't come up. Cirocco needed him in Hyperion, disabled or not. And since he could ride on Rocky, it wasn't much of a problem.

But it had been a bad break. The Titanide healers thought he would limp for a long time—possibly the rest of his life.

Gaby knelt in front of him. With effortless strength she opened the bulky cast, then put her hands on the bare ankle. She squeezed for half a second. Conal gasped, then looked surprised. He stood up and put his weight on it.

"Miracles, two for a quarter," Gaby said.

"I'll have to owe you the quarter," Conal said. "But thank you..." And he burst out laughing.

"What's the matter?"

"Thank you just seems a little . . ." He shrugged, and his mouth worked in a foolish grin. He seemed unsteady. "What's the second miracle?"

"I'll show you. Take my hands, children."

Flying seemed to upset Conal a lot more than ghosts or magic healing. Cirocco could hear his teeth chattering.

"Buck up, Conal," Gaby said. "After that trick you pulled on the Luftmorder, this ought to be a walk in the park."

He said nothing. Cirocco simply endured. She didn't *like* things that were out of her control. But during these dreams it never seemed to matter so much.

She found out she was wrong. When she realized where they were headed, she wanted to turn around and go back.

"You've trusted me this far," Gaby said, gently. "Trust me a little longer. There's nothing here for you to be afraid of."

"I know, but—"

"But you've always felt an irrational fear every time you went through Oceanus, and you've never been within a hundred kilometers of the central cable. Oceanus is the *enemy*, your mind keeps telling you. Oceanus is *Evil*. Well, for twenty years now you've known it's Gaea that is evil. So what does that make Oceanus?"

". . . I don't know. Many times I've started out to come and look the bastard in the eye . . . and I keep seeing the *Ringmaster* coming apart at the seams."

"And hearing that fancy story Gaea told us up in the hub"— Gaby paused, and made her voice sound like a petulant child— "about how poor, misunderstood Gaea tried *everything, honest* she did, and she only wanted to be *friends* with humanity, to welcome us with open *arms* . . . but that foul conniving rebellious bastard Oceanus reached out and . . . oh, you poor souls, how terrible it must have been for you, but it wasn't my *fault*, you see, it was *Oceanus*, who *used* to be a part of my titanic brain, but is really his own semi-god now, and I just have no *control* over the rascal . . ."

Gaby fell silent, and Cirocco went over it in her mind again.

"I'm not such an idiot that I haven't thought that out," Cirocco said. "But like I told you, I just couldn't come here."

"Snitch had a lot to do with that," Gaby said. "Even when you got him out of your head, he left some of his garbage behind."

Cirocco shuddered.

"Sorry, it was a pretty bad metaphor, I guess. No more metaphors. Now we get down to the reality."

They landed just outside the verge of the strand-forest of the central cable, and proceeded in on foot.

It grew warmer as they neared the center. What little light there had been failed within the first hundred meters. Neither Conal nor Cirocco carried a lantern, but Gaby had some kind of light source that streamed ahead of her like beams of moonlight, or reflections from a mirrored ballroom globe. It was enough to see by... and there was nothing to see. Cirocco had been under many cables, and there had always been the flotsam of centuries beneath them. Skeletons of long-dead creatures, fallen nests of blind flying animals, the crumpled remains of dimpled tapestries that peeled away from the cable strands and hung for hours or millennia... even old cardboard boxes and plastic sandwich wrappers and crumpled cans from the days of Gaea's tourist program, when thousands of humans had gone rafting on the Ophion or caving in the strand forests. Strand forests supported complex nocturnal ecologies, seldom seen, but indicated by animal droppings and seed-pods fallen from the unseen interstices high above.

In Oceanus, there was nothing. A cleaning team might have swept through only hours before, dusting and polishing. The ground had the texture of linoleum.

Cirocco's fears were now vaguely remembered. When she thought about it, she was amazed that she *had* been afraid. Her times with Gaby had always been spent in a pleasant, half-drugged dream state. She knew nothing could go wrong. Even in retrospect, the dreams did not seem frightening. Now she walked in her usual state of placid expectancy. In a way, she felt like a small child walking with her mother on a winding, wooded path. It was interesting, without being exciting. There would be new things around each curve, but they would not be scary. She had a sweet what-comes-next expectancy, but no sense of urgency.

She felt some of Conal's emotion, in a way difficult to describe. He was not afraid, either, but he was very curious. Gaby had to keep calling him back or he would have bounded ahead of them. Continuing her analogy, he was like a boy from the city who had never *seen* the forest; every curve held a new marvel.

At a point Cirocco knew—without understanding how she knew—to be the exact center of the cable, they saw a light. As they got nearer they saw a man sitting beside the light. They approached him, and stopped. He looked up at them.

He looked like Robinson Crusoe, or Rip Van Winkle. His hair and beard were long and gray. There were foreign objects, twigs and little bits of fishbone, matted in it, and a long brown stain in his beard below his mouth. He was crusted with dirt. He was wearing the same clothes Cirocco had last seen him in, twenty years ago, writhing in the sawdust on the floor of The Enchanted Cat taproom, in Titantown. To say the clothes were tatters did them an injustice; they were the most decrepit articles of apparel she had ever seen. Great gaps in them showed a lot of skin—gaunt, stretched tightly over the bones—and every inch of that skin had scars great and small. His face was old, but not the same way Calvin's was old. He might have been a sixty-year-old beachcomber. One of his eye sockets was empty. "Hello, Gene," Gaby said, quietly.

"How are you, Gaby?" Gene asked, in a surprisingly strong voice.

"I'm well." She turned to Conal. "Conal, let me introduce to you Gene Springfield, formerly of the *D.S.V. Ringmaster*. Gene, this is your great-great grandson, Conal Ray. He came a long way to see you."

"Sit down," Gene said, apparently to all of them. "I'm not going anywhere."

They did. Conal was staring at his ancient relative, the man he had thought dead when he came to Gaea.

The first thing Cirocco noticed upon taking a closer look at Gene was that he had a bulge on his balding forehead. The skin there was unmarked. The shape of the skull was distorted, like half a grapefruit had bulged up under his skin.

The location of the bulge was suggestive. She wondered at the pressure the thing was putting on his frontal lobes.

She saw a little more of his surroundings. There wasn't much. The fire came from a crack in the ground. It was bright and steady in the windless dark.

There was a heap of straw, apparently Gene's bed. In the distance the light reflected off a still pool of water, twenty meters across. Close to Gene was a big, galvanized pail with water in it.

That was all. A short distance away was the entrance to the stairs that would lead down to Oceanus.

"Have you been in here all this time, Gene?" Cirocco asked him.

"All this time," he confirmed. "Ever since that time in Tethys when Gaby cut my balls off." He looked at Gaby, and cackled. No, Cirocco decided, that wasn't quite the right word. There was no laughter in it. It was just a sound made by an old man. He made it again as he looked at Cirocco, Conal, then back to Gaby. "Didn't come by to apologize for that, did you?"

"No," Gaby said.

"Didn't expect you would. No matter. They grew back, just like they did the first time you cut 'em off." He cackled again.

"What do you eat?" Conal asked.

Gene eyed him with suspicion, then plunged a gnarled hand into the pail. He came up with something gray and blind that wiggled.

"You cook them on that fire?" Gaby asked.

"Cook 'em?" Gene asked, startled. He looked from the ugly thing in his hand, to the fire, then back again, and a wild surmise grew beneath the beetled brow. He grinned, showing the brown stumps of teeth. "Say, that's an idea. They's pretty tough. Like to wear your teeth down, they do. Catch 'em in that pool yonder. Slippery devils." He looked at the eel again, frowned, as if unable to remember how it had come to be there. He tossed it back in the pail.

"What do you do down here?" Conal asked.

Gene glanced up, but didn't seem to see Conal. He scratched his head—Cirocco winced when she saw how deeply his fingers went into the bulge of skin—and muttered into his beard. He didn't seem to be aware of them.

"Gaby," Cirocco whispered. "What's with . . . the way he talks, it's—"

"Backwoods? Quaint? Colloquial?" One side of her lip curled in a bitter smile. "Interesting, for a Harvard graduate, NASA-type New Yorker, wouldn't you say? Rocky, Gene is the sorriest son of a bitch that ever lived. He's had tricks played on him that make what she did to us seem like playful pranks. Look at his head. Just look at it."

Cirocco had hardly been able to take her eyes away.

Now she was seized by a compulsion to touch it. She fought it as long as she could, then she got up, knelt in front of him, and placed her palm against his forehead. It was soft. Something moved sluggishly under the skin.

She thought she should be revolted, but she was not. She stared at her hand as if it belonged to someone else, and felt a power building in her. Gene's hands came up slowly, and he put them around her forearm, making no attempt to push her away. She felt him frown. She had an absurd impulse—very close to hysteria—to shout *Heal!*

Then she was holding something wet and squirmy and vile-smelling. She looked at it dispassionately. It was covered with blood, and so was her hand. It was built along the same lines as Snitch, but bloated, grotesquely fat, with rolling eyes like peeled grapes. It made a croaking noise.

"Son of a bitch," Gene muttered. "Son of a bitch. Son of a bitch."

Cirocco heard Conal stumbling away, heard him vomiting. Somehow she knew it was important to keep staring at the creature, which continued to croak. Gaby was moving, holding something out....

It was a jar made of thick, black glass. Cirocco popped the monstrosity into it, and screwed the lid on tight.

Only then did Cirocco look at Gene. He was fingering his forehead, which had bloody fingermarks on it, but was not broken. The skin hung loosely on his head, but there was no sign of damage.

"Son of a bitch," he said.

"Like Snitch?" Cirocco asked. Now that it was over, she felt faint.

"No," Gaby said. "They're related. But Snitch only listened, and reported." She tapped her own forehead. "The one in my head only listened." She held up the black jar. "*This* one was like what spies call a mole. He burrowed deep, and he shuffled things around. When he could, without revealing himself, he made things happen. Things like rape, and war, and sabotage....He ran Gene's life after a while. Gene was like a puppet on Gaea's strings."

"Up there...on the cable?"

They had had their doubts about him, so many years ago, shortly after the wreck of the *Ringmaster*. He had tried to show the Titanides how to use new weapons in their war with the angels, in direct violation of First Contact procedures and United Nations regulations. But they had written that off as a simple desire to help the Titanides.

So they had taken him on their climb up the cable to the hub. And he had clubbed Gaby unconscious, left her for dead after raping her. Then he had raped Cirocco, and would have killed them both but for some luck and some fast footwork.

Gaby had wanted to castrate him then and there. Cirocco had not permitted it. She still didn't regret the decision, even though he had been endless trouble in the next seventy-five years, and had set events in motion that led to Gaby's death. She had regretted not *killing* him many times.

They had found he was very hard to kill. Gaby had once slit his throat and left him for dead. He had survived it.

So he had become like Snitch. When Cirocco wanted something from Snitch, she had to torture it out of it. And, over the years, whenever Gaby had encountered Gene she had left him a little less than he was—an ear, a few fingers, a testicle. He healed, but unlike Cirocco and Gaby, he scarred.

"No, not on the cable," Gaby said. "Not directly, I mean. That thing didn't jerk him around. But it whispered things to him. Gene was like a schizophrenic. I...think he had to have some tendency to rape, for the thing to egg him on to doing it. Later, it didn't matter what Gene thought about anything. In a sense, Gene was gone. In a sense, he died years ago."

Gaby sighed, and shook her head.

"It makes me feel ashamed. Because, see, if there's a miracle here, it's in how much he *resisted,* and for how long. Even to coming here...the one place in the wheel where Gaea doesn't *ever* look. She still gets reports from the mole, but she pretends they're coming from somewhere else."

"Why?"

"Why? Because she's crazy. And...something else you'll see in a minute."

Conal had rejoined them now. He still looked green.

"What did she *do* to him?" he said, with a quiet intensity.

For a moment Cirocco thought he was asking about what she had done. But he was looking at Gaby, and Gaby explained what Gaea had done, and how long ago, and what it had meant. Conal took it all in silence.

"What about Calvin?" Cirocco asked.

"He got one, too. But Whistlestop knew about it, and killed it almost immediately. I don't know how. Whistlestop didn't bother to tell us... which I blame him for, a little, even though I know he isn't wrapped up in human concerns." She shrugged. "Killing the thing in Calvin's head is the reason he's dying now."

"Who's Calvin?" Conal wanted to know.

"Remember your comic book?" Cirocco asked. "He was the black one."

"He's still alive, too?"

"Yes." Cirocco turned to Gaby again. "What about Bill?"

"When he went back to Earth, he resigned from NASA and went to work as an agent for Gaea. All quite openly, but he had clandestine activities. I *think* he got one like Gene did, but I don't know. Don't ask me about April or August; I don't know what Gaea did with them."

"How much *do* you know? Can you tell me more now?"

"Knew he was up there," Gene said. They all looked at him.

"He liked fish," Gene clarified, and gestured to the bucket. "Got hisself real fat on fish, he did. Didn't do much for me, fish." He thumped his scrawny chest. "But I knew he was up there. Pissin' on my head, he was." He cackled.

"Do you know who put him there, Gene?" Gaby asked.

"Gaea."

"What do you think of that?"

"Mean thing to do." He cackled again, and shook his head. "Been doing some thinking, down here. Been doing me some thinking."

Gaby spoke to Cirocco as if Gene could not hear. And perhaps he couldn't.

"The cornpone dialect is a parting gift from Gaea. Remember the movie analogy I told you about? She wanted him to be a character actor. A buffoon, a sidekick... I don't know. Folksy humor."

"Real funny," Conal seethed.

"Tons of fun," Gaby agreed. "Gaea always had been about as funny as cancer of the rectum."

"Poked m'own eye out," Gene said, and cackled. "Thinking real hard, I was. Like to bust a gut, thinking. It just popped right out. Hurt like the dickens. Tried to put 'er back in." He cackled again. "She'll grow back in, though. Always happens that way. Like to sawed my hand off, once, trying to stop thinking. She grew back, too." He pondered this. "Thinking hurts," he concluded.

"Did you think of something, Gene?" Gaby asked.

He squinted his one eye.

"Sure did," he said, at last. "Thought something oughta be done. Somebody oughta . . . whale the daylights out of her, that's what!" He looked at them defiantly.

"There may be a way, Gene," Gaby said.

He narrowed his eye suspiciously.

"Don't kid with ol' Gene, Gaby." He looked puzzled, then cackled, then shrugged, and regarded her in the same way a dog would if the dog had just made a mess where he knew he shouldn't.

"Are you really Gaby? Been meaning to look you up. Wanted to tell you . . . gosh, I'm really sorry for . . ." He looked even more puzzled. ". . . for killing you."

"That's all in the past, Gene," Gaby said.

Gene's laugh sounded genuine for the first time.

"All in the past. That's a good one. I'll have to tell . . ." He looked around vaguely in the darkness. Then, with difficulty, he brought himself back to his tenuous connection with the present.

"There's maybe something you can do," Gaby said. "To Gaea."

"To Gaea?"

"But it will be dangerous. I'll be honest. You might get killed."

Gene studied her. Cirocco wondered if he had understood. Then she saw a tear fall from his eye.

"You mean . . . I may be able to stop thinking?"

FIFTEEN

Gaby brought them to Oceanus by the same sort of dizzy-making teleportation she had used in the previous dream. When Cirocco got her bearings, she looked around and felt she had been here before.

But she had not. It simply looked so much like Dione. The big difference was a big, greenish tube running from the ruins of the brain that had once been Oceanus straight up into the darkness overhead. Before the tube reached floor level it split in two parts, going east and west. Cirocco tried to find the image it reminded her of, and finally got it. Old tenement buildings with bare light bulbs hanging from the ceiling—extension cords to power the toaster and the television.

The moat was deep and dry. Nothing had been alive in here for a long time. Cirocco turned to Gaby.

"What happened?"

"We'll probably never know all of it. Parts of it are still in Gaea's mind. Parts are lost. It was thousands of years ago, like she told us. But the brains were never separate. I think Oceanus just...died. Gaea couldn't accept it.

"The human analogy can only be pushed so far before it breaks down, but I don't have a better way of explaining it to you.

"Gaea felt betrayed. She refused to believe in something so fantastic as Oceanus's death. So her mind *did* split up, and she grew this nerve down to here—that part goes to the Hyperion brain, and the other one to Mnemosyne—and...*became* Oceanus. And that part of her was a bastard. Some sort of physical struggle did occur, but I don't think it was as dramatic as Gaea described it to you. It was always Gaea talking to herself. When you talk to *any* of the regional brains, you're really talking to a fragment of Gaea's personality.

"She's splitting up more and more. She...I *still* can't tell you all of it, but she evolved a...system to keep things running. That fifty-foot woman you're going to do battle with is part of the system.

414

You are, too. So am I, though that was an accident. And that's all I can tell you."

Gaby turned to Gene.

"If I tell you some things to do, will you do them? Will you remember? If you know these things will hurt Gaea?"

Gene's eye gleamed.

"Oh, yes. Gene will remember. Gene will hurt Gaea."

Gaby sighed.

"Then the last piece is in place," she said.

Gaby left them on the outskirts of the camp, but inside the outer perimeter of guards so there would be no misunderstanding. They started walking toward the light.

Conal stumbled. Cirocco reached out for him—and realized he was crying. She hesitated just a moment, wondering what would be best for him, then put her arms around him. He wept helplessly, got it under control quickly, and pulled away, embarrassed.

"Feel better?"

"I was just remembering . . . what I came here to do to you."

"Don't be a horse's ass. *I* didn't know most of what we just heard."

"That poor man. That poor, sorry son of a bitch."

"You'll feel better when you wake up."

He looked at her strangely, then squeezed her hand and went off toward his own tent.

Cirocco went to hers. The guard challenged her, then recognized her, and saluted. He didn't seem to have any trouble with the idea that she could sneak out of her tent, despite his surveillance.

If only he could see inside the tent, Cirocco thought. She sighed, and pulled back the tent flap, preparing herself for an evolution she had performed twice before but which still made her uneasy.

But there was no other Cirocco in the bunk.

After standing there for a while, pondering it, she sat on the cot and pondered some more. She eventually decided there was no point in trying to wake up if she wasn't asleep.

She glanced at the time, saw it was approaching the rev when they should move on, and went back outside to get things started.

*   *   *

The army moved into Hyperion.

Their objective had been in sight, in clear weather, since the middle of Mnemosyne. One could hardly miss the south vertical cable, which pointed directly at the heart of Pandemonium. Now, as they marched across the gently rolling hills of southwest Hyperion, they could sometimes see the circular wall that surrounded the Studio.

The bridge over the Urania River was one of the few still intact on the Circum-Gaea. Cirocco had her engineers check it out, first for booby-traps, then for structural strength. She was told it was sound, but took the precaution of spacing the wagons widely and making the troops march out of step. The bridge held.

Gaea had provided the bridge over the Calliope. The dam she had caused to be built there was earth-fill. The turbines were small, by human hydro-electric standards.

The Air Force flew in more dynamite, and after the army had crossed the dam, Cirocco had it blown. Everyone watched as a good-sized hole was punched in it, and cheered as the lake swiftly eroded it into a ruin. Cirocco destroyed the turbines, too. The dam was completely unguarded except for six Iron Master technicians, who were apparently unconcerned to see their handiwork destroyed.

Cirocco didn't know if that was a good or bad sign. She kept her patrols out, looking for Gaea troop movements, but there were none.

SIXTEEN

Gaea had been watching war movies almost exclusively for a long time.

When the power went out, it couldn't have picked a worse moment. It was during the last reel of *The Bridge on the River Kwai*. The tension was building in one of the all-time great big-budget final scenes. You could hear the little Jap choo-choo coming around the bend and it looked like the guy had gone bananas, because he was *helping* the Japs find the bombs wired to the bridge, and...

Alec Guinness, she thought sourly. It was almost like an omen.
e didn't believe in omens, of course...

So then the power goes out. Some distant, vague part of her
nd knew what had caused it, but she didn't want to think about
t. This had all started out as a lot of fun, but she was getting
re and more bored with it every day.

She was getting tired of movies, if the truth were told. She
is tired of that little brat Adam, and that stinking drunk Chris.
st of all she was tired of waiting for Cirocco Jones to show up.
e didn't think it was going to be the charge she had hoped it would
 when she mashed the bitch under her foot.

She fumed about that while they scurried around getting the
ergency generator turned on, bringing in a transformer so the
ojector could run off it... all the dreary little things the dreary
le technical people do. Didn't they know she was a *star*?

Then they finally got it running again. It clattered along for
ybe fifteen seconds, then it stopped, and the lamp burnt a hole
 the film.

Enough was enough.

She killed the projectionist and stomped out into daylight to
 if Cirocco's army was here yet.

EVENTEEN

he final encampment was only ten kilometers away from Pande-
onium. An easy march. And in Gaea, of course, a General didn't
ve to worry about what time of day to attack.

There were two things to be done.

She called Nova, Virginal, Conal, Rocky, Robin, Serpent,
aliha, and Hornpipe together in the big command tent. No one else
as present. Even the guards outside had been told to stay fifty
eters away.

She stood before them, looking at each one in turn. She was
ore than pleased at what she saw, disgusted at what she had to
y.

"Robin," she began. "I haven't lied to you. But I haven't te
you the whole truth. Nasu has maybe a one in a thousand chance
beating Gaea."

Robin looked away, then nodded slowly.

"I guess I knew that."

"Even if she *did* kill this Gaea...and I'm talking about th
giant monstrosity in Pandemonium now, not the real Gaea, w
Nasu could never beat—it wouldn't do any good. In fact, I'm cou
ing on Gaea killing her."

"Nasu's not my demon anymore, Captain," Robin said. S
looked back at Cirocco, and there were tears in her eyes. "I mea
I really can't carry her around in a gunny sack, can I?"

"No. But I can still call her back. We might get along witho
her."

Robin shook her head, and stood straighter.

"You do what you think is right, Cirocco."

It was Cirocco's turn to look away.

"I wish I could. But I don't always *know*." She looked at t
rest of them. "I've told you people more than anyone else. I'm telli
you more now. I'm not telling you *all*, even this late—and I do
even know all of it myself. But there is only one chance, and I
taking it. Nova."

The young witch inhaled quickly, surprised. Cirocco smil
tiredly at her.

"No, I don't have any big surprises for you. But I'm leveli
with everyone, and you're the only one who saw Calvin. Rememb
him?"

Nova nodded.

"He's dying. What he has *might* be curable by Titanide healers
we don't really know, because he won't let us examine him. I
used to be a doctor, so maybe he knows it's incurable. At any ra
he wants to do something for us, and it will kill him. That's wh
took you to visit him that day, to see if he was willing. He was.

"The day I got drunk," Nova said, with a wistful smile.

"Conal. You saw Gene. You must have some idea of wh
he's capable of. What Gaby told him to do...he probably wo
do it right. He probably won't survive it. Gaby and I knew that.

Conal looked at his boots for a moment, then met Cirocc
eyes.

"I never saw anybody more ready to die than he is. I think it would be a blessing if he died . . . and I think he knows *exactly* what he's doing."

Cirocco was grateful. Conal always seemed to come through. She took a deep breath, fought off her own tears.

"Virginal. Valiha. Serpent. Horn—"

Hornpipe stepped forward and put his hand gently on Cirocco's shoulder.

"Captain, since it is the time for truth-telling, I should tell you that we have already figured out that—"

"No," Cirocco said, pushing his hand away. "I have to say this. You all knew Chris might die in this encounter. I told you that saving Adam was my number one objective. That was a lie. Saving him is my second objective. It is more important to me than I can say . . . but if this ends with me, Adam, *and* Gaea dead, I'll count it a victory."

Hornpipe said nothing. Valiha stepped forward.

"We have discussed this," she said. "We obeyed your security rules and did not spread it through the race, so we four are making this decision, and will bear the weight of it. We feel the race would agree with us. There comes a time when all must be risked that a great evil be eliminated."

Cirocco shook her head.

"I hope you're right. There . . . is the *strong* possibility that even if Gaea and Adam and I are killed, the wonderful Titanide race—who, I swear to you, I love more than my own race—will survive. But if Adam and I are killed, and Gaea survives, you are doomed. And this is my *first* priority: that the thing called Gaea be erased from the universe."

"We are with you in this endeavor," Hornpipe said. "The responsibility for saving Adam will rest with us. . . ." He gestured to include the whole group. ". . . with us seven, from two races, but bound by love. This is as it should be."

"This is as it should be," the Titanides sang.

"Adam's life is in our hands now. You should put it from your mind. You have told us what we must do, and we will do these things to the best of our ability. You should now forget about it, trust us . . . and do what you must do."

"You will always be our Wizard," Serpent said, and then sang it, ringing and defiant. The other Titanides joined him.

Cirocco felt she *must* cry, but managed to hold it back. Sh
faced them again.

"This may be the last time we meet," she said.

"Then those who survive will always cherish those who fall,
Virginal said.

Cirocco moved among them, kissing each one. Then she sen
them on their way. She had thought she had all the crying done
back at the Junction, but found, when they were gone, there wer
some tears left.

It was some time before she could summon the Generals.

When they were seated around the command table, Cirocce
looked from one to the other, and felt ashamed at her conceit in
always thinking of them by the numbers of the divisions they com
manded. The impulse had sprung from her distaste for things military
But these were comrades now. They had stood beside her, and she
had an odd surprise to give them, and she knew she must end, now
and forever, this number game.

She looked at each in turn, fixing them in memory.

Park Suk Chee: a small, fiftyish Korean, in command of th
Second Division.

Nadaba Shalom: in her forties, light-skinned, impassive, and
the backbone of the Eighth.

Daegal Kurosawa: a racial mix of Japanese, Swedish, and
Swazi, who commanded the One Hundred First.

All had been in the military on Earth, but none had advance
beyond the rank of Lieutenant. There were troops under their com
mand who had ranked higher . . . but no former Generals. There ha
been a time, in Bellinzona, when the discovery of an ex-General ha
been the occasion for a rare celebration. People would get togethe
and burn the fellow at the stake. General-burning had been Bellin
zona's only indigenous sport.

There had been no lynchings for some time before Cirocce
took power. Nevertheless, it had been difficult at first to get anyone
to accept the title, and for a time the Generals had been calle
"Caesars." But common usage gradually took over, as people grew
used to the fact that these Generals had no nuclear weapons to play
with.

"Park. Shalom. Kurosawa." She nodded at each of them, and they nodded back, warily.

"First ... we won't be building siege towers."

They were surprised, but did their best not to show it. Not long ago, one of them would have asked if she planned a frontal assault over the bridges, and another would have asked about starving them out. Not now. They simply listened.

"What is going to happen here will be a little like a big parade. It'll be something like a carnival, and something like a wide-screen spectacular. It'll be a monster movie. It'll be like one of those big outdoor performances of the *1812 Overture,* complete with cannons. It'll be the Fourth of July and Cinco de mayo. What it *won't* be, my friends, is a war."

There was a silence for a while. At last Kurosawa spoke.

"Then what *will* it be?"

"I'll tell you in a minute. First ... if what I'm going to describe to you goes wrong, I will be dead. You'll have to carry on without me. I won't be so stupid as to try to give you orders from beyond the grave. You'll have to make the decisions." She pointed to Park. "You'll be in command, overall. I can do that much, and hereby promote you to Two-Star General. According to the Bellinzona laws, that makes you answerable to the Mayor, when a new one is elected, but it gives you almost total authority in field decisions."

She looked from one to the other. Their thoughts were veiled, but she had a pretty good idea how they were going. Three divisions in the field, one in Bellinzona. If Park wanted to march home and take over, nobody was likely to stop him. She had chosen him as the least likely to have ambitions toward martial law. But she knew she had created a potential monster in the army itself. If there had only been another way ...

But Gaea had wanted a war, and she had to have at least the illusion of one. She had to have her attention diverted, and nothing short of an army would be enough.

"Before we get to the orders of the day, I'll give you the benefit of my thinking about the situation you'll face if I *am* killed. You can do with it what you will.

"I advise you to retreat."

She waited for a comment, and got none.

"You might successfully breach the wall. I think you could.

Inside, you're more than a match for her people. But you're out
numbered. You'd take heavy losses...and you'd lose in the end.
If Gaea decides to pursue you...it'll be a nightmare such as you've
never imagined. She would rampage through your troops. She never
sleeps, never gets tired. She might only kill a few of you at first.
But as your troops get tired, she'll kill more. Maybe a Legion a day
until you're wiped out. That's why, if I'm killed, you should start
your pull-out *immediately*. Once you get to Oceanus, you'll be safe
for a while, because I don't think she'll go in there."

She saw she had managed to frighten at least two of them.
Park had merely narrowed his eyes, and Cirocco had no idea what
was going on behind them.

"If she lives..." Park began. His eyes got even narrower.
"She will eventually come to Bellinzona."

"I think it's inevitable."

"What do we do then?" Shalom asked.

Cirocco shrugged.

"I haven't the faintest idea. Maybe you can whip up a weapon
that can kill her. I hope you can." She jerked a thumb in the direction
of the unseen walls of Pandemonium. "Maybe your best course is
to knuckle down to her like those poor souls in there. Bow down to
her and tell her how great she is, and how much you liked her last
picture. Go to her movies three times a day like a dutiful slave, and
be thankful you're alive. I don't *know* if it's better to die on your
feet than live on your knees."

"I, personally," Park said, quietly, "would rather die. But this
is beside the point. I appreciate your evaluation of this hypothetical
situation. Could you tell us now, what we do *today?*"

That extra star sure emboldens one, Cirocco thought. She leaned
forward, putting her elbows on the table, earnest as could be. She
felt like a three-card-Monte dealer about to go into her spiel.

"Have any of you ever heard of a bullfight?"

EIGHTEEN

Chris climbed down the ladder from the top of the wall to the ground. He had been standing up there for several revs, just to the west of the Universal Gate, watching Cirocco's troops in the distance.

At first he had been impressed. It seemed like a lot of people. Through an observation telescope he had been able to make out the size and shape of the wagons, the type of uniforms the soldiers wore, and the business-like way they moved.

The longer he looked, the less sure he was. So he did his best to make an estimate of just how many soldiers were out there. He did it again and again, and even the largest number he came up with was smaller than he had hoped. There were fewer Titanides than he had expected, too.

Chris had not been completely idle. As the news of the approaching army whispered through the nervous Pandemonium grapevines, he had gone about assessing Pandemonium's strength. He had tried not to be obvious about it—though he doubted Gaea really cared. She made no attempt to conceal anything from him or anyone else in Pandemonium. In fact, she often bragged openly that she had a hundred thousand fighters.

That was true, Chris had decided . . . and deceptive. There were that many people inside the wall, and they would all fight. But he assumed Cirocco's army would know *how* to fight. What Gaea's troops had been trained to do, it seemed to Chris, was wait for the cameras to get into position, wear fierce expressions when charging, shout, and pose in attitudes of stalwart determination.

But there were some things he wished he could get to Cirocco. A spy wasn't worth much if he couldn't get his information out of the country. That thought made him want a beer. . . .

He shook his head, violently. He was determined to stay dry until the fighting was over. He had to be ready, if the chance came . . . though he didn't know if he would recognize it, if and when. He was too much in the dark. And that made him want a beer—

Damn it.

Gaea came striding along the wall. She had been going around and around, checking the deployment of her troops, ordering units back and forth, wearing them out before the fighting even started.

"Hey, Chris!" she called out. He turned and looked up at her. She gestured out to the north, where the army was assembling. "What do you think? They're real pretty, aren't they?"

"They're going to whip your ass, Gaea," he said.

She roared with laughter, stepped over the Universal globe and continued on her rounds. Increasingly, Chris found himself in the role of court jester, able to say the outrageous things permitted a comic figure. It didn't do anything to improve his morale, and it hardly even amused *him* anymore.

Damn it, if there was only some way to get word to Cirocco. She should know Gaea had cannons.

Maybe she *did* know, and Chris was worrying for nothing. And it was true they weren't very good cannons. Chris had watched the testing—from a safe distance, after one of the early models had blown up, killing sixteen.

The range of the cannons was not good, and their accuracy was low. But the Iron Masters had recently come up with some new exploding cannonballs. They sprayed thousands of nails over a wide area. They would be a problem if Cirocco planned to storm the walls.

There were the vats of boiling oil, too, but he figured Cirocco expected that. And she knew Gaea would have archers. . . .

There was other bad news. Gaea had guns. The good news was there weren't many of them, and they were primitive flintlocks that took forever to re-load, and they blew up even more often than the cannons. The men who had to carry them were scared to fire the damn things.

Chris wondered which would be worse: to carry a weapon that might blow your hands off . . . or to go into battle with a prop.

He had had a very bad moment not long ago when he saw a regiment of soldiers dressed in modern, lightweight body armor, carrying laser rifles and the big backpacks to power them. One company of such troops could massacre an entire Roman legion, Chris was sure.

Then he had encountered one of the soldiers in a commissary. From ten feet away, the deception was obvious. The laser rifles were

ust wood and glass. The backpacks were hollow shells. The armor
vas some kind of plastic.

He started back toward Tara. On his way there he had to move
side frequently for dog-trotting formations of soldiers.

There was a troop of cavalry, mounted on the horses Gaea
ised in her western epics. Their sabers were real, but their six-
hooters were carved out of wood. And he happened to know that,
t the right signal, most of those horses would fall over, pretending
o be shot, as they had been trained to do. Wouldn't it be great if
e could get that signal out to Cirocco?

Later, a Roman legion marched by, resplendent in brass shields
nd breastplates and crimson skirts. They were followed by a goose-
tepping regiment of Nazi storm troopers, and *they* were followed
y a shambling bunch of Star Wars storm troopers. Before he got
ack to Tara he saw Ghurkas from *Gunga Din*, doughboys from *All
Quiet on the Western Front*, Johnny Rebs from *Gone With the Wind*,
Huns, Mongols, Boers, *Federales*, Redcoats, Apaches, Zulus, and
Trojans.

Whatever else he thought about Pandemonium, the costume
lepartment was terrific.

He mounted the broad plantation-house steps and found Adam
n one of the huge rooms, sitting on the marble floor playing with
is train set. It was a wonder, made of silver and embellished with
ewels too big for him to swallow if he were to pry them loose—
nd Adam was always prying things loose, though he no longer tried
o eat things that weren't food. He hooked cars to the engine, then
e scooted around on his knees, jerking the train forward, cars flying
ff the end as he went, shouting *choo-choo-choo-choo-choo!*

He saw Chris, and joyously threw his priceless engine against
a wall, badly denting the soft metal (which would be repaired during
is next sleep, Chris knew).

"Wanna *fly*, Daddy!" he crowed.

So Chris went to him and picked him up and zoomed him
hrough the air like an airplane. Adam got a great case of the giggles.
Then he put the child on his hip and carried him to a second-floor
alcony. They looked out toward the north.

Gaea was still striding the wall. She had reached the Goldwyn
Gate, and was returning to Universal, which was closest to Cirocco's
oncentration of troops. It was one of Adam's top three gates: he

liked Mickey Mouse atop the Disney Gate, the big stone lion a
MGM, and the turning globe at Universal, in that order. Adam
pointed.

"There's Gaea!" he crowed. He was always proud and please
when he spotted her vast bulk from a great distance. "Want down
Daddy," he ordered, and Chris set him down.

Adam hurried to the telescope. Tara had about a hundred ver
good telescopes, just for this purpose. Adam was rough with them
as he was with all his toys. And every time he woke up, the broke
lenses had been repaired, the finger smudges had been wiped away
and the brass barrels gleamed.

He was skilled with them by now. He swung the scope bac
and forth and quickly located Gaea. Chris went to another, so h
could see what Adam saw.

She was shouting orders to troops inside the wall, pointing thi
way and that. Then she turned to face outward, her fists on her hips
Chris glanced at Adam, and saw him move the scope slightly t
focus on the beautiful fields of Hyperion, where the army was swarm
ing like a mass of ants. He pointed.

"What's that, Daddy?"

"That, my bright boy, is Cirocco Jones and her army."

Adam looked back into the scope, obviously impressed. Mayb
he thought he would get a glimpse of Jones herself. Lately, he ha
been seeing a lot of her, in movies like *The Brain Eaters*, *Ciroco
Jones Meets Dracula*, and *The Creature from the Black Lagoon*. *
few of the movies were genuine Earth product, with Cirocco sub
stituting for the monster, and additional scenes showing her trans
forming from a rather sinister but recognizable Captain Jones int
whatever latex calamity was devouring Tokyo *this* week. But mos
were new product, stamped Made in Pandemonium, with productio
credit given to "Gaea, the Great and Powerful." Gaea had a con
vincing double for Cirocco in some of the scenes, and used computer
enhancement for others. The quality was not great, but the budget
were lavish. Chris knew from commissary gossip that a lot of th
eviscerations, amputations, decapitations, and defenestrations in thes
monster adventures were not special effects and had nothing to d
with stunt men. Often, to get the effect she wanted, Gaea found i
easier to bury the extras.

It was hard to tell what effect these movies had on Adam

hey were usually flagrant morality plays, with Cirocco always cast
 the evil one, usually being killed in the end to the cheers of
nlookers. Still, Chris remembered that both Dracula and Franken-
ein, ancient cinematic bad-guys, were viewed with a certain fas-
nation by children. Adam seemed to react in the same way. He
rew excited when Cirocco appeared on the television screen.

Maybe that was part of Gaea's plan. Maybe she *wanted* Adam
 identify with the bad guy, even if it was Cirocco.

On the other hand, there was the computer-altered version of
ing Kong.

Chris had never seen *any* of these old films, but long ago
irocco had told him the plot of that one, as he had been thinking
f going into northern Phoebe to attempt the heroic slaughter of
aea's re-creation.

The version on Pandemonium television was different. Gaea
ad been cast as Kong, and Cirocco as Carl Denham. Fay Wray was
ardly in the movie. Kong/Gaea never threatened her in any way;
verything he/she did was to protect innocent bystanders from Den-
am's blundering attempts to kill Kong. At last, hounded to the top
f a tall building, horribly wounded by little biplanes, Gaea had
allen. Chris remembered the classic last line: "It was beauty killed
ae beast." In this version, Cirocco/Denham said "Now the world is
ine!"

It was impossible to think of Kong without a queasy glance
own the Twenty-four Carat Highway. Not too far from where it
aded at the gates of Tara was a big black ball with protruding ears.
 was the head of Kong. Every time Chris passed it, the mournful
ves followed him.

"What's gonna happen, Daddy?"

Chris was brought back to the present. It was Adam's favorite
uestion. When watching a movie on television, as the tension built
dam would look back at Chris with anticipation and fright, and
sk what's gonna happen.

What happens next?

It's what we all ask ourselves, Chris thought.

"I think there's going to be a war, Adam."

"Wow!" Adam said, and looked back to his telescope.

NINETEEN

The attack on Pandemonium commenced two decarevs after the las
encampment had been made. It started with a rendition, by the thre
hundred members of the Titanide Brass Band of the Army of Be
linzona, of *The Liberty Bell*, by John Philip Sousa.

Gaea, atop her wall of stone, had watched the band assembling
seen the polished instruments appear and gleam in the beautif
Hyperion light, listened to the two-bar opening phrase. Then sh
jumped up in delight.

"It's . . . Monty Python!" she shouted.

She stared in astonishment. Somehow, Cirocco had taught o
persuaded or convinced the Titanides to march. They had alway
adored march music, but had little talent for marching in step. The
usual habit was to caper about randomly—while still keeping tha
steady and invariable march tempo, as if metered by a metronome
But now they were in step, in formation, and belting it out as onl
Titanides could. And it was glorious. One of Sousa's earliest marche
The Liberty Bell had been adopted by a comedy group as their them
song, and was familiar to Gaea from many movies and televisio
tapes.

Soon she was quite caught up in it. She marched back an
forth along her stone wall, and shouted imprecations at her ow
troops inside until they wearily formed up and marched back an
forth with her.

The Titanides stayed a reasonable distance from the moat tha
encircled the walls, and began marching counterclockwise aroun
Pandemonium, heading for the United Artists gate. They finishe
The Liberty Bell, and, without a pause, swung in to *Colonel Bogey*
Gaea frowned for a moment, remembering the bad scene with th
movie not so very long ago, but quickly brightened, especially whe
half the Titanides put down their instruments and whistled the refrair

After that came *Seventy-six Trombones*. Many of the subse

428

quent numbers seemed to be identified with movies in one way or another.

As the sound faded with distance, Gaea looked back to the north, where a single black-clad figure was approaching, a good fifty meters in front of another group of three hundred Titanides. Behind them, in perfect formations, were the Legions. Only the commanding officers, at the head of each group of soldiers, wore brass brightwork, which Gaea thought was rather cheap of Cirocco. But what brass there was was polished to a high gloss, and she had to admit the common footsoldiers looked rested, alert, competent, and dedicated.

Also approaching from the northwest was a blimp. Even at twenty kilometers it was easy to see that it was Whistlestop.

The group on the ground continued to march forward, and the blimp came in closer, stopping at about five kilometers distance and three kilometers altitude. Slowly, the great mass turned until its side faced Gaea and Pandemonium.

Some humans were hurrying up beside Cirocco. These didn't look like soldiers. They set something up in front of her. Then Whistlestop's side flickered, and built up a pattern of lights that became Cirocco's face. Gaea thought it was a good trick. She hadn't known blimps could do that.

"Gaea," Cirocco's voice boomed out from the blimp.

"I hear you, Demon," Gaea shouted back. There was no need for technical tricks to amplify her voice. She could be heard in Titantown.

"Gaea, I am here with a mighty army, dedicated to the overthrow of your evil regime. We do not want to fight you. We ask you to surrender peacefully. You will not be harmed. Spare yourself the humiliation of final and total defeat. Lower the bridges to Pandemonium. We *will* be victorious."

For a fleeting moment Gaea wondered what the stupid bitch would do if she *did* surrender. She wondered if Cirocco had brought a pair of handcuffs that big. But the thought passed. This must be fought out to the end.

"Of *course* you don't want to fight," she taunted. "You will be killed, to the last soldier. My troops will march to Bellinzona and overwhelm the few who remain loyal to you. Give up, Cirocco."

The reply certainly did not seem to surprise Cirocco. There

was a long pause, then a rapid-fire series of explosions that caused a lot of unrest inside the walls of Pandemonium. People looked up, and saw the Bellinzona Air Force, all twelve operable planes, pulling out of their powerdives. All they had dropped on Pandemonium were sonic booms, however.

The planes had been traveling from east to west. Now they pulled up sharply, performed a *very* spiffy roll-over maneuver that left them traveling in a straight line, wingtips almost touching. They began emitting pulsed dots of smoke at high speed. As they passed over again, the sonic booms were heard. And the dots were forming words.

"People of Pandemonium," Cirocco's massive image on the side of Whistlestop bellowed . . . and the planes printed PEOPLE OF PANDEMONIUM across Gaea's pristine sky.

Gaea's jaw dropped. It was impressive as hell, she had to admit that. The planes went up and over, and very quickly were in position for another run.

"Throw off your chains," Cirocco boomed. THROW OFF YOUR CHAINS. Then up, and over, and straightening out. . . .

It was done with computers, obviously. Human reflexes couldn't be fast enough, at supersonic speeds, to drop all those little dots of smoke in the precise pattern. All the pilots had to do was stay in a perfectly straight line. Almost as soon as the line was written, the words were whipped away by the high winds caused by the planes' passage, leaving the sky clear for the next line.

"Reject Gaea's bondage . . . lower the drawbridges . . . flee to the hills . . . you will be protected. . . ."

That was about enough of that, Gaea decided. She gave the orders for her own display. In a few moments the sky was filled with bursting fireworks. It served to take the people's minds off the skywriting. She saw to it that a lot of the pyrotechnics were directed at the big blimp. There was no hope of reaching him, of course, but it wouldn't hurt to rattle him a bit.

It was an odd thing about Whistlestop, Gaea thought. She'd had the reports of his activities over Bellinzona. Hearing it and seeing it were two different things. A normally cautious blimp wouldn't want to be in the same airspace as those dangerous little fire-breathing planes. And a bottle rocket fired in his direction ought to be enough to send him fleeing into Rhea as fast as his massive back fins could take him, much less the huge airbursts Gaea was sending into the sky. But Whistlestop didn't seem to care.

Before long both the fireworks and the skywriting were over. They had both been symbolic, Gaea presumed. Cirocco was doing well in that direction. She wondered if she would do as well when the fighting started.

That was when the ground began to move under her feet.

Only one of her Generals had known what Cirocco was talking about when she mentioned a bullfight. Even *he* hadn't seen one.

She thought she was the last living human to have witnessed a real live bullfight. Her mother had taken her to one when she was quite young, shortly before they had been outlawed in Spain, the last country to permit them.

Cirocco's mother had felt it was wrong to shield a child from all the world's ugliness and brutality. She had not approved of bull-fighting—which was a political issue on the order of the Save the Whales movement a few decades earlier—but thought it would be an educational experience. Cirocco was a child of war, a rape-child, and her mother, a tough, self-reliant woman, had always been a little strange after her time in the Arab prison camp.

It was one of Cirocco's most vivid childhood memories.

Few spectacles are as colorful. The matador's costume was not called a suit of lights for nothing.

She had watched in fascination as the men on horseback rode up to the mighty bull and drove their lances into his back. She remembered the bright red blood dripping down the sides of the bull. By the time the matador made his appearance, the bull was a pitiful sight: dazed, confused, and angry enough to charge at anything that moved.

So then the little pissant matador moved in. With stunning machismo he toyed with the animal, faking it out time after time with his magical cape, turning his back on it as it stood in stupefied pain, unable to understand why the world had turned against it in such a grotesque manner. Cirocco had wanted to divorce herself from the crowd. She *hated* the crowd. She wanted to see the bull rip the matador from his balls to his chin, and she would cheer as his guts steamed in the hot Spanish sun.

But it didn't turn out that way. The bad guy won. The stinking little prick faced the half-dead bull and plunged his sword into its heart. Then he strutted away to deafening applause, and if Cirocco had possessed a rifle and the know-how to use it, he would have been a *dead* little prick. Instead, she threw up.

And now, she proposed to be the matador.

There were a couple of things to keep in mind, before she drowned in self-disgust. For one, Gaea was not some dumb *toro*. She was not helpless, not innocent, and not stupid. For another, Cirocco was not fighting for sport. In any sane appraisal, Gaea had most of the advantages.

To the person who knew nothing about bullfighting, it would seem at first glance that the bull had all the advantages, too. Analyzing it, watching the preparations and comparing the minds of the bull and the matador, one soon realized that only the most idiotic matador was in any danger at all. He had his moment of sport with the tired beast, killed it . . . and fooled everyone into thinking he had done something glorious instead of craven and cowardly.

But the principle was the same. Cirocco intended to keep her distracted, in pain, always watching the bright red cape, never understanding why her horns failed to do any good . . . and slipping the sword in when Gaea was mentally and emotionally exhausted.

So. The first part of the show was done. The words in the sky, the loud music. Gaea had helped out with fireworks.

"Remember," Gaby had said, when last they met. "In many ways, Gaea has regressed mentally to about the age of five. She loves spectacle. It's what attracted her to movies in the first place. It's the *basic* reason she started the war, god help us all. Give her a good one, Rocky, and I'll take care of the rest. But don't forget, even for a moment, that it's only *part* of her that's child-like. The rest of her will be alert for a trick. She doesn't know where it will come from. She doesn't suspect we know as much as we do. Both times, when you go for her, it should look like you really mean it."

Bearing all that in mind, Cirocco gestured the camera crew out of her way, stepped forward a little ways, folded her arms across her chest, and summoned Nasu.

The ground buckled under Gaea. She fell a few feet, her arms waving, then turned and watched in amazement as the Twenty-four Carat Highway exploded.

It was a rippling explosion, working its way from a point
halfway to Tara to a point just under her feet. Solid gold bricks and
clods of dirt flew in every direction—and a mammoth loop of something coiled around her ankle.

She was jerked off her feet and stared up as Nasu, pearly white
and scaled, reared three hundred meters above her.

Monty Anaconda, she thought, and rolled away.

Chris and Adam watched from the balcony of Tara.

"King Kong!" Adam screeched.

Chris glanced nervously at him. He seemed to be enjoying it.

The snake quickly looped its massive coils around Gaea. Gaea
rolled. She rolled so hard and so fast that she had demolished three
soundstages before she was able to struggle to her feet. She killed
hundreds of extras during the roll. Those who saw her get up could
barely believe their eyes. All that could be seen of Gaea was her
feet, and part of one leg.

Then an arm struggled free.

There was the sound of breaking bones. Nobody figured it was
the snake that was getting crushed. High above her, the snake looked
down impassively on her victim. It had been a long time since she
had attacked prey as satisfying as this. Heffalumps were boring.
They didn't even run.

Then the other arm was free. The hands groped, found a loop,
and started to pull at it.

Snakes don't have any facial expression. About all they can
do is open their mouths, blink, and flick their tongues. Nasu's tail
began to thrash.

Gaea, still blinded, staggered toward the wall. She hit it, seemed
to think that was a good idea, and backed off to hit it again. The
top three meters of the wall crumpled. She hit it again.

Some of Nasu's coils loosened. The top of Gaea's head was
now visible. There were more crunching sounds. Gaea's bones had
sounded like redwoods snapping off at ground level. Nasu's bones
were more flexible, and sounded like two-by-fours breaking.

Gaea started groping for the snake's head. Nasu bobbed and
weaved, and squeezed even harder. A forest of redwoods cracked
beneath the terrible pressure.

Then Gaea was on top of the wall. And she was peeling th snake away from her, ten meters at a time. Those parts she pulle away didn't move.

Nasu opened her mouth. It was all she could do.

Gaea fell backwards, and the Universal globe was knocke from its turntable and went rolling down the far side of the wall She struggled up again . . . and finally she had the snake's head. Sh opened its mouth, kept opening it and opening it.

Nasu's head cracked. Gaea pounded it against the wall ove and over, until it was a limp mass. She stood, winded and confused holding the head of the dead snake. Then she tossed it and a hundre meters of coils over the side of the wall, down into the moat. Shark quickly converged on it and began a feeding frenzy.

Gaea was . . . bent. None of her joints looked right. Her hea was a squashed melon, her back took a series of horrible turns, lik a Swiss mountain road.

Then she started to squirm. She threw one hand up high, an something snapped into place. She moved her hips, and there wa another loud cracking sound. She pressed her palms to her face setting bones back into place. Step by step, she put herself back together until she stood, whole, unmarked, and glaring out at Cir occo, who still stood impassively, arms folded.

"That was a stinking trick, you bitch!" she shouted. Then sh turned, leaped down on the inside of the wall, and shouted to th gatekeeper.

"Open this door! Lower that bridge. I'm going out to get her."

One of her military advisors tried to say something. It earne him a kick that dropped his broken body ten miles away, in Warne territory. And the man in charge of the gate was already franticall cranking it open.

Gaea put her foot on the drawbridge as it started to lower. He weight caused the pulley to turn so fast the rope smoked and caugh fire. Then she strode over the bridge and onto the Universal cause way.

She was out of the magic circle.

WENTY

hris reached into the cooler beside his chair—Gaea had been quite nd in providing all the coolers and all the beer he needed; an ice-ld bottle was never more than a few steps away—pulled out a ttle, and uncapped it. The encounter with the monster snake had een frightening at first. But, as it went on, it became more and ore like the hundreds of monster movies he had seen in the last ear. It was unreal. It was preordained. One knew the woman was oing to kill the snake, and she had done so.

He was beginning to feel a pleasant buzz from the beer. Adam till sat on the floor and stared, spellbound, through the posts of the alcony. He had never seen a movie quite like this one. From time time he would jump up and run to the telescope for a better view.

Chris had never felt so helpless. But Cirocco had been quite xplicit in her orders. He was to stay put until she came to get them ut. Well, she was out there, all right—just a black speck at the ead of an improbable army. Was he supposed to march out the Jniversal gate, side-stepping Gaea as she battled the snake? It didn't nake a lot of sense, and he had felt no impulse to do it.

Someone will come for you, Cirocco had said.

He wished that someone would get here.

Gaby tapped him on the shoulder.

He dropped his beer bottle, which shattered on the marble errace. Adam laughed when he saw the broken glass. It was just ike the Three Stooges.

"Chris, are you sober?" she asked, as her eyes narrowed.

"Sober enough."

"Then here's what you have to do."

She told him. It didn't take long. It was not too complicated, ut it was frightening. One year I sat here, he thought. One year with nothing to do but talk baby-talk. Now I have to be a super-hero.

435

He knew he would start to whine in a moment, so he nodde
his head.

And Gaby was gone.

He hurried to Adam, picked him up, and smiled as well as h
could.

"We're going to take a walk," he said.

"Don't wanna. I wanna watch Gaea fightin' some more."

"We'll do that later. This is going to be even better."

Adam looked doubtful, but said nothing as Chris hurried dow
the stairs, past the sleeping forms of Amparo and Sushi and all th
other household servants. He went out the back door of Tara, an
into the strand-forest behind it.

Gaea paused in the middle of the causeway. Something didn
feel right.

Her mind was a fragmented thing, but she was used to tha
knew how to deal with it. A growing percentage of her had com
to be concentrated in this body. While fighting the snake, she ha
been able to think of almost nothing else. It was the same way whe
she concentrated her energies on healing herself.

But now something else was happening. She'd have it in
minute. The great brow furrowed in thought.

Then there were shouts. At the same time, the other group o
Titanides, who were organized into a drum and bugle corps, bega
an exceptionally loud number, and started marching toward the eas
It left Cirocco out there alone, almost a kilometer in front of he
army.

Let's see now. The first group of Titanides must almost be t
the Disney gate by now. This new group was headed the other way
toward Goldwyn. Was Cirocco dispersing her forces, getting read
for an attack?

There were twelve explosions. Gaea looked up, saw the tin
planes passing by again, moving west to east. Another factor t
consider. The planes passed Whistlestop...who seemed shorte
somehow. And the blimp seemed to be smoking or steaming....

She figured it out. Whistlestop looked shorter because he wa
coming at her. As she watched he straightened his course even more
until he was almost nose-down. Tons of ballast water spilled fro

his rear end, and it rose and rose, until he was a huge circle in the air, getting bigger.

The "steam" was cherubs flying away from his upper vent holes, and a million creatures, some no larger than a mouse, leaping out the sides at the ends of tiny parachutes. An evacuation was under way. It was an awesome sight, accompanied by an awesome sound: a high, mournful wail that loosened her teeth.

It was a blimp's death-cry.

Luther stood alone, atop the wall near his chapel beside the Goldwyn Gate. It looked as if he would be left out of the action.

He knew he didn't have long to live. He had endured wounds at the hands of Pope Joan's Kollege of Kardinals, he had been ignored by Gaea for too long following Kali's triumph. He was out of the inner circle, and it pained him, as all he wished to do was serve Gaea.

He watched the battle with the snake. Gaea won, and he felt neither pleasure nor pain.

He saw the blimp moving into position . . .

And that tiny part of his mind still attuned to Gaea's thoughts picked up her moment of doubt before she looked up into the sky.

He fell to his knees. He tore at his flesh, and he prayed.

Luther's mind was like a truck with square wheels. It was possible to move it, but only with great effort. He strained, lifting his mind up onto the edge, and then it thumped solidly down on a new thought. Then once again he strained.

Where is the Child? he thought.

Strain, lift . . . *thump*.

The devil's army is all here, in the north. *Thump*.

What if this is all a distraction? *Thump*. What if the real attack is coming from somewhere else?

A voice whispered very close to his ear. It sounded like his wife . . . but he didn't have a wife. It was Gaea . . . of course, it was Gaea.

"The Fox Gate is due south," the voice said.

"Fox Gate, Fox Gate," Luther muttered. Well, not actually. His mouth was such a ruin now that all he could say was "Aah gay, aah gay."

There was a train waiting in the Goldwyn station. Luther climbed aboard, out onto the narrow monorail track that ran around the top of the wall.

For once there was a good head of steam in the thing. He got into the engineer's cab and pulled the big iron lever all the way back. The train started to move, and quickly gathered speed.

Chris ran through the strand-forest. Adam seemed to love it.

"Faster, Daddy, faster!" he shouted.

It would have been pitch dark, but for a mysterious blue light that floated on ahead of them. He had to hope it was leading the way, because without it, and even with a flashlight, he would soon have been hopelessly lost.

"Catch it, Daddy!"

I hope not, he thought. If I caught it, I wouldn't know what to do with it. I hope it just keeps floating on out there, fifty meters ahead, and I hope I don't stumble over anything in here.

Far away, he heard a deep, sustained, rumbling explosion.

He wondered what it was.

Calvin sat in the bombardier's seat, just under the very tip of Whistlestop's great airframe. He was swathed in rich fabrics, but he shivered. He didn't feel so good. He couldn't get rid of the chill. Everything he ate seemed to come right back up. And his head hurt most of the time.

He didn't know what he had. It could probably be diagnosed, but he doubted it could be cured. What he did know was that there came a time for a man to pack it in.

For Calvin, one hundred and twenty-six years was plenty. Old and sick, he had seen the great wheel turn just over a million times in his life, and it was enough.

"Why don't you just drop me off here?" Calvin said, to Whistlestop. "I can walk it. You're good for another twenty, thirty centuries, I guess."

He heard the gentle whistling. It did not come to him as words. It told of a relationship he knew he could never explain to a human. He and Whistlestop had grown together, shared something neither of them could tell another blimp or another human, and were ready to die together.

"Well, I figured I had to offer," he chuckled. He leaned back, and took out the cigar and lighter Gaby had left with him, and he chuckled again. This time it turned to a laugh.

"She remembered," he said. Calvin had smoked cigars so long ago he had almost forgotten it himself.

This one was fresh and aromatic. He sniffed it, bit off the end, and snapped the lighter. He got it going, took a drag. It tasted good.

Then he snapped the lighter once more, and held it to the cloth at his right side. Behind him, he heard the deep whoosh as valves opened, as air mixed with hydrogen and came rushing at him.

He did not hear the explosion.

TWENTY-ONE

All blimps die in fire. It is their destiny. Nothing else can kill them.

Cirocco watched as Whistlestop descended toward Gaea, who stood transfixed on the broad wooden bridge.

It was voluntary, she told herself. They chose to do this.

Somehow, it didn't help.

"Everyone down!" she shouted over her shoulder. "Protect yourselves behind your shields." She turned back, and Whistlestop's nose was a hundred meters above Gaea and still descending.

She had wondered if Gaea would run. She did not. She stood her ground, and as the mammoth gasbag bore down on her, she drew her fist back and would have punched it, but she was enveloped in fire.

The flame started at Whistlestop's nose, and licked up his sides faster than the eye could follow. The sound was beyond imagining. A bloom of flames fifteen kilometers high roared into the air, and the blimp's body crunched down on the spot where Gaea had been standing. It seemed to hesitate a moment, still held by internal gases not yet burning, then began a stately collapse. It took a long, long time.

Being lighter than air does not mean a blimp is not heavy. It simply means it masses less than the volume of air it displaces. The volume of Whistlestop's gasbags alone was half a billion cubic feet;

that amount of air at two atmospheres of pressure had tremendous mass.

The first half of Whistlestop seemed to accordion pretty much at the spot where Gaea had been. The rest of him tumbled, no longer held up by the hydrogen. It fell, burning, into the Universal studio and along the western wall. Everything but the rock itself began to burn.

The heat of the fire was intense at first, when it was a billowing plume that seemed to touch the sky. Cirocco did not move away, but had to hold her hand up to shield her face. She heard the ends of her hair sizzling, and thought her clothes were smoldering. Behind her, the army found their shields growing too hot to touch, and they were a kilometer away.

But that towering pyre of hydrogen died away quickly. Universal burned hot, but it was not unbearable.

The huge heap of dry canvas-like skin that had been Whistlestop was going to burn for some time. Everyone watched it. Gaea was under there. She was probably in the moat. No one knew how deep it might be.

After ten minutes of no movement, some of the troops behind her began to shout. Cirocco glanced around. They were throwing things in the air. They were daring to believe Gaea was dead. They gradually quieted when they saw that Cirocco was not moving.

She turned around, and watched the fire burn.

Two hundred panaflexes, over a thousand arriflexes, and uncounted bolexes died in the conflagration, taking with them priceless footage of the battle with the Giant Snake.

The Chief Cinematographer began ordering up battalions of photofauns from other studios . . . but it was hardly necessary. Most had stayed at their posts, morosely shooting a few feet when the Titanide bands went by their gate, but quite a few had started hurrying toward Universal when they heard the sounds of the snake tearing itself from the earth.

Then the great column of flame had erupted to the north.

Well.

They had their orders, but it was too damn much. It was like asking a hungry child to sit still and touch nothing in a room made of chocolate. It was like telling a horde of savage *papparazzi* that,

Just a block away, the Queen of England was balling the biggest television star in the world right in the middle of the road...but c'mon, fellas, please, respect their dignity, okay? They don't want any pictures.

Almost as one, every bolex, arriflex, and panaflex in Pandemonium headed toward the fire, by the shortest possible route.

Chris emerged from the strand-forest into a strange quiet.

He looked cautiously around, and didn't see anyone. They must all be at the wall, at defensive posts, he decided.

Not far from him was the northern end of the Fox Main Street. There was not much of the studio this close to the cable. There were trees, and lawns, and some shrubs. It was called Producers Park. Twice-life-size statues of past greats faced each other on each side of the road, standing on high pedestals listing their film credits. At the head of the road, with its back to Chris, was the even larger image of Irving Thalberg, presiding over the others: Goldwyn, Louis B. Mayer, Jack Warner, Zanuck, De Laurentiis, Ponti, Foreman, Lucas, Zamyatin, Fong, Cohn, Lasker—there were over a hundred of them, dwindling in the distance. They were in thoughtful poses, most of them looking downward so visitors to the park would look up and see themselves being regarded by the greats of cinema history.

All the statues regarded just then was a roadway covered with gold paint. It didn't seem to upset them.

Chris no longer had his guiding light. He wondered what it had been, feeling sure Gaby had something to do with it.

Apparently she felt his course from here was clear. She had said hurry, and there was no one in sight. So he dodged around the statue of Thalberg and ran down the road.

The producers watched him in silence.

Far away to his left, he noticed the little plume of white smoke that meant a train was heading south on the monorail. He and Adam had been on it many times. It was one of the nicer things in Pandemonium.

He wondered if the people on it were aware the track was out at Universal.

A safe distance from the Paramount Gate, the Titanide Drum and Bugle Corps stopped playing, carefully put their instruments aside, and started off at a full gallop, continuing in their clockwise direction.

On the other side of Pandemonium, the Brass Band did the same.

Both actions were observed from the walls, of course. But the Titanides made no move toward the gates. They stayed a careful distance away from the wall, just out of cannon range.

Orders were specific. Stand and fight. Defend your gate. So while small detachments ran along the walls, vainly trying to keep up with the thundering herd and to report if they attempted to cross the moat and attack between gates, the actions had little effect on the defense of the Studio.

The forest came relatively close to the Fox Gate. That had been one consideration in Gaby's mind.

It was defended by Gautama and Siddhartha, possibly the two least able military Priests. That had been important, too. That it was one hundred and eighty degrees away from Universal, as far away as one could get and still be in Pandemonium, had been a bit of luck. She felt she was due a little. She'd need some more to pull this off and not lose any of her friends.

On the bad side, Gautama had two companies of Minutemen with functional flintlock rifles. Siddhartha had a couple of cannons.

And Luther had a long way to go to reach Fox.

Gaby had been working on Luther's deteriorating mind for some time. She used the discontent she found there and built on it. There was no way to sway him in his loyalty to Gaea, but he resented her just enough that he would not be as cautious as usual. She had managed to whisper in his ear back at his post at Goldwyn, and he was on his way. And she had a few more tricks in store.

Luther was a weak reed. She hated to rely on him so much. But she could not take direct actions within the walls of Pandemonium. Putting the staff of Tara to sleep was about as far as she could go.

Gene was a weak reed, too. But what could you do? He *had* to have his part to play, she owed him that much. And . . . there was no one else who could do what Gene had to do.

She was waiting on the verge of the forest when the four Titanides and three humans showed up. She greeted each of them

y name. She noted the shocked surprise on Robin's face, wished
he had more time to talk to the little witch, who she loved dearly,
ut there was so much to do.

So she gave them their instruciton. They had brought their
eapons.

The rest was going to be up to them.

Conal sat astride Rocky and watched as the little plume of
team crawled around the rim of Pandemonium. He didn't know
hat it was. All he knew was that Gaby said that when it reached
certain mark on the wall, they were to go.

He was surprised to discover that he was not afraid for himself.
ut he was absolutely terrified Robin would die.

They had their weapons. Each Titanide had a long sword and
rifle with interchangeable magazines. The humans carried hand-
uns. They had practiced with both rifles and handguns, and found
was practically impossible to hit anything with either, even from
e relatively steady moving platform of a Titanide's back. But they
vere fractionally better with the smaller weapons. They also carried
hort swords, and hoped they didn't have to use them, because it
vas hard to see what use they would be unless they were dismounted.
o be thrown from a Titanide generally meant the Titanide was badly
urt.

The puff of steam was at the proper mark. Conal felt his hand
eing squeezed tightly. It was Robin, and her hand was very cold.
le leaned over and kissed her. There didn't seem to be anything to
ay.

The Titanides moved out into the open and began their charge.

The body of Whistlestop had almost burned out before the
emains began to stir.

Behind it, Universal was still burning madly. The waters of
e moat were full of floating debris. The corpses of a hundred
arboiled eight-meter Great White sharks floated belly-up all around
e crumpled ruin of the blimp.

As with Nasu, it was a hand that appeared first. Then, slowly,
ruggling, Gaea pulled herself out of the black mess and stood,
oking dazed, on the outer shore of the moat.

Cirocco sternly repressed an impulse to laugh. Once it started, it would never stop, it would quickly become hysteria. But Gaea . . .

She looked like some cartoon character in one of the oldest gags in the trade. Hapless cartoon animal is handed a round black bomb with a sizzling fuse, looks at it, does a double-take—eyes bug out and *BLAM!* Smoke clears to reveal character standing in exactly the same position, holding nothing, but completely black, hair standing on end, wisps of smoke curling away . . . character blinks twice—only the eyes are visible—and falls over.

Completely black but for the eyes. That was Gaea. But she didn't fall over.

She began to writhe. It was awful to watch. She stretched this way and that, and her skin began to crack. She reached down to her belly, to her legs, her feet, and scrubbed herself vigorously with her hands. And the skin began to peel away.

It came off in one big chunk, like a child's bunny-suit pajamas. Beneath was glistening white skin, blonde hair . . . a new Gaea, unhurt. She stood for a moment, having lost perhaps two feet in height, then began to walk toward Cirocco.

TWENTY-TWO

"It's time, Gene."

"I know it's time," he said. "Tarnation, didn't you tell me . . ."

He stopped his work and looked around. Gaby wasn't there. He thought he had heard her, but he couldn't be sure. He shrugged and returned to the device in his lap.

He was sitting on a big crate labeled DYNAMITE: Product of Bellinzona. It sat, in turn, on the great green nerve nexus down in the dead heart of Oceanus. Stacked all around him were similar crates.

What he had in his lap was a timing device. He had thought he understood how to use it. Hook this here dingus to that there whatchamacallit over there, wind up the little hammenframis on the back of that doohickey. . . .

Nothing. It wasn't ticking or nothing.

He was supposed to hook it up and get the hell out of there.

didn't plan to get out, so when Gaby gave him the go-on-ahead, 'd waited it out here what he figured was a goodly chunk of time, d then set to work. Now it didn't look like it was gonna work now, on account he'd hooked it up ever whichway, and nothing was ppening.

He sobbed his frustration.

It'd be nice to have him a nice hunk of fish right about now. was a wonderment, it surely was, how much better the stinking ings tasted if you charred them a bit over the fire. Now why hadn't thought of that?

He was about to get up and get him some fish, when he membered how long it would take to get up there and back. Phooey! at's why he'd waited so long before setting to work on this dingus yway, figuring in the time it would have took him to of clumb up the top of them stairs...

He was woolgathering again, and he knew it. He rearranged e parts of the detonator, wondering if he'd ever get it right.

And he kept thinking that he was forgetting something.

And it was the most important part.

The brakes on the frigging little train didn't work.

Luther cursed it mightily, then, as the station came by, he aped, and he rolled.

He got up shakily. There were little bits of Luther scattered re and there on the platform. Luckily, they weren't important bits. n ear, a fragment of skull, part of a foot.

He didn't have much time left, and he knew it.

Luther watched the little train puff away around the broad curve the track. It would keep going forever, round and round the great heel of Pandemonium, round and round the Great Gaea....

No it wouldn't. The track was broken, because... *thump* .Gaea had fought the snake because... thump, thump... irocco was attacking! And Gaea had sent him here on an important ission!

His brain was thumping along pretty good by now, actually. square wheel, if it rolls long enough, wears off some of the corners. e felt as alert as he'd been since the day he... died. What was left his brow furrowed, then he shrugged it off and hurried down the airs—

He was met by Gautama. Little fat-ass gold-painted pissa Gautama, yammering something in some godless language. Luth drew his cross—the mighty Sword of the Lord—and lopped off h head.

Which didn't kill Gautama, of course, but when Luther kick the head a hundred yards down the road it sure inconvenienced hi some. Gautama blundered around, senseless, his hands held out front of him. Luther didn't give him another thought. He was hu ming, trying to mouth the words, though there wasn't enough mou left to form many of them.

"But now a champion comes to fight, Whom God Herse elected! No strength of ours can match Her might! We would lost, rejected!"

Up on the walls, people were shooting their guns. He heard cannon go off. And he marched up to the gate and threw it ope People were shouting at him. He couldn't understand the words. H went to the drawbridge mechanism, located the proper lever to pull . .

Thump.

I'm lowering the drawbridge, he told himself. Thump.

Why am I lowering the drawbridge?

Ah . . . why, to help Gaea, of course. To help Gaea to . . .

Get in? Thump thump thump.

Maybe this was some sort of trick. His hand moved away fro the lever.

"This is not a trick, my darling Luther," said a voice close his ear.

He turned his head and saw her.

It was Gaea, it was his wife, his mother, all motherhood a womanhood and the virginmary god-help-me, with thorns wrappe around her heart and that saintly expression on her face (and it w a little brown woman) and the dazzling white robes and the halo—*halo!* Why, it was a searing, screaming light that *burst* from he the burning light of goodness/pain/death—and millions of ange were hovering above her, blowing their trumpets (and he didn't eve know the little brown woman) . . . thump—*trick?* How could it be trick?!

People were hacking at him with swords now. Absently, h saw one of his arms fall to the stone floor. But, O Lord, I hav another to do Thy bidding.

He lunged at the lever, thrust it forward, and fell into the rattling clattering chewing mechanism as the tons of drawbridge fell forward and rended him limb from limb. . . .

Arthur Lundquist's first death had been horrible. His second was glorious.

Some photofauns had somehow managed to swim the moat. There were a dozen of them clustered around Cirocco as she stood her ground and watched Gaea striding confidently forward.

The giant Monroe-thing had its arms wide, as if to cut Cirocco off no matter which way she ran. She came on like a dreadful professional wrestler, her face contorted with hate.

She was five hundred meters away. Four hundred. Three hundred.

And she stopped, listening, as Luther died.

Where is the Child?

As they neared the end of the bridge, a cannon shell burst over their heads. Conal heard something rattle off his helmet, felt something sting his arm, and heard Robin cry out.

He saw she was holding her hand to her forehead, and there was blood under it. He started to jump—

"No!" Robin shouted. "I'm all right."

There was no time, anyway. They were on the bridge now, the Titanides' hooves pounding on the thick timbers. They charged toward the big gap. The drawbridge was up. We'd better turn back, Conal thought.

Then it fell, and not a moment too soon. With part of his mind Conal noticed that Rocky was bleeding from many wounds. Up on the wall, something was making odd little barking sounds. Smoke was drifting around them. He looked up and saw people pointing rifles at them. He hoped they couldn't shoot any better than he could.

They entered the arched gate, passed quickly through it. Conal didn't have time to fire at anything. The Titanide swords were at work, and the humans that fell beneath them were probably dead before they hit the ground. Still they came charging up. Conal began to shoot at anything that moved.

There had been no time to see who he was fighting, no sense of them as individuals. Finally, he started to notice they were dressed

oddly. They wore long coats, some of them, or suits of white armo
or multi-colored green-gray-brown pants and helmets like his ow

A man came shrieking up to him, getting under Rocky's swor
thrust. He was carrying an impossibly long sword. How could h
even lift it, much less swing it?

But swing it he did, and it hit Conal on the leg, and Con
started saying his prayers, certain his leg was off and it would be
few seconds before the shock hit him.

He looked down. Part of the sword was clutched in his hand
He saw broken wood. He saw silver paint. The paint came off o
his hand as he threw it away.

It was too much for his confused mind to deal with.

My god, did they think this was a *game?*

Then he heard Valiha's shout. She was far ahead of the res
unencumbered, and she had found Chris.

"Turn around!" she screamed. "I've got them! Turn around

"Chicken!" Cirocco screamed.

Gaea paused.

"Gaea's a stinking, *gutless, yellow* COWARD! Gaea
CHICKEN!!"

The naked, sweating giant turned slowly. She had been on he
way to Fox, on her way to stop the theft of Adam. But . . . Ciroco
was right here. Adam was miles away.

"Come on back here and *fight,* you yellow *bitch!* What a
you . . . *afraid?* Gaea's afraid, Gaea's a coward, Gaea's a stinkin
whore!"

Gaea hung there, swaying back and forth, torn between goin
for Adam and taking care of this insect once and for all. She *kne*
it was a trick. She knew Cirocco wanted her to come and silenc
her filthy mouth. She knew it . . . and more than anything in th
stinking, dreary universe she wanted to go back and *crush* this ho
rible upstart.

Cirocco spat in Gaea's direction. She picked up a rock an
threw it as hard as she could. It bounced off Gaea's head, leavin
a bloody mark. She drew her sword and held it high in the swe
light of Hyperion. It flashed as Cirocco brandished it.

"God? You make me *laugh,* Gaea. You are a *pig.* Your moth
was a pig, your *grandmother* was a pig, and *her* mother fucked *dea*

gs. I *spit* on you. I *piss* on you. I *dare* you to come out and fight.
you run away, *everyone* will know you for the coward you are!"

Tears of rage were streaming from Cirocco's eyes.

Gaea might still have turned away and gone after Adam, but
irocco gave a bloodcurdling shriek . . . and charged at her.

Which was simply too much. Gaea began to move.

Toward Cirocco.

"It's time, Gene."

"I *know* it's time, Gaby. I'm sorry I ra . . . r-r-r-raped you. I'm
orry I killed you. I didn't mean to do it."

His hands fumbled with the detonator on his lap. It was a
imple mechanism, he *knew* it was simple. It was just so *horrible*.
e couldn't *remember*.

Eugene Springfield had been a flyer. He had piloted jet fighter
ircraft, rocket-powered moon landers. He had been picked over a
iousand others to fly the exploration vehicles *Ringmaster* brought
> Saturn, and there was only one reason for it. He was the *best*.

And now he couldn't sort out this jumble of wires any slack-
rained terrorist could have put together in his sleep.

He wiped away tears. Start from the beginning. What did Gaby
ay?

Take out the . . .

His eyes opened wide. *The most important part,* and he had
lmost forgotten it. By golly, his brains *must* be turning to mush.

There it was, at his feet. The black glass jar with the metal
d.

He picked it up, opened it, tossed the lid into the clattering
arkness.

The fat, toad-like parasite which had sucked his brains for
inety years hopped out and perched on the edge of the jar. Its eyes
>ok in the scene, then bulged out. It made incoherent sounds: croaks,
>bs, strangling gasps. It didn't mean jack*shit* to Gene, but Gaby
ad said it was important.

Gaea must see it, Gaby had said.

"Think you're smarter'n me, do you?" Gene whispered, staring
ie thing in its ugly bloodshot eyes. "Well, ol' Gene'll show you a
iing or two."

He looked again at the detonator.

Battery. That's this dingus right here.

Wires. Well, there's a couple of them. This one goes to here and this one goes to here. So it ought to logically follow that if fella touched *this* wire to this one over *here*, he ought to get on *hell* of a

Gaea froze as her eyes in Oceanus were uncapped, as the looked up out of the bottle, hopped up on the edge of it, and stare down at the spectacle of a brain-damaged child playing with matche and gasoline.

"Gene!" she screamed. "Don't do it!"

Cirocco charged, filled with a blood-red rage she hadn't know was in her. She ran at the monster and sank her sword in its foot.

Then Gaea screamed, and Cirocco was filled with an incredibl sense of triumph . . . which lasted about two seconds. Gaea wheele around, tossing Cirocco off like a pesky ant. Gaea had forgotte Cirocco existed.

Cirocco got to her feet, saw Gaea stop dead in her tracks. Gae put her hands to her head, then she looked slowly up at the sky.

"Gaby!" she shouted. "Gaby, *wait!* Listen, I'm . . . I'm no ready! Gaby, we've got to *talk!*"

Then the ground was shaking as Gaea ran at top speed towar the cable.

Cirocco sank to her knees and sobbed helplessly. She felt hand on her shoulder, looked up, and saw all three of her General at her side. My god, she thought. They came to me. They didn run.

All around her was the army. Swords were drawn, arrows wer fitted into bowstrings . . . and nobody had anything to shoot at. The all watched, terrified and dumbfounded, as Gaea floundered throug the moat, still shrieking at the top of her lungs.

The wall didn't stop her. She lowered one shoulder and plowe right through it. She ran through the flames of the Universal studi complex, thundered along the rutted remains of the Twenty-fou Carat Highway.

At last she came to the cable.

She leaped, her fingers dug into the incredibly hard materia of one cable strand. Gaea began to climb it, agile as any monkey.

Later, people speculated that she had been seeking the fastest ay to the hub. Gaby was there, Gaby was taking control, and it as imperative that Gaea/Monroe, which now held over ninety per-ent of the thing that was called Gaea, get up there at once and begin egotiations.

Gaea was five hundred meters up the strand when it broke off t ground level.

The strand snapped up, quick as a mousetrap. Incalculable tons f cable strand curled, twisted... and smashed the Gaea-thing against he unyielding bulk of the cable.

"Hang on!" Cirocco shouted. "Get down, and hang on!"

The ground below them dropped thirty meters.

TWENTY-THREE

ar above them, as these events were played out, a far less dramatic ut far more important drama unfolded in the region known as the ed line.

The entity known as Gaea was dispersed. It was dealing with nany things at once. The entity known as Gaby was pulled close n, in a defensive posture. One after another, horrible blows landed n the Gaea-mind. The important nerve being severed in Oceanus vas the last blow. Gaby erupted from her place of concealment.

There was no way to explain what happened to a human, or Titanide, or a blimp, or anything with time-bound senses.

The end result was simple. The mind of Gaea was destroyed. The mind of Gaby Plauget, of New Orleans, Louisiana, flew through he non-Einsteinian space of the red line, unchallenged.

TWENTY-FOUR

They waited for Valiha, Chris, and Adam to catch up with them. They waited, while hundreds of Pandemonium extras charged at them with swords of wood, cardboard . . . and, occasionally, steel.

"They're props!" Nova shouted to Virginal.

"I see that," Virginal shouted back. "But not *all* of them are."

It was horrible. Try as you might, it was hard to tell which weapon was real and which was an imposter. And the people of Pandemonium didn't seem to know the difference.

They charged out the Fox Gate. Chris was badly hurt. Valiha had a deep gash in her left hind leg. Robin was being held in place by Serpent, who had several injuries himself.

Conal felt an awful detachment. He shot at the people who came at him, but it didn't seem as if he were shooting at real things.

They went through the gate, heading straight out toward the forest. The hordes of Pandemonium followed.

They stopped, turned, and watched as the Brass Band arrived on schedule and began to slay the enemy by the hundreds.

"Stop!" they shouted. "Wait, back off! They're not armed!"

Gradually, with expressions of stunned horror, the three hundred Titanides slowed, saw what was happening . . . and moved away. The Pandemonium troops milled around aimlessly. It seemed that most of them had been fleeing what they thought was an invasion from the inside.

Conal remembered how so many of them had run. The gate to the outside must have seemed like a safe place.

He jumped down from Rocky's back and went to his knees. He swayed there, not knowing if he would throw up. He felt an arm go around his shoulders, and turned to hug her tightly to him.

But it was Nova, not Robin, and she was crying too. He hugged her, then they both hurried to Robin.

They had just enough time to learn that no one had an injury that was surely fatal—though everyone was bleeding—when the ground dropped out from under them.

The great wheel of Gaea vibrated for twenty revs.

The first three or four were the worst. Many people died in the first wave, when the strand broke. Most of them were in Pandemonium, where structures toppled. But a few of Cirocco's army were badly hurt in the pounding.

Then, on the fourth resonation, a strand in Tethys broke, and the next three bounces were bad, but not as bad as the first series.

Eventually, it all settled down. The interior of the rim was full of suspended dust motes for kilorevs, but the wheel had found a new equilibrium. Ophion rushed a little faster in some places, a little slower in others. A few lakes grew and a few shrunk. Two swamps claimed several thousand acres, and the desert of Tethys—which had always been desert, unlike Mnemosyne—advanced a few meters in each direction.

Rocky was kept busy for a while, treating the major and minor wounds of the band of seven—which had grown to nine with Chris and Adam. None of the wounds were life-threatening.

The Brass Band rounded up two thousand prisoners. It was expected that, after a short period of blockade, the holdouts in Pandemonium would surrender when they got hungry.

Adam seemed to have enjoyed the whole thing. He was unmarked. It had been just like the movies, and a little bit like flying... and he was looking forward to the sequel.

Cirocco stood at the head of her cheering army and watched the remains of the thing that had been Gaea drip wetly down the side of the cable.

She was the only one who understood why the cable had killed her, after Nasu and Whistlestop had failed—and she knew there were some questions still unanswered.

She heard a plaintive howling from her backpack. She reached into it, and came up with the bottle that held Snitch.

He was dying. She shook him out into her hand.

"Can I have a drink?" he asked her, between wheezes. Cirocco found the bottle. She didn't bother with the eyedropper. She poured a generous dollop over Snitch's body, and he lapped up several swallows.

She knew he was the last dying fragment of Gaea.

Gaea had known she might lose when she started the game. She hadn't *expected* to . . . but there it was. Gaby had outwitted her.

So she lay in Cirocco's palm. Poetic justice, she thought. You spend twenty years of your life plotting how to wipe out a traitor, and what does it get you? You get to cough out your last seconds literally in the fist of your greatest enemy.

She had devoted some thought to the matter of last words.

If you were going to go out, you ought to do it with some style. So she had thought it over, on the off chance.

There were the classic Looney Tunes cartoon words. A little too light-hearted.

There was "Rosebud." Too arty, too obscure.

In the end, she reverted to the "B" movies she loved so well.

"Mother of mercy," Snitch coughed. "Is this the end of Gaea?"

And she died.

And . . .

Long before the vibrations of the final cataclysm had died, a ray of light angled down from the Hyperion roof.

It centered on Cirocco Jones.

Cirocco stood up, facing into the light. Her feet left the ground. She was lifted, bodily, into Heaven.

FADE OUT

Include me out.

—Sam Goldwyn

Cirocco found herself on the Stairway to Paradise without remembering how she had come there.

She and Gaby had first seen it almost a century earlier, when they had reached the hub after their long climb up the cable and through the inside of the Rhea Spoke. Then, it had been riddled with special effects right out of *The Wizard of Oz*—the film, not the books, which Cirocco doubted Gaea had ever read. At the top had been a massive, pantheistic thing that had tried to convince them it was Gaea.

The stairs were not in very good shape. But looking closely, Cirocco saw that someone had been at work on them. Some dust had been swept to the side. There was the smell of disinfectant— the strong sort that is used in subway restrooms.

She climbed to the top and saw the door to Gaea's old room was ajar.

Inside was Gaby. Just Gaby. No supernatural rigamorole, no hocus-pocus.

She was down on her hands and knees, dressed in faded jeans and a blue work shirt, with a tool belt around her waist. Several of the translucent floor panels in the 2001 lounge had been removed and stacked against one wall. They were filthy, but sitting beside them were stacks of rags and bottles of blue cleanser. The furniture had been stacked against another wall.

Gaby was reaching down through the floor, working on a plain, ordinary fluorescent light fixture which was nailed to a wooden beam. The two light tubes were flickering.

She looked up at Cirocco, then sat back on her heels and wiped her forehead with the back of her hand. The hand held a wrench, and was dirty.

"Lot of work to do up here," Gaby said.

"Sure looks like it."

Gaby got up, fitted the wrench into a loop on her belt, and stood with her hands on her hips, smiling up at Cirocco.

"Can I get you anything? I've got beer, and wine."

"Just a glass of water would be fine."

"Pull up a chair."

Gaby went through a doorway. Cirocco heard water running. She found two chairs that seemed steady, and put them a few feet apart. She sat down on one. Gaby returned, pulled up a low table and set two frosted glasses of ice water on them. Cirocco took a sip of hers, then a long drink. It tasted good.

The silence was not so good. It threatened to get awkward.

"So," Gaby said. "You pulled it off. I was proud of you."

Cirocco shrugged.

"I didn't have as much to do with it as all those people down here think I did. But you know that better than anyone."

"You're the one who had to stand there and face Gaea. Not many people could have done that."

"I guess not." She looked around the room once more. There wasn't anything new to see. She gestured with her glass. "Fixing this place up, are you?"

Gaby looked embarrassed.

"Well, I have to live somewhere. This isn't just what I had in mind, but it'll do temporarily."

"Gaby . . . what *are* you?"

Gaby nodded rapidly, and swallowed hard, not looking at Cirocco. She took a deep breath, and let it out slowly. She looked at the ceiling.

"I was watching, you know. When you came up here and demanded some answers from Gaea. She didn't lie to you. She didn't feel like she needed to. She was pretty sure you were going to kill her, but that didn't matter. She was tired of that lousy little body, anyway. But she still wanted your loyalty. I'll tell you why in a minute. But you remember . . . she offered to bring me back to life, just as I was—but without that compulsion I had to make war against her. You said no. So she made another offer. She'd bring me back unchanged. She'd resurrect me. You remember what you said?"

"Pretty well."

Gaby's eyes got a faraway look.

"You said it was tempting." She focused on Cirocco again. "Thanks for that, by the way. Then you said, 'But then I wondered what Gaby would have thought of it, and knew just what a stinking, corrupt, foul deviltry it would be. She would have been horrified to

think she would be survived by a little Gaby doll made by you ou
of your own festering flesh. She would have wanted me to kill i
immediately.'"

"Maybe I overstated the case a little."

Gaby laughed, and shook her head.

"No. You were completely right. You had no way of knowing
that some part of me still *was* alive, and listening in . . . but you wer
right. If Gaea had put me back together then, I don't think I'd hav
been my own person. And you were certainly right not to trust he
about *anything*.

"She thought she got rid of me." She gestured at the ceiling
"That red line up there . . . this is going to be difficult. You want a
the answers, and I'm more than ready to tell them, but I'll warn yo
that some of it will be hard to understand . . . and you'll just have t
take my word for it. Because I *can't* explain to you what that re
line is like. There aren't any human concepts for so much of it.

"She threw me in there, and thought she'd made an end.

"I fooled her. I stayed sane. I survived . . . and I had to b
careful. She'd been in there a lot longer than I had and she knew
her way around. I had to learn to crawl, then walk, then run, and
had to do it all without her noticing me. That's why I was so mys
terious so much of the time. When I was learning to materialize m
body . . . when I did anything at all, the chances of her discoverin
me were much greater. When I told you things she didn't want yo
to know . . . it was like a security leak. She started becoming awar
there *was* a leak, but didn't know where it was. She might hav
found me in spite of my best efforts, but she wasn't really lookin
that hard. It's all that saved me. Her other obsessions took up to
much of her time. Too much of her life-force, for want of a bette
word.

"But you asked me what I am. I'm *not* a creation of Gaea.
created myself. I'm real, and I'm alive. . . . I'm me."

Cirocco kept looking at her, and Gaby had to look away agair
Then she reached out and took Cirocco's hand. She squeezed it.

"See? Feel me, Rocky. I'm real. I have a body. This body i
completely human. I live in it, just like you live in yours."

Again Cirocco said nothing. Then she rubbed her forehea
with her hand.

"But Gaby . . . you still haven't told me what you *are*."

Gaby released her hand and sat back in her chair.

"I'm what you were supposed to be. Gaea's successor. But ᴜ knew that, didn't you."

Cirocco nodded slowly.

"Gaea..." Gaby looked around the room, and laughed biⁱterly. ᴊaea! What a joke. By the time we met her, she was so crazy... she ᴐk that name out of Greek mythology. She took all her best ideas t of crappy motion pictures. I don't know what her real name ght have been.

"She came up here one day, a *very* long time ago. She wasn't human being. I don't think her race even exists in the wheel ymore. The being who occupied the seat I'm in right now talked 'Gaea.' Told her he needed a Wizard. It sounded fine to Gaea, d she was a good Wizard for a thousand years. Then, when her ᴇdecessor was all washed up, she overthrew him, and came to live here.

"We're not talking now about the being that *is* the Wheel. That ng is up there in the red line. It takes care of most of the day-to-y functioning of all the complex systems that keep the wheel nning. It is fairly god-like in a lot of ways, but it's more like a ᴍputer in others. The present system for... *governing* the wheel almost a million years old. There have been a lot of Wizards. ᴸen they die, they get to be... Gaea. Gaby. *Me*. You *may* be the ly Wizard that didn't graduate."

Cirocco looked at Gaby for a long time. She was very tired.

"Gaby... I'm so sorry."

Gaby hurled her glass of water across the room.

"Dammit, Rocky... *damn* you! Don't be sorry. It's not too e. When you had Snitch taken out of your head Gaea gave up on ᴜ. She had to have a complete and continuous set of memories ᴍm you before you could move up to take her place. That set is ᴐken now... but it can be fixed. I can record you. I can move ᴜ up here with me. It *isn't* death. It isn't anything *like* death. I ᴐught I was dead when I first got here, but I learned what life is ᴸly all about up there in the red line. We can... we can rule ᴈether, you and I. We can make this into a good place."

Cirocco sighed, and wondered how she could say it. Perhaps was best to move in on it sideways.

"Gaby... you kept telling me, over and over, how hard Gaea

would be to kill. And she was. All that we went through...all
distract her enough so you could overwhelm her up here in the hu
in a way that I'll never understand. Is there...is there any othe
way she could have died?"

Gaby looked away, and wiped at a tear. She shook her hea
violently.

"See, Gaby...it's not death I'm most afraid of."

Gaby nodded just as violently, then buried her face in he
hands. Cirocco was quiet. She was afraid to touch her old friend
Not afraid for herself, but afraid for Gaby.

"Do you know anything more about what Gaea was like whe
she first came to this place?" she finally asked.

"Oh, jesus, Rocky. I suspect she was a sweet and loving thin,
I don't doubt there was a golden age when she came to power. Som
of the blimps might know, if they'd talk. And you don't have to sa
it. God help me, I've thought about it enough. What will *I* be lik
in twenty thousand years? Huh? How can I even begin to imagin
how tired I might become of...everything? I can't see it now.
can't see that I've changed. I remember, when I turned a hundre
years old, I was so damn smug. I didn't feel any different than I d
when I was thirty. But a hundred is *nothing*."

"I can see that."

"I hope you don't think I did this because I wanted to."

"I don't."

"There was *no other choice*. It was watch you and everyor
I loved be killed by that maniac, or do what I did. I couldn't eve
opt out; I couldn't die." Once more, she leaned forward earnestl
"But Rocky, now that I've told you all those things I couldn't te
you...I'll tell you one more thing. All along I hoped you'd jo
me. I suspect it's a horrible fate in the end...but so is death, ar
way you look at it. I watched you in Bellinzona. You were so goo
You'd be a lot better than I'd be alone. We could work together.

"I was horrible, Gaby. So many people died. At my orders

"People are always going to die, Rocky."

"I know. I just don't want to be responsible for it."

"That's a cop-out. They're going to die because of the thin
you *don't* do. Stuart or Trini, or one of your Generals...they wor
be as enlightened as you were. They'll make a mess of things."

"Anybody would. It's the nature of the human being. T

Titanides speak of evil people. And there *are* evil people, people that must die. But I won't be the one who decides. I've done that, and I hate it. I won't live my life for them anymore. I won't save the world anymore. I'm through with that."

Gaby got up and went to the other room. Cirocco heard sounds that might have been sobs. She didn't want to think about it. Gaby returned with a fresh glass of water.

"Gaby, I think I'm your friend. At least I am if you'll have me."

"You're my friend," Gaby confirmed, in a husky voice.

"I hope you'll be my friend till the day I die. But this is asking too much of a friendship. I'm sorry this has happened to you. I'm sorry it fell to you instead of me, like Gaea wanted it. I hope you don't resent that."

"I don't. It was an accident."

"Then don't ask this of me. I can see that your life is going to be very interesting and very long. If somebody has to do it, I can't think of anyone better than you. I think that—if it *had* happened to me—I'd do what I think you're going to do. Make the best of it. Have as much fun as you can. Be as wise as you know how."

"It's a dirty job, being God," Gaby said. "But somebody's got to do it. Right?" There was the hint of a smile. Cirocco smiled back, tentatively.

"Right."

So they sat there beside each other, each thinking her own thoughts. It was a companionable silence. At last Cirocco shifted in her chair.

"So . . ." she said, and made a vague gesture. "What are you going to do?"

They looked at each other, and laughed.

"This and that," Gaby said.

"What about the Titanides?"

Gaby sobered.

"Don't worry about them. They won't be at your mercy, or Adam's either. There's a little thing I can do. They'll never notice it. It won't change them, except now they'll be able to have babies whenever they want to."

Cirocco was immediately wary. Gaby saw it, and shook her head.

"I'm way ahead of you. If they breed without control, the whole wheel will fill up. It's the same with humans, you know."

"Yes. I do."

Gaby shrugged.

"So something will have to be done if it starts getting out of hand. I don't know what yet. But the Earth will be habitable again in another century or two. We can repopulate it. I have all the things I need. And don't worry too much. I plan to use your principle of doing as little as possible at all times. I'm not going to be an activist god. But I *will* be the conservator for the human and Titanide races, and a lot of others, besides. There will be some hard choices."

"Exactly the ones I don't want to make."

"Let's don't get into that again. Listen . . ." Once more Gaby leaned forward. "You gave me your answer, and I accept it . . . for now. But think about this. We both know this job drove Gaea crazy as a loon. But I'm *sure* it took a long time. Thousands of years. I think I'm good for at least eight or nine centuries before I need a straitjacket. Is that reasonable?"

"I suppose so. Probably more. Gaby, you may not go crazy at *all*, I didn't mean to imply that I thought it was—"

"Hush. We have no data on that except Gaea's example, and you can't plot a curve from one point. Okay. I accept your decision not to go into partnership with me in the god business . . . for now. But in . . . two centuries, can I ask you again?"

Cirocco didn't answer for a long time. When she spoke, she did so very carefully.

"Answer a couple of questions first."

"Anything."

"How long can I expect to live?"

"With regular trips to the fountain . . . you're good for five or six centuries, easily. Probably more."

"But I'm not immortal?"

"There's no disease that can kill you. You're tougher than a normal human, also quicker. But to stay alive, you'll have to stay on your toes, just like you always have."

"I won't have any special protection? No guardian angel looking over my shoulder, ready to help out?"

Gaby shook her head.

"I will stay out of your affairs. I won't watch you. If you get

over your head, you will be on your own. And if you die, you
ill stay dead."

Cirocco saw the longing in Gaby's eyes. She knew, beyond
>ubt, that Gaby needed this.

And what could it cost her, after all?

"Please, Cirocco. I don't want to beg...but I just have this
eling that maybe the way to beat this thing that got Gaea...this
rminal boredom, I guess it was, is for two people to be up here to
ep each other honest."

Cirocco stuck out her hand.

"It's a deal. I'll see you in two centuries...if I should live
at long."

Gaby looked narrowly at her. She cleared her throat.

"You're not planning to...kill yourself or anything, are you?"

"I swear, I'm not." She smiled. "But I'm not going to be quite
s careful as I used to be, either. I'm going to take some chances.
nd who the hell knows? If I'm living just for myself now, I..."
ut she had to stop there. It wouldn't do to finish the thought for
aby.

If I'm living just for myself...

Maybe I can find someone else to live for. There are all kinds
f ways to take chances. Robin took a chance on Conal.

Taking chances...

Cirocco stood on the sloping upper rim of the Dione spoke.
elow her it flared out and down...and down almost eternally, six
undred kilometers to the ground. In the gently increasing "gravity"
f Gaea, it was about an hour to the bottom. One spin of the wheel,
s the air in the spoke gradually accelerated the falling body into a
urved trajectory.

Cirocco started to run.

It was awkward here in the hub. Her feet didn't have much
action. But she knew how to do it, and after a certain number of
age bounds she was moving at a good clip down the sloping side
f the spoke. When she was going fast enough, she jumped.

She arced out over the long dark well.

Taking chances.

It was not the first time she had fallen through a spoke. It was
ot even the first time she had done it without a parachute. After

killing the first incarnation of Gaea she had fallen through a Rhe Spoke so full of lightning bolts that it seemed impossible she woul ever reach the ground safely.

But she had.

Robin had been dropped through the spoke, back in the day when Gaea was pulling that practical joke on all her visitors. Sh had been rescued by an angel. Cirocco would be going by the nes of the Dione Supras. Maybe some of them would come out and sa her.

Chris had fallen through a spoke, too. He had landed on th back of a blimp. Maybe Cirocco would have the great good luck land on a blimp.

Maybe she would fall into Moros. She could probably surviv that.

And then again, maybe she would fly.

Stranger things had happened.

She smiled, and spread her wings.